Acclaimed Bestsellers by
DEAN KOONTZ

MR. MURDER
"A TRULY HARROWING TALE...SUPERB WORK BY A MASTER AT THE TOP OF HIS FORM."
— *Washington Post Book World*

THE FUNHOUSE
"KOONTZ IS A TERRIFIC WHAT-IF STORYTEL-TELLER."   —*People*

DRAGON TEARS
"A RAZOR-SHARP, NON-STOP, SUSPENSEFUL STORY...A FIRST-RATE LITERARY EXPERIENCE."
—*San Diego Union-Tribune*

SHADOWFIRES
"HIS PROSE MESMERIZES...KOONTZ CONSISTENTLY HITS THE BULL'S-EYE."
—*Arkansas Democrat*

HIDEAWAY
"NOT JUST A THRILLER BUT A MEDITATION ON THE NATURE OF GOOD AND EVIL."
—*Lexington Herald-Leader*

COLD FIRE
"AN EXTRAORDINARY PIECE OF FICTION... IT WILL BE A CLASSIC."   —UPI

THE HOUSE OF THUNDER
"KOONTZ IS BRILLIANT."   —*Chicago Sun-Times*

Continued...

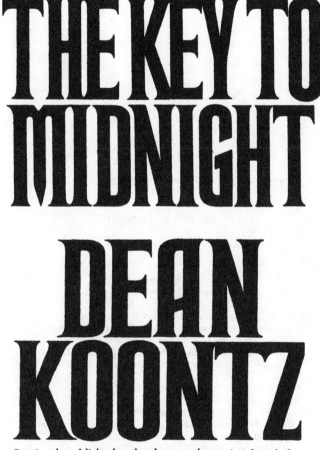

THE KEY TO MIDNIGHT

DEAN KOONTZ

Previously published under the pseudonym Leigh Nichols

BERKLEY BOOKS, NEW YORK

This better version
is for Gerda.
I can go back and improve
the earlier pen-name books
—but I'm afraid I don't
have enough energy to make
all the desperately needed
improvements in *myself!*

THE KEY TO MIDNIGHT

PART ONE

♣ ♣ ♣

JOANNA

A sound of something;
The scarecrow
    Has fallen down of itself.

—BONCHO, 1670–1714

1
✪ ✪ ✪

In the dark, Joanna Rand went to the window. Naked, trembling, she peered between the wooden slats of the blind.

Wind from the distant mountains pressed coldly against the glass and rattled a loose pane.

At four o'clock in the morning, the city of Kyoto was quiet, even in Gion, the entertainment quarter crowded with nightclubs and geisha houses. Kyoto, the spiritual heart of Japan, was a thousand years old yet as new as a fresh idea: a fascinating hodgepodge of neon signs and ancient temples, plastic gimcrackery and beautifully hand-carved stone, the worst of modern architecture thrusting up next to palaces and ornate shrines that were weathered by centuries of hot, damp summers and cold, damp winters. By a mysterious combination of tradition and popular culture, the metropolis renewed her sense of humanity's permanence and purpose, refreshed her sometimes shaky belief in the importance of the individual.

The earth revolves around the sun; society continuously changes; the city grows; new generations come forth . . . and I'll go on just as they do.

That was always a comforting thought when she was in darkness, alone, unable to sleep, morbidly energized by the powerful yet indefinable fear that came to her every night.

Calmed somewhat but not anxious to go to bed, Joanna dressed in a red silk robe and slippers. Her slender hands were still shaking, but the tremors were not as severe as they had been.

She felt violated, used, and discarded—as though the hateful creature in her nightmare had assumed a real physical form and had repeatedly, brutally raped her while she'd slept.

The man with the steel fingers reaches for the hypodermic syringe. . . .

That single image was all that she retained from the nightmare. It had been so vivid that she could recall it at will, in unsettling detail: the smooth texture of those metal fingers, the clicking and whirring of gears working in them, the gleam of light off the robotic knuckles.

She switched on the bedside lamp and studied the familiar room. Nothing was out of place. The air contained only familiar scents. Yet she wondered if she truly *had* been alone all night.

She shivered.

2

♧ ♧ ♧

Joanna stepped out of the narrow stairwell into her ground-floor office. She switched on the light and studied the room as she had inspected those upstairs, half expecting the fearsome phantom of her dream to be waiting somewhere in the real world. The soft glow from the porcelain lamp didn't reach every corner. Purple shadows draped the bookshelves, the rosewood furniture, and the rice-paper scroll paintings. Potted palms cast complex, lacy shadows across one wall. Everything was in order.

Unfinished paperwork littered the desk, but she wasn't in a bookkeeping frame of mind. She needed a drink.

The outer door of the office opened on the carpeted area that encircled the long cocktail bar at one end of the Moonglow Lounge. The club wasn't completely dark: Two low-wattage security lights glowed above the smoky blue mirrors behind the bar and made the beveled edges of the glass gleam like the blades of well-stropped knives. An eerie green bulb marked each of the four exits. Beyond the bar stools, in the main room, two hundred chairs at sixty tables faced a small stage. The nightclub was silent, deserted.

Joanna went behind the bar, took a glass from the rack, and poured a double shot of Dry Sack over ice. She sipped the sherry, sighed—and became aware of movement near the open door to her office.

Mariko Inamura, the assistant manager, had come downstairs from the apartment that she occupied on the third floor, above Joanna's quarters. As modest as always, Mariko wore a bulky green bathrobe that hung to the floor and was two sizes too large for her; lost in all that quilted fabric, she seemed less a woman than a waif. Her black hair, usually held up by ivory pins, now spilled to her shoulders. She went to the bar and sat on one of the stools.

"Like a drink?" Joanna asked.

Mariko smiled. "Water would be nice, thank you."

"Have something stronger."

"No, thank you. Just water, please."

"Trying to make me feel like a lush?"

"You aren't a lush."

"Thanks for the vote of confidence," Joanna said. "But I wonder. I seem to wind up here at the bar more nights than not, around this time." She put a glass of ice water on the counter.

Mariko turned the glass slowly in her small hands, but she didn't drink from it.

Joanna admired the woman's natural grace, which transformed every ordinary act into a moment of theater. Mariko was thirty, two years younger than Joanna, with big, dark eyes and delicate features. She seemed to be unaware of her exceptional good looks, and her humility enhanced her beauty.

Mariko had come to work at the Moonglow Lounge one week after opening night. She'd wanted the job as much for the opportunity to practice her English with Joanna as for the salary. She'd made it clear that she intended to leave after a year or two, to obtain a position as an executive secretary with one of the larger American companies with a branch office in Tokyo. But six years later, she no longer found Tokyo appealing, at least not by comparison with the life she now enjoyed.

The Moonglow had worked its spell on Mariko too. It was the main interest in her life as surely as it was the *only* interest in Joanna's.

Strangely, the insular world of the club was in some ways as sheltering and safe as a Zen monastery high in a remote mountain pass. Nightly, the place was crowded with customers, yet the outside world did not intrude to any significant extent. When the employees went home and the doors closed, the lounge—with its blue lights, mirrored walls, silver-and-black art deco appointments, and appealing air of mystery—might have been in any country, in any decade since the 1930s. It might even have been a place in a dream. Both Joanna and Mariko seemed to need that peculiar sanctuary.

Besides, an unexpected sisterly affection and concern had developed between them. Neither made friends easily. Mariko was warm and charming—but still surprisingly shy for a woman who worked in a Gion nightclub. In part she was like the retiring, soft-spoken, self-effacing Japanese women of another and less democratic age. By contrast, Joanna was vivacious, outgoing—yet she also found it difficult to permit that extra degree of closeness that allowed an acquaintance to become a friend. Therefore, she'd made a special effort to keep Mariko at the Moonglow, regularly increasing her responsibilities and her salary; Mariko had reciprocated by working hard and diligently. Without once discussing their quiet friendship, they had decided that separation was neither desirable nor necessary.

Now, not for the first time, Joanna wondered, *Why Mariko?*

Of all the people whom Joanna might have chosen for a friend, Mariko was not the obvious first choice—except that she had an unusually strong sense of privacy and considerable discretion even by Japanese standards. She would never press for details from a friend's past, never indulge in that gossipy, inquisitive, and revelatory chatter that so many people assumed was an essential part of friendship.

There's never a danger that she'll try to find out too much about me.

That thought surprised Joanna. She didn't understand herself. After all, she had no secrets, no past of which to be ashamed.

With the glass of dry sherry in her hand, Joanna came out from behind the bar and sat on a stool.

"You had a nightmare again," Mariko said.

"Just a dream."

"A nightmare," Mariko quietly insisted. "The same one you've had on a thousand other nights."

"Not a thousand," Joanna demurred.

"Two thousand? Three?"

"Did I wake you?"

"It sounded worse than ever," Mariko said.

"Just the usual."

"Thought I'd left the TV on."

"Oh?"

"Thought I was hearing some old Godzilla movie," Mariko said.

Joanna smiled. "All that screaming, huh?"

"Like Tokyo being smashed flat again, mobs running for their lives."

"All right, it was a nightmare, not just a dream. And worse than usual."

"I worry about you," Mariko said.

"No need to worry. I'm a tough girl."

"You saw him again . . . the man with the steel fingers?"

"I never see his face," Joanna said wearily. "I've never seen anything at all but his hand, those god-awful metal fingers. Or at least that's all I remember seeing. I guess there's more to the nightmare than that, but the rest of it never stays with me after I wake up." She shuddered and sipped some sherry.

Mariko put a hand on Joanna's shoulder, squeezed gently. "I have an uncle who is—"

"A hypnotist."

"Psychiatrist," Mariko said. "A doctor. He uses hypnotism only to—"

"Yes, Mariko-san, you've told me about him before. I'm really not interested."

"He could help you remember the entire dream. He might even be able to help you learn the cause of it."

Joanna stared at her own reflection in the blue bar mirror and finally said, "I don't think I ever *want* to know the cause of it."

They were silent for a while.

Eventually Mariko said, "I didn't like it when they made him into a hero."

Joanna frowned. "Who?"

"Godzilla. Those later movies, when he battles other monsters to protect Japan. So silly. We need our monsters to be scary. They don't do us any good if they don't frighten us."

"Am I about to get hit with some philosophy of the mysterious East? I didn't hear the Zen warning siren."

"Sometimes we need to be frightened," Mariko said.

Joanna softly imitated a submarine diving alarm: "*Whoop-whoop-whoop-whoop.*"

"Sometimes fear purges us, Joanna-san."

"We're deep in the unfathomable waters of the Japanese mind," Joanna whispered theatrically.

Mariko continued unfazed: "But when we confront our demons—"

"Deeper and deeper in the Japanese mind, tremendous pressure building up—"

"—and rid ourselves of those demons—"

"—deeper and deeper—"

"—we don't need the fear any more—"

"—the weight of sudden enlightenment will crush me as though I'm just a bug—"

"—don't need it to purge us—"

"—I tremble on the edge of revelation—"

"—and we are then freed."

"I'm surrounded by the light of reason," Joanna said.

"Yes, you are, but you're blind to it," said Mariko. "You are too in love with your fear to see the truth."

"That's me. A victim of phobophilia," Joanna said, and drank the rest of her sherry in one long swallow.

"And you call us Japanese inscrutable."

"Who does?" Joanna said with mock innocence.

"I hope Godzilla comes to Kyoto," Mariko said.

"Does he have a new movie to promote?"

"And if he does come, he'll be the patriotic Godzilla, seeking out new threats to the Japanese people."

"Good for him."

"When he sees all that long blond hair of yours, he'll go right for you."

"I think you've got him confused with King Kong."

"Squash you flat in the middle of the street, while the grateful citizens of Kyoto cheer wildly."

Joanna said, "You'll miss me."

"On the contrary. It'll be messy, hosing all that blood and guts off the street. But the lounge should reopen in a day or two, and then it'll be *my* place."

"Yeah? Who's going to sing when I'm gone?"

"The customers."

"Good God, you'd turn it into a karaoke bar!"

"All I need are a stack of old Engelbert Humperdinck tapes."

Joanna said, "You're scarier than Godzilla *ever* was."

They smiled at each other in the blue mirror behind the bar.

3

✛ ✛ ✛

If his employees back in the States could have seen Alex Hunter at dinner in the Moonglow Lounge, they would have been astonished by his relaxed demeanor. To them, he was a demanding boss who expected perfection and quickly dismissed employees who couldn't deliver to his standards, a man who was at all times fair but who was given to sharp and accurate criticism. They knew him to be more often silent than not, and they rarely saw him smile. In Chicago, his hometown, he was widely envied and respected, but he was well liked only by a handful of friends. His office staff and field investigators would gape in disbelief if they could see him now, because he was chatting amiably with the waiters and smiling nearly continuously.

He did not appear capable of killing anyone, but he was. A few years ago he had pumped five bullets into a man named Ross Baglio. On another occasion, he had stabbed a man in the throat with the wickedly splintered end of a broken broomstick. Both times he had acted in self-defense. Now he appeared to be nothing more than a well-dressed business executive enjoying a night on the town.

This society, this comparatively depressurized culture, which was so different from the American way, had a great deal to do with his high spirits. The relentlessly pleasant and polite Japanese inspired a smile. Alex had been in their country just ten days, on vacation, but he could not recall another period of his life during which he had felt even half as relaxed and at peace with himself as he did at that moment.

Of course, the food contributed to his excellent spirits. The Moonglow Lounge maintained a first-rate kitchen. Japanese cuisine changed with the seasons more than any style of cooking with which Alex was familiar, and late autumn provided special treats. It was also important that each item of food complement the item next to it, and that everything be served on china that—both in pattern and color—was in harmony with the food that it carried. He was enjoying a dinner perfectly suited to the cool November evening. A delicate wooden tray held a bone-white china pot that was filled with thick slices of *daikon* radish, reddish sections of octopus—and *konnyaku,* a jellylike food made from devil's tongue. A fluted green bowl contained a fragrant hot mustard in which each delicacy could be anointed. On a large gray platter stood two black-and-red bowls: One contained *akadashi* soup with mushrooms, and the other was filled with rice. An oblong plate offered sea bream and three garnishes, plus a cup of finely grated *daikon* for seasoning. It was a hearty autumn meal, of the proper somber colors.

When he finished the last morsel of bream, Alex admitted to himself that it was neither the hospitable Japanese nor the quality of the food that made him feel so fine. His good humor resulted primarily from the fact that Joanna Rand would soon appear on the small stage.

Promptly at eight o'clock, the house lights dimmed, the silvery stage curtains drew back, and the Moonglow band opened with a great rendition of "A String of Pearls." Their playing wasn't the equal of any of the famous orchestras, not a match for Goodman or Miller or either of the Dorsey brothers, but surprisingly good for house musicians who had been born, raised, and trained many thousands of miles and a few decades from the origin of the music. At the end of the number, as the audience applauded enthusiastically, the band swung into "Moonglow," and Joanna Rand entered from stage right.

Alex's heartbeat quickened.

Joanna was slim, graceful, striking, though not beautiful in any classic sense. Her chin was feminine but too strong—and her nose neither narrow enough nor straight enough—to be seen in any ancient Grecian sculpture. Her cheekbones weren't high enough to satisfy the arbiters of beauty at *Vogue,* and her startlingly blue eyes were shades darker than the washed-out blue of the ennui-drenched models currently in demand for magazine covers and television commercials. She was a vibrant, golden vision, with light amber skin and cascades of platinum-blond hair. She looked thirty, not sixteen, but her beauty was inexpressibly enhanced by every mark of experience and line of character.

She *belonged* on a stage, not merely to be seen but to be heard. Her voice was first-rate. She sang with a tremulous clarity that pierced the stuffy air and seemed to reverberate within Alex. Though the lounge was crowded and everyone had been drinking, there was none of the expected nightclub chatter when Joanna Rand performed. The audience was attentive, rapt.

He knew her from another place and time, although he could not recall where or when they'd met. Her face was hauntingly familiar, especially her eyes. In fact, he felt that he hadn't just met her once before but had known her well, even intimately.

Ridiculous. He wouldn't have forgotten a woman as striking as this one. Surely, had they met before, he would be able to remember every smallest detail of their encounter.

He watched. He listened. He wanted to hold her.

4
✪ ✪ ✪

When Joanna finished her last song and the applause finally faded, the band swung into a lively number. Couples crowded onto the dance floor. Conversation picked up again, and the lounge filled with sporadic laughter and the clatter of dinnerware.

As she did every night, Joanna briefly surveyed her domain from the edge of the stage, allowing herself a moment of pride. She ran a damn good place.

In addition to being a restaurateur, she was a practical social politician. At the end of her first of two hour-long performances, she didn't disappear behind the curtains until the ten o'clock show. Instead, she stepped down from the stage in a soft swish of pleated silk and moved slowly among the tables, acknowledging compliments, bowing and being bowed to, stopping to inquire if dinner had been enjoyable, greeting new faces and chatting at length with regular, honored customers. Good food, a romantic atmosphere, and high quality entertainment were sufficient to establish a profitable nightclub, but more than that was required for the Moonglow to become legendary. She wanted that extra degree of success. People were flattered to receive personal attention from the owner, and the forty minutes that she spent in the lounge between acts was worth uncountable yen in repeat business.

The handsome American with the neatly trimmed mustache was present for the third evening in a row. The previous two nights, they had exchanged no more than a dozen words, but Joanna had sensed that they wouldn't remain strangers. At each performance, he sat at a small table near the stage and watched her so intently that she had to avoid looking at him for fear that she would become distracted and forget the words to a song. After each show, as she mingled with the customers, she knew without looking at him that he was watching her every move. She imagined that she could feel the pressure of his gaze. Although being scrutinized by him was vaguely disturbing, it was also surprisingly pleasant.

When she reached his table, he stood and smiled. Tall, broad-shouldered, he had a European elegance in spite of his daunting size. He wore a three-piece, charcoal-gray Savile Row suit, what appeared to be a hand-tailored Egyptian-cotton shirt, and a pearl-gray tie.

He said, "When you sing 'These Foolish Things' or 'You Turned the Tables on Me,' I'm reminded of Helen Ward when she sang with Benny Goodman."

"That's fifty years ago," Joanna said. "You're not old enough to remember Helen Ward."

"Never saw her perform. But I have all her records, and you're better than she was."

"You flatter me too much. You're a jazz buff?"

"Mostly swing music."

"So we like the same corner of jazz."

Looking around at the crowd, he said, "Apparently, so do the Japanese. I was told the Moonglow was *the* nightclub for transplanted Americans. But ninety percent of your customers are Japanese."

"It surprises me, but they love the music—even though it comes from an era they otherwise prefer to forget."

"Swing is the only music I've developed a lasting enthusiasm for." He hesitated. "I'd offer you a cognac, but since you own the place, I don't suppose I can do that."

"I'll buy you one," she said.

He pulled out a chair for her, and she sat.

A white-jacketed waiter approached and bowed to them.

Joanna said, "Yamada-san, *burande wo ima omegai, shimasu.* Rémy Martin."

"*Hai, hai,*" Yamada said. "*Sugu.*" He hurried toward the bar at the back of the big room.

The American had not taken his eyes off her. "You really do have an extraordinary voice, you know. Better than Martha Tilton, Margaret McCrae, Betty Van—"

"Ella Fitzgerald?"

He appeared to consider the comparison, then said, "Well, she's really not someone you should be compared to."

"Oh?"

"I mean, her style is utterly different from yours. It'd be like comparing oranges to apples."

Joanna laughed at his diplomacy. "So I'm not better than Ella Fitzgerald."

He smiled. "Hell, no."

"Good. I'm glad you said that. I was beginning to think you had no standards at all."

"I have very high standards," he said quietly.

His dark eyes were instruments of power. His unwavering stare seemed to establish an electrical current between them, sending an extended series of pleasant tremors through her. She felt not only as though he had undressed her with his eyes—men had done as much every night that she'd stepped onto the stage—but as though he had stripped her mind bare as well and had discovered, in one minute, everything worth knowing about her, every private fold of flesh and thought. She'd never before met a man who concentrated on a woman with such intensity, as if everyone else on earth had ceased to exist. Again she felt that peculiar combination of uneasiness and pleasure at being the focus of his undivided attention.

When the two snifters of Rémy Martin were served, she used the interruption as an excuse to glance away from him. She closed her eyes and sipped the cognac as if to savor it without distraction. In that self-imposed darkness, she realized that while he had been staring into her eyes, he had transmitted some of his own intensity to her. She had lost all awareness of the noisy club around her: the clinking of glasses, the laughter and buzz of conversation, even the music. Now all that clamor returned to her with the gradualness of silence reasserting itself in the wake of a tremendous explosion.

Finally she opened her eyes. "I'm at a disadvantage. I don't know your name."

"You're sure you don't? I've felt . . . perhaps we've met before."

She frowned. "I'm sure not."

"Maybe it's just that I *wish* we'd met sooner. I'm Alex Hunter. From Chicago."

"You work for an American company here?"

"No. I'm on vacation for a month. I landed in Tokyo eight days ago. I planned on spending two days in Kyoto, but I've already been here longer than that. I've got three weeks left. Maybe I'll spend them all in Kyoto and cancel the rest of my schedule. *Anata no machi wa hijo ni kyomi ga arimatsu.*"

"Yes," she said, "it is an interesting city, the most beautiful in Japan. But the entire country is fascinating, Mr. Hunter."

"Call me Alex."

"There's much to see in these islands, Alex."

"Maybe I should come back next year and take in all those other places. Right now, everything I could want to see in Japan is here."

She stared at him, braving those insistent dark eyes, not certain what to think of him. He was quite the male animal, making his intentions known.

Joanna prided herself on her strength, not merely in business but in her emotional life. She seldom wept and never lost her temper. She valued self-control, and she was almost obsessively self-reliant. Always, she preferred to be the dominant partner in her relations with men, to choose when and how a friendship with a man would develop, to be the one who decided when—and if—they would become more than friends. She had her own ideas about the proper, desirable pace of a romance. Ordinarily she wouldn't have liked a man as direct as Alex Hunter, so she was surprised that she found his stylishly aggressive approach to be appealing.

Nevertheless, she pretended not to see that he was more than casually interested in her. She glanced around as if checking on the waiters and gauging the happiness of her customers, sipped the cognac, and said, "You speak Japanese so well."

He bowed his head an inch or two. *"Arigato."*

"Do itashimashite."

"Languages are a hobby of mine," he said. "Like swing music. And good restaurants. Speaking of which, since the Moonglow is open only evenings, do you know a place that serves lunch?"

"In the next block. A lovely little restaurant built around a garden with a fountain. It's called Mizutani."

"That sounds perfect. Shall we meet at Mizutani for lunch tomorrow?"

Joanna was startled by the question but even more surprised to hear herself answer without hesitation. "Yes. That would be nice."

"Noon?"

"Yes. Noon."

She sensed that whatever happened between her and this unusual man, whether good or bad, would be entirely different from anything she'd experienced before.

5

✚ ✚ ✚

The man with the steel fingers reaches for the hypodermic syringe. . . .

Joanna sat straight up in bed, soaked in perspiration, gasping for breath, clawing at the unyielding darkness before she regained control of herself and switched on the nightstand lamp.

She was alone.

She pushed back the covers and got out of bed with an urgency sparked by some deep-seated anxiety that she could not understand. She walked unsteadily to the center of the room and stood there, trembling in fear and confusion.

The air was cool and somehow *wrong*. She smelled a combination of strong antiseptics that hadn't been used in that room: ammonia, Lysol, alcohol, a pungent brew of germicidal substances unpleasant enough to make her eyes water. She drew a long breath, then another, but the vapors faded as she attempted to pinpoint their source.

When the stink was gone altogether, she reluctantly admitted that the odors hadn't actually existed. They were left over from the dream, figments of her imagination.

Or perhaps they were fragments of memory.

Although she had no recollection of ever having been seriously ill or injured, she half believed that once she must have been in a hospital room that had reeked with an abnormally powerful odor of antiseptics. A hospital . . . in which something terrible had happened to her, something that was the cause of the repeating nightmare about the man with steel fingers.

Silly. But the dream always left her rattled and irrational.

She went into the bathroom and drew a glass of water from the tap. She returned to the bed, sat on the edge of it, drank the water, and then slipped under the covers once more. After a brief hesitation, she switched off the lamp.

Outside, in the predawn stillness, a bird cried. A large bird, a piercing cry. The flutter of wings. Past the window. Feathers brushing the glass. Then the bird sailed off into the night, its thin screams growing thinner, fainter.

6

✪ ✪ ✪

Suddenly, as he sat in bed reading, Alex recalled where and when he'd previously seen the woman. Joanna Rand wasn't her real name.

He had awakened at six-thirty Wednesday morning in his suite at the Kyoto Hotel. Whether vacationing or working, he was always up early and to bed late, requiring never more than five hours of rest to feel alert and refreshed.

He was grateful for his uncommon metabolism, because he knew that by spending fewer hours in bed, he was at an advantage in any dealings with people who were greater slaves to the mattress than he was. To Alex, who was an overachiever by choice as well as by nature, sleep was a detestable form of slavery, insidious. Each night was a temporary death to be endured but never enjoyed. Time spent in sleep was time wasted, surrendered, stolen. By saving three hours a night, he was gaining eleven hundred hours of waking life each year, *eleven hundred hours* in which to read books and watch films and make love, more than forty-five "found" days in which to study, observe, learn—and make money.

It was a cliché but also true that time was money. And in Alex Hunter's philosophy, money was the only sure way to obtain the two most important things in life: independence and dignity, either of which meant immeasurably more to him than did love, sex, friendship, praise, or anything else.

He had been born poor, raised by a pair of hopeless alcoholics to whom the word "dignity" was as empty of meaning as the word "responsibility." As a child, he had resolved to discover the secret of obtaining wealth, and he'd found it before he had turned twenty: *time.* The secret of wealth was time. Having learned that lesson, he applied it with fervor. In more than twenty years of judiciously managed time, his net worth had increased from a thousand dollars to more than twelve million. His habit of being late to bed and early to rise, while half at odds with Ben Franklin's immortal advice, was a major factor in his phenomenal success.

Ordinarily he would begin the day by showering, shaving, and dressing precisely within twenty minutes of waking, but this morning he allowed himself the routine-shattering luxury of reading in bed. He was on vacation, after all.

Now, as he sat propped up by pillows, with a book in his lap, he realized who Joanna Rand really was. While he read, his subconscious mind, loath to squander time, apparently remained occupied with the mystery of Joanna, for although he hadn't been consciously thinking of her, he suddenly made the connection between her and an important face out of his past.

"Lisa," he whispered.

He put the book aside.

Lisa. She was twelve years older. A different hairstyle. All the baby fat of a twenty-year-old girl was gone from her face, and she was a mature woman now. But she was still Lisa.

Agitated, he got up, showered, and shaved.

Staring into his own eyes in the bathroom mirror, he said, "Slow down. Maybe the resemblance isn't as remarkable as you think."

He hadn't seen a photograph of Lisa Chelgrin in at least ten years. When he got his hands on a picture, he might discover that Joanna looked like Lisa only to the extent that a robin resembled a bluejay.

He dressed, sat at the writing desk in the suite's sparsely furnished living room, and tried to convince himself that everyone in the world had a doppelgänger, an unrelated twin. Even if Joanna *was* a dead ringer for Lisa, the resemblance might be pure chance.

For a while he stared at the telephone on the desk, and finally he said aloud, "Yeah. Only thing is, I never did believe in chance."

He'd built one of the largest security and private-investigation firms in the United States, and experience had taught him that every apparent coincidence was likely to be the visible tip on an iceberg of truth, with much more below the waterline than above.

He pulled the telephone closer and placed an overseas call through the hotel switchboard. By eight-thirty in the morning, Kyoto time (four-thirty in the afternoon, Chicago time), he got hold of Ted Blankenship, his top man in the home office. "Ted, I want you to go personally to the dead-file room and pull everything we've got on Lisa Chelgrin. I want that file in Kyoto as soon as possible. Don't trust it to an air courier service. Keep it inside the company. Give it to one of our junior field ops who doesn't have anything better to do, and put him on the first available flight."

Blankenship chose his words carefully, slowly. "Alex . . . does this mean the case . . . is being . . . reactivated?"

"I'm not sure."

"Is there a chance you've found her after all this time?"

"I'm probably chasing shadows. Most likely, nothing will come of it. So don't talk about this, not even with your wife."

"Of course."

"Go to the dead files yourself. Don't send a secretary. I don't want any rumors getting started."

"I understand."

"And the field operative who brings it shouldn't know what he's carrying."

"I'll keep him in the dark. But, Alex . . . if you've found her . . . it's very big news."

"Very big," Alex agreed. "Call me back after you've arranged things, and let me know when I can expect the file."

"Will do."

Alex put down the telephone and went to one of the living-room windows, from which he watched the bicyclists and motorists in the crowded street below. They were in a hurry, as though they clearly comprehended the value of time. As he watched, one cyclist made an error in judgment, tried to pass between two cars where there wasn't sufficient space. A white Honda bumped the bike, and the cyclist went down in a skidding-rolling-bouncing tangle of skinned legs, bent bicycle wheels, broken arms, and twisted handlebars. Brakes squealed, traffic halted, and people rushed toward the injured man.

Although Alex was not superstitious, he had the eerie feeling that the sudden violence in the street below was an omen and that he himself was rushing headlong toward an ugly crash of his own.

✪ ✪ ✪

7

At noon Alex met Joanna at Mizutani for lunch.

When he saw her again, he realized that the mental picture of her that he carried with him captured her beauty no more accurately than a snapshot of Niagara Falls could convey the beauty of wildly tumbling water. She was more golden, more vibrant and *alive*—her eyes a far deeper and more electrifying blue—than he remembered.

He kissed her hand. He was not accustomed to European manners; he just needed an excuse to touch his lips to her warm skin.

Mizutani was an *o-zashiki* restaurant, divided by rice-paper partitions into many private dining rooms where meals were served strictly Japanese style. The ceiling wasn't high, less than eighteen inches above Alex's head, and the floor was of brilliantly polished pine that seemed transparent and as unplumbable as a sea. In the vestibule, Alex and Joanna exchanged their street shoes for soft slippers. They followed a petite young hostess to a small room where they sat on the floor, side by side on thin but comfortable cushions, in front of a low table.

They faced a six-foot-square window, beyond which lay a walled garden. That late in the year, no flowers brightened the view, but there were several varieties of well-tended evergreens, and a carpet of moss had not yet turned brown for the winter. In the center of the garden, water fountained from a seven-foot-high pyramid of rocks and spilled down the stones to a shallow, trembling pool.

They ate *mizutaki*, the white meat of a chicken stewed in an earthenware pot and flavored with scallions, icicle radish, and many herbs. This was accompanied by several tiny cups of steaming sake, delicious when piping hot but like a spoiled sauterne when cool.

Throughout lunch they talked about music, Japanese customs, art, and books. Alex wanted to mention the magic name—Lisa Chelgrin—because at times he had an almost psychic ability to read guilt or innocence in the reactions of a suspect, in fleeting expressions at the instant that accusations were made, in the nuances of a voice. But he wasn't eager to discuss the Chelgrin disappearance with Joanna until he heard where she'd been born and raised, where she'd learned to sing, and why she'd come to Japan. Her biography might have enough substance to convince him that she was who she claimed to be, that her resemblance to the long-missing Chelgrin woman was coincidental, in which case he wouldn't raise the subject. It was essential that he induce her to talk unselfconsciously about herself, but she resisted—evidently not out of any sinister motive but out of sheer modesty. Ordinarily Alex was also reluctant to talk about himself, even with close friends; curiously, in Joanna's company, those inhibitions dissolved. While trying unsuccessfully to probe into her past, he told her a great deal about his own.

"Are you really a private detective?" she asked. "It's hard to believe. Where's your trench coat?"

"At the cleaners. They're removing the unsightly bloodstains."

"You aren't wearing a shoulder holster."

"It chafes my shoulder."

"Aren't you carrying a gun at all?"

"There's a miniature derringer in my left nostril."

"Come on. I'm serious."

"I'm not here on business, and the Japanese government tends to frown on pistol-packing American tourists."

"I'd expect a private detective to be . . . well, slightly seedy."

"Oh, thank you very much."

"Tough, squint-eyed, sentimental but at the same time cynical."

"Sam Spade played by Humphrey Bogart. The business isn't like that any more," Alex said. "If it ever was. Mostly mundane work, seldom anything dangerous. Divorce investigations. Skip tracing. Gathering evidence for defense attorneys in criminal cases. Providing bodyguards for the rich and famous, security guards for department stores. Not half as romantic or glamorous as Bogart, I'm afraid."

"Well, it's more romantic than being an accountant." She savored a tender piece of chicken, eating as daintily as did the Japanese, but with a healthy and decidedly erotic appetite.

Alex watched her surreptitiously: the clenching of her jaw muscles, the sinuous movement of her throat as she swallowed, and the exquisite line of her lips as she sipped the hot sake.

She put down the cup. "How'd you get into such an unusual line of work?"

"As a kid, I decided not to live my life on the edge of poverty, like my parents, and I thought every attorney on earth was filthy rich. So with a few scholarships and a long string of night jobs, I got through college and law school."

"Summa cum laude?"

Surprised, he said, "How'd you know that?"

"You're obsessive-compulsive."

"Am I? You should be a private detective."

"Samantha Spade. What happened after graduation?"

"I spent a year with a major Chicago firm that specialized in corporate law. Hated it."

"But that's an easier road to riches than being a P.I."

"The average income for an attorney these days is around maybe eighty thousand. Less back then. As a kid, it looked like riches, because what does a kid know. But after taxes, it would never be enough to put me behind the wheel of a Rolls-Royce."

"And is that what you wanted—a Rolls-Royce lifestyle?"

"Why not? I had the opposite as a child. There's nothing ennobling about poverty. Anyway, after a couple of months of writing briefs and doing legal research, I knew the really enormous money was only for senior partners of the big firms. By the time I could have worked my way to the top, I'd have been in my fifties."

When he was twenty-five, confident that the private security field would be a major growth industry for several decades, Alex had left the law firm to work for the fifty-man Bonner Agency, where he intended to learn the business from the inside. By the time he was thirty, he arranged a bank loan to buy the agency from Martin Bonner. Under his guidance, the company moved aggressively into all areas of the industry, including installation and maintenance of electronic security systems. Now Bonner-Hunter Security had offices in eleven cities and employed two thousand people.

"You have your Rolls-Royce?" Joanna asked.

"Two."

"Is life better for having two?"

"Sounds like a Zen question."

"And *that* sounds like an evasion."

"Money's neither dirty nor noble. It's a neutral substance, an inevitable part of civilization. But your voice, your talent—that's a gift from God."

For a long moment she regarded him in silence, and he knew she was judging him. She put down her chopsticks and patted her mouth with a napkin. "Most men who started out with nothing and piled up a fortune by the age of forty would be insufferable egomaniacs."

"Not at all. There's nothing special about me. I know quite a few wealthy, self-made men and women, and most of them have every bit as much humility as any office clerk. Maybe more."

Their waitress, a pleasant round-faced woman dressed in a white *yukata* and short maroon jacket, brought dessert: peeled mandarin orange slices coated with finely shredded almonds and coconut.

"Now we've talked too much about me," Alex said. "What about you? How did you get to Japan, to the Moonglow? I want to hear all about you."

"There's not a lot to hear."

"Nonsense."

"My life seems boring compared to yours."

She was either secretive about her past or genuinely intimidated by him. He couldn't decide which, but he continued to encourage her until she finally opened up.

"I was born in New York City," she said, "but I don't remember it well. My father was an executive with one of those hydra-headed conglomerates. When I was ten, he was promoted to a top management position in a British subsidiary, so then I grew up in London and attended university there."

"What did you study?"

"Music for a while . . . then Asian languages. I became interested in the Orient because of a brief, intense infatuation with a Japanese exchange student. He and I shared an apartment for a year. Our affair didn't last, but my interest in the Orient grew."

"When did you come to Japan?"

"Almost twelve years ago."

Coincidental with the disappearance of Lisa Chelgrin, he thought. But he said nothing.

With her chopsticks, Joanna picked up another slice of orange, ate it with visible delight, and licked away a paper-thin curl of coconut that clung to the corner of her mouth.

To Alex, she resembled a tawny cat: sleek-muscled, full of kinetic energy.

As though she had heard his thought, she turned her head with feline fluidity to gaze at him. Her eyes had that catlike quality of harmoniously blended opposites: sleepiness combined with total awareness, watchfulness mixed with cool indifference, and a proud isolation that coexisted with a longing for affection.

She said, "My parents were killed in an auto accident while they were on vacation in Brighton. I had no relatives in the States, no great desire to return there. And England seemed terribly dreary all of a sudden, full of bad memories. When my dad's life insurance was paid and the estate was settled, I took the money and came to Japan."

"Looking for that exchange student?"

"Oh, no. That was over. I came because I thought I'd like it here. And I did. I spent a few months playing tourist. Then I put together an act and got a gig singing Japanese and American pop music in a Yokohama nightclub. I've always had a good voice but not always much stage presence. I was dreadful at the start, but I learned."

"How'd you get to Kyoto?"

"There was a stopover in Tokyo, a better job than the one in Yokohama. A big club called Ongaku, Ongaku."

"Music, Music," Alex translated. "I know the place. I was there only five days ago!"

"The club had a reasonably good house band back then, and they were willing to take chances. Some of them were familiar with jazz, and I taught them what I knew. The management was skeptical at first, but the customers loved the Big Band sound. A Japanese audience is usually more reserved than a Western audience, but the people at Ongaku really let down their hair when they heard us."

That first triumph was, Alex saw, a sweet recollection for Joanna. Smiling faintly, she stared at the garden without seeing it, eyes glazed, looking back along the curve of time.

"It was a crazy place for a while. It really jumped. I surprised even myself. I was the main attraction for two years. If I'd wanted to stay, I'd still be there. But I realized I'd do better with my own club."

"Ongaku, Ongaku is changed, not like you describe it," Alex said. "It must've lost a lot when you left. It doesn't jump these days. It doesn't even twitch."

Joanna laughed and tossed her head to get a long wave of hair out of her face. With that gesture, she looked like a schoolgirl, fresh, innocent—and more than ever like Lisa Chelgrin. Indeed, for a moment, she was not merely a Chelgrin look-alike: She was a dead ringer for the missing woman.

"I came to Kyoto for a vacation in July, more than six years ago," she said. "It was during the annual Gion Matsuri."

"Matsuri . . . a festival."

"It's Kyoto's most elaborate celebration. Parties, exhibits, art shows. The beautiful old houses on Muromachi were open to the public with displays of family treasures and heirlooms, and there was a parade of the most enormous ornate floats you ever saw. Absolutely enchanting. I stayed an extra week and fell in love with Kyoto even when it wasn't in the midst of a festival. Used a lot of my savings to buy the building that's now the Moonglow. The rest is history. I warned you it was dull compared to your life. Not a single murder mystery or Rolls-Royce in the entire tale."

"I didn't yawn once."

"I try to make the Moonglow a little like the Café Americain, in *Casablanca,* but the dangerous, romantic stuff that happened to Bogart doesn't happen to me and never will. I'm a lightning rod for the *ordinary* forces in life. The last major crisis I can recall was when the dishwasher broke down for two days."

Alex wasn't certain that everything Joanna had told him was true, but he was favorably impressed. Her capsule biography was generally convincing, as much for the manner in which it was delivered as for its detail. Although she'd been reluctant to talk about herself, there had been no hesitation in her voice once she'd begun, not the slightest hint of a liar's discomfort. Her history as a nightclub singer in Yokohama and Tokyo was undoubtedly true. If she'd needed to invent a story to cover those years, she wouldn't have created one that was so easy to investigate and disprove. The part about England and the parents who'd been killed while on holiday in Brighton . . . well, he wasn't sure what to make of that. As a device for totally sealing off her life prior to Japan, it was effective but far too pat. Furthermore, at a few points, her biography intersected with that of Lisa Chelgrin, which seemed to be piling coincidence on coincidence.

Joanna turned on her cushion to face him directly. Her knee pressed against his leg, sending a pleasant shiver through him. "Do you have any plans for the afternoon?" she asked. "If you'd like to do some sightseeing, I'll be your guide for a few hours."

"Thanks for the offer, but you must have business to attend to."

"Mariko can handle things at the club until it opens. I don't have to put in an appearance until at least six o'clock."

"Mariko?"

"Mariko Inamura. My assistant manager. The best thing that's happened to me since I came to Japan. She's smart, trustworthy, and works like a demon."

Alex repeated the name to himself until he was sure that he would remember it. If he had a chance to talk with Mariko, she might inadvertently reveal more about her boss than he could learn from Joanna herself.

"Well," he said, "if you're sure you have the time, I'd like nothing better than a tour."

He had expected to make up his mind about her during lunch, but he had reached no conclusions.

Her uncommonly dark blue eyes seemed to grow darker still. He stared into them, entranced.

Joanna Rand or Lisa Chelgrin?

He couldn't decide which.

At Joanna's request, the hostess at Mizutani telephoned the Sogo Taxi Company. The cab arrived in less than five minutes, a black car with red lettering.

Joanna was delighted with the driver. No one could have been better suited than he was for the little tour that she had in mind. He was a wrinkled, white-haired old man with an appealing smile that lacked one tooth. He sensed romance between her and Alex, so he interrupted their conversation only to make certain that they didn't miss special scenery here and there, using his rearview mirror to glance furtively at them, always with bright-eyed approval.

For more than an hour, at the driver's discretion, they cruised the ancient city. Joanna drew Alex's attention to interesting houses and temples, and she kept up a stream of patter about Japanese history and architecture. He smiled, laughed frequently, and asked questions about what he was seeing. But he looked at her as much as at the city, and again she felt the incredible power of his dark eyes and direct stare.

They were stopped at a traffic light near the National Museum when he said, "Your accent intrigues me."

She blinked. "What accent?"

"It isn't New York, is it?"

"I wasn't aware I *had* an accent."

"No, it's certainly not New York. Boston?"

"I've never been to Boston."

"It's not Boston, anyway. Difficult to pin down. Maybe there's a slight trace of British English in it. Maybe that's it."

"I hope not," Joanna said. "I've always disliked Americans who assume an English accent after living a few years there. So phony."

"It's not English." He studied her while he pondered the problem, and as the cab started up again, he said, "I know what it sounds like! Chicago."

"You're from Chicago, and I don't sound like you."

"Oh, but you do. Just a little. A very little."

"Not at all. And I've never been to Chicago, either."

"You must have lived somewhere in Illinois," he insisted.

Suddenly his smile seemed to be false, maintained only with considerable effort.

"No," she said, "I've never been to Illinois."

He shrugged. "Then I'm wrong." He pointed to a building ahead, on the left. "That's an odd-looking place. What is it?"

Joanna resumed her role as his guide, although with the uneasy feeling that the questions about her accent had not been casual. That sudden turn in the conversation had a purpose that eluded her.

A shiver passed through Joanna, and it felt like an echo of the chills that she endured every night, when waking from the nightmare.

✛ ✛ ✛

At Nijo Castle, they paid the cab fare and continued sightseeing on foot. Turning away from the small Sogo taxi as it roared off into traffic, they followed three other tourists toward the palace's huge iron-plated East Gate.

Joanna glanced at Alex and saw that he was impressed. "It's something, huh?"

"Now *this* is my idea of a castle!" Then he shook his head. "But it looks too . . . garish for Japan."

Joanna sighed. "I'm glad you said that. If you admired Nijo Castle too much, then how could I ever like you?"

"You mean I'm supposed to find it garish?"

"Most sensitive people do . . . if they understand Japanese style, that is."

"I thought it was a landmark."

"It is, historically. But it's an attraction with more appeal for tourists than for the Japanese."

They entered through the main gate and passed a second gate, the *Karamon*, which was richly ornamented with metalwork and elaborate wood carvings. Ahead lay a wide courtyard and then the palace itself.

As they crossed the courtyard, Joanna said, "Most Westerners expect ancient palaces to be massive, lavish. They're disappointed to find so few imposing monuments here—but they like Nijo Castle. Its rococo grandeur is something they can relate to. But Nijo doesn't actually represent the fundamental qualities of Japanese life and philosophy."

She was beginning to babble, but she couldn't stop. Over lunch and in the taxi, she had grown aware of a building sexual tension between them. She welcomed it, yet at the same time was frightened of the commitment that she might have to make. For more than ten months, she'd had no lover, and her loneliness had become as heavy as cast-iron shackles. Now she wanted Alex, wanted the pleasure of being with him, giving and taking, sharing that special tenderness, animal closeness. But if she opened herself to joy, she would only have to endure another painful separation, and that prospect made her nervous.

Separation was inevitable—and not because he would go back to Chicago. She ended every love affair the same way: badly. She harbored a strong, inexplicable, destructive urge—no, a *need*—to demolish anything good and right that developed between her and any man. All of her adult life, she had wanted a permanent relationship and had sought it with quiet desperation. Yet she rebelled against marriage when it was proposed, fled from affection when it threatened to ripen into love. She worried that any would-be fiancé might have more curiosity about her when he was her husband than he'd exhibited when he was her lover; she worried that he'd probe too deeply into her past and learn the truth. *The truth.* The worry always swelled into fear, and the fear swiftly became debilitating, unbearable. But why? *Why?* She had nothing to hide. Her life story *was* singularly lacking in momentous events and dark secrets, just as she had told Alex. Nevertheless, she knew that if she had an affair with him, and if he began to feel that they had a future together, she would reject and alienate him with a suddenness and viciousness that would leave him stunned. And when he was gone, when she was alone, she would be crushed by the loss and unable to understand why she had treated him so cruelly. Her fear was irrational, but she knew by now that she would never conquer it.

With Alex, she sensed the potential for a deeper relationship than she had ever known, which meant that she was walking the edge of an emotional precipice, foolishly testing her balance. Consequently, as they crossed the courtyard of Nijo Castle, she talked incessantly and filled all possible silences with trivial chatter that left no room for anything of a personal nature. She didn't think she could bear the pain of loving him and then driving him away.

"Westerners," she told him pedantically, "seek constant action and excitement from morning to night, then complain about the awful pressures that deform their lives. Life here is the opposite—calm and sane. The key words of the Japanese experience, at least for most of its philosophical history, are 'serenity' and 'simplicity.' "

Alex grinned winningly. "No offense meant . . . but judging by the hyperactive state you've been in since we left the restaurant, you're still more American than Japanese."

"Sorry. It's just that I love Kyoto and Japan so much that I tend to run on. I'm so anxious for you to like it too."

They stopped at the main entrance to the largest of the castle's five connected buildings. "Joanna, are you worried about something?"

"Me? No. Nothing."

She was unsettled by his perception. Again, she sensed that she could hide nothing from him.

"Are you certain you have the time for this today?"

"Really, I'm enjoying myself. I have all the time in the world."

He stared thoughtfully at her. With two pinched fingers, he tugged at one point of his neatly trimmed mustache.

"Come along," she said brightly, trying to cover her uneasiness. "There's so much to see here."

They followed a group of tourists through the ornate chambers, and Joanna shared with him the colorful history of Nijo Castle. The place was a trove of priceless art, even if a large measure of it tended to gaudiness. The first buildings had been erected in 1603, to serve as the Kyoto residence of the first shogun of the honorable Tokugawa family, and later enlarged with sections of Hideyoshi's dismantled Fushimi Castle. In spite of its moat and turrets and magnificent iron gate, the castle had been constructed by a man who had no doubts about his safety; with its low walls and broad gardens, it never could have withstood a determined enemy. Although the palace was not representative of Japanese style, it was quite successful as the meant-to-be impressive home of a rich and powerful military dictator who commanded absolute obedience and could afford to live as well as the emperor himself.

In the middle of the tour, when the other visitors had drifted far ahead, as Joanna was explaining the meaning and the value of a beautiful and complex mural, Alex said, "Nijo Castle is wonderful, but I'm more impressed with you than with it."

"How so?"

"If you came to Chicago, I wouldn't be able to do anything like this. I don't know a damn thing about the history of my own hometown. I couldn't even tell you the year that the great fire burned it all to the ground. Yet here you are, an American in a strange country, and you know everything."

"It amazes me too," she said quietly. "I know Kyoto better than most of the people who were born here. Japanese history has been a hobby ever since I moved here from England. More than hobby, I guess. Almost an avocation. Sometimes . . . an obsession."

His eyes narrowed slightly and seemed to shine with professional curiosity. "Obsession? That's an odd way of putting it."

Again the conversation had ceased to be casual. He was leading her, probing gently but insistently, motivated by more than friendly interest. What did this man want from her? Sometimes he made her feel as though she was concealing a dreadful crime. She wished that she could change the subject before another word was said, but she couldn't see any polite way to do so.

"I read a lot of books on Japanese history," she said, "and I attend lectures in history. Spend most of my holidays poking around ancient shrines, museums. It's almost as if I . . ."

"As if you what?" Alex prompted.

She looked at the mural again. "It's as if I'm obsessed with Japanese history because I've no real roots of my own. Born in the U.S., raised in England, parents dead for nearly twelve years now, Yokohama to Tokyo to Kyoto, no living relatives . . ."

"Is that true?"

"Is what true?"

"That you have no relatives."

"None living."

"Not any grandparents or—"

"Like I said."

"Not even an aunt or uncle?"

"Not a one."

"Not even a cousin—"

"No."

"How odd."

"It happens."

"Not often."

She turned to face him, and she couldn't be sure whether his handsome face was lined with sympathy or calculation, concern for her or suspicion. "I came to Japan because there was nowhere else for me to go, no one I could turn to."

He frowned. "Almost anyone your age can claim at least one relative kicking around somewhere . . . maybe not someone you know well or really care about, but a bona fide relative nonetheless."

Joanna shrugged, wishing he'd drop the subject. "Well, if I do have any folks out there, I don't know about them."

His response was quick. "I could help you search for them. After all, investigations are my trade."

"I couldn't afford your rates."

"Oh, I'm very reasonable."

"Yeah? You *do* buy Rolls-Royces with your fees."

"Just for you, I'd do it for the cost of a bicycle."

"A very large and ornate bicycle, I'll bet."

"I'll do it for a smile, Joanna."

She smiled. "That's generous of you, but I couldn't accept."

"I'd charge it to overhead. The cost would be a tax write-off."

Although she couldn't imagine his reasons, he was eager to dig into her past. This time, she wasn't suffering from her usual, irrational paranoia: He really *was* too curious.

Nevertheless, she wanted to talk to him and be with him. There was good chemistry between them. He was a medicine for loneliness.

"No," she said. "Forget it, Alex. Even if I've got folks out there someplace, they're strangers. I mean nothing to them. That's why it's important to me to get a solid grip on the history of Kyoto and Japan. This is my hometown now. It's my past and present and future. They've accepted me here."

"Which is rather odd, isn't it? The Japanese are pretty insular. They rarely accept immigrants who aren't at least half Japanese."

Ignoring his question, she said, "I don't have roots like other people do. Mine have been dug up and burned. So maybe I can *create* new roots for myself, grow them right here, and maybe they'll be as strong and meaningful as the roots that were destroyed. In fact, it's something I *have* to do. I don't have any choice. I need to belong, not just as a successful immigrant but as an integral part of this lovely country. Belonging . . . being securely and deeply connected to it all, like a fiber in the cloth . . . that's what counts. I need to lose myself in Japan. A lot of days there's a terrible emptiness in me. Not all the time. Now and then. But when it comes, it's almost too much to bear. And I think . . . I *know* that if I melt completely into this society, then I won't have to suffer that emptiness any longer."

She amazed herself, because with Alex Hunter, she was allowing an unusual intimacy. She was telling him things that she had never told anyone before.

He spoke so quietly that she could barely hear. " 'Emptiness.' That's another odd word choice."

"I guess it is."

"What do you mean by it?"

Joanna groped for words that could convey the hollowness, the cold feeling of being different from all other people, the cancerous alienation that sometimes crept over her, usually when she least expected it. Periodically she fell victim to a brutal, disabling loneliness that bordered on despair. Bleak, unremitting loneliness, yet more than that, worse than that. *Aloneness.* That was a better term for it. Without apparent reason, she sometimes felt certain that she was separate, hideously unique. *Aloneness.* The depression that accompanied one of these inexplicable moods was a black pit out of which she could claw only with fierce determination.

Haltingly she said, "The emptiness is like . . . well, it's like I'm nobody."

"You mean . . . you're bothered that you have no one."

"No. That's not it. I feel that I *am* no one."

"I still don't understand."

"It's as if I'm not Joanna Rand . . . not anybody at all . . . just a shell . . . a cipher . . . hollow . . . not the same as other people . . . not even human. And when I'm like that, I wonder why I'm alive . . . what purpose I have. My connections seem so tenuous. . . ."

He was silent for a while, but she was aware that he was staring at her while she gazed blindly at the mural. At last he said, "How can you live with this attitude, this emptiness, and still be . . . the way you are?"

"The way I am?"

"Generally so outgoing, cheerful."

"Oh," Joanna said quickly, "I don't feel alienated all the time. The mood comes over me only now and then, and never for longer than a day or two. I fight it off."

He touched her cheek with his fingertips.

Abruptly Joanna was aware of how intently he was staring, and she saw a trace of pity mixed with the compassion in his eyes. The reality of Nijo Castle and the actuality of the limited relationship that they shared now flooded back to her, and she was surprised—even shocked—by how much she had said and by how far she had opened herself to him. Why had she cast aside the armor of her privacy in front of this man rather than at the feet of someone before him? Why was she willing to reveal herself to Alex Hunter in a way and to a degree that she had never allowed Mariko Inamura to know her? She wondered if her hunger for companionship and love was much greater than she had ever realized until this disturbing moment.

She blushed. "Enough of this soul baring. How'd you get me to do that? You aren't a psychoanalyst, are you?"

"Every private detective has to be a bit of a psychiatrist . . . just like any popular bartender."

"Well, I don't know what in the world got me started on that."

"I don't mind listening."

"You're sweet."

"I mean it."

"Maybe you don't mind listening," she said, "but I mind talking about it."

"Why?"

"It's private. And silly."

"Didn't sound silly to me. It's probably good for you to talk about it."

"Probably," she admitted. "But it's not like me to babble on about myself to a perfect stranger."

"Hey, I'm not a perfect stranger."

"Well, almost."

"Oh, I see," he said. "I understand. You mean I'm perfect but not a stranger. I can live with that."

Joanna smiled. She wanted to touch him, but she didn't. "Well, anyway, we're here to show you the palace, not to have long boring Freudian discussions. There are a thousand things to see, and every one of them is more interesting than my psyche."

"You underestimate yourself."

Another group of chattering tourists rounded the corner and approached from behind Joanna. She turned toward them, using them as an excuse to avoid Alex's eyes for the few seconds required to regain her composure, but what she saw made her gasp.

A man with no right hand.

Twenty feet away.

Walking toward her.

A. Man. With. No. Right. Hand.

He was at the front of the group: a smiling, grandfatherly Korean gentleman with a softly creased face and iron-gray hair. He wore sharply pressed slacks, a white shirt, a blue tie, and a light blue sweater with the right sleeve rolled up a few inches. His arm was deformed at the wrist: There was nothing but a smooth, knobby, pinkish stub where the hand should have been.

"Are you all right?" Alex asked, apparently sensing the sudden tension in her.

She wasn't able to speak.

The one-handed man drew closer.

Fifteen feet away now.

She could smell antiseptics. Alcohol. Lysol. Lye soap.

That was ridiculous. She couldn't *really* smell antiseptics. Imagination. Nothing to fear. Nothing to fear in Nijo Castle.

Lysol.

Alcohol.

No. Nothing to fear. The one-handed Korean was a stranger, a kindly little *ojii-san* who couldn't possibly hurt anyone. She had to get a grip on herself.

Lysol.

Alcohol.

"Joanna? What's happening? What's wrong?" Alex asked, touching her shoulder.

The elderly Korean seemed to advance with the slow-motion single-mindedness of a monster in a horror film or in a nightmare. Joanna felt trapped in the unearthly, oppressive gravity of her dream, in that same syrupy flow of time.

Her tongue was thick. A bad taste filled her mouth, the coppery flavor of blood, which was no doubt as imaginary as the miasma of antiseptics, although it was as sickening as if it had been real. Her throat was constricted. She felt as if she might begin to gag. She heard herself straining for air.

Lysol.

Alcohol.

She blinked, and the flutter of her eyelids magically altered reality even further, so the Korean's pinkish stump now ended in a mechanical hand.

Incredibly, she could hear the compact servo-mechanisms purring with power, the oiled push-pull rods sliding in their tracks, and the gears *click-click-click*ing as the fingers opened from a clenched fist.

No. That was imagination too.

"Joanna?"

When the Korean was less than three yards from her, he raised his twisted limb and pointed with the mechanical hand that wasn't really there. Intellectually Joanna knew that he was interested only in the mural that she and Alex had been studying, but on a more primitive and affecting emotional level, she reacted with the certainty that he was pointing at *her,* reaching for *her* with unmistakably malevolent purpose.

"Joanna."

It was Alex speaking her name, but she could almost believe that it had been the Korean.

From the deepest reaches of memory came a frightening sound: a gravelly, jagged, icy voice seething with hatred and bitterness. A familiar voice, synonymous with pain and terror. She wanted to scream. Although the man in her nightmare, the faceless bastard with steel fingers, had never spoken to her in sleep, she knew this was his voice. With a jolt, she realized that while she had never heard him speak in the nightmare, she *had* heard him when she was awake, a long time ago . . . somehow, somewhere. The words he spoke to her now were not imagined or dredged up from her worst dreams, but recollected. The voice was a cold, dark effervescence bubbling up from a long-forgotten place and time: *"Once more the needle, my lovely little lady. Once more the needle."* It grew louder, reverberating in her mind, a voice to which the rest of the world was deaf—*"Once more the needle, once more the needle, once more the needle"*—booming with firecracker repetitiveness, until she thought her head would explode.

The Korean stopped two feet from her.

Lysol.

Alcohol.

Once more the needle, my lovely little lady . . .

Joanna ran. She cried out like a wounded animal and turned away from the startled Korean, pushed at Alex without fully realizing who he was, pushed so hard that she almost knocked him down, and darted past him, her heels tapping noisily on the hardwood floor. She hurried into the next chamber, trying to scream but unable to find her voice, ran without looking back, convinced that the Korean was pursuing her, ran past the dazzling seventeenth-century artworks of the master Kano Tan'yu and his students, fled between strikingly beautiful wood sculptures, and all the while she struggled to draw a breath, but the air was like a thick dust that clogged her lungs. She ran past richly carved transoms, past intricate scenes painted on sliding doors, footsteps echoing off the coffered ceilings, ran past a surprised guard who called to her, dashed through an exit into cool November air, started across the big courtyard, heard a familiar voice calling her name, *not* the cold voice of the man with the steel hand, so she finally stopped, stunned, in the center of the Nijo garden, shaking, shaking.

10
✛ ✛ ✛

Alex led her to a garden bench and sat beside her in the brisk autumn breeze. Her eyes were unnaturally wide, and her face was as pale and fragile as bridal lace. He held her hand. Her fingers were cold and chalky white, and she squeezed his hand so hard that her manicured nails bit into his skin.

"Should I get you to a doctor?"

"No. It's over. I'll be all right. I just . . . I need to sit here for a while."

She still appeared to be ill, but a trace of color slowly began to return to her cheeks.

"What happened, Joanna?"

Her lower lip quivered like a suspended bead of water about to surrender to the insistent pull of gravity. Bright tears glistened in the corners of her eyes.

"Hey. Hey now," he said softly.

"Alex, I'm so sorry."

"About what?"

"I made such a fool of myself."

"Nonsense."

"Embarrassed you," she said.

"Not a chance."

Her eyes brimmed with tears.

"It's okay," he told her.

"I was just . . . scared."

"Of what?"

"The Korean."

"What Korean?"

"The man with one hand."

"Was he Korean? Do you know him?"

"Never saw him before."

"Then what? Did he say something?"

She shook her head. "No. He . . . he reminded me of something awful . . . and I panicked." Her hand tightened on his.

"Reminded you of what?"

She was silent, biting her lower lip.

He said, "It might help to talk about it."

For a long moment she gazed up into the lowering sky, as if reading enigmatic messages into the patterns of the swift-moving clouds. Finally she told him about the nightmare.

"You have it *every* night?" he asked.

"For as far back as I can remember."

"When you were a child?"

"I guess . . . no . . . not then."

"Exactly how far back?"

"Seven or eight years. Maybe ten."

"Maybe twelve?"

Through her shimmering tears she regarded him curiously. "What do you mean?"

Rather than answer, he said, "The odd thing about it is the frequency. *Every night.* That must be unbearable. It must drain you. The dream itself isn't particularly strange. I've had worse. But the endless repetition—"

"Everyone's had worse," Joanna said. "When I try to describe the nightmare, it doesn't sound all that terrifying or threatening. But at night . . . I feel as if I'm dying. There aren't words for what I go through, what it does to me."

Alex felt her stiffen as though steeling herself against the recollected impact of the nightly ordeal. She bit her lip and for a while said nothing, merely stared at the funereal gray-black clouds that moved in an endless cortege from east to west across the city.

When at last she looked at him again, her eyes were haunted. "Years ago, I'd wake up from the dream and be so damned scared I'd throw up. Physically ill with fear, hysterical. These days, it's not so acute . . . though more often than not, I can't get back to sleep. Not right away. The mechanical hand, the needle . . . it makes me feel so . . . slimy . . . sick in my soul."

Alex held her hand in both of his hands, cupping her frigid fingers in his warmth. "Have you ever talked to anyone about this dream?"

"Just Mariko . . . and now you."

"I was thinking of a doctor."

"Psychiatrist?"

"It might help."

"He'd try to free me of the dream by discovering the cause of it," she said tensely.

"What's wrong with that?"

She huddled on the bench, silent, the image of despair.

"Joanna?"

"I don't want to know the cause."

"If it'll help cure—"

"I don't want to know," she said firmly.

"All right. But why not?"

She didn't answer.

"Joanna?"

"Knowing would destroy me."

Frowning, he said, "Destroy? How?"

"I can't explain . . . but I feel it."

"It's *not* knowing that's tearing you apart."

She was silent again. She withdrew her hand from his, rummaged in her purse for a handkerchief, and blew her nose.

After a while he said, "Okay, forget the psychiatrist. What do *you* suppose is the cause of the nightmare?"

She shrugged.

"You must have given it a lot of thought over the years."

"Thousands of hours," Joanna said bleakly.

"And? Not even one idea?"

"Alex, I'm tired. And still embarrassed. Can we just . . . not talk about it any more?"

"All right."

She cocked her head. "You'll really drop it that easily?"

"What right do I have to pry?"

She smiled thinly. It was her first smile since they had sat down, and it looked unnatural. "Shouldn't a private detective be pushy at a time like this, inquisitive, absolutely relentless?"

Although her question was meant to sound casual, flippant, Alex saw that she was genuinely afraid of him probing too far. "I'm not a private detective here. I'm not investigating you. I'm just a friend who's offering a shoulder if you feel like crying on one." As he spoke, a pang of guilt pierced him, because he actually *was* investigating her.

"Can we get a taxi?" she asked. "I'm not up to any more sightseeing."

"Sure."

She clung to his arm as they crossed the palace garden toward the *Karamon*, the ornate inner gate.

Overhead, a pair of crows wheeled against the somber sky, cawing as they dived and soared. With a dry flutter of wings, they settled into the exquisitely sculptured branches of a large bonsai pine.

Wanting to pursue the conversation but resigned to Joanna's silence, Alex was surprised when she suddenly began to talk about the nightmare again.

Evidently, on some level and in spite of what she'd said, she *wanted* him to be an aggressive inquisitor, so she would have an excuse to tell him more.

"For a long time," she continued as they walked, "I've thought it's a symbolic dream, totally Freudian. I figured the mechanical hand and hypodermic syringe weren't what they seemed. You know? That they represented other things. I thought maybe the nightmare was symbolic of some real-life trauma that I couldn't face up to even when I was asleep. But . . ." She faltered. Her voice grew shaky on the last few words and then faded altogether.

"Go on," he said softly.

"A few minutes ago in the palace, when I saw that man with one hand . . . what scared me so much was . . . for the first time I realized the dream isn't symbolic at all. It's a memory. A memory that comes to me in sleep. It really happened."

"When?"

"I don't know."

"Where?"

"I don't know."

They passed the *Kara-mon*. No other tourists were in sight. Alex stopped Joanna in the space between the inner and outer gates of the castle. Even the nippy autumn breeze hadn't restored significant color to her cheeks. She was as white-faced as any powdered geisha.

"So somewhere in your past . . . there actually *was* a man with a mechanical hand?"

She nodded.

"And for reasons you don't understand, he used a hypodermic needle on you?"

"Yeah. And when I saw the Korean, something . . . snapped in me. I remembered the voice of the man in the dream. He just kept saying, 'Once more the needle, once more the needle,' over and over again."

"But you don't know who he was?"

"Or where or when or why. But I swear to God it happened. I'm not crazy. Something happened to me . . . was done to me . . . something I can't remember."

"Something you don't *want* to remember. That's what you said before."

She spoke in a whisper, as if afraid that the beast in her nightmare might hear her. "That man hurt me . . . did something to me that was . . . a sort of death. Worse than death."

Each whispered sibilant in her voice was like the hissing of an electrical current leaping in a bright blue arc across the tiny gap between two wires. Alex shivered.

Instinctively he opened his arms. She moved against him, and he held her.

A gust of wind passed through the trees with a sound like scarecrows on the march.

"I know it sounds . . . so bizarre," she said miserably. "A man with a mechanical hand, like a villain out of a comic book. But I swear, Alex—"

"I believe you."

Still in his embrace, she looked up. "You do?"

He watched her closely as he said, "Yes, I really do—Lisa."

She blinked. "What?"

"Lisa Chelgrin."

Puzzled, she slipped out of his arms, stepped back from him.

He waited, watched.

"Who's Lisa Chelgrin?" she asked.

He studied her.

"Alex?"

"I think maybe you honestly don't know."

"I don't."

"*You* are Lisa Chelgrin," he said.

He was intent upon catching any fleeting expression that might betray her, a brief glimpse of hidden knowledge, the look of the hunted in her eyes, or perhaps guilt expressed in briefly visible lines of tension at the corners of her mouth. She seemed genuinely perplexed. If Joanna Rand and the long-lost Lisa Chelgrin were one and the same—and Alex was certain now that she could be no one else—then all memory of her true identity had been scrubbed from her either by accident or by intent.

"Lisa Chelgrin?" She seemed dazed. "I don't get it."

"Neither do I."

"Who is she? What's the joke?"

"No joke. But it's a long story. Too long for me to tell it while we're standing here in the cold."

11

♣ ♣ ♣

During the return trip to the Moonglow Lounge, Joanna huddled in one corner of the rear seat of the taxi while Alex told her who he thought she was. Her face remained blank. Her dark-blue eyes were guarded, and she would not look at him directly. He was unable to determine how his words were affecting her.

The driver didn't speak English. He hummed along softly with the music on a Sony Discman.

"Thomas Moore Chelgrin," Alex told Joanna. "Ring a bell?"

"No."

"Never heard of him?"

She shook her head.

"He's been a United States Senator from Illinois for almost fourteen years. Before that, he served two terms in the House of Representatives—a liberal on social issues, to the right on defense and foreign policy. He's well liked in Washington, primarily because he's a team player. And he throws some of the best shindigs in the capital, which makes him popular too. They're a bunch of partying fools in Washington. They appreciate a man who knows how to set a table and pour whiskey. Apparently Tom Chelgrin satisfies his constituents too, because they keep returning him to office with ever larger vote totals. I've never seen a more clever politician, and I hope I never do. He knows how to manipulate the voters—white, brown, black, Catholics and Protestants and Jews and atheists, young and old, right and left. Out of six times at bat, he's lost only one election, and that was his first. He's an imposing man— tall, lean, with the trained voice of an actor. His hair turned silver when he was in his early thirties, and his opponents attribute his success to the fact that he *looks* like a senator. That's damned cynical, and it's a simplification, but there's some truth in it."

When Alex paused, waiting for her reaction, she only said, "Go on."

"Can you place him yet?"

"I never met him."

"I think you know him as well as anyone."

"Not me."

The cabdriver tried to speed through a changing traffic signal, decided not to risk it after all, and tramped on the brakes. When the car stopped rocking, he glanced at Alex in the rearview mirror, grinned disarmingly, and apologized: *"Gomen-nasai, jokyaku-san."*

Alex inclined his head respectfully and said, *"Yoroshii desu. Karedomo . . . untenshu-san yukkuri."*

The driver nodded vigorously in agreement. *"Hai."* Henceforth he would go slowly, as requested.

Alex turned to Joanna. "When Tom Chelgrin was thirteen, his father died. The family already had been on the edge of poverty, and now they plunged all the way in. Tom worked through high school and college, earned a degree in business. In his early twenties, he was drafted into the army, wound up in Vietnam. While on a search-and-destroy mission, he was taken prisoner by the Viet Cong. Do you know anything about what happened to our POWs during that war?"

"Not much. Not really."

"During World Wars One and Two, nearly all our POWs had been stubborn in captivity, difficult to contain. They conspired against their keepers, resisted, engineered elaborate escapes. Starting with the Korean War, all that changed. With brutal physical torture and sophisticated brainwashing, by applying continuous psychological stress, the Communists broke their spirit. Not many attempted to escape, and those who actually got away can just about be counted on my fingers. It was the same in Vietnam. If anything, the torture our POWs were subjected to was worse than in Korea. But Chelgrin was one of the few who refused to be passive, cooperative. After fourteen months in captivity, he escaped, made it back to friendly territory. *Time* devoted a cover story to him, and he wrote a successful book about his adventures. He ran for office a few years later, and he milked his service record for every vote it was worth."

"I've never heard of him," Joanna insisted.

As the taxi moved through the heavy traffic on Horikawa Street, Alex said, "When Tom Chelgrin got out of the army, he met a girl, got married, and fathered a child. His mother had died while he was in that North Vietnamese prison camp, and he'd inherited seventy-five or eighty thousand dollars after taxes, which was a good chunk in those pre-inflation days. He put that money with his book earnings and whatever he could borrow, and he purchased a Honda dealership. Soon it seemed like half the people in the country were driving Japanese cars, especially Hondas. Tom added three more dealerships, got into other businesses, and became a rich man. He did a lot of charity work, earned a reputation as a humanitarian in his community, and finally campaigned for a congressional seat. He lost the first time, but came back two years later and won. Won again. And then moved on to the U.S. Senate, where he's been since—"

Joanna interrupted him. "What about the name you used, what you called me?"

"Lisa Chelgrin."

"How's she fit in?"

"She was Thomas Chelgrin's only child."

Joanna's eyes widened. Again, Alex was unable to detect any deception in her response. With genuine surprise, she said, "You think I'm this man's *daughter?*"

"I believe there's a chance you might be."

"Are you crazy?"

"Am I?"

"I'm beginning to wonder," she said.

"Considering the—"

"I *know* whose daughter I am, for God's sake."

"Do you?"

"Of course. Robert and Elizabeth Rand were my parents."

"And they died in an accident near Brighton," he said.

"Yes. A long time ago."

"And you've no living relatives."

"So?"

"Convenient, don't you think?"

"Why would I lie to you?" she asked, not just baffled by his peculiar conviction that she was living under a false identity but increasingly angered by it. "I'm not a liar."

The driver clearly sensed the antagonism in her voice. He glanced at them in the rearview mirror, and then he looked straight ahead, humming a bit louder than the music on the Sony Discman, too polite to eavesdrop even when he didn't understand the language that they were speaking.

"I'm not calling you a liar," Alex said quietly.

"That's sure what I'm hearing."

"You're overreacting."

"The hell I am. This is weird."

"I agree. It is weird. Your repeating nightmare, your reaction to the Korean with one hand, your resemblance to Lisa Chelgrin. It's definitely weird."

She didn't reply, just glared at him.

"Maybe you're afraid of what I'm leading up to."

"I'm not afraid of you," she said curtly.

"Then what *are* you afraid of?"

"What are you accusing me of?"

"Joanna, I'm not accusing you of anything. I'm only—"

"I feel like you *are* accusing me, and I don't like it. I don't understand it, and I don't like it. All right?"

She looked away from him and out the side window at the cars and cyclists on Shijo Street.

For a moment Alex was silent, but then he continued as if her outburst had never occurred. "One night in July, more than twelve years ago, the summer after Lisa Chelgrin's junior year at Georgetown University, she vanished from her father's vacation villa in Jamaica. Someone got into her bedroom through an unlocked window. Although there were signs of a struggle, even a few smears of her blood on the bedclothes and one windowsill, no one in the house heard her scream. Clearly, she'd been kidnapped, but no ransom demand was received. The police believed she'd been abducted and murdered. A sex maniac, they said. On the other hand, they weren't able to find her body, so they couldn't just assume she was dead. At least not right away, not until they went through the motions of an exhaustive search. After three weeks, Chelgrin lost all confidence in the island police—which he should have done the second day he had to deal with them. Because he was from the Chicago area, because a friend of his had used my company and recommended me, Chelgrin asked me to fly to Jamaica to look for Lisa—even though Bonner-Hunter was still a relatively small company back then and I was just turning thirty. My people worked on the case for ten months before Tom Chelgrin gave up. We used eight damned good men full time and hired as many Jamaicans to do a lot of footwork. It was an expensive deal for the senator, but he didn't care. Still . . . it wouldn't have mattered if we'd had ten thousand men on the case. It was a perfect crime. It's one of only two major investigations that we've failed to wrap up successfully since I took over the business."

The taxi swung around another corner. The Moonglow Lounge stood half a block ahead.

Joanna finally spoke again, although she still wouldn't look at him. "But why do you think I'm Lisa Chelgrin?"

"Lots of reasons. For one thing, you're the same age she'd be if she were still alive. More important, you're a dead ringer for her, just twelve years older."

Frowning, she looked at him at last. "Do you have a photograph of her?"

"Not on me. But I'll get one."

The taxi slowed, pulled to the curb, and stopped in front of the Moonglow Lounge. The driver switched off the meter, opened his door, and got out.

"When you have a photo," Joanna said, "I'd like to see it." She shook hands with him as if they'd experienced nothing more together than a pleasant business lunch. "Thanks for lunch. Sorry I spoiled the sightseeing."

Alex realized that she was dismissing him. "Can't we have a drink and—"

"I don't feel well," she said.

The cabdriver opened her door, and she started to get out.

Alex held on to her hand, forcing her to look at him again. "Joanna, we have a lot to talk about. We—"

"Maybe later."

"Aren't you still curious, for God's sake?"

"Not nearly as curious as I am ill. Queasy stomach, headache. It must be something I ate. Or maybe all the excitement."

"Do you want a doctor?"

"I just need to lie down a while."

"When *can* we talk?" He sensed a widening gulf between them that had not existed a few minutes ago. "Tonight? Between shows?"

"Yes. We can chat then."

"Promise?"

"Really, Alex, the poor driver will catch pneumonia if he stands there holding the door for me any longer. It's gotten fifteen degrees colder since lunch."

Reluctantly he let go of her.

As she got out of the taxi, a blast of frigid air rushed past her and struck Alex in the face.

12

Joanna felt threatened.

She was overcome by the unshakable conviction that her every move was being watched and recorded.

She locked the door of her apartment. She went into the bedroom and latched that door as well.

For a minute she stood in the center of the room, listening. Then she poured a double brandy from a crystal decanter, drank it quickly, poured another shot, and put the snifter on the nightstand.

The room was too warm.

Stifling. Tropical.

She was sweating.

Each breath seemed to scorch her lungs.

She opened a window two inches to let in a cold draft, took off her clothes, and stretched out nude atop the silk bedspread.

Nevertheless, she still felt that she was smothering. Her pulse raced. She was dizzy. The room began to move around her as if the bed had become a slowly revolving carousel. She experienced a series of mild hallucinations too, none new to her, images that had been a part of other days and moods like the one that now gripped her. The ceiling appeared to descend between the walls, like the ceiling of an execution chamber in one of those corny old Tarzan movie serials. And the mattress, which she'd chosen for its firmness, suddenly softened to her touch, not in reality but in her mind: It became marshmallowy, gradually closing around her, relentlessly engulfing her, as though it were a living, amoeboid creature.

Imagination. Nothing to fear.

Gritting her teeth, fisting her hands, she strained to suppress all sensations that she knew to be false. But they were beyond her control.

She shut her eyes—but then opened them at once, suffocated and terrified by the brief self-imposed darkness.

She was dismayingly familiar with that peculiar state of mind, those emotions, that unfocused dread. She suffered the same terrors every time that she allowed a friendship to develop into more than a casual relationship, every time that she traveled beyond mere desire and approached the special intimacy of love. The panic attacks had just begun sooner this time, much sooner than usual. She desired Alex Hunter, but she didn't love him. Not yet. She hadn't known him long enough to feel more than strong affection. A bond was forming between them, however, and she sensed that their relationship would be special, that it would evolve far faster than usual—which was sufficient to trigger the anguish that had washed like a dark tide over her. And now events, people, inanimate objects, and the very air itself seemed to acquire evil purpose that was focused upon her. She felt a malevolent pressure, squeezing her from all sides, like a vast weight of water, as though she had sunk to the bottom of a deep sea. Already it was unbearable. The pressure would not relent until she turned forever from Alex Hunter and put behind her any danger of emotional intimacy. Intense fear lay dormant in her at all times; now it had been translated into a physical power that squeezed all hope out of her. She knew how it would have to end. She needed to break off the relationship that sparked her claustrophobia; only then would she obtain relief from the crushing, closed-in, listened-to, watched-over feeling that made her heart pound painfully against her ribs.

She would never see Alex Hunter again.

He would come to the Moonglow, of course. Tonight. Maybe other nights. He would sit through both performances.

Until the man left Kyoto, however, Joanna would not mingle with the audience between shows.

He'd telephone. She'd hang up.

If he came around to visit in the afternoon, she would be unavailable.

If he wrote to her, she would throw his letters in the trash without reading them.

Joanna could be cruel. She'd had plenty of experience with other men when simple attraction had threatened to develop into something deeper . . . and more dangerous.

The decision to freeze Alex out of her life had a markedly beneficial effect on her. Almost imperceptibly at first, but then more rapidly, the immobilizing fear diminished. The bedroom grew steadily cooler, and the sweat began to dry on her naked body. The humid air became less oppressive, breathable. The ceiling rose to its proper height, and the mattress beneath her grew firm once more.

13

❖ ❖ ❖

The Kyoto Hotel, the largest first-class hotel in the city, was Western style in most regards, and the telephones in Alex's suite featured beeping-flashing message indicators, which were signaling him when he returned from the eventful afternoon with Joanna Rand. He called the operator for messages, certain that Joanna had phoned during his trip from the Moonglow to the hotel.

But it wasn't Joanna. The front desk was holding a fax for him. At his request a bellhop brought it to the suite.

Alex exchanged polite greetings and bows with the man, accepted the cable, tipped him, and went through the bowing again. When he was alone, he sat at the drawing-room desk and tore open the flimsy envelope. The message was from Ted Blankenship in Chicago, on Bonner-Hunter letterhead:

Courier arrives at your hotel noon Thursday, your time.

By noon tomorrow Alex would have the complete Chelgrin file, which had been closed for more than ten years but which definitely had now been reopened. In addition to hundreds of field-agent reports and meticulously transcribed interviews, the file contained several excellent photographs of Lisa that had been taken just days before she disappeared. Perhaps those pictures would shock Joanna out of her eerie detachment.

Alex thought of her as she had been when she'd gotten out of the taxi a short while ago, and he wondered why she'd so suddenly turned cold toward him. If she was Lisa Chelgrin, she didn't seem to know it. Yet she acted like a woman with dangerous secrets and a sordid past to hide.

He suspected that amnesia was the explanation for her situation—perhaps the result of a head injury or even psychological trauma. Of course, amnesia didn't explain where and why she had come up with an alternate past history.

He looked at his watch: 4:30.

At six-thirty he would take his nightly stroll through the bustling Gion district to the Moonglow Lounge for drinks and dinner—and for that important conversation with Joanna. He had time for a leisurely soak in the tub, and he looked forward to balancing the steamy heat with sips of cold beer.

After fetching an ice-cold bottle of Asahi from the softly humming bar refrigerator, he left the drawing room and went halfway across the bedroom before he stopped dead, aware that something was wrong. He surveyed his surroundings, tense, baffled. The chambermaid had straightened the pile of paperbacks, magazines, and newspapers on the dresser, and she'd remade the bed while he'd been gone. The drapes were open; he preferred to keep them drawn. What else? He couldn't see anything out of the ordinary—and certainly nothing sinister. But something was wrong. Call it intuition: He'd experienced it before, and usually he'd found it worth heeding.

Alex set the bottle of Asahi on the vanity bench and approached the bathroom with caution. He put his left hand against the heavy swinging door, listened, heard nothing, hesitated, then pushed the door inward and stepped quickly across the threshold.

The late-afternoon sun pierced a frosted window high in one wall, and the bathroom glowed with golden light. He was alone.

This time his sixth sense had misled him. A false alarm. He felt slightly foolish.

He was jumpy. And no wonder. Although lunch with Joanna had been immensely enjoyable, the rest of the day had been a grinding emery wheel that had put a sharp edge on his nerves: her irrational flight from the Korean at Nijo Castle; her description of the oft-repeated nightmare; and his growing belief that the unexplained disappearance of Lisa Jean Chelgrin had been an event with powerful causes and effects, with layers of complex and mysterious meaning that went far deeper than anything that he had uncovered or even imagined at the time it had happened. He had a right to be jumpy.

Alex stripped off his shirt and put it in the laundry bag. He brought a magazine and the bottle of beer from the other room and put them on a low utility table that he had moved next to the bath. He bent down at the tub, turned on the water, adjusted the temperature.

In the bedroom again, he went to the walk-in closet to choose a suit for the evening. The door was ajar. As Alex pulled it open, a man leapt at him from the darkness beyond. *Dorobo.* A burglar. The guy was Japanese, short, stocky, muscular, very quick. He swung a fistful of wire shirt hangers. The bristling cluster of hooked ends struck Alex in the face, could have blinded him, and he cried out, but the hangers spared his sight, stung one cheek, and rained around him in a burst of dissonant music.

Counting on the element of surprise, the stranger tried to push past Alex to the bedroom door, but Alex clutched the guy's jacket and spun him around. Unbalanced, they fell against the side of the bed, then to the floor, with the intruder on top.

Alex took a punch in the ribs, another, and a punch in the face. He wasn't in a good position to use his own fists, but he heaved hard enough to pitch off his assailant.

The stranger rolled into the vanity bench and knocked it over. Cursing continuously in Japanese, he scrambled to his feet.

Still on the floor, dazed only for an instant, Alex seized the intruder's ankle. The stocky man toppled to the floor, kicking as he fell. Alex howled as a kick caught his left elbow. Sharp pain crackled the length of his arm and brought a stinging flood of tears to his eyes.

The Japanese was on his feet again, moving through the open doorway, into the drawing room, toward the suite's entrance foyer.

Blinking away the involuntary tears that blurred his vision, Alex got up, staggered to the doorway. In the drawing room, when he saw that he couldn't reach the intruder in time to prevent him from getting to the hotel corridor, he plucked a vase from a decorative pedestal and threw it with anger and accuracy. The heavy ceramic exploded against the back of the *dorobo*'s skull, instantly dropping him to his knees, and Alex slipped past him to block the only exit.

They were breathing like long-distance runners.

Shaking his head, flicking shards of the vase from his broad shoulders, the *dorobo* got up. He glared at Alex and motioned for him to move away from the door. "Don't be a hero," he said in heavily accented English.

"What're you doing here?" Alex demanded.

"Get out of my way."

"What are you doing here? A *dorobo*? No. You're more than just a cheap burglar, aren't you?"

The stranger said nothing.

"It's the Chelgrin case, isn't it?"

"Move."

"Who's your boss?" Alex asked.

The intruder balled his chunky hands into formidable fists and advanced a single threatening step.

Alex refused to stand aside.

The *dorobo* withdrew a bone-handled switchblade from a jacket pocket. He touched a button on the handle, and faster than the eye could follow, a seven-inch blade popped into sight. "Move."

Alex licked his lips. His mouth was dry. While he considered his alternatives—none appealing—he divided his attention between the man's hard black eyes and the point of the blade.

Thinking he sensed fear and imminent surrender, the stranger waved the knife and smiled.

"It's not going to be that easy," Alex said.

"I can break you."

At first glance, the intruder seemed soft, out of shape. On closer inspection, however, Alex realized that the guy was iron hard beneath the masking layer of fat. A sumo wrestler had the same look in the early days of training, before attaining his gross physique.

Brandishing the switchblade again, the intruder said, "Move."

"Are you familiar with the English expression 'Fuck you'?"

The stranger moved faster than any man Alex had ever seen, as fluid as a dancer in spite of his bulk. Alex clutched the thick wrist of the knife hand, but with the amazing dexterity of a magician, the *dorobo* tossed the weapon from one hand to the other—and struck. The cold blade sliced smoothly, lightly along the underside of Alex's left arm, which still tingled from being kicked.

The stocky intruder stepped back as abruptly as he had attacked. "Gave you just a scratch, Mr. Hunter."

The blade had skipped across the flesh: Two wounds glistened, thin and scarlet, the first about three inches long, the other marginally longer. Alex stared at the shallow cuts as if they had opened utterly without cause, miraculous stigmata. Blood oozed down his arm, trickled into his hand, dripped from his fingertips, but it didn't spurt; no major artery or vein was violated, and the flow was stanchable.

He was badly shaken by the lightning-swift attack. It had happened so fast that he still hadn't begun to feel any pain.

"Won't require stitches," the stranger said. "But if you make me cut again . . . no promises next time."

"There won't be a next time," Alex said. He found it difficult to admit defeat, but he wasn't a fool. "You're too good."

The intruder smiled like a malevolent Buddha. "Go across the room. Sit on the couch."

Alex did as instructed, cradling his bloodied arm and thinking furiously, hoping to come up with a wonderful trick that would turn defeat into triumph. But he wasn't a sorcerer. There was nothing he could do.

The burglar remained in the foyer until Alex was seated. Then he left, slamming the door behind him.

The instant he was alone, Alex sprinted to the telephone on the desk. He punched the single number for hotel security. He changed his mind, however, and hung up before anyone answered.

Hotel security would call in the police. He didn't want the cops involved. Not yet. Maybe never.

He went to the door and locked the deadbolt. He also braced the door shut by jamming the straight-backed desk chair at an angle under the knob.

Hugging himself with his injured arm so the blood would soak into his undershirt instead of dripping on the carpet, he went into the bathroom. He shut off the taps just as the water was about to overflow the tub, and he opened the drain.

The bastard hadn't been a burglar. No way. He was someone—or worked for someone—who was worried that Alex would uncover the truth about Joanna, someone who wanted the suite searched for evidence that Alex had already made the link between the singer and the long-lost girl.

The knife wounds were beginning to burn and throb. He hugged himself harder, attempting to stop or slow the bleeding by applying direct pressure to the cuts. The entire front and side of his undershirt were crimson.

He sat on the edge of the tub.

Perspiration seeped into the corners of his eyes, making him blink. He wiped his forehead with a washcloth. He was thirsty. He picked up the bottle of Asahi beer and chugged a third of it.

The knife man was working for people with good connections. International connections. They might even have a man planted in the Chicago office. How else had they managed to put someone on his ass so soon after he had spoken on the phone with Blankenship?

The tub was half empty. He turned on the cold water.

More likely than a plant in Chicago: His hotel phone must be tapped. He had probably been followed since he'd arrived in Kyoto.

Gingerly he moved his arm, held it away from his chest. Although the wounds continued to bleed freely, they weren't serious enough to require a doctor's attention. He hadn't any desire to explain the injury to anyone other than Joanna.

The burning-stinging had grown worse, intolerable. He plunged his arm under the cold water that foamed out of the faucet. Relief was instantaneous, and he sat for a couple of minutes, just thinking.

The first time he'd seen Joanna Rand at the Moonglow, when he'd first suspected that she might be Lisa Chelgrin, he'd figured that she must have engineered her own kidnapping in Jamaica, twelve years ago. He couldn't imagine *why* she would have done such a thing, but his years as a detective had taught him that people committed drastic acts for the thinnest and strangest reasons. Sometimes they hurtled off the rails in a simple quest for freedom or new thrills or self-destruction. They sought change for the sake of change, for better or worse.

After talking to Joanna, however, he'd known she wasn't one of those reckless types. Besides, it was ludicrous to suppose that she could have planned her own abduction and confused Bonner-Hunter's best investigators, especially when, at that time, she had been an inexperienced college girl.

He considered amnesia again, but that was as unsatisfying as the other explanations. As an amnesiac, she might have forgotten every detail of her previous life, but she would not have fabricated and come to believe a completely false set of memories in order to fill the gap, which was precisely what Joanna seemed to have done.

Okay, she was not consciously deceiving anyone, and she was not an amnesiac, at least not in the classic sense. What possibilities were left?

He withdrew his arm from the cold water. The flow of blood had been reduced. He wrapped the arm tightly in a towel. Eventually blood would seep through, but as a temporary bandage, the towel was adequate.

He returned to the drawing room and telephoned the bell captain in the hotel lobby. He asked for a bottle of rubbing alcohol, a bottle of Mercurochrome, a box of gauze pads, a roll of gauze, and adhesive tape. "If the man who brings it is fast, there'll be an especially generous tip for him."

The bell captain said, "If there's been an accident, we have a house doctor who—"

"Only a minor accident. No need for a doctor, thank you. Just those items I requested."

While he waited for the bandages and antiseptics, Alex made himself presentable. In the bathroom, he stripped out of his blood-drenched undershirt, scrubbed his chest with the washcloth, and combed his hair.

The worst of the stinging pain in the wounds had subsided to a pounding but tolerable ache. The arm was stiff, as if undergoing a medusan metamorphosis: flesh into stone.

In the drawing room, he picked up most of the shattered vase and dropped the pieces in the wastebasket. He took the straight-backed chair from under the doorknob and returned it to the desk.

Blood was beginning to work through the layers of the towel that was wrapped around his arm.

He sat at the desk to wait for the bellhop, and the room seemed to move slowly around him.

If he ruled out deception and classic amnesia, he was left with only one credible explanation for Joanna's condition: brainwashing.

"Crazy," he said aloud.

With drugs, hypnosis, and subliminal reeducation, they could have wiped her mind clean. Absolutely spotless. Actually, he was not a hundred percent certain that such a thing was possible, but he thought it was a good bet. The modern menu of psychological-conditioning and brainwashing techniques was far more extensive than it had been in the Korean or Vietnam wars. In the past ten years there had been truly amazing advances in those areas of research—psychopharmacology, biochemistry, psychosurgery, clinical psychology—that directly and indirectly contributed to the less reputable but nonetheless hotly pursued science of mind control.

He hoped that something far less severe had been done to Lisa. If the complete eradication of a life-set of memories still eluded modern science, then the girl's kidnappers might have been able to do no more than repress her original personality. In which case, Lisa might still be buried deep beneath the Joanna cover, missing but not gone forever. She might still be reached, resurrected, and helped to remember the circumstances of her premature burial.

In either case, the kidnappers had stuffed her full of fake memories. They had provided her with phony identification and turned her loose in Japan with a substantial bankroll that had supposedly come from the settlement of her make-believe father's estate.

But for God's sake, *why?*

Alex got to his feet and paced nervously. His legs felt more rubbery with every step.

Who could have done it to her? Why? And why were they still interested in her?

He had no idea what the stakes of the game might be. If they thought it was important enough to keep Joanna's true identity a secret, they might kill him if he was on the verge of proving who she really was. Indeed, if he managed to convince Joanna of the truth, they might even kill *her* to keep the whole story from being revealed.

Regardless of the risk, he was determined to have the answers that he wanted. His rooms had been searched, and he had been cut. He owed these people a measure of humiliation and pain.

14

West of Kyoto, the last light of day gradually faded like the glow in a bank of dying embers. The city smoldered into evening under an ash-colored sky.

The streets of the Gion district were crowded. In the bars, clubs, restaurants, and geisha houses, another night of escape from reality had begun.

On his way to the Moonglow Lounge, immaculately dressed in a charcoal-gray suit, matching vest, pale-gray shirt, and green tie, with a gray top-coat thrown capelike across his shoulders, Alex walked at a tourist's pace. Although he pretended to be engrossed by the passing scene, he paid scant attention to the whirl of color and activity on all sides. Instead, he was trying to learn if the opposition had put a tail on him. In the busy throng that hurried over the washed-stone pavement, Alex had difficulty detecting any one person who might have been following him. Every time he turned a corner or stopped at a crosswalk, he glanced casually behind, as if taking a second look at some landmark of the Gion, and without appearing to do so, he studied the people in his wake.

Eventually he grew suspicious of three men, each walking alone, each caught watching him at one point or another, each remaining behind him block after block. The first was a fat man with deeply set eyes, enormous jowls, and a wispy chin beard. His size made him the least likely of the three candidates, because he was highly visible; this was a line of work that favored nondescript men. The second suspect was slender, in his forties, with a narrow, bony face. The third was young, perhaps twenty-five, dressed in blue jeans and a yellow nylon windbreaker; as he walked, he puffed nervously on a cigarette. By the time Alex reached the Moonglow Lounge, he still hadn't decided which of the three men was tailing him, but he had committed every detail of their faces to memory for future reference.

Just inside the front door of Moonglow, an easel supported a yard-square posterboard sign. The red-and-black announcement was neatly handprinted, first in Japanese characters and then in English.

DUE TO ILLNESS
JOANNA RAND
WILL NOT PERFORM TONIGHT

THE MOONGLOW ORCHESTRA
WILL PROVIDE MUSIC FOR DANCING

Alex left his topcoat with the hat-check girl and went to the bar for a drink. The restaurant was doing a lot of business, but only six customers were in the lounge. He sat alone at the curved end of the bar and ordered Old Suntory. When the bartender brought the whiskey, Alex said, "I hope Miss Rand's illness isn't serious."

"Not serious," the bartender assured him in heavily accented English. "Only sore throat."

"Would you please call upstairs and tell her that Alex Hunter is here?"

"Too sick see anyone," the man said, nodding and smiling.

"I'm a friend."

"Much too sick."

"She'll talk to me."

"Sore throat."

"We have an appointment."

"So sorry."

They went around and around for a while, until the bartender finally surrendered and picked up a phone beside the cash register. As he spoke with Joanna, he glanced repeatedly at Alex. When he hung up and returned to Alex, he said, "Sorry. She say can't see you."

"You must be mistaken. Call her again, please."

The bartender was clearly embarrassed for him. "She say don't know anyone name Alex Hunter."

"But she does."

The bartender said nothing.

"We had lunch together," Alex said.

The man shrugged.

"Just this afternoon."

A pained smile. And: "So sorry."

A customer asked for service at the far end of the bar, and the bartender hurried away with obvious relief.

Alex stared at his reflection in the bluish bar mirror. He sipped the Old Suntory.

Softly he said, "What the hell's going on here?"

15

$\oplus$ $\oplus$ $\oplus$

When Alex asked for Mariko Inamura, the bartender was at first no more inclined to cooperate than when he'd been asked to put in a call to Joanna. At last, however, he relented and summoned Mariko on the house phone.

A few minutes later she entered the lounge through a door marked PRIVATE. She was Joanna's age and quite lovely. Her thick black hair was held up with ivory pins.

Alex stood and bowed to her.

After she returned the bow, they introduced themselves, and she sat on the stool next to his.

As he sat again, he said, "Mariko-san, I've heard many good things about you."

"Likewise, Mr. Hunter." Her English was flawless. She didn't have the slightest difficulty pronouncing the L sound, which had no equivalent in her native tongue.

"How's Joanna?"

"She has a sore throat."

He sipped his whiskey. "Excuse me if I act like a stereotypical American. I don't mean to be blunt and boorish, but I wonder if that is really the truth—that story about a sore throat."

Mariko was silent. She looked away from him, down at her hands.

Alex said, "Joanna told the bartender she didn't know anyone named Alex Hunter."

Mariko sighed.

"What's wrong here, Mariko-san?"

"She spoke so well of you. She was like a young girl. I began to hope it would be different this time."

"What's wrong with her?"

Mariko continued to stare at the polished bartop in front of her and said nothing. The Japanese had a highly developed sense of propriety, a complex system of social graces, and a very rigid set of standards concerning the conduct of personal relationships. She was reluctant to talk about her friend, for in doing so, she would not be conducting herself according to those standards.

"I already know about the bad dream she has every night," Alex prodded gently.

Mariko was clearly surprised. "Joanna's never told anyone about that—except me."

"And now me."

She glanced at Alex, and he saw a greater warmth in her coal-colored eyes than he'd seen a minute ago. Nevertheless, to stall, she signaled the bartender and ordered Old Suntory over ice.

Alex sensed that Mariko was basically conservative and old-fashioned. She couldn't easily overcome the traditional Japanese respect for other people's privacy.

When her drink came, she sipped it slowly, rattled the ice in the glass, and at last said, "If Joanna's told you about her nightmare, then she's probably told you as much about herself as she ever tells anyone."

"She's secretive?"

"Not that, exactly."

"Modest?"

"That's part of it. But only part. It's also as if . . . as if she's afraid to talk about herself too much."

He watched Mariko closely. "Afraid? What do you mean?"

"I can't explain it. . . ."

He waited, aware that she had capitulated. She needed a moment to decide where to begin.

After another sip of Old Suntory, she said, "What Joanna did to you tonight . . . pretending not to know you . . . this isn't the first time she's behaved that way."

"It doesn't seem to be her style."

"Every time she does it, I'm shocked. It's out of character. She's really the sweetest, kindest person. Yet, whenever she begins to feel close to a man, when she begins perhaps to fall in love with him—or he with her—she kills the romance. And she's never nice about it. A different woman. Almost . . . mean. Cold."

"But I don't see how that applies to me. We've only had one date, an innocent lunch together."

Mariko nodded solemnly. "But she's fallen for you. Fast."

"No. You're wrong about that."

"Just before you came on the scene, she was deeply depressed."

"She didn't seem that way to me."

"That's what I mean. You had an instant effect on her. She's always in bad shape for a few weeks or even months after she drops someone she cares for, but recently she'd reached new lows. She felt so alone, lost. You lifted her spirits overnight."

"If she's really so lonely . . . why does she keep destroying every relationship?"

"She never wants to. But she seems compelled to shatter every hope of companionship."

"Has she tried therapy?"

Mariko frowned. "My uncle's a fine psychologist. I've urged her to see him about this and the nightmare, but she refuses. I worry about her all the time. At its deepest and blackest, her depression is contagious. It infects me at times, a little. If she didn't need me and if I didn't care for her so much, like my own sister, I'd have left long ago. She needs to share her life with friends, a partner. The last few months she's pushed people away harder than usual, even me to some extent. In fact, it's been so bad I'd just about decided to get out no matter what—and then you came along. Her immediate reaction to you was . . . Well, this time it seemed as if she might overcome her fear and form something permanent."

Alex shifted on the bar stool. "Mariko-san, you're making me uneasy. You're seeing a lot more in this relationship than there really is. She doesn't love me, for heaven's sake. Love doesn't happen this fast."

"Don't you believe in love at first sight?"

"That's a poet's conceit."

"I think it can happen," she demurred.

"Good luck. Fact is, I don't think I believe in love at all, much less in love at first sight."

She regarded him with amazement. "Not believe in love? Then what do you call it when a man and woman—"

"I call it lust—"

"Not just that."

"—and affection, mutual dependence, sometimes even temporary insanity."

"That's all you've ever felt? I don't believe it."

He shrugged. "It's true."

"Love is the only thing we can depend on in this world. To deny that it exists—"

"Love is the *last* thing we can depend on. People say they're in love. But it never lasts. The only constants are death and taxes."

"Some men don't work," Mariko said, "therefore, they pay no taxes. And there are many wise men who believe in life everlasting."

He opened his mouth to argue but grinned instead. "I have a hunch you're a natural-born debater. I'd better stop while I'm only slightly behind."

"What about Joanna?" she asked. "Don't you care for her?"

"Yes, of course, I do."

"But you don't believe in love."

"I *like* Joanna enormously. But as for love—"

Mariko raised one hand to silence him. "I'm sorry. This is rude of me. You've no reason to reveal so much of yourself."

"If I didn't want to talk, you couldn't pry a word out of me."

"I just wanted you to know that regardless of what you feel for her, Joanna is drawn to you. Strongly. Perhaps it's even love. That's why she rejected you so bluntly—because she's afraid of such a deep commitment."

As Mariko drank the last of her whiskey and got up to leave, Alex said, "Wait. I've got to see her."

"Why?"

"Because . . . I've got to."

"Lust, I suppose."

"Maybe."

"Not love, of course."

He said nothing.

"Because you don't believe in love," she said.

He nodded.

Mariko smiled knowingly.

Alex didn't want to explain about Lisa Chelgrin, so he let Mariko think that, after all, he felt more for Joanna than he was willing to admit. "It's important, Mariko-san."

"Come back tomorrow night. Joanna can't take off work forever."

"Won't you just go upstairs now and persuade her to see me?"

"It wouldn't help. She's at her worst just after she's broken off with someone. When she's in this mood, she won't listen to me or anyone."

"I'll be back tomorrow."

"She'll be cold to you."

He smiled weakly. "I'll charm her."

"Other good men have given up."

"I won't."

Mariko put one hand on his arm. "Pursue her, Alex-san. I think you need her every bit as much as she needs you."

She walked away from him and disappeared through the door marked PRIVATE.

For a while after she left, Alex stared at himself in the blue mirror behind the bar.

The Moonglow orchestra played dance music. A Glenn Miller tune. The legendary Miller was long dead. Lost in a mysterious plane crash in World War II. His body had never been found.

Sometimes people vanish. The world goes on.

16
✪ ✪ ✪

Alex was surprised by his reaction to Joanna's rejection. He had the irrational urge to punch someone, anyone, and to pitch his whiskey glass at the bar mirror.

He restrained himself but only because surrender to the urge would be an admission of how powerfully this woman affected him. He'd always thought that he was immune to the sickness of romance. Now he was uneasy about his response to her—and as yet unwilling to think seriously about it.

He ate a light dinner at the Moonglow and left before the orchestra had finished its first set of the evening. The brassy, bouncy music—"A String of Pearls"—followed him into the street.

The sun had abandoned Kyoto. The city gave forth its own cold, electric illumination. With the arrival of darkness, the temperature had plummeted below freezing. Fat snowflakes circled lazily through the light from windows, open doors, neon signs, and passing cars, but they melted upon contact with the pavement, where the same lights were reflected in a skin of icy water.

Instead of putting on his topcoat, Alex draped it capelike over his shoulders. He could foresee several circumstances in which he might wish to be quickly free of such a bulky, encumbering garment.

Standing outside the Moonglow Lounge, he looked around as if deciding where to go next. In seconds, he spotted one of the three men who had appeared to be following him earlier in the evening.

The gaunt, middle-aged Japanese with a narrow face and prominent cheekbones waited thirty yards away, in front of a neon-emblazoned nightclub called Serene Dragon. Coat collar turned up, shoulders hunched against the wintry wind, he tried to blend with the pleasure-seekers streaming through the Gion, but his furtive manner made him conspicuous.

Smiling, pretending to be unaware of being watched, Alex considered the possibilities. He could take an uneventful stroll to the Kyoto Hotel, return to his suite, and go to bed for the night—still buzzing with energy, tied in knots of frustration, and none the wiser about the people behind the Chelgrin kidnapping. Or he could have some fun with the man who had him under surveillance.

The choice was easy.

Whistling happily, Alex walked deeper into the glittering Gion. After five minutes, having changed streets twice, he glanced behind and saw the operative following at a discreet distance.

In spite of the rising wind and shatters of snowflakes, the streets were still busy. Sometimes the nightlife in Kyoto seemed too frantic for Japan—perhaps because it was squeezed into fewer hours than in Tokyo and most Western cities. The nightclubs opened in late afternoon and usually closed by eleven-thirty. The two million residents of Kyoto had the provincial habit of going to bed before midnight. Already, by their schedule, half the night was gone, and they were in a rush to enjoy themselves.

Alex was fascinated by the Gion: a complex maze of streets, alleys, winding passages, and covered footpaths, all crowded with nightclubs, bars, craft shops, short-time hotels, sedate inns, restaurants, public baths, temples, movie theaters, shrines, snack shops, geisha houses. The larger streets were noisy, exciting, garish, ablaze with rainbow neon that was reflected and refracted in acres of glass, polished steel, and plastic. Here, the wholesale adoption of the worst elements of Western style proved that not *all* of the Japanese possessed the good taste and highly refined sense of design for which the country was noted. In many alleyways and cobbled lanes, however, a more appealing Gion flourished. Off major thoroughfares, pockets of traditional architecture survived: houses that still served as homes, as well as old-style houses that had been transformed into expensive spas, restaurants, bars, or intimate cabarets; and all shared the time-honored construction of satiny, weather-smoothed woods and polished stones and heavy bronze or ironwork.

Alex walked the backstreets, thinking furiously, searching for an opportunity to play turnabout with the man who was tailing him.

The tail also assumed the role of a tourist. He did his phony window-shopping half a block behind Alex and, amusingly, in perfect harmony with him.

Of course, the guy might be more than merely a hired shadow. If Joanna was really Senator Tom Chelgrin's daughter, the stakes in this mysterious game were likely to be so high that the rules might allow murder.

Finally, seeking respite from the chill wind, Alex went into a bar and ordered sake. He drank several small cups of the hot brew, and when he went outside again, the gaunt man was waiting, a shadow among shadows, twenty yards away.

Fewer people were on the street than when Alex had gone into the bar, but the Gion was still far too busy for the stranger to risk an assault—if, in fact, his mission was to do anything more than conduct surveillance. The Japanese people were generally not as apathetic about crime as were most Americans. They respected tradition, stability, order, and the law. Most would attempt to apprehend a man who committed a crime in public.

Alex went into a beverage shop and bought a bottle of Awamori, an Okinawa sweet-potato brandy that was smooth and delicious to the Japanese palate but coarse and acrid by Western standards. He wasn't concerned about the taste, because he didn't intend to drink it.

When Alex came out of the shop, the gaunt man was standing fifty or sixty feet to the north, at a jewelry-store window. He didn't look up, but when Alex headed south, the hired shadow drifted after him.

Alex turned right at the first crossroads and ventured into a lane that was only open to pedestrians. The beauty of the old buildings was tainted by only a small amount of neon: Fewer than a dozen signs shone in the snowy night, and all were much smaller than the flashing monstrosities elsewhere in the Gion. Spirals of snow spun around half-century-old, globe-type street lamps. He passed a shrine that was flanked by cocktail lounges and bathed in dim yellow light, where worshipers practiced ancient central Asian temple dances to the accompaniment of finger bells and eerie string music. People were walking in that block too; though considerably fewer than in the lane that he'd just left, they were still numerous enough to discourage murder or even assault.

With the stranger tagging along, Alex tried other branches of the maze. He progressed from commercial blocks to areas that were half residential. The gaunt man became increasingly conspicuous in the thinning crowd and fell back more than thirty yards.

Eventually Alex found a quiet, deserted lane that fronted single-family homes and apartments. The only lights were those above the doors of the houses: accordionlike paper lanterns, waterproofed with oil and suspended on electric cords. The lanterns swung in the wind, and macabre shadows capered demonically across the snow-wet cobblestones.

The next alleyway was precisely what he needed: a six-foot-wide, brick-paved serviceway. On both sides, the backs of houses faced the passage. The first block featured three lights, one at each end and one in the middle. Among shadows that pooled between the alleyway lamps, there were groups of trash barrels and a few bicycles tethered to fences, but no people were anywhere to be seen.

Alex hurried into the alley, pulling off his topcoat as he went. Holding the coat, and with the bottle of Awamori gripped firmly in his right hand, he broke into a run. His shoes slipped on the damp bricks, but he didn't fall.

His heart pounded as he sprinted out of the light into the first long patch of darkness, ran under the midpoint lamp, and dashed into another stretch of deep gloom. His breath exploded in bursts of steam, and his injured arm bumped painfully against his side. When he reached the well-illuminated circle of brick pavement beneath the third and final street lamp, he stopped and turned and looked back.

The gaunt man was not yet in sight.

Alex dropped his topcoat in the center of the puddle of light. He hurried back the way he had come, but only ten or fifteen feet, until he was out of the reach of the street lamp and in the embrace of darkness once more.

He was still alone.

He quickly slipped behind a row of five enormous trash barrels and hunkered down. From the space between the barrels and the back wall of the house, he had an unobstructed view of the intersection where the gaunt man would soon appear.

Footsteps. Sound carried well in the cold air.

Alex strove to quiet his own ragged breathing.

The stranger entered the far end of the serviceway and stopped abruptly, surprised by the disappearance of his prey.

In spite of the apprehension that had pulled him as taut as a drumhead, Alex smiled.

The stranger stood without moving, without making a sound.

Come on, you bastard.

Finally the man approached along the serviceway. Warier than he had been a minute ago, he moved as lightly as a cat, making no noise to betray himself.

Alex cupped one hand over his mouth, directing the crystallized plumes of his breath toward the ground, hoping they would dissipate before they could rise like ghosts in the darkness and possibly betray his position.

As the stranger approached, he cautiously checked behind the trash cans on both sides of the alley. He moved in a half crouch. His right hand was jammed in his coat pocket.

Holding a gun?

The gaunt man walked out of the first circle of light and into darkness, visible only as a silhouette.

Although the night was cold and Alex was without a coat, he began to perspire.

The stranger reached the midpoint light. Methodically he continued to inspect every object and shadow behind which—or in which—a man might hide.

Beside Alex, the garbage cans exuded the nauseating odor of spoiled fish and rancid cooking oil. He'd been aware of the stench from the moment he'd hidden behind the barrels, and second by second, it grew riper, more disgusting. He imagined that he could taste as well as smell the fish. He resisted the urge to gag, to clear his throat, and to spit out the offending substance.

The gaunt man was almost out of the light at the halfway point, about to step into the second stretch of darkness, when again he stopped and stood as if quick-frozen.

He had seen the topcoat. Perhaps he was thinking that the coat had slipped off Alex's shoulder and that, in a panic, Alex had not stopped to retrieve it.

The stranger moved again—not slowly, as before, and not with caution either. He strode purposefully toward the third streetlight and the discarded topcoat. The hard echoes of his footsteps bounced back and forth between the houses that bracketed him, and he didn't look closely at any more of the trash barrels.

Alex held his breath.

The stranger was twenty feet away.

Ten feet.

Five.

As soon as the guy passed by, literally close enough to touch, Alex rose in the shadows.

The stranger's attention was fixed on the coat.

Alex slipped soundlessly into the passageway behind his adversary. What little noise he made was masked by the other man's footsteps.

The stranger stopped in the circle of light, bent down, and picked up the topcoat.

Because it fell behind, Alex's shadow did not betray him as he moved into the light, but the stranger sensed the danger. He gasped and began to turn.

Alex swung the Awamori with all his strength. The bottle exploded against the side of the stranger's head, and a rain of glass rang down on the brick pavement. The night was filled with the aroma of sweet-potato brandy.

The stranger staggered, dropped the coat, put one hand to his head, reached feebly for Alex with the other hand, and then fell as if his flesh had been transformed into lead by some perverse alchemy.

Glancing left and right along the alleyway, Alex expected people to come out of the houses to see what was happening. The pop of the bottle as it broke and the clink of glass had seemed loud. He stood with the neck of the bottle still clamped in his right hand, ready to flee at the first sign of response, but after half a minute he realized that he hadn't been heard.

17

♣ ♣ ♣

The flurries of snow had grown into a squall. Dense sheets of fat white flakes swirled through the passageway.

The gaunt man was unconscious but not seriously hurt. His heart was beating strongly, and his breathing was shallow but steady. The ugly red precursor of a bruise marked the spot where the bottle had shattered against his temple, but the superficial cuts in his face had already begun to clot.

Alex searched the stranger's pockets. He found coins, a wad of paper money, a book of matches that bore no advertising, a packet of facial tissues, breath mints, and a comb. He didn't find a wallet, credit cards, a driver's license, or any other identification, and the absence of ID told him almost as much as he could hope to learn: He was dealing with a cautious professional.

The guy was carrying a gun: a Japanese-made 9mm automatic with a sound suppressor. It was in his right overcoat pocket, which was much deeper than the left pocket. Evidently he carried the pistol so routinely that he had modified his wardrobe to accommodate it. He also had a spare magazine of ammunition.

Alex propped him against a wall on one side of the alleyway. The gunman sat where he was placed, hands at his sides, palms turned up. His chin rested on his chest.

After retrieving his soiled topcoat, Alex slipped it on, not just cape style this time. The knife wounds flared with pain as he eased his bandaged left arm into the coat sleeve.

By now a thin, icy lace of snow covered the unconscious man's hair. In his battered condition, with the snowflake mantilla, he looked like a pathetic yet determinedly jaunty drunk who was trying to get laughs by wearing a doily on his head.

Alex stooped beside him and slapped his face a couple of times to bring him around.

The gunman stirred, opened his eyes, and blinked stupidly. Comprehension came gradually to him.

Alex pointed the pistol at the guy's heart. When he was sure that his captive was no longer disoriented, he said, "I have a few questions."

"Go to hell," the guy said in Japanese.

Alex spoke in the same language. "Why were you following me?"

"I wasn't."

"You think I'm a fool?"

"Yes."

Alex poked him hard in the stomach with the gun, then again.

Wincing, the stranger said, "I was going to rob you."

"No. Nothing that simple. Someone ordered you to watch me."

The man said nothing.

"Who's your boss?" Alex asked.

"I'm my own boss."

"Don't lie." Alex poked him hard with the gun once more.

The stranger gasped in pain, glared at him, but didn't respond.

Although Alex was incapable of using physical abuse to extract information, he was willing to engage in light psychological torture. He put the cold muzzle of the weapon against the man's left eye.

With his right eye, the stranger stared back unwaveringly. He didn't appear to be intimidated.

"Who's your boss?" Alex asked.

No response.

"One round, through the brain."

The stranger remained silent.

"I'll do it," Alex said quietly.

"You're not a killer."

"Is that what they told you?" Alex pressed the muzzle against the guy's left eye just hard enough to hurt him.

The wind fluted through the clusters of trash barrels, playing them as though they were organ pipes, producing a crude, hollow, ululant, unearthly music.

Finally Alex sighed and rose to his feet. Staring down at the stranger, still training the gun on him, he said, "Tell your bosses I'll get to the truth one way or another. If they want to save me time, if they want to cooperate, maybe I'll keep my mouth shut when I know what this is all about."

The gaunt man virtually spat out his response: "You're dead."

"We're all dead sooner or later."

"In your case, sooner."

"I'm not going to drop this case. I'm going to be a bulldog. Tell them that," Alex said. "You people don't scare me."

"We haven't tried yet."

Still holding the pistol, Alex backed off. When he and the stranger were separated by twenty yards of pavement, he turned and walked away.

At the end of the alley, when Alex glanced back, the gaunt man had vanished into the gloom and the snow.

Alex rounded the corner and walked swiftly through the Gion maze toward more major thoroughfares.

The blackness above the city seemed to be something other than an ordinary night sky, something worse, an astronomical oddity that bled all the heat from the world below, that sucked away the light as well, until even the dazzling spectacle of the Gion dimmed to a somber glow, until every bright-yellow bulb began to radiate a thin and sour aura, until red neon darkened to the muddy maroon of cold, coagulating blood.

The late-autumn chill pierced him and scraped like a steel scalpel along his bones.

It was not a night for sleeping alone, but the bed that awaited him would be empty, the sheets as crisp and cool as morgue shrouds.

18

In the lightless room, in bed, staring at the shadowy ceiling, Joanna startled herself by saying aloud: "Alex." That involuntary word seemed to have been spoken by someone else, and it sounded like a soft cry for help.

The name reverberated in her mind while she contemplated all the meanings that it had for her.

Misery was her only companion. She was being forced yet again to choose between a man and her obsessive need for an extraordinary degree of privacy. This time, however, either choice would destroy her. She was teetering on the brink of mental collapse.

Her joy in life—and therefore her strength—had been drained by years of compulsive solitude.

Nevertheless, if she dared to pursue Alex, the world would close like a vise around her, as it had done more than once before. In a waking nightmare, the ceiling, the walls, and the floor would appear to draw together from all sides, tighter, tighter, until she was reduced by claustrophobia to unreasoning animal panic. Huddled. Shaking. Unable to breathe. Gripped by an unshakable sense of doom.

On the other hand, if she didn't pursue him, she would finally have to accept that she would always be alone. Forever. He was her last chance. Resigning herself to unending loneliness was a heavier weight than she could carry.

Either way, whether she reached out to Alex or shunned him, she would be unable to endure the consequences. She was so tired of the struggle of living.

She longed for sleep. Her head ached. Her eyes burned. She felt as though innumerable lead weights encumbered her limbs. In sleep she would be briefly free.

She raised herself from the sheets and sat on the edge of the bed. Without switching on the lamp, she opened the nightstand drawer and located the small bottle of the prescription drug on which she depended more nights than not. Although she'd taken one sedative an hour ago, she wasn't even drowsy. One more couldn't do any harm.

But then she thought, *Why just one more? Why not five, ten, an entire bottleful?*

Her exhaustion, her fear, and her depression at the prospect of perpetual loneliness were so grave that she didn't reject the idea immediately, as she would have done only a day ago.

In the darkness, like a penitent reverently fingering rosary beads, Joanna counted pills.

Twenty.

That was surely enough for a long sleep.

No. She must not call it sleep. No euphemisms. She would hold on to at least some self-respect. She must be honest with herself, if nothing else. Call it by its true name. Suicide.

She wasn't frightened, repelled, or embarrassed by the word, and she realized that her weary acceptance represented a terrible loss of will. For as long as she could remember, she had been tough enough to face anything, but she had no resources left. She was so tired.

Twenty pills.

No more loneliness. No longer would she have to yearn for intimacy that she could never allow herself to accept. No more alienation. No more doubts. No more pain. No more nightmares, visions of syringes, and grasping mechanical hands. No more.

She no longer had to choose between Alex Hunter and her sick compulsion to smash love when and where it arose. Now the choice was much simpler yet far more profound. For the moment she had to decide only whether to take one more pill—or all twenty.

She held them in her cupped hands.

They were as smooth and cool as tiny pebbles fished from a mountain stream.

19

♣ ♣ ♣

Alex was accustomed to sleeping as little as possible. If time was money, then every minute spent in sleep was an act of financial irresponsibility. This night, however, he was not going to get even the few hours of rest that he usually required. His mind raced, and he couldn't downshift it.

Finally he got a bottle of beer from the refrigerator in the suite's wet bar and sat in an armchair in the drawing room. The only light was that which came through the windows—the pale, ghostly radiance of predawn Kyoto.

He was not worried about the people who had sent the *dorobo* to his hotel room and had him followed in the Gion. The single cause of his insomnia was Joanna. A torrent of images cascaded through his mind: Joanna in the pantsuit that she'd worn to lunch at Mizutani; Joanna on the stage of the Moonglow Lounge, moving sinuously in a clinging, red silk dress; Joanna laughing; Joanna so vibrant and *alive* in the Kyoto sun; Joanna frightened and huddled in the shade of the trees in the garden at Nijo Castle.

He was filled with an almost painful desire, but more surprising was the tenderness that he felt toward her, something deeper than affection, deeper even than friendship.

Not love.

He didn't believe in love.

His parents had proved to him that love was a word that had no meaning. Love was a sham, a hoax. It was a drug with which people deluded themselves, repressing their true feelings and all awareness of the primitive jungle reality of existence. Occasionally, and always with apparent sincerity, his mother and father had told him that they loved him. Sometimes, when the mood seized them—usually after their morning hangovers abated but before the new day's intake of whiskey had awakened the dragons in them—they hugged him and wept and loudly despised themselves for what they had done the night before, for the latest black eye or bruise or burn or cut that they had administered.

When they felt especially guilty, they bought lots of inexpensive gifts for him—comic books, small toys, candy, ice cream—as if a war had ended and reparations were required. They called it love, but it never lasted. In hours it faded, and it vanished altogether by nightfall. Eventually Alex had learned to dread his parents' slobbering, boozy displays of "love," because when love waned, as it always did, their anger and brutality seemed worse by comparison with the preceding brief moment of peace. At its best, love was just a seasoning like pepper and salt, enhancing the bitter flavor of loneliness, hatred, and pain.

Therefore, he had not, would not, *could* not fall in love with Joanna Rand. His feelings for her were strong, more than lust, more than affection. Something new. And strange. If he was not falling in love, then he was at least sailing in uncharted waters, and the guide that he most needed was caution.

He drank two bottles of beer and returned to bed. He couldn't get comfortable. He lay in every position permitted by his injured left arm, yet sleep eluded him. The injury wasn't the problem: Joanna was. He tried to banish all thoughts of her by picturing the hypnotic motion of the sea, the gracefully rolling masses of water, endless chains of waves surging through the night. After a time, he did grow drowsy, although even the primordial rhythms and mesmeric power of the sea couldn't bar Joanna from his mind: She was the only swimmer in the currents of his dreams.

He was awakened by the phone.

According to the luminous number on the travel clock, it was four-thirty in the morning. He had been asleep less than an hour.

He picked up the handset and recognized Mariko's voice. "Alex-san, Joanna asked me to call you. Can you come here right away? A very bad thing has happened."

He sat up in bed, shuddering and suddenly nauseous. "What have they done to her?"

"She's done it to herself, Alex-san." Mariko's voice broke. "She tried to commit suicide."

✪ ✪ ✪

The sky was still spitting snow, but the accumulation on the streets was no more than a quarter of an inch by the time that the taxi dropped Alex at the Moonglow Lounge.

Black hair cascading over her shoulders, ivory pins forgotten, Mariko was waiting for him at the front door of the club. "Joanna's upstairs. The doctor's with her."

"Will she be okay?"

"He says she will."

"Is he a good doctor?"

"Dr. Mifuni has been treating her for years."

"But is he any *good?*" he demanded, surprised by the vehemence in his voice.

"Yes, Alex-san. He's a good doctor."

He followed Mariko past the bar with the blue mirror into an elegantly decorated office and up a set of stairs to Joanna's apartment.

The living room was furnished with cane, rattan, and rosewood. There were half a dozen excellent watercolors on scrolls, and numerous potted plants.

"She's in the bedroom with Dr. Mifuni. We'll wait here," said Mariko, indicating a couch.

Sitting beside her, Alex said, "Was it . . . a gun?"

"Oh, no. No. Thank God. Sleeping tablets."

"Who found her?"

"She found me. I have a three-room apartment on the floor above this one. I was asleep . . . and she came to my room, woke me." Mariko's voice faltered. "She said, 'Mariko-san, I'm afraid I'm making a goddamned silly fool of myself, as usual.'"

"Dear God."

"There were twenty pills in the bottle. She'd taken eighteen before she'd realized that suicide wasn't the answer. I called an ambulance."

"Why isn't she in a hospital?"

"The paramedics came, made her swallow a tube... pumped out her stomach right here." She closed her eyes and grimaced at the memory.

"I've seen it done," Alex said. "It isn't pleasant."

"I held her hand. By the time they were finished, Dr. Mifuni arrived. He didn't think a hospital was necessary."

Alex glanced at the bedroom door. The silence behind it seemed ominous, and he had to resist an impulse to cross the living room and yank the door open to see if Joanna was all right.

Looking at Mariko again, he said, "Is this the first time she tried to kill herself?"

"Of course!"

"Do you think she actually intended to go through with it?"

"Yes, at first."

"What changed her mind?"

"She realized it was wrong."

"Some people only pretend suicide. They're looking for sympathy, or maybe for—"

She interrupted him. Her voice was as cold as the vapor rising from a block of dry ice. "If you think Joanna would stoop to such a thing, then you don't know her at all." Mariko was stiff with anger. Her small hands were fisted on her lap.

After a while he nodded. "You're right. She's not that mixed up . . . or that selfish."

Gradually the stiffness left Mariko.

He said, "But I wouldn't think she's the type to seriously consider suicide, either."

"She was so depressed before she met you. Then after she . . . rejected you . . . it got worse. At one moment she was so far down that death seemed the only way out. But she's strong. Even stronger than my mama-san, who is an iron lady."

The bedroom door opened, and Dr. Mifuni entered the living room. He was a short man with a round face and thick black hair. When meeting someone new, the Japanese were usually quick to smile, but Mifuni was somber.

Alex was sure that something had gone wrong, that Joanna had taken a turn for the worse. His mouth went as dry as talcum.

Even under these less than ideal circumstances, Mariko took the time to introduce the two men formally, with a good word said about the qualities of each. Now there were bows and smiles all around.

The introductory ritual almost shattered Alex's brittle nerves. He nearly pushed past the physician and into the bedroom. But he controlled himself and said, "Isha-san *dozo yoroshiku.*"

Mufini bowed too. "I am honored to make your acquaintance, Mr. Hunter."

"Is Joanna feeling better?" Mariko asked.

"I've given her something to calm her. But there's still time for Mr. Hunter to talk with her before the sedative takes effect." He smiled at Alex again. "In fact, she insists on seeing you."

Unnerved by the emotional turmoil that gripped him, Alex went into the bedroom and closed the door behind him.

21

⊕ ⊕ ⊕

Joanna was sitting in bed, propped against pillows, wearing blue silk pajamas. Although her hair was damp and lank, although she was so pale that her skin seemed translucent, although vague dark smudges of weariness encircled her eyes, she was still beautiful to him. The suffering showed only in her amethyst-blue eyes; that evidence of her pain and fear made Alex weak as he sat on the edge of the bed.

"Hi," she said softly.

"Hi."

"After they pumped all the sleeping pills out of me, I've been given a sedative. Isn't that ironic?"

He could think of nothing to say.

"Before I fall asleep," she said, "I want to know . . . do you still think I'm really . . . not who I think I am?"

"Lisa Chelgrin? Yes. I do."

"How can you be so positive?"

"There've been developments since we had lunch. I'm being followed everywhere I go."

"By whom?"

"I need time to explain."

"I'm not going anywhere," she said.

"But your eyes are beginning to droop."

She blinked rapidly. "I reached the breaking point tonight. Almost did a stupid thing."

"Hush. It's over."

"I wanted to die. If I don't have the courage to die . . . then I've got to find out why I behave the way I do."

He held her hand and said nothing.

"There's something wrong with me, Alex. I've always felt so hollow, empty . . . detached. Something happened to me a long time ago, something to make me the way I am. I'm not just . . . not just making excuses for myself."

"I realize that. God knows what they did to you—or why."

"I have to find out what it was."

"You will."

"I've got to know his name."

"Whose name?" he asked.

"The man with the mechanical hand."

"We'll find him."

"He's dangerous," she said sleepily.

"So am I."

Joanna slid down on the bed until she was flat on her back. "Damn it, I don't want to go to sleep yet."

He took one of the two pillows from beneath her head and drew the covers to her chin.

Her voice was growing thick. "There was a room . . . a room that stank of antiseptics . . . maybe a hospital somewhere."

"We'll find it."

"I want to hire you to help me."

"I've already been hired. Senator Chelgrin paid me a small fortune to find his daughter. It's about time I gave him something for his money."

"You'll come back tomorrow?"

"Yes. Whenever you want."

"One o'clock."

"I'll be here."

Her eyes fluttered, closed. "What if I'm not . . . not awake by then?"

"I'll wait."

She was silent so long that he was sure she had fallen asleep. Then she said, "I was so scared."

"Everything will be fine. It's okay."

"I'm glad you're here, Alex."

"So am I."

She turned on her side.

She slept.

The only sound was the faint hum of the electric clock.

Neither of us used the word "love," Alex thought.

After a while he kissed her forehead and left the room.

22

Mariko was sitting on the living-room couch. Mifuni had gone.

"The sedative worked," Alex said.

"The doctor said she'll sleep five or six hours. He'll be back this afternoon."

"You'll stay here with her?"

"Of course." She rose from the couch and straightened the collar of her shapeless brown robe. "Would you like tea?"

"Thank you. That would be nice."

While they sat at the small kitchen table, sipping hot tea and nibbling almond wafers, Alex told Mariko Inamura about the Chelgrin case, about the burglar he had encountered in his hotel suite, and about the man who had followed him in the Gion a few hours ago.

"Incredible," she said. "But *why?* Why would they change the girl's name . . . *change her complete set of memories* . . . and bring her here to Kyoto?"

"I haven't any idea. But I'll find out. Listen, Mariko, I've told you all this so you'll understand there are dangerous people manipulating Joanna. I don't know what they're trying to cover up, but it's obvious that the stakes are high. Tonight when you opened the door for me downstairs, you didn't ask who was there. You've got to be more careful."

"But I was expecting you."

"From now on, always expect the worst. Do you have a gun?"

Frowning, she said, "We can't protect her every minute. What about when she appears on stage? She's a perfect target then."

"If I have anything to say about it, she won't perform again until this is settled."

"But in spite of everything they've done to her, they've never hurt her physically."

"If they know she's investigating her past and might learn enough to expose them, God knows what they'll do."

She stared into her tea for a long moment, as if she had the power to read the future in that brew. "All right, Alex-san. I'll be more careful."

"Good."

He finished his tea while she telephoned the taxi company.

At the downstairs door, as he stepped into the street, Mariko said, "Alex-san, you won't be sorry that you helped her."

"I didn't expect to be."

"You'll find what you've been looking for in life."

He raised his eyebrows. "I thought I'd found it already."

"Men are the same."

"As what?"

"Men of all cultures, societies, races are equally capable of being such fools."

"We pride ourselves in our dependability," he said with a small smile.

"You need Joanna as much as she needs you."

"You've told me that before."

"Have I?"

"You know you have."

She smiled mischievously, bowed to him, and assumed an air of Asian wisdom that was partly a joke and partly serious. "Honorable detective should know that repetition of a truth does not make it any less true, and resistance to the truth can never be more than a brief folly."

She closed the door, and Alex didn't move until he heard the lock bolt slide into place.

The black taxi was waiting for him in the snow-skinned street. A few snowflakes still spiraled out of the morning sky.

A red Toyota followed his cab all the way to the hotel.

Exhaustion overcame insomnia. Alex slept four hours and got out of bed at twenty past eleven, Thursday morning.

He shaved, showered, and quickly changed the bandage on his arm, concerned that he wouldn't be ready to meet the courier from Chicago if the man arrived on time.

As he was dressing, the telephone rang. He snatched up the handset on the nightstand.

"Mr. Hunter?"

The voice was familiar, and Alex said, "Yes?"

"We met last night."

"Dr. Mifuni?"

"No, Mr. Hunter. You have my pistol." It was the gaunt-faced man from the alleyway. "You'll be receiving a message soon."

"What message?"

"You'll see," the man said, and he hung up.

After Alex hurriedly finished dressing, he removed the silencer from the 9mm automatic. He put the sound suppressor in an inside pocket of his suit coat and tucked the gun itself under his belt. He was sure that it was no more legal to carry a concealed handgun without a permit in Japan than it was in the U.S., but he preferred risking arrest to being defense-less.

At six minutes past noon, just as he buttoned his suit coat over the pistol, a sharp knock came at the door.

He went into the foyer. "Who's there?" he asked in Japanese.

"Bellhop, Mr. Hunter."

The view through the fish-eye lens revealed the bellman who had brought his luggage upstairs when he had checked into the hotel. The man was clearly distressed, fidgeting.

When Alex opened the door, the bellman bowed and said, "I'm so sorry to disturb you, sir, but do you know a Mr. Wayne Kennedy?"

"Yes, of course. He works for me."

"There's been an accident. Almost fifteen minutes ago," the bellman said anxiously. "A car, this pedestrian, very terrible, right here in front of the hotel."

Although Blakenship hadn't mentioned the courier in the fax that he had sent yesterday, Kennedy was no doubt the man.

The bellman said, "The ambulance crew wants to take Mr. Kennedy to the hospital, but every time they get close to him, he kicks and punches and tries to bite them."

Because they were speaking Japanese and because the bellman was speaking very fast, Alex thought he had misunderstood. "Kicking and punching, you said?"

"Yes, sir. He refuses to let anyone touch him or take him away until he talks to you. The police don't want to handle him because they're afraid of aggravating his injuries."

They hurried to the elevator alcove. Another bellman was holding open the doors at one of the elevators.

On the way down, Alex said, "Did you see it happen?"

"Yes, sir," said the first bellman. "Mr. Kennedy got out of the taxi, and a car angled through the traffic, jumped the curb, hit him."

"Do they have the driver?"

"He got away."

"Didn't stop?"

"No, sir," the bellman said, clearly embarrassed that any Japanese citizen could behave so lawlessly.

"What's Mr. Kennedy's condition?"

"It's his leg," said the bellman uneasily.

"Broken?" Alex asked.

"There's a lot of blood."

The hotel lobby was nearly deserted. Everyone except the desk clerks was at the scene of the accident in the street.

Alex pushed through the crowd and saw Wayne Kennedy sitting on the sidewalk with his back against the building, flanked by two blood-smeared and badly battered suitcases. The wide-eyed onlookers kept a respectful distance on three sides of him, as if he were a wild animal that no one dared approach. He was shouting furiously at a uniformed ambulance attendant who had ventured within six or seven feet of him.

Kennedy was an impressive sight: a handsome black man, about thirty years old, six foot five, two hundred forty pounds, with fierce dark eyes. Cursing at the top of his voice, shaking one huge fist at the paramedics, he looked as if he might be constructed of concrete, iron, two-by-fours, and railroad ties,

23

✪ ✪ ✪

and in spite of his incapacity, he didn't seem to be an ordinary mortal man.

When Alex glimpsed the courier's injuries, he was stunned and doubly impressed by all the shrieking, fist-shaking bravado. The leg wasn't merely broken: It was crushed. Splinters of bone had pierced the flesh and the blood-soaked trousers.

"Thank God you're here," Kennedy said as Alex knelt beside him.

The courier slumped against the wall as if someone had cut a set of supporting wires. He seemed to grow smaller, and the maniacal energy that had sustained him suddenly vanished. He was streaming sweat, shivering violently, in tremendous pain. It was amazing that he had summoned sufficient strength to hold everyone off for nearly a quarter of an hour.

"Have you really punched at the medics?" Alex asked.

"The bastards don't speak English!" Kennedy said, as if Chicagoans faced with an injured tourist from Kyoto would have held forth in fluent Japanese. "Jesus, what I had to go through to find someone . . . who could understand me. I couldn't let them cart me off until I'd delivered . . . the file." He indicated one of the suitcases at his side.

"Good God, man, the file isn't *that* important."

"It must be," Kennedy said shakily. "Someone tried . . . to kill me for it. This wasn't an accident."

"How do you know that?"

"Saw the stinking sonofabitch coming." Kennedy grimaced with pain. "A red Toyota."

Alex remembered the car that had followed his taxi from the Moonglow Lounge earlier that same morning.

"I stepped . . . out of the way . . . but he turned straight toward me."

When Alex signaled the waiting paramedics, two men rushed in with a stretcher.

"Two guys . . . in the Toyota," Kennedy said.

"Save your strength. You can tell me about it later."

"I'd rather . . . talk now," Kennedy said as the paramedics cut open his pants leg to examine his injury and to stabilize the broken bones with an inflatable splint before moving him. "Takes my mind off . . . the pain. The Toyota hit me . . . knocked me into the wall . . . ass over teakettle . . . pinned me there . . . then backed off. The guy on the passenger side got out . . . grabbed for the suitcase. We played . . . tug of war. Then I bit his hand . . . hard. He gave up."

Alex had been warned to expect a message. This was it.

With considerable effort—and a little lingering wariness—the paramedics lifted Wayne Kennedy onto the wheeled stretcher.

The courier howled as he was moved. Tears of pain streamed down his face.

The wheeled legs of the gurney folded under it as it was shoved into the van-style ambulance.

Alex picked up both suitcases and followed Kennedy. No one tried to stop him. In the van, he sat on the suitcases.

The rear doors slammed shut. One of the paramedics remained with Kennedy and began to prepare a bottle of plasma for intravenous transfusion.

The ambulance began to move, and the siren wailed.

Without raising his head from the stretcher, Wayne Kennedy said, "You still there, boss?"

"Right here," Alex assured him.

Kennedy's voice was twisted with pain, but he wouldn't be quiet. "You think I'm an idiot?"

Alex stared at the hideously crumpled leg. "Wayne, for God's sake, you were sitting there bleeding to death."

"If you'd been in my shoes . . . you'd have done the same."

"Not in a million years."

"Oh, yeah. You would've. I know you," Kennedy insisted. "You hate to lose."

The paramedic cut away the coat and shirt sleeves on Kennedy's left arm. He swabbed the ebony skin with an alcohol-damp sterile pad, then quickly placed the needle in the vein.

Kennedy's bad leg twitched. He groaned and said, "I've got something to say . . . Mr. Hunter. But maybe I shouldn't."

"Say it before you choke on it," Alex told him. "Then please shut the hell up before you talk yourself to death."

The ambulance turned the corner so sharply that Alex had to grab at the safety railing beside him to keep from sliding off the pair of suitcases.

Kennedy said, "You and me . . . we're an awful lot alike in some ways. I mean . . . like you started out with nothing . . . and so did I. You were damned determined to make it . . . to the top . . . and you did. *I'm* determined . . . to make it . . . and I will. We're both smooth on the surface and street fighters underneath."

Alex wondered if the courier was delirious. "I know all that, Wayne. Why do you think I hired you? I knew you'd be the same kind of field op that I was when I started."

Grinding the words out between clenched teeth, Kennedy said, "So I'd like to suggest . . . when you get back to the States . . . you've got to make a decision about filling Bob Feldman's job. Don't forget me."

Bob Feldman was in charge of the company's entire force of field operatives, and he was retiring in two months.

"I get things done," Kennedy said. "I'm right . . . for the job . . . Mr. Hunter."

Alex shook his head in amazement. "I can almost believe you traveled around the world and *arranged* to be hit by that car just to trap me in here for this sales pitch."

"Bob Feldman . . . retiring . . . keep me in mind," Kennedy said, his speech beginning to slur.

"I'll do better than that. I'll give you the job."

Kennedy tried to raise his head but couldn't manage to do so. "You . . . mean it?"

"I said it, didn't I?"

"Every cloud," Kennedy said, "has a silver lining," and at last he relinquished his tenuous grip on consciousness.

24

✛ ✛ ✛

After Wayne Kennedy was taken into surgery, Alex used a hospital pay phone to call Joanna.

Mariko answered. "She's still asleep, Alex-san."

He told her what had happened. "So I'm going to stay here until Wayne comes out of surgery and the doctors can tell me whether the leg stays or goes."

"It's that bad?"

"Yes. So I won't be able to get there by one o'clock, like I promised Joanna."

"You belong with your friend. She'll understand."

"I don't want her to think I'm backing out."

"She knows you better than that."

"Does Joanna have a spare bedroom?"

"For your Mr. Kennedy?"

"No. He'll be staying here. The room would be for me. Neither you nor Joanna should be alone until this is finished. Besides, it's better strategy to work out of one place. Saves time. I'd like to check out of the hotel and move in there—if it won't ruin anyone's reputation."

"I'll prepare the spare room, Alex-san."

"I'll be there as soon as I can. Keep the doors locked. And Mariko . . . we aren't quitting until we know what was done to Joanna and why."

"Good," Mariko said.

"We're going to nail these bastards to the barn wall."

"Nail them to a barn wall? Whatever that means exactly, I think it will be most excellent," Mariko agreed.

Alex was far more energized than he'd been in years. Until this moment, he hadn't fully realized that all his financial success had to some degree dampened the fire in him. His fortune, his twenty-two-room estate, and his pair of Rolls-Royces had mellowed him. But now, once again, he was a driven man.

PART TWO

♣ ♣ ♣

CLUES

The hanging bridge
Creeping vines
    Entwine our life.

—BASHO, 1644–1694

✪ ✪ ✪

25

At six o'clock the chief surgeon, Dr. Ito, came to the hospital waiting room where Alex was pacing. The doctor was a thin, elegant man in his fifties. He had been working on Wayne Kennedy for five hours. He looked tired, but he smiled because he had good news: Amputation would not be necessary. Kennedy was not entirely out of danger; all manner of complications could yet arise. More likely than not, even without complications, he would have a pronounced limp for the rest of his life, but at least he'd walk on his own two legs.

Dr. Ito was leaving the lounge when Mariko Inamura arrived to take over the vigil from Alex and free him to move his belongings from the hotel to the spare bedroom above the Moonglow Lounge. When Wayne Kennedy came out of anesthesia, he would need to see a friendly face other than those of the nurses and physicians, and he would want someone close by who spoke fluent English. Dr. Mifuni was staying with Joanna until Alex could get to the Moonglow.

Alex led Mariko to a corner of the waiting room. They sat on a yellow leatherette couch and spoke in whispers.

"The police will want to talk to Wayne," Alex told her.

"Tonight? The way he is?"

"Probably not until tomorrow when he's got his wits about him. So when he wakes up and you're certain he understands what you're saying, tell him that I want him to cooperate with the police—"

"Of course."

"—but only to a point."

Mariko frowned.

"He should give them a description of the car and the men in it," Alex said, "but he shouldn't tell them about the file he was carrying from Chicago. He'll have to pretend he's just an ordinary tourist. He hasn't any idea why they were trying to steal his suitcase. Nothing in it but shirts and underwear. Got that?"

Mariko's traditional Japanese upbringing had instilled in her a respect for authority that was as much a part of her as grain is a part of wood. "But wouldn't it be better to tell the police everything and have them working for us? They have the facilities, the manpower—"

"If Joanna is really Lisa Chelgrin, do you think her forged passport and phony identification are so convincing that no one's ever doubted them? Not for a minute? No one?"

"Well, I don't know, but—"

"Japan is insular. It doesn't welcome non-Japanese immigrants with open arms. Yet the authorities have allowed this woman to take up residence and open a business, evidently with no serious check of her background."

"You're saying this is some big international conspiracy? That the Japanese government might be involved? Alex-san, excuse me, but isn't this paranoid?"

"Joanna . . . *Lisa* isn't just an ordinary missing person. This is a damned strange situation. We're dealing with the daughter of a United States Senator. We don't know what political forces and interests are at work in this."

"In Japan the police are—"

"Do you want to take chances with Joanna's life?"

"No. But . . ."

"Trust me."

She hesitated. "All right."

Alex got to his feet. "I've arranged a private room for Wayne. You'd better go up there now. They'll be transferring him from the recovery room in a few minutes."

"Is it safe for you to leave here alone?" Mariko asked.

He picked up the suitcase that contained the Chelgrin file, having left the other bag in Wayne's room. "They think they've scared me off. For a while they'll be lying low, just watching."

Outside the hospital, the night was cold, but the snow flurries had long ago stopped. Backlighted by the moon, fast-moving trains of clouds tracked west to east.

Alex took a taxicab to the hotel, packed his bags, and checked out of his suite. From the hospital to the hotel, then from the hotel to the Moonglow Lounge, he was followed by two men in a white Honda.

By seven-thirty at Joanna's place, he had unpacked. The spare bedroom was cozy, with a low, slanted ceiling and a pair of dormer windows.

Shortly before Dr. Mifuni left, Joanna went into the kitchen to check on dinner, and the physician took advantage of her absence to draw Alex aside and speak with him. "Once or twice a night, you should look in on her to be certain she's only sleeping."

"You don't think she'd try it again?"

"No, no," Mifuni said. "There's virtually no chance. What she did last night was strictly impulsive, and she's not really impulsive by nature. Nevertheless . . ."

"I'll watch over her," Alex said softly.

"Good," Mifuni said. "I've known her since she came to Kyoto. A singer who performs more evenings than not is bound to have throat problems once in a while. But she's more than a patient. She's a friend too."

"Right now she needs all the friends she can get."

"But she's an amazingly resilient woman. She's got that going for her. Last night's experience appears to have left only minor psychological scars. And physically, she doesn't seem marked at all. Untouched. It almost seems a month has passed, not just one day."

Joanna returned from the kitchen to say good-bye to the doctor, and indeed she did look splendid. Even in faded jeans and a midnight-blue sweater worn to a smooth shine at the elbows and frayed at the cuffs, she was a vision, the golden girl once more.

"*Arigato, Isha-san.*"

"*Do itashimashita.*"

"*Konbanwa.*"

"*Konbanwa.*"

Suddenly, as Alex watched Joanna and Mifuni bowing to each other at the apartment door, he was caught in a powerful wave of desire that swept him into a strange state of mind. He seemed to be looking back and down at himself, somewhere between a condition of heightened consciousness and an out-of-body experience. He saw the familiar Alex Hunter, the carefully crafted persona that he put on view to the world—the quiet, self-assured, self-contained, determined, no-nonsense businessman—but he was also aware of an aspect of himself that had never before been visible to him. Within the cool and analytical detective was an insecure, lonely, desperately seeking, hungry creature driven by emotional need. Regarding this heretofore hidden aspect of himself, he understood that the power to see deeper into himself came from his desire for Joanna, from his need to share a life with her.

For the first time in his experience, Alex was overwhelmed by a desire that couldn't be satisfied solely through hard work and the application of his intellect. He was filled with a longing for something more abstract and spiritual than the drive for success, money, and status that had always motivated him. Joanna. He wanted Joanna. He wanted to touch her. He wanted to hold her, make love to her, be as close to her as one human being could ever get to another. But he required far more than mere physical intimacy. He sought from her a number of things that he couldn't entirely understand: a kind of peace that he could not describe; satisfactions he had never known; feelings for which he had no words. After a lifetime shaped by his unwavering denial of love's existence, he wanted love from Joanna Rand.

Old convictions and reliable psychic crutches were not easily cast aside. He couldn't yet accept the reality of love, but a part of him desperately *wanted* to believe.

The prospect of belief, however, scared the hell out of him.

26
✿ ✿ ✿

Joanna wanted the dinner to be perfect. She needed to prove to herself, as much as to Alex, that she was coping again, that life was going on, that the event of the past night was an aberration.

She served at the low table in her Japanese-style dining room, using royal-blue placemats, several shades of gray dinnerware, and dark red napkins. Six fresh white carnations were spread in a fan on one end of the table.

The food was hearty but not heavy. *Igaguri:* thorny shrimp balls filled with sweet chestnuts. *Sumashi wan:* clear soup with soybean curd and shrimp. *Tatsuta age:* sliced beef garnished with red peppers and radish. *Yuan zuke:* grilled fish in a soy-and-sake marinade. *Umani:* chicken and vegetables simmered in a richly seasoned broth. And of course they also had steamed rice—a staple of the Japanese menu—and they accompanied everything with cups of hot tea.

The dinner was a success, and Joanna felt better than she had in months. In a curious way, the suicide attempt was beneficial. Having sunk to the depths of ultimate despair, having reached even a brief moment during which she'd had no reason to go on living, she could now face anything that might come. Even by acting halfheartedly on her death wish, she seemed to have been purged of it. For the first time, she felt that she would be able to overcome the periodic paranoia and the strange claustrophobia that had destroyed so many opportunities for happiness in the past.

Immediately after they had eaten, Joanna had a chance to test her newfound strength. She and Alex moved into the living room, sat together on the sofa, and began to look through the Chelgrin file, which filled the large suitcase—and which, according to Alex, held the true story of the first two decades of her life. There were thick stacks of field investigators' reports in the gray-and-green folders of the Bonner-Hunter Security Corporation, Alex's company, scores of transcriptions of interviews with potential witnesses as well as with friends and relatives of Lisa Chelgrin, plus copies of the Jamaican police records and other official documents. The sight of all that evidence had a negative effect on Joanna, and for the first time all day, she felt threatened. The familiar strains of paranoia were a distant, ominous music in her mind— but growing louder.

More than anything else in the suitcase, the photographs disturbed her. Here was Lisa Chelgrin in blue jeans and a T-shirt, standing in front of a Cadillac convertible, smiling and waving at the camera. Here was Lisa Chelgrin in a bikini, posed at the foot of an enormous palm tree. Several close-ups, in all of which she was smiling. A dozen photos in all. All were snapshots except for the professional portrait taken for the high-school yearbook when she had been a senior. The settings in which Lisa posed and the people with whom she was photographed meant nothing whatsoever to Joanna. Nevertheless, the young girl herself—blond, with a full but lithe figure—was as familiar as the image in any mirror. As Joanna stared in disbelief at the face of the missing woman, a chill crept along her spine.

Finally she got up and retrieved half a dozen photographs of her own from a box in the bedroom closet. These shots had been taken the first year she'd lived in Japan, when she'd been working in Yokohama. She spread them on the coffee table, next to the old photos from the Chelgrin file. As she studied the resemblance between Lisa's face and her own as she had looked more than a decade ago, a dynamic but formless fear stirred in her.

"It's a remarkable likeness, isn't it?" Alex asked.

"Identical," she said weakly.

"You can see why I was convinced almost from the moment I saw you in the Moonglow."

Suddenly the air seemed too thick to breathe comfortably. The room was warm. Hot. She stood, intending to open a window to get a breath of fresh air, but she sat down again at once, too dizzy to remain on her feet. The walls moved in and out like living membranes, and the ceiling was descending, coming down, slowly but relentlessly down. Although she knew the shrinkage of the room was occurring only in her imagination, she was nevertheless terrified of being crushed to death.

"Joanna?"

She closed her eyes.

"Is something wrong?" he asked.

She was overcome by an irrational urge to tell him to pack up his pictures and his reports, and get out. His presence now seemed to be a terrible intrusion into her life, an unconscionable intimacy, and a flutter of nausea went through her at the thought that he might touch her. *He's dangerous,* she thought.

"Joanna?"

Restraining herself from lashing out at him, she said in a whisper: "The walls are closing in again."

"Walls?" Alex looked around, perplexed.

To her, the room appeared to be only a third of its former size.

The air was so hot and dry that it scorched her lungs, parched her lips.

"And the ceiling," she said. "Coming lower."

She broke into a sweat. Dissolving in the heat. Melting. As if made of wax. Unable to breathe. The heat was going to kill her.

"Is that really what you see?" he asked. "Walls closing in?"

"Y-yes."

She stared at the walls, trying to make them roll back, willing the room to return to its former proportions. She was determined not to let fear get the better of her this time.

"You're hallucinating," Alex said.

"I know. Because of you. Because of feeling . . . too close to you. This is always what happens. I've never told anyone . . . not even Mariko. I've never told anyone about the spells of paranoia either. Sometimes I think the whole world's against me, out to get me. Seems like nothing's real, all just a clever stage setting. When I start thinking like that, I want to run off and hide where no one can find me, hurt me." She was speaking rapidly, in part because she was afraid that she would lose the courage she needed to reveal these things, and in part because she hoped that talking would distract her from the advancing walls and the steadily lowering ceiling. "I've never told anyone about it because I've been afraid people will think I'm crazy. But I'm not nuts. If I were crazy, I'd accept paranoia as a perfectly normal state of mind. I wouldn't even realize I was *having* spells of paranoia."

The hallucinations grew worse. Although she was sitting, the ceiling appeared to be no more than ten or twelve inches above her head. The walls were only a few feet away on every side, rolling closer on well-oiled tracks. The atmosphere was being compressed within this space, molecules jamming against molecules, until the air ceased to be a gas and became a liquid, first as dense as water, then syrup. When she breathed, she was convinced against all reason that her throat and lungs were filling with fluid. She heard herself whimpering, and she despised her weakness, but she couldn't silence herself.

Alex took her hand. "None of it's real. You can turn it off if you try."

The air became so thick that she choked on it. She bent forward, coughed, gagged.

Alex tried to guide her through the seizure. "You've been brainwashed, Joanna. That's got to be it. The answer. Somehow. All the memories of your true past have been eradicated, replaced with totally false recollections."

100   DEAN KOONTZ

She understood, but that understanding didn't stop the ceiling from descending farther.

"After they did that to you," Alex said, holding fast to her hand as she tried to pull away from him, "they must have implanted a couple of posthypnotic suggestions that have twisted your life ever since. One of those suggestions is affecting you right this minute. Every time you meet someone who's interested in your past, anyone who might uncover the deception, then you suffer attacks of paranoia and claustrophobia *because the people who brainwashed you told you this would happen.*"

To Joanna's ear, at least, his voice boomed and echoed within the shrinking room. He was loud, demanding, as fearsome as the relentless advance of the viselike walls.

"And each time you reject the person with whom you've become close," he continued, "the claustrophobia goes away, the paranoid fear declines—*because they told you it would.* That's a damn effective method for keeping inquisitive people out of your life. You're programmed to be a loner, Joanna. *Programmed.*"

He was so plausible, so earnest—but he was not a friend. He was one of *Them.* He was one of the people who had been trying to kill her, part of the conspiracy. He couldn't be trusted. He was the worst of them all, a conniving and despicable—

As if reading her mind, he said, "No, Joanna. I'm with you. I'm here for you. I'm the best friend and the best hope you have."

She jerked reflexively as the ceiling shuddered and dropped closer to her, and she wrenched her hand out of his. She slid down on the couch.

The air had been compressed to such a degree that she could feel it against her skin. Insistent. Heavy. Metallic. All around her. Like a suit of armor. A suit of armor that was constantly growing tighter, smaller, more confining. Inside that defensive garment, she was drenched with perspiration. Her flesh was bruised by the steel embrace of her armor, and the bones ached in every torturously compressed joint.

"Fight it," Alex said.

"The walls, the walls," she keened, because the room began to close around her more quickly. No previous attack of claustrophobia had been as fierce as this one. She gasped. Her lungs were clogged. She tasted blood and realized that she had bitten her tongue. The room was rapidly shrinking to the size of a coffin, and she foresaw the conditions of the grave so clearly that she could actually *feel* the cold, damp embrace of eternity.

"Close your eyes," Alex said urgently.

"No!" That would be intolerable. If she closed her eyes, she would be surrendering to the grave. She would never be able to open her eyes again. The darkness would seize her and drag her down, the cold and the dampness, the silence, down into the bottomless black maw of forever. "Oh, my *God*," she groaned miserably.

"Close your eyes," Alex insisted.

He put one hand on her shoulder, and she tried to pull away, but his grip tightened.

"Let me alone. Get away," she demanded.

"Trust me."

"I know what you are."

"I'm your best hope."

She found the strength to draw herself into a sitting position from which she could confront him. For the moment she was able to bear up under the colossal weight of the descending ceiling. The most important thing was to get rid of him. "Get out."

"No, Joanna."

"Now. I mean it. Get out."

"No."

"I don't want you here. I don't need you. *Get out!*"

"No."

"This is *my* place, you sonofabitch. I *hate* you, get out, get out, damn you!"

"It's not your place. It's Joanna's place. Right now you aren't Joanna. You don't act like her at all."

She knew that what he said was true. She was behaving like a woman possessed. In her heart, she didn't want to argue with him or drive him away, but she could not stop herself. She struck at his face, and he blocked the blow, so she tried to claw at his eyes, but he seized her wrist.

"You creep, you sick sonofabitch!"

They struggled on the couch. She was atop him, trying to hurt him, so badly *needing* to hurt him, but he was holding her off, and the longer that he prevented her from drawing his blood the more enraged she became.

"I know what you are," she shrieked, "I know *exactly* what you are, oh, yes, you *rotten* bastard."

Her heart was thudding with terror that she couldn't understand. Her vision blurred with a fierce anger that wasn't real, for she had nothing to be angry *about*, yet her fury was so powerful that it was shaking her to pieces.

"You're one of *Them!*" she cried, and she had no idea what she meant by that.

"Who?"

"*Them!*"

"*Who?*"

"I hate your guts," she said, trying to jam her knee into his crotch and break his hold on her.

"Listen, listen to me," he demanded, holding both her wrists, struggling against her determined assault. "Listen, damn it!"

But she dared not listen, because if she listened, the walls would complete their inward journey, and she would be crushed. Listening to him was what had gotten her into this trouble in the first place.

"Stop it, Joanna!"

She rolled off the couch, pulling him with her, kicking at him, twisting in his grasp. She tore loose and scrambled to her feet. "Get out! I'll call the police. Get the hell out of my house," she shouted, and she could feel that her face was wrenched into a mask of blind fury.

It was an inexplicable rage—except somehow she knew that she would be all right if she could force him to leave. When he was gone, when she was alone, the walls would roll back. The air would no longer be so thick, so difficult to breathe. The terror would subside when at last he went away, and thereafter she would find peace again.

"You don't really want me to go," he said, getting to his own feet, calmly challenging her.

She slapped his face so hard that her hand stung as if an electrical current had blasted through it.

He didn't move.

She slapped him again, harder, leaving the imprint of her hand on his cheek.

With no anger in his face, with an infuriating compassion in his eyes, he reached out to touch her.

She shrank back.

"Give me your hand," he pleaded.

"Get away."

"I'm going to lead you through this."

"Get out of my life."

"Give me your hand."

She backed into one corner of the living room. Nowhere to go. He stood in front of her. Trapped.

She was shaking violently with fear. Her heart was knocking in her breast. She couldn't get her breath; each inhalation was shaken out of her before she could draw it all the way into her lungs.

He took her hand before she realized what he'd done. She no longer had the strength to wrench away from him.

"I'm going to stay here until you close your eyes and cooperate with me," he said quietly. "Or until the walls crush you or the ceiling presses you into the floor. Which will it be?"

She slumped against the wall.

"Close your eyes," he said.

Tears blurred her vision so completely that she couldn't see his face. He might have been anyone.

"Close your eyes."

Weeping, she slid down the wall, her back in the corner, until she was sitting on the floor.

He dropped to his knees in front of her. Now he was holding both of her hands. "Close your eyes, Joanna. Please. Trust me."

Sobbing uncontrollably, Joanna closed her eyes, and immediately she felt that she was in a coffin, one of those hulking bronze models with a lead lining, and the lid was bolted down just inches above her face. Such a narrow space, shallow and dark, as black as the heart of a moonless midnight, so utterly lightless that the darkness might have been a living thing, an amorphous entity that flowed all around her and molded to her shape, sucking the heat of life out of her.

Nevertheless, cornered and in an extreme state of helplessness, she could do nothing but keep her eyes closed and listen to Alex. His voice was a beacon that marked the way to release, to freedom.

"Keep your eyes closed. No need to look," Alex said softly. "I'll be your eyes. I'll tell you what's happening."

She couldn't stop sobbing.

"The walls aren't closing in as fast as they were. Barely creeping inward now. Barely creeping . . . and now . . . now they've stopped altogether. The ceiling too . . . not descending any more. Everything's stopped. Stable. Do you hear me, Joanna?"

"Y-yes."

"No, don't open your eyes yet. Squeeze them tight shut. Just visualize what I'm telling you. See the world through me."

She nodded.

The air wasn't normal, but it was thinner than it had been since the seizure had stricken her. Breathable. Sweet.

"Eyes closed . . . closed . . . but see what's happening," Alex said as softly and lullingly as a hypnotist. "The ceiling is starting to withdraw . . . moving up where it belongs. The walls too . . . pulling back from you, back from us, away . . . slowly away. You understand? The room is getting larger . . . a lot of space now. Do you feel the room gradually getting bigger, Joanna?"

"Yes," she said, and though hot tears were still streaming from her eyes, she was no longer sobbing.

Alex spoke to her in that fashion for several minutes, and Joanna listened closely to each word and visualized each statement. Eventually the air pressure returned to normal; she was no longer suffocating.

When her tears had dried and when her breathing had become rhythmic, relaxed, almost normal, he said, "Okay, open your eyes."

She opened them, although reluctantly. The living room was as it should be.

"You made it all go away," she said wonderingly. "You made it right again."

He was still holding her hands. He gently squeezed them, smiled, and said, "Not just me. We did it together. And from now on, I'm pretty sure you'll be able to do it alone."

"Oh, no. Never by myself."

"Yes, you will. Because this phobia isn't a natural part of your psychological makeup. I'd bet everything I own that it's just posthypnotic suggestion. You don't need psychoanalysis to get rid of it. From now on, when a seizure hits you, just close your eyes and picture everything opening up and moving away from you."

"But I've tried that before. It never worked . . . until now, until you. . . ."

"Just once, you needed someone to hold your hand and force you to face up to the fear, someone who wouldn't be driven away. Until tonight, you thought it was an interior problem, an embarrassing mental illness. Now you know it's an *exterior* problem, not your fault, like a curse someone placed on you."

Joanna looked at the ceiling, daring it to descend.

Alex said, "Subsequent attacks ought to be less and less fierce—until they finally stop altogether. Neither the paranoia nor the claustrophobia has any genuine roots in you. They were both grafted onto you by the bastards who transformed you from Lisa into Joanna. You've been programmed. Now you have the power to *re*program yourself to be like other people."

To be like other people . . .

For the first time in more than a decade, Joanna felt that she had at least some control of her life. She could at last deal with the malignant forces that had made a loner of her. From this day forward, if she wanted an intimate relationship with Alex or with anyone else, nothing within her could prevent her from having what she wanted. The only obstacles remaining were external. That thought was exhilarating, like a rejuvenation drug, water from the fountain of youth. The years dropped from her. Time ran backward. She felt as though she were a girl again. She would never hereafter cringe in fear as the ceiling descended and the walls closed in on her, nor would spells of irrational paranoia keep her from the succor and sanctuary of her friends.

To be like other people . . .

The cage door had been opened. She was free.

27

The photographs no longer disturbed Joanna. She studied them in the same spirit of awe that people must have known when gazing into the first mirrors many centuries ago—with a superstitious fascination but not with fear.

Alex sat beside her on the sofa, reading aloud from some of the reports in the massive Chelgrin file. They discussed what he read, trying to see the information from every angle, searching for a perspective that might have been overlooked at the time of the investigation.

As the evening wore on, Joanna made a list of the ways in which she and Lisa Chelgrin were alike. Intellectually, she was more than half convinced that Alex was right, that she was indeed the missing daughter of the senator. But emotionally, she lacked conviction. Could it really be possible that the mother and father she remembered so well—Elizabeth and Robert Rand—were merely phantoms, that they had never existed except in her mind? And the apartment in London—was it conceivable that she had never actually lived in that place? She needed to see the evidence in black and white, a list of reasons why she should seriously consider such outrageous concepts.

LISA	ME
1) She looks like me.	1) Therefore, I look like her.
2) She is five foot six.	2) Same height.
3) She weighed 115 pounds.	3) So do I, give or take.
4) She studied music.	4) Likewise.
5) She had a fine voice.	5) So do I.
6) Her mother died when she was ten.	6) My mother is dead too.
7) Wherever she is, she's separated from her father.	7) My father is dead.

8) She had appendicitis sur-   8) I have an appendix scar.
gery when she was nine.

9) She had a brown birth-   9) So do I.
mark as big as a dime on
her right hip.

As Joanna was reading the list yet again, Alex pulled another report from the file, glanced at it, and said, "Here's something damned curious. I'd forgotten all about it."

"What?"

"It's an interview with Mr. and Mrs. Morimoto."

"Who're they?"

"Lovely people," Alex said. "Domestic servants. They've been employed by Tom Chelgrin since Lisa . . . since you were five years old."

"The senator brought a couple from Japan to work in his home?"

"No, no. They're both second-generation Japanese Americans. From San Francisco, I think."

"Still, like you said, it's curious. Now there's a Japanese link between me and Lisa."

"You haven't heard the half of it."

Frowning, she said, "You think the Morimotos had something to do with my . . . with Lisa's disappearance?"

"Not at all. They're good people. Not a drop of larceny in them. Besides, they weren't in Jamaica when Lisa disappeared. They were at the senator's house in Virginia, near Washington."

"So what is it exactly that you find so curious about them?"

Paging through the transcript of the Morimoto interview, he said, "Well . . . the Morimotos were around the house all day, every day when Lisa was growing up. Fumi was the cook. She did a little light housekeeping too. Her husband, Koji, was a combination house manager and butler. They both were Lisa's baby-sitters when she was growing up, and she adored them. She picked up a lot of Japanese from them. The senator was all in favor of that. He thought it was a good idea to teach languages to children when they were very young and had fewer mental blocks against learning. He sent Lisa to an elementary school where she was taught French beginning in the first grade—"

"I speak French."

"—and where she was taught German starting in the third grade."

"I speak German too," Joanna said.

She added those items to her list of similarities. The pen trembled slightly in her fingers.

"So what I'm leading up to," Alex said, "is that Tom Chelgrin used the

Morimotos to tutor Lisa in Japanese. She spoke it fluently. Better than she spoke either French or German."

Joanna looked up from the list that she was making. She felt dizzy. "My God."

"Yeah. Too incredible to be coincidence."

"But I learned Japanese in England," she insisted.

"Did you?"

"At the university—and from my boyfriend."

"Did you?"

They stared at each other.

For Joanna, the impossible now seemed probable.

28
✪ ✪ ✪

Joanna found the letters in her bedroom closet, at the bottom of a box of snapshots and other mementos. They were in one thin bundle, tied together with faded yellow ribbon. She brought them back to the living room and gave them to Alex. "I don't really know why I've held on to them all these years."

"You probably kept them because you were *told* to keep them."

"Told—by whom?"

"By the people who kidnapped Lisa. By the people who tinkered with your mind. Letters like these are superficial proof of your Joanna Rand identity."

"Only superficial?"

"We'll see."

The packet contained five letters, three of which were from J. Compton Woolrich, a London solicitor and the executor of the Robert and Elizabeth Rand estate. The final letter from Woolrich mentioned the enclosure of an after-tax, estate-settlement check in excess of three hundred thousand dollars.

As far as Joanna could see, that money from Woolrich blasted an enormous hole in Alex's conspiracy theory.

"You actually received that check?" he asked.

"Yes."

"And it cleared? You got the money?"

"Every dime. And if there was such a large estate, then my father and mother—Robert and Elizabeth—must have been real people."

"Maybe," Alex said doubtfully. "Real people. But even if they did exist, that doesn't mean you were their daughter."

"How else could I inherit from them?"

Instead of responding, he read the last two of the five letters, both of which were from the claims office of the United British-Continental Insurance

Association, Limited. Upon its receipt of the medical examiner's official certification of the death of Robert and Elizabeth (née Henderson) Rand, British-Continental had honored Robert's life insurance policy and had paid the full death benefits to Joanna, the sole surviving heir. The sum received—which was in addition to the three hundred thousand dollars that had been realized from the liquidation of the estate—was a hundred thousand pounds Sterling, minus the applicable taxes.

"A hundred thousand pounds. More than another hundred and fifty thousand bucks. And you received this too?" Alex asked.

"Yes."

"Quite a lot of money."

"It was," Joanna agreed. "But I needed virtually all of it to purchase this building and renovate it. The place needed a lot of work. Then I had to use most of what was left to operate the Moonglow until it became profitable—which, thank God, wasn't all that long."

Alex shuffled the letters, stopped when he found the last one from the London solicitor, and said, "This Woolrich guy—did you do all of your business with him by mail and on the phone?"

"Of course not."

"You met him face-to-face?"

"Sure. Lots of times."

"When? Where?"

"He was my father's . . . He was Robert Rand's personal attorney. They were also friends. He was a dinner guest at our apartment in London at least three or four times a year."

"What was he like?"

"Very kind, gentle," Joanna said. "After my parents were killed in the accident near Brighton—well, if they *were* my parents—Mr. Woolrich came to see me a number of times. And not just when he needed my approval or my signature to proceed with the settlement of the estate. He paid me frequent visits. I was horribly depressed. He worried about keeping my spirits up. I don't know how I'd have gotten through without him. He loved jokes. He always had a couple of new jokes to tell me every time he came by. Usually quite funny jokes too. Always trying to get a little laugh out of me. He was extraordinarily considerate. He never made me go to his office on business. He always came to me. He never put me out in the least. He was warm and considerate. He was a nice man. I liked him."

Alex studied her with narrowed eyes, very much the detective again. "Did you listen to yourself just now?"

"What?"

"The way you sounded."

"How did I sound?"

Rather than answer, he got up from the couch and began to pace. "Tell me one of his jokes."

"Jokes?"

"Yes. Tell me one."

"You can't be serious. I don't remember any. Not after all these years."

"His jokes were usually quite funny. You stressed that. Seems reasonable to assume you might remember at least one."

She was puzzled by his interest. "Well, I don't. Sorry. Why does it matter anyway?"

He stopped pacing and stared down at her.

Those eyes. Once again she was aware of their power. They opened her with a glance and left her defenseless. She had thought she was armored against their effect, but she wasn't. Paranoia surged in her, the stark terror of having no secrets and no place to hide. She fought off that brief madness and retained her composure.

"If you could recall one of his jokes," Alex said, "you'd provide some much needed detail. You'd be adding verisimilitude to what are now, frankly, very thin recollections of him."

"I'm not trying to hide anything. I'm giving you all the details I can."

"I know. That's what bothers me." Alex sat beside her again. "Didn't you notice anything odd about the way you summed up Woolrich a moment ago?"

"Odd?"

"Your voice changed. In fact, your whole manner changed. Subtly. But I noticed it. As soon as you started talking about this Woolrich, you spoke in . . . almost a monotone, choppy sentences . . . as if you were reciting something you'd memorized."

"Really now, Alex. You make me sound like a zombie. You were imagining it."

"My business is observation, not imagination. Tell me more about Woolrich. What does he look like?"

"Does it really matter?"

Alex was quick to press the point. "Don't you remember that either?"

She sighed. "He was in his forties when my parents died. A slender man. Five foot ten. Maybe a hundred forty or a hundred fifty pounds. Very nervous. Talked rather fast. Energetic. He had a pinched face. Pale. Thin lips. Brown eyes. Brown, thinning hair. He wore heavy tortoiseshell glasses, and he—"

Joanna stopped in midsentence, because suddenly she could hear what Alex had heard before. She sounded as if she were standing at attention in front of a class of schoolchildren, reciting an assigned poem. It was eerie, and she shivered.

"Do you correspond with Woolrich?" Alex asked.

"Write letters to him? Why should I?"

"He was your father's friend."

"They were casual friends, not best buddies."

"But he was your friend too."

"Yes, well, in a way he was."

"And after all he did for you when you were feeling so low—"

"Maybe I should have kept in touch with him."

"That would have been more in character, don't you think? You aren't a thoughtless person."

"You know how it is. Friends drift apart."

"Not always."

"Well, they generally do when you put twelve thousand miles between them." She frowned. "You're making me feel guilty."

Alex shook his head. "You're missing my point. Look, if Woolrich was really a friend of your father's and if he actually was extraordinarily helpful to you after the accident in Brighton, you would have maintained contact with him at least for a couple of years. That would be like you. From what I know of you, it's entirely out of character for you to forget a friend so quickly and easily."

Joanna smiled ruefully. "You have an idealized image of me."

"No. I'm aware of your faults. But ingratitude isn't one of them. I think this J. Compton Woolrich never existed—which is why you couldn't possibly have kept in touch with him."

"But I remember him!" Joanna said exasperatedly.

"As I said, you may have been made to remember a lot of things that never happened."

"Programmed," she said sarcastically.

"I'm close to the truth," he said confidently. "Do you realize how tense it's made you to have to listen to me?"

She realized that she was leaning forward, shoulders drawn up, hunched as if in anticipation of a blow to the back of the neck. She was even biting her fingernails. She sat back on the couch and tried to relax.

"I heard the change in my voice when I was telling you what Woolrich looked like. A monotone. It's spooky. And when I try to expand on those few memories of him . . . I can't recall anything new. There's no color, no detail. It all seems . . . flat. Like photographs or a painting. But I *did* receive those letters from him."

"That's another thing that bothers me. You said that after the accident, Woolrich came to visit you frequently."

"Yes, that's right."

"So why would he write to you at all?"

"Well, of course, he had to be careful. . . ." Joanna frowned. "I'll be damned. I don't know. I hadn't thought about that."

Alex shook the thin packet of correspondence as if he hoped a secret would drop out of it. "There isn't anything in these three letters that requires a written notice to you. He could have conducted all this business in person. He didn't even have to deliver the settlement check by mail." Alex tossed the letters on the coffee table. "The only reason that these were sent to you was so you'd have superficial proof of your phony background."

"If Mr. Woolrich never existed . . . and if Robert and Elizabeth Rand never existed . . . then who the hell sent me that three hundred thousand dollars?"

"Maybe it came from the people who kidnapped you when you were Lisa Chelgrin. For some reason, they wanted to set you up well in your new identity."

Amazed, she said, "You've got it all backward. Kidnappers are out to get money, not to give it away."

"These weren't ordinary kidnappers. They never sent a ransom demand to the senator. Their motives apparently were unique."

"Yeah? So who were they?"

"Maybe we can find out." He pointed to the telephone that stood on a rosewood desk in one corner of the living room. "As a start, maybe you should make a call to J. Compton Woolrich."

"I thought you'd decided he doesn't exist."

"There's a telephone number on his stationery. We're obliged to try it, even if it won't get us anywhere. And it won't. After that, we'll make a call to the United British-Continental Insurance Association."

"Will that get us anywhere?"

"No. But I want you to make the call for the same reason that a curious little boy might poke a stick into a hornet's nest: to see what will happen."

29

Joanna sat at the small rosewood desk on which stood the telephone. Alex pulled up a chair beside her and sat close enough to hear the other end of the conversation when she turned the receiver half away from her ear.

Midnight Kyoto time was two o'clock in the afternoon in London, and the insurance company's switchboard operator answered on the second ring. She had a sweet, girlish voice. "May I help you?"

Joanna said, "Is this British-Continental Insurance?"

After a pause the operator said, "Yes."

"I need to speak to someone in your claims department."

"Do you know the name of the claims officer you want?"

"No," Joanna said. "Anyone will do."

"What sort of policy does the claim involve?"

"Life insurance."

"One moment, please."

For a while the line carried nothing but background static: a steady hissing, intermittent sputtering.

The man in the claims department finally came on the line. He clipped his words with crisp efficiency as sharp as any scissors. "Phillips speaking. Something I can help you with?"

Joanna told him the story that she and Alex had concocted: After all these years, the Japanese tax authorities wanted to be certain that the funds with which she had started life in Japan had not, in fact, been earned there either by her or someone else. She needed to prove the provenance of her original capital in order to avoid paying back taxes. Unfortunately, she had thrown away the cover letter that had come with the insurance company's check.

She felt that she was convincing. Even Alex seemed to think so, for he nodded at her several times to indicate that she was doing a good job.

"Now I was wondering, Mr. Phillips, if you can possibly send me a copy of that letter, so I can satisfy the tax authorities here."

Phillips said, "When did you receive our check?"

Joanna gave him the date.

"Oh, then I can't help. Our records don't go back that far."

"What happened to them?"

"Threw them out. We're always short of file space. We're legally obligated to store them only seven years. In fact, I'm surprised it's still a worry to you. Don't they have a statute of limitations in Japan?"

"Not in tax matters," Joanna said. She hadn't the slightest idea whether that was true. "With everything on computer these days, I would think nothing ever gets thrown out."

"Well, I'm sorry, but they're gone."

She thought for a moment and then said, "Mr. Phillips, were you working for British-Continental when my claim was paid?"

"No. I've been here only eight years."

"What about other people in your department? Weren't some of them working there twelve years ago?"

"Oh, yes. Quite a few."

"Do you think one of them might remember?"

"Remember back twelve years to the payoff on an ordinary life policy?" Phillips asked, incredulous. "Highly unlikely."

"Just the same, would you ask around for me?"

"You don't mean now, while you hold long distance from Japan?"

"Oh, no. If you'd just make inquiries when you've got the time, I'd appreciate it. And if anyone does remember anything, please write me immediately."

"A memory isn't a legal record," Phillips said doubtfully. "I'm not sure what good someone's recollections would be to you."

"Can't do any harm," she said.

"I suppose not. All right. I'll ask."

Joanna gave Phillips her address, thanked him, and hung up.

"Threw out all the records. Convenient," Alex said sourly.

"But it doesn't prove anything."

"Exactly. It doesn't prove anything—one way or the other."

At twenty minutes past midnight, Kyoto time, Joanna reached the number that they had found on J. Compton Woolrich's impressively heavy vellum stationery.

The woman who answered the phone in London had never heard of a solicitor named Woolrich. She was the owner and manager of an antique shop on Jermyn Street. The number had belonged to her for more than eight years. She didn't know to whom it might have been assigned prior to the opening of her shop.

Another blank wall.

30

The Moonglow Lounge had closed early, at eleven-thirty, nearly an hour ago, and the staff had gone home by the time Joanna concluded the second call to London. Music no longer drifted up through the floor, and without a background melody, the winter night seemed preternaturally quiet, impossibly dark at the windows.

Joanna switched on the CD player. Bach.

She sat beside Alex on the sofa, and they continued to leaf through the gray-and-green Bonner-Hunter Security Corporation file folders that were stacked on the coffee table.

Suddenly Alex said, "I'll be damned!" He took a pair of eight-by-ten, black-and-white glossies from one of the folders. "Look at this. Photographic enlargements of Lisa Chelgrin's thumbprints. We got one from her driver's license application and lifted the other from the clock radio in her bedroom. I'd forgotten about them."

"Hard proof," Joanna said softly, half wishing that the prints did not exist.

"We'll need an ink pad. And paper with a soft finish . . . but nothing too absorbent. We want a clear print, not a meaningless blot. And we've got to have a magnifying glass."

"The paper I have," she said. "And the ink pad. But not the magnifying glass . . . unless. There's a paperweight that might do."

She led him out of the living room, down the narrow stairs, and into her first-floor office.

The paperweight was a clear, two-inch-thick lens, four inches in diameter. It had no frame or handle, and it wasn't optically flawless. But when Alex held it above the open accounts ledger that was filled with Joanna's neat handwriting, the letters and figures appeared three to five times larger than they did to the unassisted eye.

"It'll do," he said.

Joanna got the ink and paper from the center drawer of her desk. After several tries, she managed to make two smudge-free thumbprints.

Alex placed them beside the photographs. While Joanna scrubbed her inky fingers with paper tissues and spit, he used the lens to compare the prints.

When Joanna had cleaned up as best she could without soap and hot water, Alex passed the magnifying glass to her.

"I don't know what to look for," she said.

"Here. I'll show you."

"Can we cut to the chase?" she asked impatiently.

"Sure." He hesitated. "Your prints and Lisa's are identical."

31

When at last Mariko returned to the Moonglow Lounge from the hospital where she had been at the bedside of Wayne Kennedy, Joanna and Alex were waiting for her at the table in the kitchen. They had made hot tea and a stack of small sandwiches.

Mariko was exhausted, having slept less than three hours in the past thirty-six. Her face felt grimy, and her eyes burned. Her feet and legs were as leaden and swollen as those of an old woman.

Joanna and Alex wanted a report on Wayne Kennedy, but Mariko had little to tell, other than that she was impressed by his strength and vitality. Kennedy had come out of anesthesia at six forty-five, but he had not been fully coherent until nine o'clock, when he had complained about a dry mouth and gnawing hunger. The nurses gave him chips of ice to suck, but his dinner came from an intravenous-drip bottle even though he demanded eggs and bacon.

"Is he in a lot of pain?" Alex asked.

"A little. But drugs mask most of it."

When Wayne had been told by Dr. Ito that he would be in the hospital for a month and might need additional surgery, he had not been depressed in the least but had predicted that he'd be out in a week and back at work in two. Mariko had been prepared for the hard job of cheering him up, but he had been in good spirits and, before he had finally fallen asleep, had told her a lot of funny stories about his work with the security agency in Chicago.

"Have the police questioned him?" Alex asked.

"Not yet," Mariko said. "In the morning. I don't envy them if they hope to get more out of Wayne than you told him to give, Alex-san. Even in a sickbed, with one leg in traction, he'll be more than a match for them."

As she'd told them about Wayne, Mariko had been content to sip tea. Now she was ravenous. She devoured her share of the sandwiches while Joanna and Alex told her about the Chelgrin file, the two calls to London, and the thumbprints.

Although their stunning revelations made Mariko forget her weariness, she was as intrigued by their demeanor as by what they told her. They were relaxed with each other. Joanna regarded Alex with obvious affection, trust—and a certain proprietary concern. For once, he was without his omnipresent jacket and tie, and his shirtsleeves were rolled up. He had even kicked off his shoes, although Joanna didn't maintain the traditional shoeless Japanese house. Mariko didn't think they'd been to bed together. Not yet. But soon. In their eyes and voices, she could see and hear that special, sweet anticipation.

She wondered how much longer Alex would argue that love did not actually exist.

She smiled, sipped her tea. "Now that you've matched the thumbprints, what will you do? Call the senator and tell him?"

"No. Not yet," Alex said.

"Why not?"

"I have a hunch . . . he's somehow part of this whole thing."

This was evidently a thought that he had not previously shared with Joanna, because she seemed surprised.

Alex said, "I think the senator knows you're here in Kyoto, Joanna. I think he's always known who kidnapped his daughter—and maybe even arranged the whole thing himself."

"But for God's sake, why?"

He took hold of Joanna's hand, and Mariko smiled again.

"It's just a hunch," he said, "but it explains a few things. Like where you got all that money to start a new life. We know now it didn't come from the Rand estate or Robert Rand's life insurance."

Mariko put down her teacup and patted her lips with a napkin. "Let me get this straight. The senator had his own daughter kidnapped from the vacation house in Jamaica, brainwashed her, then arranged for her to be set up in a new life with an entirely new identity?"

Alex nodded. "I don't pretend to know *why*. But where else would all the money come from—if not from Tom Chelgrin?"

Perplexed, Mariko said, "How could any father send his daughter away? How could he ever be happy if he could not see her any more?"

"Here in Japan," Alex said, "you're aware of the continuity of generations, you have a strong sense of family. It isn't always like that where I come from. My own parents were alcoholics. They nearly destroyed me—emotionally and physically."

"We have a few like that. Human animals."

"Fewer than we do."

"Even one is too many. But this thing you say Joanna's father did . . . it's still beyond my comprehension."

Alex smiled so beautifully that for an instant Mariko wished that she had found him first, before Joanna had ever seen him and before he had seen Joanna.

He said, "It's beyond your comprehension because you're so exquisitely civilized, Mariko."

She blushed and acknowledged the compliment with a slow bow of her head.

"There's something you haven't accounted for," Joanna told Alex. "The senator hired you to find his daughter, spent a small fortune on the search. Why would he do that if he knew where she was?"

Pouring more tea for himself, Alex said, "Misdirection. He was playing the stricken father who'd stop at nothing, spend anything, to get his child back. Who could suspect him of involvement? And he could afford to play expensive games."

Joanna was grim. "What he did to me—*if* he did it to me—was not a game. Since you first mentioned Tom Chelgrin on Wednesday, in the taxi, you've made it clear you don't like him or trust him. But why not?"

"He manipulates people."

"Don't all politicians?"

"I don't have to like them for it. And Chelgrin is smoother than most politicians. He's oily." Alex picked up another sandwich, hesitated, and put it down again without taking a bite. He seemed to have lost his appetite. "I was around Chelgrin a lot, and I finally figured he had only four facial expressions he put on for the public: a somber, attentive look when he pretended to be listening to the views of a constituent; a fatherly smile that crinkled his whole face but was maybe one micron deep; a stern frown when he wanted to be perceived as a hard-nosed negotiator; and grief for when his wife died, for when his daughter disappeared, for occasions when American soldiers were killed in one far place or another. Masks. He has all these masks. I think he enjoys manipulating people even more than the average politician. For him it's almost a form of masturbation."

"*Whew!*" Joanna said.

"Sorry if I come on a bit strong about him," Alex said. "But this is the first time I've had an opportunity to tell anyone what I really think of the man. He was an important client, so I always hid my true feelings. But in spite of the money he spent to find Lisa and all his weeping about his lost little girl, I never believed he was as devastated about her disappearance as everyone thought. He seemed . . . hollow. There was a coldness, a deep emptiness about him."

"Then maybe we should just stop right here."

"That's not an option."

Joanna frowned. "But if the senator is the kind of man you say, if he's capable of anything . . . we might all be better off if we forget him. At least now I know a little bit about why I've made a loner of myself. Programmed. I don't really have to know any more. I can live without knowing how it was done or who did it or why."

Mariko glanced at Alex. He met her eyes, and he was clearly as dismayed as she herself was. "Joanna-san, maybe right now you feel that you can live without knowing, but later you'll change your mind. You'll be curious. It'll eat at you like an acid. Everyone needs to know who he is, where he's come from. Ignorance isn't bliss."

"Besides," Alex said, taking a less philosophical approach, "it's too late for us to walk away from this. They won't let us. We've learned too much."

Joanna looked skeptical. "You think they might try to kill us?"

"Or worse."

"What's worse?"

Alex got up, went to the small window, and stood with his back to them, staring at the Gion and the dark city beyond. "Maybe one day we'll all wake up in other parts of the world with new names, new pasts, new sets of memories, troubled by nightmares but unaware that we were once Joanna Rand, Mariko Inamura, and Alex Hunter."

Mariko saw Joanna turn sickly white, as if pale moonlight had pierced the window and lit nothing in the room but her face.

"Would they really do it again?" Mariko asked.

Alex turned from the window. "Why not? It's an effective way of silencing us—without leaving behind any dead bodies to excite the police."

"No," Joanna said, and she looked haunted. "Everything that's happened to me in Japan, everything I am and want to become—all of it wiped out of my mind? No."

Mariko shuddered at the thought of being erased, remade, so utterly *controlled.*

"But *why?*" Joanna demanded. In frustration she slammed one fist onto the table, rattling the teacups and saucers. "Why did all of this happen? It's insane. It makes no sense."

"It makes perfect sense to the people who did it," Alex said.

"And it would make sense to us too, if we knew what they know," Mariko added.

Alex nodded. "Right. And we won't be safe until we *do* know what they know. As soon as we understand what motivated the Lisa-Joanna switch, we can go public, make headlines. When all the secrets are out in the open, the people behind this won't have any reason either to kill us or brainwash us."

"No reason except revenge," Joanna said.

"There's that," he admitted. "But maybe it won't matter to them once the game is over."

"All right. Then what's next?" Joanna asked.

Alex said, "Mariko-san, you have an uncle who's a psychiatrist. Sometimes does he use hypnotic regression to help his patients?"

"Yes." For years Mariko had tried to persuade Joanna to see Uncle Omi, but always without success.

To Joanna, Alex said, "He can pry open the memory block and help you recall things we need to know."

Joanna was skeptical. "Yeah? Like what?"

"Like the name of the man with the mechanical hand."

Joanna bit her lip, scowled. "Him? But what's it matter. He's just a man in a nightmare."

"Oh? Don't you remember what you said about him on Wednesday?"

Joanna shifted uneasily in her chair, glanced at Mariko, looked down at the table, and focused on her own pale, interlocked hands.

"At Nijo Castle?" Alex prompted.

"I was hysterical."

"You said that you suddenly realized the man in your nightmare was someone you'd actually known, not just a figment of a dream."

Reluctantly she said, "Yes. All right. But I'm not sure I want to find him."

"Until you find him and know what he did to you and understand why, the dreams aren't going to go away," Alex said.

Joanna continued to stare at her hands, which were clasped so tightly that the knuckles were sharp and bone-white.

"When you meet this man with the mechanical hand," Mariko said, "when you confront him face-to-face, you'll discover he isn't half as frightening in reality as he is in the nightmare."

"I wish I could believe that," Joanna said.

"The known," Mariko said, "is never as terrifying as the unknown. Damn it, Joanna, you *must* talk to Uncle Omi."

Joanna was clearly surprised to hear Mariko swear.

Mariko was a little surprised as well. She pressed on. "I'll call him in the morning."

Joanna hesitated, then nodded. "All right. But, Alex, you've got to go with me."

"A psychiatrist might not want me looking over his shoulder."

"If you can't go with me, I won't go."

Mariko said, "I'm sure Uncle Omi won't mind. After all, this is a very special case."

Relieved, Joanna leaned back in her chair.

"It won't be so bad, Joanna-san. My Uncle Omi isn't as scary as Godzilla. No radioactive breath. No giant tail to knock over skyscrapers."

Joanna found a smile. "You're a good friend, Mariko-san."

"Patients *are* sometimes spooked by his mechanical hand," Mariko said, and she was rewarded with Joanna's laughter like the music of silver bells, which reverberated in the windowpane that separated them from the cold, watchful face of the night.

32

✪ ✪ ✪

Ignacio Carrera's breathing was violent but metronomical, as if he was exercising to Prussian martial music that no one else could hear. The barbells with which he struggled were heavier than he was, and judging by his cries of agony, which echoed through the private gym, the weight was too difficult for him.

Nevertheless, he continued without pause. If the task had been nearer possibility, it wouldn't have been worthwhile. His strenuous efforts distilled alcohol-clear drops of sweat from him; perspiration streamed down his slick flesh, dripped off his earlobes, nose, chin, elbows, and fingertips. He wore only a pair of royal-blue workout shorts, and his strikingly powerful body glistened like every boy's dream of brute masculine strength. The sound of tortured tissues being torn down and stronger muscle fibers growing in their place was almost audible.

On Mondays, Wednesdays, and Fridays, without exception, Ignacio Carrera worked diligently on his calves, thighs, buttocks, hips, waist, lower back, and stomach. He had a prodigious set of stomach muscles: His belly was hard and concave, like a sheet of corrugated steel. On Tuesdays, Thursdays, and Saturdays, he labored to improve his chest, upper back, neck, shoulders, biceps, triceps, and forearms. On the seventh day he rested, although inactivity made him nervous.

Ignacio yearned for the transmutation of his flesh—every ounce, every cell. For relaxation, he read science fiction, and he longed to have the body of the perfect robot that occasionally appeared in those books—flexible yet invulnerable, precise in its movements and capable of grace yet charged with crude power.

He was only thirty-eight years old, but he looked much younger than his true age. His hair was coarse, thick, and black, and while he exercised, he wore a bright yellow ribbon around his head to keep the hair out of his face.

With his strong features, prominent nose, dark and deeply set eyes, dusky complexion, and headband, he could have passed for an American Indian.

He did not claim to be an Indian, American or otherwise. He told people that he was a Brazilian. That was a lie.

In more genteel times, the gymnasium on the first floor of the Carrera house had been a music room in which guests in formal attire had frequently attended evenings of chamber music. At one end of the room was a circular dais on which a piano had stood. Now the enormous space—thirty by thirty feet—was carpeted solely with scattered vinyl mats and furnished largely with exercise machines. The high ceiling featured richly carved moldings, painted white with accents of gold leaf, and the plaster was pale blue.

Carrera was on the dais, imitating a machine, grimly working through yet another set of two-arm, standing presses. His obsessive-compulsive behavior in his private gym was similar to his approach to everything in life. He would almost rather die than lose, even when his only competition was himself. He pressed the great weight up, up, up again, through a haze of pain that, like a fog, engulfed him. He was determined to make it through the set of ten repetitions, just as he had endured tens of thousands of other sets over the years.

Antonio Paz, another bodybuilder who served as bodyguard and exercise partner to Carrera, stood slightly behind and to one side of his boss, counting aloud as each repetition was concluded. Paz was forty years old, but he also appeared to be younger than he was. At six-two, Paz was three inches taller than Carrera and twenty-five pounds heavier. He had none of his employer's good looks: His face was broad, flat, with a low brow. He also claimed to be Brazilian, but he was not.

Paz said, "Three." Seven repetitions remained in the set.

The telephone rang. Carrera could barely hear it above his own labored breathing. Through a veil of sweat and tears of pain, he watched Paz cross the room to answer the call.

All the way up with the barbell. Hold it at any cost. Four. Bring it down. Rest. Take it up. Hold. Five. Lungs burning. Bring it down. Machinelike.

Paz spoke rapidly into the phone, but Carrera could not hear what he was saying. The only sounds were his own breathing and the fierce thudding of his heart.

Up again. Hold. Arms quivering. Back spasming. Neck bulging. The pain! *Glorious.* Bring it down.

Paz left the telephone handset off the hook and returned to the dais. He resumed his former position and waited.

Carrera did four more presses, and when at last he dropped the barbell at the end of the set, he felt as though quarts of adrenaline were pumping through him. He was soaring, lighter than air. Pumping iron never left him tired. On the contrary, he was filled with an effervescent feeling of freedom.

In fact, the only other act that gave him as much of a rush was killing. Carrera loved to kill. Men. Women. Children. He didn't care about the sex or age of the prey.

He didn't often get the chance to kill, of course. Certainly not as frequently as he lifted weights and not as often as he would have liked.

Paz picked up a towel from a chair at the edge of the dais. He handed it to Carrera. "Marlowe is on the line from London."

"What does he want?"

"He wouldn't say. Except that it's urgent."

Both men spoke English as if they had learned the language at an upper-class school in England, but neither had ever attended any such institution.

Carrera stepped off the platform and went to the telephone to deal with Marlowe. He didn't move with the heavy, purposeful steps of his bodyguard but with such lightness and grace that he appeared to know the secret of levitation.

The telephone was on a table by one of the tall, mullioned windows. The tapestry drapes were drawn aside, but most of the light in the room came from the huge chandelier that hung above the dais; its hundreds of crystal beads and finely cut pendants shimmered with rainbow beauty. Now, in the late afternoon, the winter sunlight was thin, tinted gray by curdled masses of snow clouds; it seemed barely able to pierce the panes of the windows. Beyond the leaded glass lay Zurich, Switzerland: the clear blue lake, the crystalline Limmat River, the massive churches, the discreet banks, the solidly built houses, the glass office buildings, the ancient guildhalls, the twelfth-century Grossmunster Cathedral, the smokeless factories—a fascinating mix of oppressive Gothic somberness and alpine charm, modern and medieval. The city shelved down the hills and spread along the shores of the lake, and the Carrera house stood above it all. The view was spectacular, and the telephone table seemed to be perched on top of the world.

Carrera picked up the receiver. "Marlowe?"

"Good afternoon, Ignacio."

Rolling his shoulders and stretching as he spoke, Carrera said, "What's wrong?"

He could be direct with Marlowe, because both his phone and the one in London were equipped with state-of-the-art scrambler devices, which made it nearly impossible for anyone to eavesdrop.

Marlowe said, "A couple hours ago Joanna Rand called British-Continental to ask about the payoff on her father's life insurance."

"You spoke to her?"

"Someone else. And a few minutes ago I was finally told about it, as if it wasn't terribly important. We have some idiots here."

"What did your idiot say to her?"

"He told her we hadn't any files that old. He used the Phillips name, of course. Now what do we do?"

"Nothing yet," Carrera said.

"I should think time is of the essence."

"It's not actually necessary that you think."

"Obviously the whole charade is crumbling."

"Perhaps."

"You're damned cool. What am I to do if she comes calling?"

"She won't," Carrera said confidently.

"If she's beginning to question her entire past, what's to keep her from popping up here in London for a closer inspection?"

"For one thing," Carrera said, "she carries a posthypnotic suggestion that makes it impossible for her to leave Japan. When she attempts to board a plane—or a ship, for that matter—she'll be overwhelmed by fear. She'll become violently ill. She'll need a doctor, and she'll miss her flight."

"Oh." Marlowe considered that information for a moment. "But maybe a posthypnotic suggestion won't have much force after all these years. What if she finds a way around it?"

"She might. But I'm getting daily reports from Kyoto. If she gets out of Japan, I'll know within an hour. You'll be warned."

"Nevertheless, I simply can't have her nosing around here. Far too much is at stake."

"If she gets to England," Carrera said, "she won't stay long."

"She can cause irreparable damage in just a day or two."

"If she gets to London, she'll be seeking an unraveled thread of the conspiracy. We'll provide several she can't overlook, and all of them will lead to Zurich. She'll decide this is where the mystery can be solved, and she'll come here. Then I'll deal with her."

"Look here, if she *does* slip past your people in Kyoto and out of the country, if she *does* show up in London by surprise, I'll make my own decisions about how to handle her. I'll have to move fast."

"That wouldn't be wise," Carrera said with a softness that was more ominous than any shouted threat could have been.

"I'm not just part of your game, you know. In fact, it's little more than a sideline to me. I've got a lot of things going on, a lot of interests to protect. If the woman comes knocking at my door without warning, and if I feel she's endangering my entire operation, then I'll have her terminated. I'll have no choice. Is that clear?"

"She won't arrive without notice," Carrera said. "And if you harm her without permission, she won't be the only termination."

"Are you threatening me?"

"I'm merely explaining the consequences."

"I don't like to be threatened."

"I haven't the authority to whack you," Carrera said. "You know that. I'm just telling you what others will surely decide to do with you if you make a wrong move with this woman."

"Oh? And who would pull the trigger on me?" Marlowe asked.

Carrera named a singularly powerful and ruthless man.

The name had the desired effect. Marlowe hesitated and then said, "Are you serious?"

"I'll arrange for you to receive a phone call from him."

"For God's sake, Ignacio, why would a man of his position be so intently interested in one of these relocations?"

"Because it's not simply another relocation. She's special."

"What makes her different from the others? Who is she?"

"I can't tell you that."

"You can, but you won't."

"That's right."

"I've never seen her," Marlowe said. "She's liable to show up on my doorstep, and I wouldn't even recognize her."

"If the need arises, you'll be shown a photograph," Carrera said impatiently, eager to end the conversation and return to his exercises.

A moment ago Marlowe had been securely wrapped in that false but unshakable sense of superiority that came from pride in lineage, from years at Eton and then Oxford, and from the upper-crust, old-boy circles in which he moved. Now he was worried about being relegated to a secondary role in a major operation. To a man like Marlowe, who felt that he had been born to special privilege, any indication that he was *not* regarded as an insider was not merely a blow to his sense of job security but to his entire self-image. Carrera could hear a burgeoning anxiety in the Brit's voice, and it amused him.

Marlowe said, "You must be exaggerating the need for security. After all, I'm on your side. Surely a description of this woman can't hurt anything."

"I can't give you even a description. Not yet."

"What's her name?"

"Joanna Rand."

"I know *that* name. I mean, what's her real name?"

"You shouldn't even ask," Carrera said, and he hung up.

A strong gust of wind pressed suddenly and insistently against the window. A few specks of powdery snow spun through the ash-gray afternoon light. A storm was coming.

33

Shortly after six o'clock in the morning, Alex was awakened by Joanna's cries for help.

He was sleeping in the room next to hers, lying atop the covers in pants and T-shirt. His shoes were beside the bed, and he stepped into them as he plucked the pistol off the nightstand.

When he burst into Joanna's room and switched on the lights, she sat up in bed, blinking, dazed. She had been asleep and calling for help in a nightmare.

"The man with the mechanical hand?" he asked as he sat on the edge of her bed.

"Yeah."

"Want to tell me about it?"

"I already have. It's always the same."

Her face was pale. Her mouth was soft and slack from sleep, and her golden hair was damp with perspiration, yet she was a vision in yellow silk pajamas.

She leaned against him, wanting to be held—and they were kissing before he realized the depth of comfort that both of them needed. He slid his hands down her silk-sheathed back, up along her sides, to her breasts, and she whispered "yes," between kisses. He was overcome not merely by desire but by a great tenderness unlike anything he had ever felt before, by something that for a moment he couldn't name. But then he *did* have a name for it—love. He wanted her, needed her, but he also loved her, and in that moment he half believed in love even though he still struggled to resist its pull. The very thought of that freighted word brought to mind his parents' faces, their voices, their protestations of affection always followed swiftly by anger, shouts, curses, blows, pain. He must have become tense, because the quality of their kiss changed. Joanna felt it too, and when she pulled away, Alex didn't try to hold her.

"What's wrong?" she asked.

"I'm confused."

"Don't you want me?"

"More than anything."

"Then what're you confused about?"

"About what we can have together. Beyond tonight."

She touched his face. "Let the future take care of itself."

"I can't. I've got to know what you expect . . . what you think we can have together."

"Everything. If we want it."

"I don't want to disappoint you, Joanna."

"You won't."

"You don't know me. In some ways, commitment hasn't been any easier for me than it's been for you. I'm . . . an emotional cripple." He was amazed that he had admitted it even to himself, let alone to her. "A part of me is . . . missing."

"There's nothing wrong with you that I can see," she said.

"I've never said, 'I love you.' "

"But I've known it."

"I mean . . . I've never said it to *anyone*."

"Good. Then I'm the first."

"You still don't understand. I've never believed love exists. I don't know if I can say it . . . and *mean* it. Not even to you."

She was the first person to whom he had ever revealed anything of what had happened to him, and he talked for an hour, dredging up both familiar and long-repressed details of his nightmare childhood. The beatings. The bruises, the split lips, the blackened eyes, the broken bones. Scalded once with a pan of hot water that his mother threw at him. The scar was still between his shoulders. He'd turned from her just in time. Otherwise, his face would have borne the scar, and he might have been blinded. He recalled the psychological torture that filled every potential empty space between the physical assaults, like mortar in a stone wall. The insults, vicious teasing. The shouting, cursing. The unrelenting denigration and humiliation. Periodically they had locked him in a closet, sometimes for a few hours, sometimes for two or three days. No light. Food and water only if they remembered to provide it. . . .

At first, as he journeyed through his troubled past, his voice was supercharged with hatred, but gradually hatred gave way to hurt, and he found that he was grieving for the child he might have been and for the man into which that child might have grown. That was another Alex Hunter, lost forever, who perhaps would have been a better—certainly a happier—person than the Alex who had survived. As he talked, the memory sludge gushed from him in much the way that guilt might flow from a devout Catholic in a confessional, and when at last he stopped, he felt mercifully cleaner and freer than ever before in his life.

She kissed his eyes.

"Sorry," he said, ashamed of the pent-up tears that blurred his vision and that he was barely able to hold back.

"What for?"

"I never cry."

"That's part of your problem."

"I never wanted them to have the satisfaction of seeing me cry, so I learned to keep everything inside." He forced a smile. "This is the man you're relying on. Still have any confidence in him?"

"More confidence than ever. You seem human now."

More than ever, she wanted to make love, and so did he. But he needed to exercise the iron will and self-control that his monstrous parents had unwittingly taught him. "With you, Joanna, it's got to be right. Special. With you I want to wait until I *can* say those three little words and mean them. For the rest of my life, I'll carry with me every detail of the first time we make love, and from now on I don't intend to lug around anything but *good* memories."

"And neither do I. We'll wait."

She turned out the lights, and they lay together on the bed.

Shadows pooled around them. They were beyond the direct reach of the thin streams of morning sun that drizzled through the narrow gaps in the draperies.

Holding each other, kissing chastely, they were neither lovers nor would-be lovers. Rather, they were like animals in a burrow, pressing against each other for reassurance, warmth, and protection from the mysterious forces of a hostile universe.

Eventually he dozed off. When he woke, he was alone on the bed. At first he thought that he heard rain beating on the windows, but then he realized it was the sound of the shower, coming through the half-open door from the adjacent bathroom.

In a peculiar but comfortably domestic mood, he returned to the guest room, showered, and changed the bandage on his left arm. The shallow knife wounds were healing well.

By the time he dressed and got to the kitchen, Joanna was preparing a light breakfast: *shiro dashi,* white *miso*-flavored soup. Floating in each bowl was a neat tie of *kanpyo,* paper-thin gourd shavings, topped by a dab of hot mustard. The soup was properly served in a red dish with a gold rim, in keeping with the Japanese belief that a man "eats with his eyes as well as his mouth."

In this instance, however, Alex was at odds with traditional Japanese wisdom. He couldn't look away from Joanna long enough to appreciate the presentation of the *shiro dashi.*

Outside, a chill wind stripped dead leaves from a nearby mulberry tree and blew them against the kitchen window, startling him. It was a scarecrow sound, dry and brittle—and somehow more ominous than it should have been.

Streaked with rust-maroon the same shade as dried blood, the crisp brown leaves spun against the glass, and for a moment he half thought that they were about to coalesce into a monstrous face. Instead, the capricious wind suddenly carried them up and out of sight into the dead sky.

For a long time Joanna stared at the mulberry tree. Her mood, like his, had inexplicably changed.

After breakfast, Alex called Ted Blankenship's home number in Chicago. He wanted Ted to use Bonner-Hunter's contacts in England, respected colleagues in the private-security trade, to dig up all available information on the United British-Continental Insurance Association and on the solicitor J. Compton Woolrich.

He and Joanna passed the remainder of the morning with the Chelgrin file, searching for new clues. They didn't find any.

Mariko joined them for lunch at a restaurant two blocks from the Moonglow, and then Joanna drove them directly to the hospital to see Wayne Kennedy. The police had already been there. Wayne had told them only what Alex wanted him to reveal, and they'd seemed satisfied—or at least not terribly suspicious. Wayne was just as Mariko had described him the previous night: brimming with energy in spite of his condition, joking with everyone, demanding to know when he would be permitted to walk, "because if I lay here much longer, my legs will atrophy." One of the nurses spoke English, and Wayne tried to convince her that he'd come to Japan to enter a tap-dancing contest and was determined to participate on crutches if necessary. The nurse was amused, but Wayne's best audience was Mariko. Alex had never seen her so animated and cheerful as she was in that small, clean, but decidedly dreary hospital room.

At three o'clock he and Joanna left to keep an appointment with Dr. Omi Inamura, but Mariko remained at the hospital.

The leaden sky had darkened and descended since they'd arrived at the hospital, as if a solar eclipse was in progress behind the vault of clouds.

In Joanna's Lexus, as she drove across the busy city, Alex said, "From now on, Mariko's going to put her matchmaking energy to work for herself."

"What do you mean?"

"You didn't notice the attraction between them?"

"Who? Mariko and Wayne?"

"It was obvious to me."

On the sidewalks, pedestrians hurried stoop-shouldered through a cold, brisk wind that flapped their coattails.

"I don't doubt Mariko and Wayne are attracted to each other, but nothing'll come of it," Joanna predicted. "Sad to say, but there's a strong cultural bias here against interracial relationships. If you aren't Japanese, then you're regarded as one degree of barbarian or another. It's almost not something you can become angry about when you encounter their prejudice, because they're so unfailingly polite about it, and they do treat everyone with great respect. It's just been a part of their worldview so long that it's in their bones."

Alex frowned. "Mariko doesn't think of *you* as a barbarian."

"Not entirely. She's a modern woman, but in some deep recess of her Japanese soul, the attitude is still present. On a subconscious level maybe, but it's there. And she's definitely not modern enough . . . for Wayne."

"I suspect you're wrong about that. She believes in love at first sight, you know."

"Mariko?"

"She told me."

"She was talking about Wayne?"

"About you and me. But she believes in it for herself too. Love at first sight."

"Is he good enough for her?" Joanna asked.

"He's first-rate, I think."

"Well, then, I hope she's even more of a modern woman than I think she is."

Joanna parked half a block from Omi Inamura's office but did not switch off the engine. Staring at his building through the windshield, she said, "Maybe this is a mistake."

"Why?"

"I'm scared."

"I'll be with you."

"What if Inamura *can* help me remember the face and name of the man with the mechanical hand? Then we'll have to go looking for him, won't we?"

"Yes."

"And when we find him . . ."

"Don't worry. It's like Mariko said last night. When you finally find him, he won't be as frightening as he is in your nightmares."

"No. Not as frightening. Maybe worse."

"Think positive," he said.

He reached out and took her hand. It was cold and moist.

A piercing wail rose in the distance. Traffic pulled aside to allow an ambulance to pass. The shrieking siren filled the world for a moment. In the gray-on-gray day, the fierce red light from the revolving emergency beacons seemed to have preternatural substance: It splashed like blood across the street, washed through the car in an intangible tide, and briefly transformed

Joanna's face into a mask that might have been the universal face of any spattered victim, blue eyes wide but sightless and darkened by a glimpse of Death's own cold face in the penultimate moment.

Alex shivered.

"I'm ready," she said. She let go of his hand and switched off the car engine.

The siren had dwindled beyond hearing. The splashing red light was gone. Once again, the day was dead gray.

34

♣ ♣ ♣

Bowing not from the waist but with a discreet inclination of his head and a rounding of his shoulders, not with any disrespect but with a sense that he understood the need for the old traditions while being personally somewhat above them, Dr. Omi Inamura welcomed Joanna and Alex into his inner office. He was in his early fifties, an inch shorter than Joanna, with slightly crinkled, papery skin and brown eyes as warm as his quick smile. In black slacks, suspenders, white shirt, baggy gray cardigan, and half-lens reading glasses, he seemed more like a literature professor than a psychiatrist.

The inner office, where Inamura treated his patients, was reassuringly cozy. One wall featured floor-to-ceiling shelves crammed with books, and another was covered by a tapestry depicting a wooded mountainside, a foaming water-fall, and a river where accordion-sail boats were running with the wind toward a small village just below the cataracts. Instead of a traditional analyst's couch, four dark-green armchairs were arranged around a low coffee table. The pine-slat blinds closed out the ashen daylight, and the electric lighting was indirect, soft, relaxing. A sweet, elusive fragrance threaded the air: perhaps lemon incense.

In one corner, a large birdcage hung from a brass stand. On a perch in the cage was a coal-black myna with eyes that were simultaneously bright and dark, like little drops of oil glistening in moonlight. From Mariko, they had learned that its name was Freud.

They sat in the armchairs, and Alex told Omi Inamura about Lisa Chelgrin's inexplicable metamorphosis into Joanna Rand. Mariko had prepared her uncle to expect a strange case, so the doctor was neither greatly surprised nor disbe-lieving. He was even cautiously optimistic about the chances of conducting a successful program of hypnotic regression therapy.

"However," Omi Inamura said, "ordinarily, I wouldn't employ hypnosis until I'd done extensive groundwork with you, Miss Rand. I find that it's always wise to begin with certain standard tests, a series of casual conversations, another series of investigative dialogues. I progress slowly, and I thoroughly explore the patient's problems until trust has been established. *Then* I use hypnosis only if it is indicated. This takes time. Weeks. Months."

"I appreciate your concern for the patient," Joanna said, "but we don't have months. Or even weeks."

Alex said, "What these people did to Wayne Kennedy was meant to be a warning. They'll give us a day or two to learn from it. When they see we aren't scared off, they'll try something . . . more violent."

The doctor frowned, still unconvinced that standard procedure should be set aside under even these circumstances.

"*Isha-san,*" Joanna said, "all your other patients suffer from neuroses that they developed subtly and unconsciously over a period of many years. Am I correct?"

"Not entirely. Essentially—yes."

"But, you see, everything that I suffer from was *implanted* in me twelve years ago, in that room in my nightmare, by the man with the mechanical hand. With your other patients, of course, you must do a lot of groundwork to discover the sources of their illnesses. But in my case, we know the source. We just don't know *why* or *who*. So couldn't you just this once set aside your customary procedures?"

Alex was impressed by the vigor with which Joanna made her argument. He knew that she dreaded what she might discover when she was regressed, but she was not afraid to make that journey.

Omi Inamura was careful and conscientious. For a quarter of an hour they discussed the situation, studied it from various points of view, before he finally agreed to begin the regression therapy.

"But you must realize," he said, "that we very likely won't finish today. Indeed, it would be amazing if we did."

"How long?" Joanna asked.

The doctor shook his head. "I can't say. Therapy creates its own pace, which is different for each patient. But I understand how urgent this is, and I'll see you for at least an hour or two every day until we've learned what you need to know."

"That's kind of you, *Isha-san,* but I don't want you to interfere with your regularly scheduled appointments just because I'm a friend of Mariko's."

Dr. Inamura waved one slender hand dismissively and insisted that she was not causing him any trouble. "In Japan a psychiatrist is in somewhat the same position as that proverbial salesman who tries to sell refrigerators to the Eskimos. Because they live in a society that values tradition, teaches meditation, and encourages a code of etiquette and mutual respect, my people are generally at peace with themselves." With typical Japanese modesty, Inamura said, "While some colleagues might be so kind as to say I am moderately successful in my profession, I nevertheless have open appointments every day. Believe me, Miss Rand, you are not an inconvenience. Quite the opposite. It is an honor to provide treatment for you."

She inclined her head toward the doctor. "It is a privilege to be your patient, *Isha-san*."

"You regard me too highly, Joanna-san."

"As you do me."

"Shall we begin now?"

"Yes, please." She tried to appear calm, but a tremor in her voice betrayed her fear.

Alex put his hand on her arm. "It'll be okay."

After picking up a remote control from the coffee table, the doctor rose from his chair and came around the table, soundless on the thick carpet. He stood by Joanna's chair. "Lean back, please. Relax. Put your hands in your lap with the palms up. Very good."

He pointed the remote control at the tapestry, and the room lights, although not bright to begin with, slowly dimmed. Like cautious predators, shadows crept out of the corners.

"Ahhhhh," Freud said softly and appreciatively from his brass cage. "Ahhhhh."

The vanes of the highly lacquered pine shutters had previously glimmered with a liquid amber luminescence, but now they faded into gloom. Only the tapestry remained clearly revealed—and in the altered light it was transformed. It appeared to be mysteriously illuminated from within, and in spite of the stylized and idealized nature of the scene, it acquired such a strong aspect of reality that it almost seemed to be a view from a window.

"Look straight ahead," Inamura told Joanna. "Do you see the lovely tapestry on the wall?"

"Yes."

"Do you see the river in the tapestry?"

"Yes."

"Do you see the small boats?"

"I see them."

The tapestry light was subtly cycling up and down on a rheostat, within a narrow range of brightness: a hypnotic pulse.

"Concentrate on those boats, Joanna. Look closely at those little boats. Imagine yourself on one of them. You are standing on the deck. Water is lapping at the hull. Lapping gently at the hull. The water makes a soothing, rhythmic sound. The boat sways in the current. Gently. Gently. The boat sways gently in the water. Can you feel it swaying?"

"Yes," Joanna said.

Alex looked away from the tapestry and blinked rapidly. Omi Inamura's voice was so remarkably mellow and entrancing that Alex actually had felt the sway of the boat and had heard the faintest lapping of water.

Joanna continued to stare straight ahead.

"The boat is like a baby's cradle." Inamura's voice grew even softer and more intimate than it had been at the start. "It rocks gently, gently like a cradle. Gently like a cradle, rocking, rocking. Putting the baby to sleep. If you feel your eyes getting heavy now, you may close them."

Joanna closed her eyes.

The tapestry light stopped pulsing.

"Now I'm going to tilt your chair back slightly," Inamura said. "To help you relax."

Pointing the remote control at her, he touched another button, and her armchair changed positions until it was halfway between being a chair and a couch.

"Now I want you to think of your forehead, Joanna. You are frowning. Your forehead is lined. It should be smooth. As smooth as glass. You will relax. I will touch you, and those lines will vanish."

He placed his fingertips on her forehead, on her eyelids. The lines in her brow did, indeed, vanish.

"Joanna, you're clenching your teeth. I want you to relax the muscles in your face."

He lightly pressed his fingertips to her left temple, her right temple, her cheekbones, her chin. His touch was magical, smoothing away all visible signs of her anxiety.

"And now your neck . . . relax your neck muscles . . . now your left shoulder . . . very relaxed . . . your right shoulder . . . both arms . . . so very relaxed . . . deeper . . . deeper . . . your abdomen and your hips . . . limp . . . no tension . . . relaxed . . . and now your legs, your feet . . . even into your toes, all relaxed, totally and wonderfully relaxed. You feel as if you are floating on a vast body of water . . . floating on blue water under blue sky . . . drowsy . . . drowsy . . . drowsier . . . until you are now in a deep and natural sleep."

Joanna's breathing had become slow and regular, but Inamura continued:

"I am taking hold of your right hand, Joanna. I'm lifting your right arm. And now your arm is becoming stiff . . . rigid . . . cannot be moved . . . cannot be lowered. It is impossible for you to lower your arm. It is rigid and will stay where I have put it. I'm going to count down from three, and when I say 'one,' you will be unable to put your arm down. Three . . . you are sleeping deeply . . . two . . . deeper and deeper into a relaxed, natural sleep . . . one . . . your arm is rigid. Rigid. But try to prove me wrong, Joanna. Try to move your arm."

She tried, but the arm trembled, and she could not lower it.

Inamura nodded with satisfaction. "You may now lower your arm, Joanna. I am now *allowing* you to lower it. Indeed, your arm is now so limp that you cannot possibly hold it up."

Her arm dropped into her lap.

"And now you are in a deep, deep, very relaxed sleep, and you will answer a number of questions for me. You will enjoy answering them. Do you understand?"

"Yes," she murmured.

"Speak more clearly, please."

"Yes."

Inamura returned to his chair. He put the remote control on the coffee table.

"Fly away," said the myna in the cage. A wistfulness colored those two words, as if the bird actually understood their meaning.

Joanna was limp, but now Alex was tense. He slid to the edge of his chair and turned to his right, so he could look directly at her.

To Alex, Inamura said, "She's an excellent subject for hypnosis. Usually, there's a little resistance, but not with her."

"Perhaps she's had a lot of practice."

"Quite a lot of it, I think," said Inamura.

Joanna waited.

The doctor leaned back in his chair, every bit as relaxed as his patient. His face was half in shadow. One eye was dark, the other gilded by a soft golden light, a reflection off the brass birdcage. He thought for a moment, then said, "Joanna, what is your full name?"

"Joanna Louise Rand," she said.

"Is that truly your name?"

"Yes."

"Recently you learned that Joanna Rand is a false name and that you were once called something else. Is that true?"

"No."

"You don't remember making that discovery?"

"My name is Joanna Louise Rand."

"Have you heard the name 'Lisa Chelgrin'?"

"No."

"Think about it before answering."

Silence. Then: "I've never heard the name."

"Do you know a man named Alex Hunter?"

"Of course. He's here."

"Did he mention Lisa Chelgrin to you?"

"I've never heard that name."

"Joanna, you can't lie to me. Understand?"

"Yes."

"You must always tell me the truth."

"Always."

"It is utterly impossible for you to lie to me."

"Impossible. I understand."

"Have you ever heard the name 'Lisa Chelgrin'?"

"No."

Alex glanced at the doctor. "What's happening?"

Inamura stared at Joanna for a while, tilting his head just far enough so the reflected spot of golden light shifted from his right eye to his cheek, where it shimmered like a strange stigmata. Finally he said, "She might have been programmed with this response to this particular question."

"Then how do we get around the program?" Alex asked.

"Patience."

"I haven't much of that at the moment."

Inamura said, "Joanna, we will now do something amazing. Something you might think impossible. But it is not impossible and is not even difficult. It is simple, easy. We are going to make time run backward. You are going to get younger. It is beginning to happen already. You can't resist it. You don't want to resist it. It is a lovely, sweet, flowing feeling . . . getting younger . . . and younger. The hands of the clock are turning backward . . . and you feel yourself floating in time . . . getting younger . . . rapidly younger . . . and now you are thirty-one years old, not thirty-two any more . . . and now thirty . . . and now twenty-nine . . . floating back through time." He continued in that fashion until he had regressed Joanna to her twentieth year, where he stopped her. "You are in London, Joanna. The apartment in London. You are sitting in . . . let's make it the kitchen. You are sitting at the kitchen table. Your mother is cooking something. It smells delicious. Makes your mouth water. What is your mother cooking, Joanna?"

Silence.

"What is your mother cooking, Joanna?"

"Nothing."

"She is not cooking?"

"No."

"Then what smells so delicious?"

"Nothing. There's no smell."

"What is your mother doing if not cooking?"

"Nothing."

"Are you in the kitchen?"

"Yes."

"What's happening?"

"Nothing."

"All right then. What is your mother's name?"

"My mother's name is Elizabeth Rand."

"What does she look like?"

"She has blond hair like mine."

"What color are her eyes?"

"Blue. Like mine."

"Is she pretty?"

"Yes."

"Heavy or thin."

"Slender."

"How tall is she, Joanna?"

Silence.

"How tall is your mother?"

"I don't know."

"Is she tall, short, or of medium height?"

"I don't know."

"Okay. All right. But you are there in the kitchen."

"Yes."

"Now . . . does your mother *like* to cook, Joanna?"

"I don't know."

"What is her favorite food?"

Silence.

"What is your mother's favorite food, Joanna?"

"I don't know."

"She must like to eat certain things in particular."

"I suppose so."

"What kind of meals does she prepare for you?"

"Regular meals."

"All right . . . what about beef? Does she favor beef dishes?"

After a hesitation Joanna sighed and said, "My mother's name is Elizabeth Rand."

Frowning, Inamura said, "Answer my question, Joanna. Does your mother prepare beef for you?"

"I don't remember."

"Yes, you do," he said gently, encouragingly. "You're in the kitchen. What is your mother cooking for you, Joanna?"

She said nothing.

Inamura was silent, pondering her blank face. He changed the subject. "Joanna, does your mother like to go to the movies?"

Joanna shifted uneasily in the armchair but kept her eyes shut.

Inamura said, "Does your mother like the theater, perhaps?"

"I guess she does."

"Does she like the movies too?"

"I guess she does."

"Don't you know for sure?"

Joanna made no response.

"Does your mother like to read?"

Silence.

"Does your mother enjoy books, Joanna?"

"I . . . I don't know."

"Does it seem strange to you that you know so little about your own mother?"

Joanna squirmed in her chair.

Inamura said, "What's your mother's name, Joanna?"

"My mother's name is Elizabeth Rand."

"Tell me everything you know about her."

"She has blond hair and blue eyes like mine."

"Tell me more."

"She's slender and pretty."

"More, Joanna. Tell me more."

Silence.

"Surely you know more, Joanna."

"She's very pretty."

"And?"

"Slender."

"And?"

"I can't remember, damn it!" Her face contorted. "Leave me alone!"

"Relax, Joanna," Inamura said. "You will relax."

Joanna's hands were no longer in her lap. She was fiercely gripping the arms of the chair, digging her fingernails into the upholstery. Under her closed lids, her eyes moved rapidly, like those of a sleeper caught in a bad dream.

Alex wanted to touch and comfort her, but he was afraid that he might break the spell that the doctor had cast.

"Relax and be calm," Inamura instructed. "You are very relaxed and calm. In deep sleep . . . deep natural sleep . . . yes . . . yes, that's better . . . deep relaxation. Joanna, perhaps you can't remember these things because you never knew them. And perhaps you never knew them . . . because Elizabeth Rand never existed."

"My mother's name is Elizabeth Rand," Joanna said woodenly.

"And perhaps Robert Rand never existed either."

"My father's name is Robert Rand."

"And perhaps you cannot picture the activity in that kitchen," Inamura pressed on, "because it never existed. Nor the apartment in London. So I want you to float freely in time . . . drift . . . just drift in time . . . backward . . . backward in time. You are looking for a special place, a unique and important place in your life . . . a place that reeks strongly of antiseptics, disinfectants. You know the place I mean. You dream of it repeatedly. Now you're searching for it . . . drifting toward it . . . drifting toward that special place and time . . . settling into it . . . and now . . . *there* . . . you are there in that room."

"Yes," she whispered.

"Are you sitting or standing?"

A tremor passed through her.

"Easy, relax. You're safe, Joanna. Answer all my questions, and you will be perfectly safe. Are you sitting or standing in that room?"

"Lying down."

"On the floor or on a bed?"

"Yes. I'm . . ."

"What?"

"I'm . . ."

"You're what, Joanna?"

"I'm n-naked."

"You seem frightened. Are you frightened?"

"Yes. S-scared."

"What are you frightened of?"

"I'm . . . s-strapped down."

"Restrained?"

"Oh, God."

"Relax, Joanna."

"Oh, God. My ankles, my wrists."

"Fly away," said the myna bird. "Fly away."

Inamura said, "Who did this to you, Joanna?"

"The straps are so tight."

"Who did this to you?"

"They hurt."

"Who strapped you to this bed, Joanna? You must answer me."

"I smell ammonia. Strong. Makes me sick."

"Look around the room, Joanna."

She grimaced at the stench of ammonia.

"Look around the room," Inamura repeated.

She lifted her head from the chair in which she reclined, opened her eyes, and looked obediently from left to right. She didn't see Alex or the office. She now existed in another day and place. In her haunted eyes, a veil of weeks and months and years seemed to shimmer like a sheet of tears.

"What do you see?" Inamura asked.

Joanna lowered her head. Closed her eyes.

"What do you see in that room?" Inamura persisted.

A strange, guttural sound issued from her.

Inamura repeated the question.

Joanna made the peculiar noise again, then louder: an ugly, asthmatic wheezing. Suddenly her eyes popped open and rolled up until only the whites were visible. She tried to lift her hands from the arms of the chair, but apparently she believed they were strapped down, and her wheezing grew worse.

Alex rose to his feet in alarm. "She can't breathe."

Joanna began to jerk and twitch violently, as if great jolts of electricity were slamming through her.

"She's choking to death!"

"Don't touch her," Inamura said.

Although the psychiatrist hadn't raised his voice, his tone halted Alex.

Inamura's left eye gleamed from deep in the shadows that fell across that side of his face, and the reflection of gold light was over his right eye again, a bright cataract that gave him an eerie aspect. He seemed to have no concern about Joanna's apparent agony.

As Alex watched, Joanna's blank white eyes bulged. Her face flushed, darkened. Flecks of spittle glistened on her lips. Her wheezing grew louder, louder.

"For God's sake, help her!" Alex demanded.

Inamura said, "Joanna, you will be calm and relaxed. Let your throat muscles relax. You will do as I say. You *must* do as I say. Relax . . . tension draining out of you . . . breath coming easier . . . easier. Breathe slowly . . . slowly and deeply . . . deeply . . . evenly . . . very relaxed. You are in a deep and natural sleep . . . perfectly safe . . . in a deep and peaceful sleep. . . ."

Joanna gradually grew quiet. Her eyes, which had been rolled back in her head, came down where they belonged. She closed them. She was breathing normally again.

"What the hell was that all about?" Alex asked, badly shaken.

Inamura waved him back into his chair, and Alex sat reluctantly.

The doctor said, "Do you hear me, Joanna?"

"Yes."

"I never lie to you, Joanna. I tell you only the truth. I'm here only to help you. Do you understand that?"

"Yes."

"Now, I'm going to tell you why you had that little respiratory problem. And when you understand, you will not allow such a thing to happen ever again."

"I can't control it," she said.

"Yes, you can. I'm telling you the truth now, and you are well aware of that truth. You had difficulty breathing only because *they* told you that you'd be unable to breathe, that you'd suffocate, that you'd spiral down into uncontrollable panic if you were questioned thoroughly under the influence of drugs or hypnosis. They implanted a posthypnotic suggestion that caused this attack when I probed too deeply, evidently with the hope your seizure would terminate this interrogation."

Joanna scowled. "That's the same thing that caused my claustrophobia."

"Precisely," Inamura said. "And now that you're aware of it, you won't allow it to happen again."

"I hate them," she said bitterly.

"Will you allow it to happen again, Joanna?"

"No."

"Good," Inamura said.

Even in the dimly lighted room, Joanna looked so pale that Alex said, "Maybe we shouldn't continue with this."

"It's perfectly safe," the doctor said.

"I'm not so sure."

Inamura said, "Joanna, are you still in the room, that special room, the place that reeks of ammonia?"

"Ammonia . . . alcohol . . . other things," she said. "Sickening. It's so strong I can smell it and *taste* it."

"You are unclothed—"

"—naked—"

"—and strapped to the bed."

"The straps are too tight. I can't move. Can't get up. I've got to get up and out of here."

"Relax," Inamura said. "Easy. Easy."

Alex watched her anxiously.

"Be calm," Inamura said. "You will remember all of it, but you will do so quietly. You will be calm and relaxed, and you will not be afraid."

"At least the room's warm," she said.

"That's the spirit. Now, I want you to look around and tell me what you see."

"Not much."

"Is it a large place?"

"No. Small."

"Any furniture other than the bed?"

She didn't reply. He repeated the question, and she said, "I don't know if you'd call it furniture."

"All right. But what is it? Can you describe what's in the room with you?"

"Beside my bed . . . it's . . . I guess it's one of those cardiac monitors . . . you know . . . like in an intensive-care ward or hospital operating theater."

"An electrocardiograph."

"Yes. And beside it . . . maybe . . . a brainwave machine."

"An electroencephalograph. Are you in a hospital?"

"No. I don't think so."

"Are you hooked up to the machines now?"

"Sometimes. Not now. No beeping. No wiggly lines of light. Machines are . . . shut off."

"Is there anything else in the room?"

"A chair. And a cabinet . . . with a glass door."

"What's in the cabinet, Joanna?"

"Lots of small bottles . . . vials . . . ampules . . ."

"Drugs?"

"Yes. And hypodermic syringes wrapped in plastic."

"Are those drugs used on you?"

"Yes. I hate . . ." Her hands closed into fists, opened, closed. "I hate . . ."
"Go on."

"I hate the needle." She twitched at the word "needle."

"What else do you see?"

"Nothing."

"Does the room have a window?"

"Yes. One."

"Good. Does it have a blind or drapes?"

"A blind."

"Is the blind open or shut?"

"Open."

"What do you see through the window, Joanna?"

She was silent again.

"What do you see through the window?"

Her voice suddenly changed. It was so hard, flat, and cold that it might have been the voice of an altogether different person. "Tension, apprehension, and dissension have begun."

Omi Inamura gazed at her, captured by a silence of his own. At last he repeated the question. "What do you see beyond the window?"

She chanted—not woodenly but with a strange, cold anger. "Tension, apprehension, and dissension have begun."

"You are relaxed and calm. You are not tense or apprehensive. You are completely safe, utterly relaxed, calm, in a deep and natural sleep."

"Tension, apprehension, and dissension have begun."

Alex put one hand to the nape of his neck where a chill crept across his skin.

Inamura said, "What do you mean by that, Joanna?"

She was rigid in her reclining chair. Her hands were fisted against her abdomen. "Tension, apprehension, and dissension have begun."

A dry scratching noise rose from the shadows across the room. Freud was scraping his talons against his wooden perch.

"Tension, apprehension, and dissension have begun," Joanna repeated.

"Very well," Inamura said. "Forget about the window for the time being. Let's talk about the people who came to see you when you were kept in that room. Were there many of them?"

Shaking with what seemed to be anger but which Alex now realized might be the physical evidence of a fierce internal struggle to break free of the implanted psychological bonds that imprisoned her memory, she repeated, "Tension, apprehension, and dissension have begun."

"Now what?" Alex asked.

Omi Inamura was silent for so long that Alex thought he hadn't heard the question. Then: "The posthypnotic suggestion that triggered her breathing difficulties was their first line of defense. This is their second. I suspect this one is going to be harder to crack."

✣ ✣ ✣

"Tension, apprehension, and dissension have begun."

"Do you hear me, Joanna?" the psychiatrist asked.

"Tension, apprehension, and dissension have begun."

Alex closed his eyes, silently repeating her chant along with her. He was teased by a vague sense of familiarity, as though he had heard it somewhere before.

Inamura said, "At the moment, Joanna, I'm not trying to pry any of your secrets out of you. I just want to know if you are listening, if you can hear my voice."

"Yes," she said.

"That sentence you keep repeating is a memory block. It must have been implanted posthypnotically. You will not use that sentence—'Tension, apprehension, and dissension have begun'—when you talk with me. You neither need nor want to avoid my questions. You came here to learn the truth. So just relax. Be calm. You are in a deep and natural sleep, safe in a deep sleep, and you will answer all my questions. I want you to *see* that memory block. It's lying in your mind, rather like a fallen tree lying across a highway, preventing you from going deeper into your memories. Visualize it, Joanna. A fallen tree. Or a boulder. Lying across the highway of memory. You can see it now . . . and you can even put your hands on it. You're getting a grip on it . . . such a powerful grip . . . and you feel a sudden rush of superhuman strength . . . so very strong, you are, so powerful . . . straining . . . lifting . . . lifting the boulder . . . casting it aside . . . out of the way. It's gone. The highway is open. No obstacle any more. Now you will remember. You will cooperate. Is that clear?"

"Yes," she said.

"Good. Very good. Now, Joanna, you are still in that room. You smell the alcohol . . . ammonia. Such a stench that you can even taste it. You're strapped to the bed . . . and the straps are biting into you. The blind is open at the window. Look at the window, Joanna. What do you see beyond the window?"

"Tension, apprehension, and dissension have begun."

"As I expected," Inamura said. "A difficult barrier."

Alex opened his eyes. "I've heard that chant before."

Inamura blinked and leaned forward in his chair. "You have? Where? When?"

"I can't recall. But it's strangely familiar."

"If you can remember, it would be enormously helpful," Inamura said. "I've got several tools with which I might be able to reach her, but I wouldn't be surprised if none of them worked. She's been programmed by clever and capable people, and more likely than not, they've anticipated most methods of treatment. I suspect there are only two ways I might be able to break through the memory block. And under the circumstances, with time so short, the first method—years of intensive therapy—isn't really acceptable."

"Not really," Alex agreed. "What's the second way?"

"An answering sentence."

"Answering sentence?"

Inamura nodded. "She might be requesting a password, you see. It's un- likely. But possible. Once she gives me the first line—'Tension, appre- hension, and dissension have begun'—she might be waiting for me to respond with the appropriate second line. A sort of code. If that's the case, she won't answer my questions until I've given her the correct answering sentence."

Alex was impressed by the doctor's insight and imagination. "A two-piece puzzle. She's got the first piece, and we've got to find the second before we can proceed."

"Perhaps."

"I'll be damned."

"If we knew the source of the line she uses, we might be able to come up with the answering sentence. For instance, perhaps she's giving us the first line of a couplet of poetry."

"I believe it's from a book," Alex said. He rose to his feet, stepped out of the circle of chairs, and began to pace around the shadow-shrouded room, because pacing sometimes helped him think. "Something I read once a long time ago."

"While you think," said Omi Inamura, "I'll see what I can do with her."

For thirty minutes the doctor strove to break down the memory block. He cajoled and argued and reasoned with Joanna; he used humor and discipline and logic; he demanded, asked, pleaded; he pried and probed and thrust and picked at her resistance.

Nothing worked. She continued to answer with those same six words, grating them out in a tone of barely contained rage: "Tension, apprehension, and dissension have begun."

For a while Alex stood at the cage, eye to eye with the myna. It was a small bird, but its stare was fierce. Most of the time, the myna worked its orange beak without producing any sound, but once it said, "Nevermore," as though it were perched on a plaster bust above a study door, lamenting Poe's lost Lenore.

Alex wondered why the myna spoke in English rather than in Japanese. Omi Inamura spoke English well, but with most of his patients, he would converse in his native language.

"Freud," said the myna. "Freud. Fly away."

The creature's speech was simple mimicry, of course; it didn't understand anything it said. Still, Alex was intrigued by the quick intelligence in its eyes, and he wondered what thoughts went through the mind of a bird. Somewhere he'd read that birds were descended from flying reptiles. Although the myna was cute and appealing, its basically reptilian view of the world was most likely cold, strange, and utterly alien. If he'd been able to read its mind, no doubt he'd have recoiled in horror and disgust from—

Read its mind.

Mind reading.

Telepathy.

Tension, apprehension, and dissension have begun.

"I've got it," he said, turning away from the bird and hurrying back to the circle of armchairs. "The line. It's from a science fiction novel." He sat down on the edge of his chair. "I read it years and years ago."

"What's the title?" Inamura asked.

"The Demolished Man."

"You're certain?"

"Absolutely. It's a classic of the genre. When I was young, I read a lot of science fiction. It was the perfect escape from . . . well, from everything."

"Do you remember the author?"

"Alfred Bester."

"And the line Joanna keeps repeating? What's the significance of it?"

Alex closed his eyes and cast his mind back into his childhood, when the covers of books had been doors through which he escaped to far places where there had been no monsters as terrible as drunken and abusive parents. He could see the futuristic artwork on the paperback almost as clearly as if he'd held it in his hands only a week ago.

"The novel's set a few hundred years in the future, during a time when the police use telepathy to enforce the law. They're mind readers. It's impossible for anyone to commit murder and get away with it in the society Bester envisions, but there's one character who's determined to kill someone and escape punishment. He finds a way to conceal his incriminating innermost thoughts. To prevent the telepathic detectives from reading his guilt in his own mind, he mentally recites a cleverly constructed, infectious jingle while retaining the ability to concentrate on other things at the same time. The monotonous repetition of the jingle acts like a shield to deflect the snooping telepaths."

Inamura said, "And one of the lines he recites is 'Tension, apprehension, and dissension have begun.' "

"Yeah."

"Then if there *is* an answering sentence that will dispose of Joanna's memory block, it's almost certainly another line of that jingle. Do you remember the rest of it?"

"No," Alex said. "We'll have to get the book. I'll call my office in Chicago and have someone track down a copy. We—"

"That might not be necessary," Dr. Inamura said. "If the novel is a classic in its field, there's a good chance it's been translated into Japanese. I'll be able to obtain it from a bookstore here or from a man I know who deals in rare and out-of-print titles."

That put an end to their first session. There was no point in continuing until Inamura had a copy of *The Demolished Man*. Once more the doctor turned his attention to Joanna. He told her that upon waking she'd remember all that had transpired between them—and would be more easily hypnotized the next time that he treated her.

"In fact," Inamura told her, "in the future you will slip into a deep trance upon hearing me speak just two words: 'dancing butterflies.' "

"Dancing butterflies," Joanna repeated, at his request.

The psychiatrist brought her slowly back from the past to the present, used the remote control to tilt her chair into the full upright position, and then woke her.

Outside, when Alex and Joanna left Inamura's building, the day had grown colder. The huffing wind seemed like a living presence, pulling and shoving with malicious intent.

As they walked toward Joanna's Lexus, a large black-and-yellow cat scurried along the gutter. It jumped the curb to the sidewalk, directly into their path, glanced warily at them, and then dashed down a set of shadow-filled basement steps. Alex was glad for the touch of yellow in its coat.

"Dancing butterflies," Joanna said.

"You find that curious?"

"I find it very Japanese. Dancing butterflies. Such a lovely, delicate image to be associated with a grim business like this."

The afternoon was giving way to evening. The low clouds were as dark as slate, and the sky looked too hard to be the home of any but malevolent gods.

36

❂ ❂ ❂

Twenty-four hours later. Saturday afternoon.

The myna climbed the curved walls of its cage, and from time to time its talons plucked a reverberant note from the brass, which to Alex sounded like a piano wire snapping under too much tension.

"Dancing butterflies," said Omi Inamura.

Joanna's eyes fluttered and closed. Her breathing changed. She went limp in the big reclining chair.

With great skill, the psychiatrist took her back through the years until she was once again deep in the past, in the room that stank of antiseptics and disinfectants.

"There is a window in that room, isn't there, Joanna?" Inamura asked.

"Yes. One."

"Is the blind open?"

"Yes."

The doctor hesitated, then asked, "What do you see beyond that window?"

"Tension, apprehension, and dissension have begun."

Inamura opened a copy of the Japanese edition of *The Demolished Man,* one page of which he had marked with a blue silk ribbon. Joanna had recited the last line of the jingle that was an integral part of Bester's story. Inamura read aloud the next to last line, hoping that it would prove to be the answering sentence—if there was such a thing. " 'Tenser, said the Tensor.' "

Although the doctor had not asked a question, Joanna responded. "Tension, apprehension, and dissension have begun."

" 'Tenser, said the Tensor.' "

Joanna did not respond this time.

Inamura leaned forward in his armchair. "You are in the room that smells of alcohol . . . ammonia. You're strapped to the bed."

"Yes."

"There is a window. An open window. What do you see beyond the window, Joanna?"

"The roof of a house," she said without hesitation. "It's a mansard roof. Black slate. No windows in it. I can see two brick chimneys."

"By God, it worked!" Alex said.

"I got the Bester novel last evening," Inamura said, "and read it in a single sitting. It's engrossing science fiction. Do you remember what happens to the killer at the end of the novel?"

"He's caught by the telepathic police," Alex said.

"Yes. Caught in spite of all his cleverness. And after they apprehend him, rather than imprison or execute him, they 'demolish' the man. They tear down his psyche, wipe out his memory. They remove every twist and quirk that made it possible for him to commit murder. Then they reconstruct him as a model citizen. *They make an entirely new person out of him.*"

"So in some ways it's similar to Joanna's experience. Except that she's an innocent victim."

"Some things that were science fiction thirty years ago are fact today. For better or worse."

"I've never doubted that modern brainwashing techniques could produce a total identity change," Alex said. "I just want to know why the hell it was done to Joanna."

"Perhaps we'll find the answer today," the psychiatrist said. He faced his patient again. "What else do you see beyond the window, Joanna?"

"Just the sky."

"Do you know what city you're in?"

"No."

"What country?"

"No."

"Let's talk about the people who visit you in that room. Are there many of them?"

"A nurse. Heavyset. Gray hair. I don't like her. She has a . . . strange smile."

"Do you know her name?"

"I can't remember."

"Take your time."

Her face clouded with puzzlement as she struggled to recall the nurse's name. At last: "No. It's gone."

"Who else visits you?"

"A woman with brown hair, brown eyes. Sharp features. She's very brisk, businesslike. She's a doctor."

"How do you know that?"

"I . . . I guess maybe she told me. And she does things . . . doctor things."

"Such as?"

"She takes my blood pressure and gives me injections and runs all kinds of tests on me."

"What's her name?"

"I don't know."

"Have you just forgotten—or did she never tell you her name?"

"I don't think she ever told me."

"Is there anyone else who comes to see you in that room?"

Joanna shuddered. Although she didn't reply, she crossed her arms protectively across her breasts, and a shadow of fear fell across her face.

"There is someone," said Inamura. "Who, Joanna? Who else comes to see you?"

She chewed on her lower lip. Her hands were fisted. Her voice faded to a tremulous whisper: "Oh, God, no. No. No."

"Relax. Be calm," Inamura instructed.

Alex fidgeted in his chair. He wanted to take her in his arms and hold her, let her know that she was safe.

Inamura persisted: "Who else comes to see you, Joanna?"

"The Hand," she said thinly.

"The Hand? Do you mean the man with the prosthetic device, the mechanical hand?"

"Him."

"Is he a doctor too?"

"Yes."

"How do you know that?"

"The woman doctor and the nurse call him 'Herr Doktor.' "

"Did you say *Herr,* the German form of address?"

"Yes."

"Are the women German?"

"I don't know."

"Is the man German?"

"The . . . The Hand? I don't know."

"Do they speak German?"

"Not to me. Only English to me."

"What language do they speak among themselves?"

"Sometimes English."

"And at other times?"

"Something else."

"Might it be German?"

"I guess. Maybe."

"When they're speaking in English, do they have German accents?"

"I . . . I'm not sure. Accents. All of them have accents. But not necessarily German."

"Do you think this room could be somewhere in Germany?"

"No. Maybe. Well . . . I don't know where it is."

"The doctor, this man who—"

"Do we have to talk about him?" she asked plaintively.

"Yes, Joanna. We must talk about him. Just relax. He can't hurt you now. Tell me—what does he look like?"

"Brown hair. He's going bald."

"What color eyes?"

"Light brown. Pale. Almost yellow."

"Tall or short? Thin or fat?"

"Tall and thin."

"What does he do to you in that room?"

She rolled her head slowly from side to side on the chair, declining to answer.

"What does he do to you?"

The myna was suddenly frantic, rapidly circling the walls of its cage, plucking at the brass bars with its talons and beak.

"What does he do to you, Joanna?"

The *plink-plonk-plink* of brass was a cold, flat music, as though a draft out of Hell were stirring the music of damnation from a set of wind chimes.

Inamura was insistent. "What does he do to you, Joanna?"

At last she said shakily: "Treatments."

"What sort of treatments?"

Her lashes fluttered, and from her closed eyes came slow tears.

Alex reached out for her from his chair.

"No," the doctor said almost sotto voce but forcefully.

"But she needs—"

"She needs to remember."

Alex said, "But I can't—"

"Trust me, Mr. Hunter."

Anguished, Alex drew back from Joanna.

"What sort of treatments?" Inamura asked again.

"I'm dying." She shuddered. She pressed her arms even tighter across her chest, shrank back defensively into the chair. "Each time I d-d-die just a little more. Why not kill me all at once? Why not get it over with?" She was crying openly now. "Please, just get it over with."

"You aren't dying," Inamura assured her. "You're safe. I am protecting you, Joanna. Just tell me about these treatments. What are they like?"

She could not speak.

"All right," the psychiatrist said gently. "Relax. Be calm. You are calm and relaxed . . . relaxed . . . safe and at peace and relaxed . . . sleeping deeply . . . such sweet tranquillity."

Her shaking subsided. Her tears stopped flowing. But she kept her arms crossed defensively.

"You are still in that room," Inamura said when Joanna was ready to go on. "Alone in that room, on the bed, strapped down."

"Naked," she said. "Under a sheet."

"You haven't yet had your daily treatment. Herr Doktor will be here in a moment, and you will describe what happens after he arrives. You will describe it calmly, serenely. Begin."

Joanna swallowed hard. "The woman doctor . . . comes into the room and pulls the sheet down to my waist. She makes me feel so helpless, utterly defenseless. She hooks me up to the machines."

"To the electrocardiograph and electroencephalograph?"

"Yes. She tapes electrodes to me. Cold against my skin. The machine keeps beeping . . . beeping . . . beeping. It drives me crazy. She slips a board under my arm. Tapes it in place. Hooks me up to the bottle."

"Do you mean that you're being fed intravenously?"

"That's always how the treatment starts." Gradually Joanna's speech became slower and thicker than normal. "And she covers my breasts with the sheet . . . watches me . . . watches me . . . takes my blood pressure . . . and after a while . . . I begin to float . . . light, so light, like a feather . . . but aware of everything . . . too aware, painfully aware . . . a sharp, terrible awareness . . . but all the time floating . . . floating."

"Joanna, why is your speech slurring?"

"Floating . . . numb . . . drifting . . ."

"Does the IV bottle contain a drug in addition to glucose?"

"Don't know. Maybe. Up, up, up like a balloon."

"It must be a drug," Alex said.

Inamura nodded. "Joanna, I don't want you to speak in that thick, sluggish manner. Speak normally. The drug is still being administered to you, but it won't affect your speech. You'll continue to experience this treatment, and you will tell me about it in your usual, unaffected voice."

"All right."

"Good. Continue."

"The woman leaves. I'm alone again. Still floating. But I don't feel high or happy. Never do. Just scared. Then . . ."

"What happens then?" Inamura encouraged.

"Then . . . then . . . the door opens and he enters. The Hand."

"Herr Doktor?"

"Him, him."

"What's he doing?"

"I want out of here."

"What is the doctor doing, Joanna?"

"Please. Please let me out."

"Be calm. You are in no danger. What is he doing?"

She continued reluctantly: "Pushing the cart."

"What cart is he pushing?"

"It's covered with medical instruments."

"Go on."

"He comes to the bed. His hand . . ."

"What about his hand, Joanna?"

"He . . . he . . . he . . . he holds his hand in front of my face."

"Yes?"

"Opens and closes his steel fingers."

"Does he say anything?"

"No. Just the s-sound of his fingers. Clicking."

"How long does this go on?"

"Until I'm crying."

"Is that what he wants—to see you cry?"

She was shivering.

The room seemed cold to Alex too.

"He wants to scare me," she said. "He enjoys it."

"How do you know he enjoys it?" asked Inamura.

"I know him. The Hand. I know him so well by now. I hate him. Standing over me. Looking down. The clicking fingers. He grins."

"So he makes you cry. He likes watching you cry. But then what does he do?"

"No," she said miserably. She turned onto her side in the big reclining chair, facing Alex, eyes still closed, arms still tucked against her breast. She drew her knees up slightly, into the fetal position. "No . . . please."

"Relax, Joanna," Inamura said. "You are there but detached from the experience now, insulated from the feelings this time. You are there only as an observer."

"No . . . no." But her protests were merely weak denials of the horror of those memories, not a refusal to proceed with the session.

Alex was suffering with her, because the helplessness that she had felt while strapped to that bed was akin to the sense of helplessness that had informed his entire childhood.

"What is Herr Doktor doing now?" Inamura asked.

"The needle."

"The IV?"

"No. Another. Oh, God."

"A hypodermic?"

"It'll kill me this time," she said with pathetic conviction.

"Rest easy. Be calm. You're safe now. What's so special about this needle?"

"It's so big. Huge. It's filled with fire."

"You're afraid the needle will sting?"

"Burn. Burn like acid. Squirting acid into me."

"Not this time," Inamura assured her. "No pain this time."

Beyond the closed pine shutters, a sudden gust of wind shrieked at the windows, and the glass thrummed.

Alex almost felt as if the man with the mechanical hand was in Omi Inamura's office. He could feel an evil presence, a sudden and chilling change in the air.

"Let's continue," the psychiatrist said. "The doctor uses this needle, gives you an injection, and then—"

"No. Not my neck. Not my neck. Jesus, *no!*"

She thrashed on the reclining chair, wrenching herself out of the fetal position almost as if racked by an extreme epileptic spasm, flopping onto her back, rigid, shaking, tossing her head from side to side.

Inamura said, "What's wrong with your neck, Joanna?"

"The needle!"

"He puts the needle in your neck?"

Alex felt ill. He touched his own neck.

Mentally, emotionally, spiritually, Joanna was not in Inamura's office. She was deep in the past, living through hell once more. And though the doctor had told her that she would remain emotionally detached from the memory and would report upon it in an objective fashion, she was unable to maintain the distance he demanded of her. She was convulsed by the memory of pain as if she were suffering the real agony at that very moment.

"It hurts, everything hurts, my veins are on fire, blood's boiling, bubbling, oh, God, Jesus, God, it's eating me up, eating me up, like acid, lye, turning me black inside. *Somebody, please, please help me!*"

Her eyes were squeezed tightly shut, as if she could not bear what she would see if she opened them. The arteries throbbed at her temples, and the muscles in her neck were taut. She writhed and cried out wordlessly, and her back raised up from the reclining chair in such an extreme arch that only her feet, her shoulders, and the back of her head were touching the upholstery.

Dr. Inamura spoke comfortingly to her, trying to talk her down from the ledge of hysteria on which she was precariously balanced.

Joanna responded to him but not as quickly as she had done earlier. She slowly relaxed—although not as completely as before. Still in a trance, she rested for a few minutes, though she never quite stopped trembling. Now and then her hands fluttered up from the arms of her chair and described meaningless patterns in the air before settling down again.

Dr. Inamura and Alex waited silently for her to be calm enough to go on with the session.

The wind huffed at the shuttered windows again, harder than before, and then keened shrilly, as if in disappointment, when it was unable to get inside.

At last Inamura said, "Joanna, you are in the room that smells of antiseptics, disinfectants. The odor is so heavy that you can taste it. You are strapped to the bed, and the treatment has begun. Now dispassionately, quietly, I want you to tell me what they do to you, what the treatment is like."

"Floating. Floating and burning at the same time."

"What does Herr Doktor do?"

"I'm not sure."

"What do you see?"

"Brilliant colors. Whirling, pulsing colors."

"What else do you see?"

"Nothing else. Just the colors."

"What do you hear?"

"The Hand. He's talking. Very distant."

"What's he saying?"

"Too distant. I can't make out the words."

"Is he talking to you?"

"Yes. And sometimes I answer him."

"What do you say to him?"

"My voice is as distant as his. I can barely hear myself. I'm so far away, high above, high up and floating in the fire, in the pain, lost in the pain."

"If you try now, you'll be able to hear yourself. Just listen to your voice, and you will hear it clearly."

"No. Can't make it out. I'm flying a thousand miles above myself, too high to hear."

"Joanna, he's talking to your subconscious. Your conscious awareness is being suppressed by drugs, and your subconscious is wide open to him."

"High, high above myself," she insisted.

"It's only your conscious mind that's floating up there. On a conscious level, perhaps you can't hear him, but your subconscious hears him clearly, every word, every nuance. I want you to let your subconscious speak. What is Herr Doktor saying?"

Joanna fell into silence and became deathly still.

"What does he say to you?"

"I don't know, but I'm scared."

"What are you scared of, Joanna?"

"Losing things."

"What things?"

"Everything."

"Please be more specific."

"Pieces of myself."

"You're afraid of losing pieces of yourself?"

"Pieces are falling away. I'm like a leper."

"Pieces of memory?" Alex guessed.

"I'm crumbling," Joanna said. "High above, I'm floating and burning, but down here I'm crumbling."

"Is it memory you're losing?" Inamura pressed.

"I don't know. But I feel it going."

"What does he say to you to make you forget?"

"Can't quite hear."

"Strain for it. You can remember."

"No. He took that away from me too."

Inamura followed that line of questioning until he was convinced that he would learn nothing more from it. "You've done well, Joanna. Very well, indeed. And now the treatment is finished. The needle has been removed from your neck. The other needle has been removed from your arm. You are gradually settling down, down."

"No. I'm still floating. Not burning any more, not being eaten up inside any more, but floating. I keep floating for a long time afterward. For at least an hour. Longer."

"All right. You're floating, but the needles are out of you. What happens now?"

She covered her face with her hands.

"Joanna," Inamura said, "what's happening to you?"

"I'm ashamed," she said miserably.

"There's no need to be ashamed."

"You don't know," she said from behind her hands. "You can't ever know."

"Nothing to be ashamed of at all. Put your hands down, Joanna. Put them down. It's okay. That's right. You haven't done anything wrong. You're a good person. You have a good heart. You're the victim here, not the criminal."

She could not speak. She tried and failed.

The wind at the windows.

The bird in the cage. Talons on the brass.

She struggled to tell Inamura what he wanted to know, and it was clear by her tortured expression that she needed to spill those secrets and be rid of them. But her mouth worked without producing a sound.

Alex could hardly bear to watch her as she lay torn between shame and the need to confess, between fear and freedom. Yet he couldn't look away from her.

Finally she said, "If only . . . I could die."

"You don't really want to die," Inamura assured her.

"More than anything."

"No."

"It's the only way to stop him . . . what he does to me."

"It's already stopped. Years ago. You're only plagued by the memory now, because you haven't been able to face it. Confront it and be freed, Joanna. Tell me the rest of it and be free."

Her voice was so faint that Alex had to lean forward in his chair to catch what she said: "Hear it? Hear it?"

"What do you hear?" Inamura asked.

"The clicking."

"Clicking?"

"Click, click, click," she said softly.

"What is this clicking?"

"The gears."

"Ah. In his hand?"

"Soft at first. Then louder. Then as loud as gunshots. The gears in his fingers."

She shuddered and made a pitiful sound that weighed like a stone on Alex's heart.

Inamura said, "Where is Herr Doktor now?"

In her still small voice, she said, "Beside the bed. He strokes my face. With those steel fingers. Click, click, click."

"Go on."

Her hands moved from her face to her throat.

"He massages my throat," she said. "I try to pry his hand away. I really do try. But I can't. It's steel. So powerful. Hear the little motors purring in it?"

She opened her eyes, staring at the ceiling. Tears shimmered.

"Go on," said Inamura.

"He grins," she said. "I'm floating very high, but I can see his grin. I'm way up high, but I can feel what he's doing. I ask God to stop him, just to stop him, that's all, because I'm too weak, I need God's help, but it . . . never . . . it never comes."

"Don't bottle this up," the psychiatrist said gently. "Don't continue to make a secret of it. Tell me everything, Joanna. Free yourself of it."

Her hands were trembling. She lowered them from her throat to her breasts.

"The clicking," she said. "It's so loud I can't hear anything else. It fills the room. Deafening."

"What does he do?"

"He pulls the sheet away. He draws it to the bottom of the bed. Uncovers me. I'm naked."

Her cheeks were wet with tears again, but she was not sobbing.

"Go on," Inamura said.

"He stands there. Grinning. Takes the electrodes off me. Touches me. He has no right to touch me like that, not like that, but I can't do anything. I'm flying high and weak."

"Where is he touching you?"

"My breasts. Stroking, squeezing with those steel fingers. Hurting me. He knows he's hurting me. He likes to hurt me. Then he touches me with the other hand too, the real hand. It's sweaty. He's rough with that hand too . . . rough . . . demanding . . . using me. . . ."

Joanna's voice faded word by word, until she couldn't speak any more. Her face was wrenched into the most devastating expression of anguish that Alex had ever seen, yet she made only the softest sounds, as though her shame and sense of violation were so heavy that her voice was crushed beneath them.

The sight of her in such excruciating emotional pain struck Alex with the force of a thunderbolt. In the past few days he had learned to feel things he'd never felt before. In himself, he'd discovered possibilities of which he'd been ignorant all his life. Joanna had sensitized him. But everything that he had experienced since meeting her was only as powerful as a spring breeze compared to the emotional storm that shook him now. He couldn't bear to see her like this. The horror of her experiences with the man she called "The Hand" affected Alex more profoundly than if her suffering had been his own. If he had incurred the wound himself, he could grit his teeth and stitch it up with the stoicism he had long cultivated, but because it was her wound, he could do little to influence the healing of it. He was shattered by the full and unwelcome realization of his helplessness.

For a few minutes Dr. Inamura patiently reassured her, until at last she regained her composure. When she was still and no longer crying, he urged her to pick up her story where she had left it. "What is Herr Doktor doing now, Joanna?"

Alex interrupted. "Surely, *Isha-san,* you don't have to pursue this thing any further."

"But I must," Inamura disagreed.

"I think we know all too well what he did to her."

"Yes, of course, we know. And I understand how you feel," the psychiatrist said sympathetically. "But it's essential that she say it. She's got to reveal everything, not for your benefit or mine but for her own. If I allow her to stop now, the ugly details will remain in her forever, festering like filthy splinters."

"But it's so hard on her."

"Finding the truth is never easy."

"She's suffering such—"

"She'll suffer even more if I let her stop now, prematurely."

"Maybe we should give her a rest and pick up here tomorrow."

"Tomorrow we have other tasks," said Inamura. "I need only a few minutes to finish this line of questioning."

Without enthusiasm, Alex admitted the superiority of Inamura's argument.

The doctor said, "Joanna, where are Herr Doktor's hands now?"

"On me. On my breasts," she said.

There was a new, peculiar, and disturbing flatness in her voice, as though a part of her had died and was speaking from a dark, frigid place on the other side of life.

"What does he do next?" Inamura asked.

"The steel hand moves down my body."

"Go on."

"Down to my thighs," she said flatly.

"And then?"

"Everything's taken."

"What is taken?" Inamura asked.

"Hope. All gone. Nothing left to cling to."

"No, Joanna. Hope can never be taken away forever. It's the one thing in us that's always renewed. He took your hope away only for a short while. He can't win in the long run unless you allow him to win. What does he do now? Please tell me, Joanna."

"He touches me there."

"Where does he touch you?"

"Between my legs."

"And then?"

"He's grinning."

"And then?"

"Click, click, click."

"Go on."

She was silent.

"Joanna?"

She said, "I need . . ."

"Yes?"

". . . a minute."

"Take your time," Inamura said. He glanced at Alex, and his eyes revealed an infinite sadness.

Alex looked down at his hands. They were fisted on his knees. He wanted to beat Herr Doktor until his knuckles were scraped and raw, until every bone in his hands was broken, until his arms were so weary that he could no longer lift them from his sides.

On its perch in the cage, the myna erupted in a brief rage, flapping its wings frenziedly before abruptly going as still as though it had spotted a predator.

In that drab voice borrowed from someone dead, as though she were channeling a despairing spirit that was trapped in Hell, she said, "Touching me between the legs. Cold steel. Clicking so loud. Like explosions."

"And then?"

"He opens me."

"And then?"

"Puts one."

"Does what?"

"Puts one of his steel fingers."

"Puts it where?"

"Inside me."

"Be more specific."

"Isn't that enough—what I said?"

"No. You mustn't be afraid to say it clearly."

"Into . . . my vagina."

"You're doing well. You were used terribly. But in order to forget, you must first remember. Go on."

Her hands were still clasped protectively over her breasts. "The clicking noise fills me, fills me inside, so loud, echoing through me."

"And then?"

"I'm afraid he'll hurt me."

"Does he hurt you?"

"He threatens me."

"What does he threaten to do?"

"He says he'll . . . tear me apart."

"And then?"

"He grins."

"And then?"

And then? And then? And then? Go on. Go on. And then? And then? Go on.

Alex wanted to press his hands over his ears. He forced himself to listen, because if he hoped to share the best of life with her, he must be prepared to share the worst as well.

Inamura probed at Joanna's psyche in the manner of a dentist meticulously drilling away every trace of rotten matter and bacteria in an infected tooth.

The brutal revelations of repeated rape and perverse sex—in addition to the even more chilling story of the "treatment" that she had endured—left Alex weak. He nurtured the blackest imaginable hatred for the people who had stolen her past and who had dealt with her as they might have dealt with any animal. He was determined to find the man with the mechanical hand and every one of that bastard's associates. But revenge would have to come later. At the moment, shell-shocked by the hideous events that Joanna was recalling for Dr. Omi Inamura, Alex didn't have even enough strength to speak.

The remainder of the interrogation lasted only five or six minutes. When Joanna answered the last question, she turned on her side and drew her knees up, assuming the fetal position once more.

Unconcerned about what the doctor might say, Alex got out of his chair and knelt beside her. With one hand, he smoothed her hair away from her face.

"Enough," he told Inamura. "That's enough for today. Bring her back to me."

37

✪ ✪ ✪

At six o'clock Sunday morning, Joanna was awakened by thirst. Her lips were chapped, and her throat was dry. She felt dehydrated. The previous night, after the exhausting session in Inamura's office, they had eaten a large dinner: thick steaks, Kobe beef, the finest meat in the world, from cattle that had been hand-massaged daily and fed nothing but rice, beans, and plenty of beer. With the steaks, they had finished two bottles of fine French wine, a rare and expensive luxury in Japan. Now the alcohol had leached moisture from her and had left a sour taste.

She went into the bathroom and greedily drank two glasses of water. It tasted almost as good as wine.

Returning to bed, she realized that for the first time in twelve years, her sleep had not been interrupted by the familiar nightmare. She had not dreamed about the man with the mechanical hand.

She was free at last, and she stood very still for a moment, stunned. Then she laughed aloud.

Free!

In bed, wrapped in a newfound sense of security as well as in blankets and sheets, she sought sleep again and found it quickly after her head touched the pillow.

She woke naturally, three hours later, at nine o'clock. Though her sleep had been dreamless, she was less enthusiastic about her new freedom than she had been in the middle of the night. She wasn't certain why her attitude had changed; but whatever the reason, the mood of innocent optimism was gone. She was wary, cautious, tempered by an intuition that told her more—and worse—trouble was coming.

Curious about the weather, she went to the nearest window and drew back the drapes. A storm had passed through during the night. The sky was clear, but Kyoto lay under six or seven inches of fresh, dry snow. The streets held little traffic.

In addition to the snow, something else had arrived in the night. Across the street, on the second floor of a popular geisha house, a man stood at a window. He was watching her apartment through a pair of binoculars.

He saw her at the same moment that she saw him. He lowered the glasses and stepped back, out of sight.

That was why her mood had changed. Subconsciously she had been expecting something like the man with the binoculars. They were out there. Waiting. Watching. Biding their time. Platoons of them, for all she knew. Until she and Alex could discover who they were and why they had stolen her past, she was neither safe nor free. In spite of the fact that the bad dream no longer had the power to disrupt her sleep, the sense of security that she enjoyed during the night was false. Although she'd lived through several kinds of hell, the worst of them all might be ahead of her.

In the morning sun, the snow was bright. The Gion looked pure. In the distance, a temple bell rang.

38

That morning, at eleven o'clock Kyoto time, Ted Blankenship called from Chicago. He had received detailed reports from the company's associates in London, in answer to the questions that Alex had asked two days ago.

According to the investigators in England, the solicitor who had acted as the executor of the Rand estate, J. Compton Woolrich, was a phantom. There was no record that he had ever existed. No birth certificate. No passport in that name. No driver's license. No file under that name with the tax authorities at Inland Revenue. No work or identity card of any sort. Nothing. No one named J. Compton Woolrich had been licensed to practice law at any time in this century. Nor had anyone with that name possessed a telephone number in greater London since 1946. As Joanna had discovered on Friday, Woolrich's telephone was actually that of an antique shop on Jermyn Street. Likewise, the return address on Compton's stationery was neither a home nor a law office; it was actually that of a library that had been established prior to the Second World War.

"What about British-Continental Insurance?" Alex asked.

"Another phony," Blankenship said. "There's no such firm registered or paying taxes in England."

"And though by some fluke they might have escaped registration, no one there escapes taxes."

"Exactly."

"But we talked to Phillips at British-Continental."

"Not his real name. A deception."

"Yes, I suppose so. What about the address on their stationery?"

"Oh, that's real enough," Blankenship said. "But it sure as hell isn't the headquarters for a major corporation. Our British friends say it's just a grimy, three-story office building in Soho."

"And there's not even a branch office of an insurance company in the place?"

"No. About a dozen other businesses operate there, all more or less cubby-hole outfits, nothing particularly successful—at least not on the surface of it. Importers. Exporters. A mail-forwarding service. A couple of talent bookers who service the cheapest clubs in the city. But no British-Continental."

"What about the telephone number?"

"It's listed to one of the importers at that address. Fielding Athison, Limited. They deal in furniture, clothes, dinnerware, crafts, jewelry, and a lot of other stuff that's made in South Korea, Taiwan, Indonesia, Hong Kong, Singapore, and Thailand."

"And they don't have a Mr. Phillips at that number?"

"That's what they say."

"They're playing games."

"I wish you'd tell me what kind of games," Blankenship said. "And how does this tie in with Tom Chelgrin and his missing daughter? I have to tell you, curiosity's got me in nearly as bad shape as the proverbial cat."

"It's not a good idea for me to talk too much about my plans," Alex said. "At least not on this phone."

"Tapped?"

"I suspect it's been transformed into a regular party line."

"In that case, should we be talking at all?" Blankenship asked worriedly.

"It doesn't matter if they hear what you're going to tell me," Alex said. "None of it's news to them. What else have you got on this Fielding Athison company?"

"Well, it's a profitable business, but only by a hair. In fact, they're so overstaffed it's a miracle they manage to stay afloat."

"What does that suggest to you?"

"Other important companies of similar size make do with ten or twelve employees. Fielding Athison has twenty-seven, the majority of them in sales. There just doesn't appear to be enough work to keep them all busy."

"So the importing business is a front," Alex said.

"In the diplomatic phrasing of our English friends, 'The distinct possibility exists that the employees of Fielding Athison engage in some sort of unpublicized work in addition to the importation of Asian goods.'"

"A front for what? For whom?"

"If you want to find out," Blankenship said, "it's going to cost us dearly. And it's not the sort of thing that can be dug up quickly—if at all. I'd bet a thousand to one that the people using Fielding Athison are breaking a serious law or two. But they've been in business for fourteen years, and no one's tumbled to them yet, so they're good at keeping secrets. Do you want me to tell London to try to dig deeper?"

"No," Alex said. "Not right now. I'll see what develops here in the next couple of days. If it's necessary to put the Englishmen on the job again, I'll call you back."

"How's Wayne?" Blankenship asked.

"Better. He'll keep the leg."

"Thank God. Look, Alex, do you want me to send help?"

"I'm all right."

"I've got a few good men free at the moment."

"If they came, they'd only be targets. Like Wayne."

"Aren't you a target?"

"Yeah. But the fewer the better."

"A little protection—"

"I don't need protection."

"Wayne needed protection. But I guess you know best."

"What I need," Alex said, "is divine guidance."

"If a voice comes to me from a burning bush anytime soon, I'll let you know right away what it says."

"Seriously, Ted, I want you to keep a lid on this. I don't want to attack the problem with an army. I'd like to find the answers I'm after without, in the process, filling up Japanese hospitals with my employees."

"It's still an odd way to handle it—alone."

"I realize that," Alex said. "But I've thought about it . . . and it seems to me that these people, whoever they might be, have given me quite a lot of slack already. There's something odd about the fact that they haven't just blown my head off by now."

"You think they're playing two sides of some game? Using you?"

"Maybe. And maybe if I bring in a platoon from Chicago, they won't cut me any more slack. Maybe they want to keep the game quiet, with a limited number of players."

"Why?"

"If I knew that, then there wouldn't be any need for the game, would there?"

39

✣ ✣ ✣

Five o'clock Sunday afternoon. Dr. Inamura's office. Pastel lighting. Lemon incense. The watchful bird in the brass cage.

The pine shutters were open, and purple twilight pressed at the windows.

"Dancing butterflies," said the psychiatrist.

In the final session with Omi Inamura, Joanna recalled the exact wording of the three posthypnotic suggestions that had been deeply implanted by the man with the mechanical hand. The first involved the memory block—"Tension, apprehension, and dissension have begun"—with which they had already dealt. The second concerned the devastating attacks of claustrophobia and paranoia that she suffered when anyone became more than casually interested in her. Inamura finished administering the cure that Alex had begun several days ago, patiently convincing Joanna that the words of Herr Doktor no longer had any power over her and that her fears were not valid. They never had been valid. Not surprisingly, the third of Herr Doktor's directives was that she would never leave Japan; and if she *did* attempt to get out of the country, if she *did* board a ship or an aircraft that was bound for any port beyond Japan's borders, she would become nauseous and extremely disoriented. Any attempt to escape from the prison to which she was assigned would end in an attack of blind terror and hysteria. Her faceless masters had boxed her up every way that they could: emotionally, intellectually, psychologically, chronologically, and now even geographically. Omi Inamura relieved her of that last restriction.

Alex was impressed by the cleverness with which Herr Doktor had programmed Joanna. Whoever and whatever else he might be, the man was a genius in his field.

When Inamura was positive that Joanna could not remember any more about what Herr Doktor had done to her, he took the session in a new direction. He urged her to move further into her past.

She squirmed in the chair. "But there's nowhere to go."

"Of course there is. You weren't born in that room, Joanna."

"Nowhere to go."

"Listen carefully," Inamura said. "You're strapped in that bed. There's one window. Outside there's a mansard roof against a blue sky. Are you there?"

"Yes," she said, more relaxed in this trance than she had been in any of the previous sessions. "Big black birds are sitting on the chimneys. A dozen big black birds."

"You're approximately twenty years old," Inamura said. "But now you're growing younger. Minute by minute, you're growing younger. You have not been in that room for a long time. In fact you've just come there, and you haven't yet even met the man with the mechanical hand. You haven't yet undergone a treatment. You're drifting back, back in time. You have just come awake in that room. And now time is running backward even faster . . . back beyond the moment you were brought into that room . . . hours slipping away . . . faster, faster . . . now days instead of hours . . . backward in time, flowing like a great river . . . carrying you back, back, back . . . Where are you now, Joanna?"

She didn't respond.

Inamura repeated the question.

"Nowhere," she said hollowly.

"Look around you."

"Nothing."

"What is your name?"

She didn't reply.

"Are you Joanna Rand?"

"Who?" she asked.

"Are you Lisa Chelgrin?"

"Who's she? Do I know her?"

"What's your name?"

"I . . . I don't have a name."

"Who are you?"

"Nobody."

"You must be somebody."

"I'm waiting to become."

"To become Joanna Rand?"

"I'm waiting," she said simply.

"Concentrate for me."

"I'm so cold. Freezing."

"Where are you?"

"Nowhere."

"What do you see?"

"Nothing," she insisted.

"What do you feel?"

"Dead."

Alex said, "Jesus."

Inamura stared thoughtfully at her. After a while he said, "I'll tell you where you are, Joanna."

"Okay."

"You are standing in front of a door. An iron door. Very imposing. Like the door to a fortress. Do you see it?"

"No."

"Try to visualize it," Inamura said. "Look closely. You really cannot miss it. The door is huge, absolutely massive. Solid iron. If you could see through to the far side of it, you would find four large hinges, each as thick as your wrist. The iron is pitted and spotted with rust, but the door nevertheless appears impregnable. It's five feet wide, nine feet high, rounded at the top, set in an arch in the middle of a great stone wall."

What the devil's he doing? Alex wondered.

"You see the door now, I'm sure," Inamura said.

"Yes," Joanna agreed.

"Touch it."

Lying in her chair but obviously believing herself to be in front of the door, Joanna raised one hand and tested the empty air.

"What does the door feel like?" Inamura asked.

"Cold and rough," she said.

"Rap your knuckles on it."

She rapped silently on nothing.

"What do you hear, Joanna?"

"A dull ringing sound. It's a very thick door."

"Yes, it is," Inamura said. "And it's locked."

Resting in the reclining chair but simultaneously existing in another time and place, Joanna tried the door that only she could see. "Yeah. Locked."

"But you've got to open it," Inamura said.

"Why?"

"Because beyond it lies twenty years of your life. The first twenty years. That's why you can't remember any of it. They've put it behind the door. They've locked it away from you."

"Oh. Yes. I see."

"Luckily, I've found the key that will unlock the door," said Inamura. "I have it right here."

Alex smiled, pleased with the doctor's creative approach to the problem.

"It's a large iron key," Inamura said. "A large iron key attached to an iron ring. I'll shake it. There. Do you hear it rattling, Joanna?"

"I hear it," she said.

Inamura was so skillful that Alex almost heard it too.

"I'm putting the key in your hand," Inamura told her, even though he didn't move from his armchair. "There. You have it now."

"I've got it," Joanna said, closing her right hand around the imaginary key.

"Now put the key in the door and give it a full turn. That's right. Just like that. Fine. You've unlocked it."

"What happens next?" Joanna asked apprehensively.

"Push the door open," the doctor said.

"It's so heavy."

"Yes, but it's coming open just the same. Hear the hinges creaking? It's been closed a long time. A long, long time. But it's coming open . . . open . . . open all the way. There. You've done it. Now step across the threshold."

"All right."

"Are you across?"

"Yes."

"Good. What do you see?"

Silence.

At the windows, twilight had given way to night. No wind pressed at the glass. Even the bird was still and attentive in its cage.

"What do you see?" Inamura repeated.

"No stars," Joanna said.

Frowning, Inamura said, "What do you mean?"

She fell silent again.

"Take another step," Inamura instructed.

"Whatever you say."

"And another. Five steps in all."

She counted them off: ". . . three . . . four . . . five."

"Now stop and look around, Joanna."

"I'm looking."

"Where are you?"

"I don't know."

"What do you see?"

"No stars, no moon."

"Joanna, what do you see?"

"Midnight."

"Be more specific, please."

"Just midnight," she said.

"Explain, please."

Joanna took a deep breath. "I see midnight. The most perfect midnight imaginable. Silky. Almost liquid. A fluid midnight sky runs all the way to the earth on all sides, sealing everything up tight, melting like tar over the whole world, over everything that comes before, over everywhere I've been and everything I've done and everything I've seen. No stars at all. Flawless blackness. Not a speck of light. And not a sound either. No wind. No odors. The earth itself is black. All darkness on all sides. Blackness is the only thing, and it goes on forever."

"No," Inamura said. "That's not true. Twenty years of your life will begin to unfold around you. It's starting to happen even as I speak. You see it now, a world coming to life all around you."

"Nothing."

"Look closer, Joanna. It may not be easy to see at first, but it's all there. I've given you the key to your past."

"You've only given me the key to midnight," Joanna said. A new despair echoed in her voice.

"The key to the past," Inamura insisted.

"To midnight," she said miserably. "A key to darkness and hopelessness. I am nobody. I am nowhere. I'm alone. All alone. I don't like it here."

40

By the time they left the psychiatrist's office, night had claimed Kyoto. From the north came a great wind that drove the bitter air through clothes and skin and flesh all the way to the bone. The light of the street lamps cast stark shadows on the wet pavement, on the dirty slush in the gutters, and on the piled-up snow that had fallen during the previous night.

Saying nothing, going nowhere, Alex and Joanna sat in her Lexus, shivering, steaming the windshield with their breath, waiting to get warm. The exhaust vapors plumed up from the tailpipe and rushed forward past the windows, like multitudes of ghosts hurrying to some otherworldly event.

"Omi Inamura can't do anything more for me," Joanna said.

Alex reluctantly agreed. The doctor had brought to the surface every existing scrap of memory involving the man with the mechanical hand, but he hadn't been able to help her recall enough to provide new leads. Thanks to the genius of those who had tampered with her memory, the specifics of the horrors perpetrated in that strange room had been scattered like the ashes of a long-extinguished fire; and the two thirds of her life spent as Lisa Chelgrin had been thoroughly, painstakingly eradicated beyond recall.

The dashboard fans pushed warm air through the vents, and the patches of condensation on the windshield shrank steadily.

Finally Joanna said, "I can accept that I've forgotten . . . Lisa. They stole my other life, but Joanna Rand is a good person to be."

"And to be with," he added.

"I can accept the loss. I can live without a past if I have to. I'm strong enough."

"I've no doubt about that."

She faced him. "But I can't just pick up and go on without knowing *why?*" she said angrily.

"We'll find out why."

"How? There's no more in me for Inamura to pull out."

"And I don't believe there's anything more to be discovered here in Kyoto. Not anything important."

"What about the man who followed you into that alleyway—or the man in your hotel room, the one who cut you?"

"Small fish. Minnows."

"Where are the big fish?" she asked. "In Jamaica—where Lisa disappeared?"

"More likely Chicago. That's Senator Tom's stomping grounds. Or in London."

"London? But you proved I never lived there. That entire background's fake."

"But Fielding Athison is there, the place that fronts on the phone as United British-Continental Insurance. I'm pretty sure they aren't just small fish."

"Will you put your British contacts on the case again?"

"No. At least not by long distance. I'd prefer to deal with these Fielding Athison people myself."

"Go to London? When?"

"As soon as possible. Tomorrow or the day after. I'll take the train to Tokyo and fly from there."

"*We'll* fly from there."

"You might be safer here. I'll bring in protection from the agency in Chicago."

"You're the only protection I can trust," she said. "I'm going to London with you."

41

✢ ✢ ✢

Senator Thomas Chelgrin stood at a window in his second-floor study, watching the sparse traffic on the street below, waiting for the telephone to ring.

Monday night, December first, Washington, D.C., lay under a heavy blanket of cool, humid air. Occasionally people hurried from houses to parked cars or from cars to welcoming doorways, their shoulders hunched and heads tucked down and hands jammed in pockets. It wasn't quite cold enough for snow. Weather reports called for icy rain before morning.

Though he was in a warm room, Chelgrin felt as cold as any of the scurrying pedestrians who from time to time passed below.

His chill arose from the cold hand of guilt on his heart, the same guilt that always touched him on the first day of every month.

During most of the year, when the upper house of the United States Congress was in session or when other government business waited to be done, the senator made his home in a twenty-five-room house on a tree-lined street in Georgetown. He lived in Illinois less than one month of every year.

Although he hadn't remarried after the death of his wife, and although his only child had been kidnapped twelve years ago and had never been found, the enormous house was not too large for him. Tom Chelgrin wanted the best of everything, and he had the money to buy it all. His extensive collections, which ranged from rare coins to the finest antique Chippendale furniture, required a great deal of space. He was not driven merely by an investor's or a collector's passion; his need to acquire valuable and beautiful things was no less than an obsession. He had more than five thousand first editions of American novels and collections of poetry—Walt Whitman, Herman Melville, Edgar Allan Poe, Nathaniel Hawthorne, James Fenimore Cooper, Stephen Vincent Benet, Thoreau, Emerson, Dreiser, Henry James, Robert Frost. Hundreds of fine antique porcelains were displayed throughout his rooms, from the simplicity of Chinese pieces of the Han and Sung dynasties to elaborate Satsuma vases from Japan. His stamp collection was worth five million dollars. The walls of his house were hung with the world's largest collection of paintings by Childe Harold. He collected Chinese tapestries and screens, antique Persian carpets, Paul Storr silver, Tiffany lamps, Dore bronzes, Chinese export porcelain, French marquetry furniture from the nineteenth century, and much more—in fact, so much that he owned a small warehouse to store the overflow.

He didn't share the house only with inanimate objects. A butler, cook, two maids, and a chauffeur all lived in, and he entertained frequently. He didn't like to be alone, because solitude gave him too much time to think about certain terrible decisions he had made over the years, certain dark roads taken.

The telephone rang. The back line, a number known only to two or three people.

Chelgrin rushed to his desk and snatched up the receiver. "Hello."

"Senator, what a lovely night for it," said Peterson.

"Miserable night," Chelgrin disagreed.

"It's going to rain," Peterson said. "I like rain. It washes the world clean, and we need that now and then. It's a damned dirty world we live in. Enough?"

Chelgrin hesitated.

"Looks clean to me," said Peterson.

Chelgrin was studying the video display of an electronic device to which the phone was connected. It would reveal the presence of any tap on the line. "Okay," Chelgrin said at last.

"Good. We've got this month's report."

Chelgrin could hear his own pounding heartbeat. "Where do you want to meet?"

"We haven't used the market for a while."

"When?"

"Thirty minutes."

"I'll be there."

"Of course you will, dear Tom," Peterson said with amusement. "I know you wouldn't miss it for the world."

"I'm not a dog on a leash," Chelgrin said. "Don't think you can jerk me around."

"Dear Tom, don't get yourself in a snit."

Chelgrin hung up. His hands were shaking.

He went to the wet bar in one corner of the study and poured two ounces of scotch. He drank it in two long swallows, without benefit of ice or water.

"God help me," he said softly.

42

✪ ✪ ✪

Chelgrin had given the servants the day off, so he drove himself to the market in his dark-gray Cadillac. He could have driven any of three Rolls-Royces, a Mercedes sports coup, an Excalibur, or one of the other cars in his collection. He chose the Cadillac because it was the least conspicuous of the group.

He arrived at the rendezvous five minutes early. The supermarket was the cornerstone of a small shopping center, and even at eight o'clock on a blustery winter night, the place was busy. He parked at the end of a row of cars, sixty or seventy yards from the market entrance. After waiting a couple of minutes, he got out, locked the doors, and stood self-consciously near the rear bumper.

He turned up the collar of his gray Bally jacket, pulled down his leather cap, and kept his distinctive face away from the light. He was trying to appear casual, but he feared that he looked like a man playing at spies.

If he didn't take precautions, however, he would be recognized. He wasn't merely a United States Senator from Illinois: He aspired to the office of the presidency, and he spent a lot of hours in front of television cameras and in the poor company of obnoxious but powerful reporters, laying the foundation for a campaign in either two or six years, depending on the fate of the new man who'd won the White House just two years ago. (Considering the sanctimonious and self-righteous lecturing, the numerous episodes of undisguised political duplicity, and the incredible bungling that marked the new man's first twenty-two months at the helm, Chelgrin was confident that his chance would come in two years rather than six.) If someone recognized him, the meeting with Peterson would have to be rescheduled for another night.

Two rows away, the lights of a Chevrolet snapped on, and the car pulled from its parking slip. It came down one aisle, around another, and stopped directly beside the senator's Cadillac.

Chelgrin opened the front passenger door, bent down, and looked inside. He knew the driver from other nights—a short, stout fellow with a prim mouth and thick glasses—but he didn't know his name. He had never asked. Now he got in and buckled his seat belt.

"Anybody on your tail?" the driver asked.

"If there were, I wouldn't be here."

"We'll play it safe just the same."

For ten minutes they traveled a maze of residential streets. The driver watched the rearview mirror as much as the road ahead.

Finally, when it was clear that they were not being followed, they went to a roadhouse seven miles from the supermarket. The place was called Smooth Joe's, and on the roof it boasted a pair of ten-foot-tall neon cowboy dancers.

Business was good for so early in the week: sixty or seventy cars surrounded the building. One was a chocolate-brown Mercedes with Maryland plates, and the stout man pulled in beside it.

Without another word to the driver, Chelgrin got out of the Chevrolet. The night air was vibrating with a thunderous rendition of Garth Brooks's "Friends in Low Places." He got quickly into the rear seat of the Mercedes, where Anson Peterson was waiting.

The instant the senator slammed the door, Peterson said, "Let's roll, Harry."

The driver was big, broad-shouldered, and totally bald. He held the steering wheel almost at arm's length, and he drove well. They headed from the suburbs into the Virginia countryside.

The interior of the car smelled of butter-rum Life Savers. They were an addiction of Peterson's.

"You're looking very well, Tom."

"And you."

In fact, Anson Peterson did not look well at all. Although he was only five feet nine, he weighed considerably in excess of three hundred pounds. His suit pants strained to encompass his enormous thighs. The buttons on his shirt met, but he had no hope of buttoning his jacket. As always, he wore a hand-knotted bow tie—this time white polka dots on a field of deep blue, to match his blue suit—which emphasized the extraordinary circumference of his neck. His face was a great, round pudding paler than vanilla—but within it shone two tar-black eyes that were bright with a fierce intelligence.

Offering the roll of candy, Peterson said, "Would you like one?"

"No, thank you."

Peterson took a circlet of butter-rum for himself and, with a girlish daintiness, popped it into his mouth. He carefully folded shut the end of the roll, as if it must be done just so to please a stern nanny, and put it in one of his jacket pockets. From another pocket he withdrew a clean white handkerchief; he shook it out and scrubbed vigorously at his fingertips.

In spite of his great size—or perhaps because of it—he was compulsively neat. His clothes were always immaculate, never a spot on shirt or tie. His hands were pink, the nails manicured and highly polished. He always looked as if he had just come from the barber: Not a hair was out of place on his round head. Occasionally Chelgrin had eaten dinner with the fat man, and Peterson had finished double servings without leaving a solitary crumb or drop of sauce on the tablecloth. The senator, hardly a sloppy man, always felt like a pig when, after dinner, he compared his place with Peterson's absolutely virginal expanse of linen.

Now they cruised along wide streets with half-acre estates and large houses, heading out to hunt country. Their monthly meetings were always conducted on the move, because a car could be checked for electronic listening devices and stripped of them more easily than could a room in any building. Furthermore, a moving car with a well-trained and observant chauffeur was almost proof against an eavesdropping directional microphone focused on them from a distance.

Of course it wasn't likely that Peterson would ever become the target of electronic surveillance. His cover as a successful real-estate entrepreneur was faultless. His secret work, done in addition to the real-estate dealing, was punishable by life imprisonment or even death if he were caught, so he was motivated to be methodical, circumspect, and security conscious.

As they sped toward the countryside, the fat man talked around his candy. "If I didn't know better, I'd think you engineered the election of this man in the White House. He seems to be determined to set himself up so precisely that you can knock him down with a single puff of breath."

"I'm not here to talk politics," Chelgrin said shortly. "May I see the report?"

"Dear Tom, since we must work together, we should try our best to be friendly. It really takes so little time to be sociable."

"The report."

Peterson sighed. "As you wish."

Chelgrin held out one hand for the file folder.

Peterson made no move to give it to him. Instead, he said, "There's nothing in writing this month. Just a *spoken* report."

Chelgrin stared at him in disbelief. "That's unacceptable."

Peterson crunched what remained of his Life Saver and swallowed. When he spoke, he expelled butter-rum fumes. "That's the way it is, I'm afraid."

The senator strove to control his temper, for to lose it would be to give the fat man an advantage. "These reports are important to me, Anson. Very personal, very private."

Peterson smiled. "You know perfectly well that they're read by at least a dozen other people. Including me."

"Yes, but then I always get to read them too. If you just summarize them instead . . . then suddenly you become an interpreter. It's not as private that way. I wouldn't feel as close to her."

Everything he knew about his daughter's current activities was third-hand information. In twelve years not one spoken word had passed between him and Lisa; therefore, he jealously guarded these few minutes of reading, the first of every month.

"That day in Jamaica," he said, "you promised I'd get written reports of her progress, her life. Always written. You hand it to me, I read it by a flashlight in a moving car, then I give it back to you, and you destroy it. That's how it works. I haven't agreed to any changes in the routine, and I never will."

"Calm down, dear Tom."

"Don't call me that, you bastard."

Peterson said, "I'll take no offense. You're distraught."

They rode in silence until Chelgrin said, "Do you have photos?"

"Oh, yes. We have photos, as we do every month. Though these are exceptionally interesting."

"Let me see them."

"They need a bit of explanation."

The senator's mouth went dry. He closed his eyes. All anger had been chased out by fear. "Is she . . . is she hurt? Dead?"

"Oh, no. Nothing like that, Tom. If it was anything like that, I wouldn't break the news this way. I'm not an insensitive man."

Relief brought anger back with it. Chelgrin opened his eyes. "Then what the hell is this all about?"

As the driver slowed the Mercedes, turned left onto a narrow lane, and accelerated again, Peterson picked up his attaché case and put it on his lap. From it, he withdrew a white envelope of the type that usually contained photographs of Lisa.

Chelgrin reached for it.

Peterson wasn't ready to relinquish the prize. As he undid the clasp and opened the flap, he said, "The report is spoken this time only because it's too complex and important to be committed to paper. We have a crisis of sorts."

The fat man took several eight-by-ten glossies from the white envelope, and Chelgrin accepted them with trepidation.

A flashlight lay on the seat between them. Chelgrin picked it up and switched it on.

In the first photograph, Lisa and a man were sitting on a bench in a tree-shaded plaza.

"Who's she with?" the senator asked.

"You know him."

Chelgrin held the flashlight at an angle to avoid casting glare on the photograph. "Something familiar . . ."

"You'll have to go back in time. Before he had the mustache. Go back at least ten years to the last time you might've seen him."

"My God, it's the detective. Hunter."

"He's become bored with his business and with Chicago," Peterson said. "So he's been taking a couple of month-long vacations every year. Last spring he went to Brazil. Two weeks ago—Japan."

Chelgrin couldn't look away from the photograph, which ceased to be merely a picture and became an omen of disaster. "But Hunter turning up in the Moonglow Lounge, that place of all places—the odds must be a million to one."

"Easily."

"She's changed over the years. Maybe he—"

"He recognized her at once. He's compared her fingerprints to Lisa's. Encouraged her to call London. Took her to a psychiatrist for hypnotic regression therapy. We had the office bugged."

As Chelgrin listened to what Dr. Omi Inamura had achieved with Joanna, the motion of the car began to make him nauseous.

"But why was this allowed to happen?" he demanded.

"We didn't expect this Inamura to be successful. By the time we realized that he was achieving a breakthrough with her, it seemed pointless to threaten or kill him."

Jagged lightning stepped down the dark sky, gouging the thick cloud cover with its spurred heels.

"And why hasn't Hunter contacted me?" the senator wondered. "I was his client. I paid him a hell of a lot of money to find her."

"He hasn't contacted you because he suspects you're part of the conspiracy that put her in Japan. He now thinks you hired him in the first place just to make yourself look good, playing the concerned father for political purposes. Which is true, of course."

Another flash of lightning illuminated the countryside beyond the car, briefly outlining clusters of leafless black trees.

Fat droplets of rain snapped against the windshield. The driver slowed the Mercedes and switched on the wipers.

"What's he going to do?" Chelgrin asked. "Go to the media?"

"Not yet," Peterson assured him. "He figures that if we wanted to remove the girl permanently, we could've killed her a long time ago. He realizes that after we've gone to all the trouble of giving her a new identity, we intend to keep her alive at nearly any cost. So he assumes she's safe in pushing this

DEAN KOONTZ

thing, at least up to a point. He figures we're most likely to turn nasty and try to kill them only when they go public. Therefore, he wants to be absolutely certain he's got most of the story before he dares to speak out."

Chelgrin frowned. "I don't like all this talk about killing."

"Dear Tom, I didn't mean we'd actually kill Lisa! Of course, that's not an option. Besides, good heavens, I feel almost as close to her as if she were my own daughter. A darling girl. No one would lift a finger against her. But Hunter's another matter altogether. He'll have to be taken out at the proper time. Soon."

"You should have killed him the moment he showed up in Kyoto. You screwed up."

Peterson was not disturbed by the accusation. "We didn't know he was going until he was there. We weren't watching him. No reason to. It's a long time since he investigated Lisa's disappearance."

"So after he's been eliminated, what will we do with her?" the senator worried.

Peterson shifted his great bulk, and the springs in the car seat protested. "She can't live as Joanna Rand any longer. She's finished with that life. We think the best thing is to send her home now."

"Back to Illinois?" Chelgrin asked, baffled by that impractical suggestion.

"No, no. That's not her real home. Neither is Jamaica nor even Washington."

Chelgrin's heart pounded faster, but he tried not to let the fat man see how alarmed he was. He stared at the photograph and then out at the rain-swept night. "Where you want to send her . . . that's your home and mine, but it's not hers."

"Neither was Japan."

Chelgrin said nothing.

"We'll send her home," Peterson said.

"No."

"She'll be well taken care of. She'll be happy there."

Chelgrin took a couple of deep breaths before responding. "This is the same argument we had in Jamaica all those years ago. I won't let you send her home. Period. End of discussion."

"Why are you so set against it?" Peterson asked, clearly amused by the senator's distress. "And why is it that we even need to hold your daughter hostage in order to ensure your continued cooperation?"

"You don't have to do any such thing," Chelgrin said, but he could hear the lack of conviction in his voice.

"But we do," said Peterson. "That's clear to us. And why? Aren't we on the same side? Aren't we working toward the same goal?"

Chelgrin switched off the flashlight and gazed out the window at the dark land rushing past. He wished the interior of the car were even darker than it was, so the fat man couldn't see his face at all.

"Aren't we on the same side?" Peterson persisted.

Chelgrin cleared his throat. "It's just that . . . sending her home . . . Well, that's an entirely alien way of life to her. She was born and raised in America. She's used to certain . . . freedoms."

"She'd have freedom at home. It's all the rage now—freedom."

"And you'll change that if you get a chance."

"Restore order, yes, if we get a chance. But even then she would move in the very highest circles, with special privileges."

"None of which would equal what she could have here or what she has now in Japan."

"Listen, Tom, the likelihood is that we'll never be able to restore the old order at home. This freedom is a virulent disease. We're working hard to disrupt the economy, to keep the bureaucracy intact. And thanks to you and other politicians, the U.S. is helping us. But the disease is hard to eradicate. Freedom will most likely grow, not diminish."

"No," Chelgrin said adamantly. "She wouldn't be able to adapt. We'll have to put her somewhere else. That's final."

Peterson was delighted with Chelgrin's bravado—perhaps because he knew that it was hollow, merely the tremulous defiance of a child crossing a grave-yard at night—and he giggled almost girlishly. The giggle swiftly became a full-fledged laugh. He gripped the senator's leg just above the knee and squeezed affectionately. Edgy, Chelgrin misinterpreted the action, detected a threat where none existed, and jerked away. The overreaction tickled the fat man. Peterson laughed and chortled and cackled, spraying spittle and expelling clouds of butter-rum fumes, until he had to gasp for breath.

"I wish I knew what was so funny," Chelgrin said.

At last Peterson got control of himself. He mopped his big moon face with his handkerchief.

"Dear Tom, why don't you just admit it? You don't want Lisa to go home to Mother Russia because you don't believe in what either of the major power blocs wants to do there. You lost faith in Marx and communism a long time ago, while we still ruled. And you don't like the crowd of socialists and thugs who're contesting for power these days. You still work for us because you have no choice, but you hate yourself for it. The good life here diverted you, dear Tom. Diverted, subverted, and thoroughly converted you. If you could get away with it, you'd make a clean break with us, cast us out of your life after all we've done for you. But you can't do that, because we've acted like wise capitalists in the way we've handled you over the years. We repossessed your daughter. We have a mortgage on your political career. Your fortune is built on credit we've extended to you. And we have a substantial—actually, *enormous*—lien against your soul."

Though Peterson now appeared willing to accept a relationship without pretense, Chelgrin remained wary about admitting to his true convictions. "I don't know where you get these ideas. I'm committed to the proletarian revolution and the people's state every bit as much as I was thirty years ago."

That statement elicited another spate of giggling from the fat man. "Dear Tom, be frank with me. We've known about the changes in you for twenty years, maybe even before you yourself were aware of them. We know the capitalist facade isn't just a facade any longer. But it doesn't matter. We aren't going to give you the axe merely because you've had a change of heart. There'll be no garroting, no bullets in the night, no poison in the wine, dear Tom. You're still an extremely valuable property. You help us enormously—though in a different way and for much different reasons now than when we all started on this little adventure."

For many years, as a congressman and then a senator, Chelgrin had passed military secrets to the Soviet regime. Since the fall of the Soviet, he'd been instrumental in arranging for tens of billions of dollars in loans to the new elected government of Russia, aware that none of it would ever be repaid. A large portion of those loans were misappropriated by the still Byzantine bureaucracy, going not to help the Russian people but to line the pockets of the same thugs who had ruled under the Soviet banner and to maintain a war chest for their indefatigable campaign to return to the pinnacle of power.

"All right. Honesty," said Chelgrin. "Every day of my life, I pray to God that the help I give you will never be enough to ensure your success, never enough to harm this big, bustling, freewheeling, wonderful country. I want you all to fail and rot in Hell."

"Good. Very good," said Peterson. "Refreshing to be open and direct for a change, isn't it?"

"All I care about now is my daughter."

"Would you like to see the other photographs?" Peterson asked.

Chelgrin switched on the flashlight and took the stack of eight-by-ten glossies from the fat man.

Rain drummed relentlessly on the roof of the car. The spinning tires sang sibilantly on the wet macadam.

After a while the senator said, "What'll happen to Lisa?"

"We didn't actually expect you to be enthusiastic about sending her home," Peterson acknowledged. "So we've worked out something else. We'll turn her over to Dr. Rotenhausen—"

"The one-armed wonder."

"—and he'll treat her at the clinic again."

"He gives me the creeps," Chelgrin said.

"Rotenhausen will erase all the Joanna Rand memories and give her yet another identity. When he's finished, we'll provide forged papers and set her up in a new life in Germany."

"Why Germany?"

"Why not? We knew you'd insist on a capitalist country with the so-called 'freedoms' you cherish."

"I thought perhaps she could . . . come back."

"Back here?" Peterson asked incredulously. "Impossible."

"I don't mean to Illinois or Washington."

"There's not a safe place in the States."

"But surely if we gave her a solid new identity and stuck her in a small town in Utah or rural Colorado or maybe Wyoming—"

"Too chancy."

"You won't even consider it?"

"Dear Tom, this trouble with Alex Hunter should make it obvious why I *can't* consider it. And I can't resist reminding you that she could've been here in the States all along, instead of Japan, if you had only agreed to plastic surgery along with the memory tampering."

"I won't even discuss the possibility."

"Your ego leaves no room for common sense. You see elements of your face in hers, and you can't bear to have them altered."

"I said I won't discuss it. I'll never let a surgeon touch her face. She won't be changed in any way."

"Stupid, dear Tom. Very stupid. If the surgery had been done immediately after the screw-up in Jamaica, Alex Hunter wouldn't have recognized her last week. We wouldn't be in trouble now."

"She's a beautiful woman. She'll stay that way."

"The point of the surgery wouldn't be to make her ugly! She'd still be beautiful. It would just be a different beauty."

"Any difference would make her less than she is now," Chelgrin insisted. "I won't allow her to be carved into someone else."

Outside, the storm grew more violent by the minute. Rain fell in dense cataracts. The driver slowed the Mercedes to a crawl.

Peterson smiled and shook his head. "You amaze me, Tom. It's so strange that you'll fight to the death to preserve her face—in which you can so readily see yourself—yet you don't feel any remorse for letting us carve away at her *mind.*"

"There's nothing strange about it," Chelgrin said defensively.

"I suspect you didn't care about the brainwashing because she wasn't intellectually or emotionally your disciple. Her beliefs, her goals, her dreams, her hopes, were different from yours. So it didn't matter to you if we erased all that. Preservation of the physical Lisa—the color of her hair, the shape of her nose and jaw and lips, the proportions of her body—was enormously important to your ego, but the preservation of the actual *person* called Lisa—those special patterns of the mind, that unique creature of wants and needs and attitudes so different from your own—was none of your concern."

"So you're calling me an egotistical bastard," Chelgrin said. "So what? What am I supposed to do? Try to change your opinion of me? Promise to be a better person? What do you want from me?"

"Dear Tom, let me put it this way—"

"Put it any way you like."

"I don't think it was a loss to our side when you were won over to their philosophy," the fat man said. "And I'd bet that the average capitalist wouldn't look at you as much of a prize either."

"If this is meant to wear me down somehow and make me agree to plastic surgery for her, you're just wasting your time."

Peterson laughed softly. "You've got thick armor, Tom. It's impossible to insult you."

Chelgrin hated him.

For a while they rode in silence.

They passed through woodlands and open fields between suburbs. Thin patches of fog drifted across the road, and when lightning flashed, the ground mist briefly glowed as if it might be an unearthly, incandescent gas.

Finally the fat man said, "There's some danger involved if we tamper with the girl's memory a second time."

"Danger?"

"The good Dr. Rotenhausen has never worked his magic twice on the same patient. He has doubts. This time the treatment might not take. It might even end badly."

"What do you mean? What could happen?"

"Madness perhaps. Or she might wind up in a catatonic state. You know—just sitting, staring into space, a vegetable, unable to talk or feed herself. She might even die."

Chelgrin stared at Peterson, trying to read his round, smiling, inscrutable face. "I don't believe it. You're making this up so I'll be afraid to send her to Rotenhausen. Then my only choice would be to let you take her home. Forget it."

"I'm being honest with you, Tom. Rotenhausen says her chances of coming through a second time are poor, less than fifty-fifty."

"You're lying. But even if you were telling the truth, I'd rather send her to Rotenhausen. I refuse to have her taken to Russia. I'd rather see her dead."

"You might," said Peterson.

Rain was falling with such force and in such tremendous quantity that the driver had to pull off the road. Visibility was no more than twenty to thirty feet. They parked in a roadside rest area, near trash barrels and picnic tables.

Peterson slipped another butter-rum circlet between his pursed lips, scrubbed his fingers with his handkerchief, and made a small wordless sound of delight as the candy began to melt on his tongue.

The roar of the rain was so loud that Chelgrin raised his voice. "Moving her secretly from Jamaica to Switzerland was a nightmare."

"I remember it all too well."

"How will you get her out of Japan, all the way to Rotenhausen?"

"She's making it easy for us. She and Hunter are going to England to look into the British-Continental Insurance scam."

"When?"

"The day after tomorrow. We've got a scenario planned for them. We'll drop clues they can't miss, steer them away from London and straight to Switzerland. We'll put them on to Rotenhausen, and when they go after him, we'll let the trap fall shut."

"You sound so confident."

"By Friday or Saturday, Hunter will be dead, and your lovely daughter will be back in Rotenhausen's clinic."

43

Wednesday afternoon, when the time came for Joanna to leave the Moonglow with Alex and take a taxi to the train depot, she didn't want to leave. Each step out of the second-floor apartment, down the narrow stairs, and across the lounge was difficult. She seemed to be walking through deep water. She stopped several times on one pretense or another—a forgotten passport; a last-minute decision to wear a different pair of traveling shoes; a sudden desire to say good-bye to the head chef, who was even then preparing the sauces and soups for that evening's customers—but eventually Alex insisted that she hurry lest they miss their train.

Her delaying tactics resulted not from worry about what would happen to the business in her absence. She trusted Mariko to manage the club efficiently and profitably.

Instead, her reluctance to depart was the result of a surprising homesickness that seized her even before she left home. She had come to this country under queer circumstances, a stranger in a strange land, and she had prospered. She loved Japan and Kyoto and the Gion district and the Moonglow Lounge. She loved the musical quality of the language, the extravagant politeness of the people, the merry ringing of finger bells at worship services, the beauty of the temple dancers, the scattered ancient structures that had survived both war and the encroachment of Western-style architecture. She loved the taste of sake and tempura, the delicious fragrance of hot brown *kamo yorshino-ni*. She felt a part of this ancient yet ever blossoming culture. This was her world now, the only place to which she had ever truly belonged, and she dreaded leaving it even temporarily.

Nevertheless, she was determined not to let Alex go to England alone.

While Alex went outside to be sure the taxi waited, Joanna and Mariko stood just inside the front door, hugging one last time.

"I'll miss you, Mariko-san."

"I'm scared for you," Mariko said.

"I have Alex. But you're at risk too. Someone may decide that you know too much."

"Me and Uncle Omi and my whole family know too much. Too many of us know too much. There's safety in numbers. Besides, we don't actually have proof of anything. Just your fingerprints—and you're taking those with you. I think these people are less of a danger to me than old Godzilla."

"I just realized—we'll be staying overnight in Tokyo. His favorite stomping grounds."

"I don't know why they keep rebuilding the city when they know he's just going to come back and knock it down again."

Joanna smiled. "Maybe they figure one day he'll learn the error of his ways. The Japanese are infinitely patient."

Mariko inclined her head. "Thank you for not saying 'stubborn,' Joanna-san."

"One more thing, Mariko-san . . . Is it true what Alex says about you and Wayne? That a certain attraction exists?"

Mariko blushed fiercely. "He's in the hospital. I've only sat at his bedside a few times to keep him company."

"And?"

Lowering her eyes, Mariko said, "He is an interesting man."

"But?"

"These things don't happen, Joanna-san. You know how it is."

"Wayne is different, and there will be many people you love who will be unhappy with you. You don't want them to feel that you've dishonored them. Yes, I know how it is. But life is short. A chance for great happiness doesn't come along all that often."

Mariko said nothing.

"When the bright-winged bird sees a fallen cherry on the ground beneath a tree," Joanna said, "it seizes the fruit and flies, full of joy, and deals with the pit later."

Amused, Mariko met her eyes. "I didn't hear the Zen warning siren."

Hugging her friend again, Joanna whispered: *"Whoop-whoop-whoop."*

"Too late," said Mariko. "I think I might already have been enlightened."

The front door opened, and Alex leaned inside. "We're going to miss that train if we don't hurry."

As they drove away in the black-and-red taxi, Joanna looked back at the Moonglow Lounge and at Mariko in the open door. "It can all evaporate like a dream."

"What can?" Alex asked.

"Happiness. Places. People. Everything."

He took her hand.

The taxi turned a corner.

The Moonglow Lounge was gone. Mariko too.

❖

The superexpress to Tokyo was a luxurious train with a buffet car, plush seats, and, considering the great speed it attained, surprisingly little rail noise and lateral motion. She wanted Alex to sit by the window for the four-hour trip, but he insisted that she have that privilege, and the porter was amused by their argument.

At the Western-style hotel in Tokyo, a two-bedroom suite was reserved for them. The employees at the front desk were unable to conceal their amazement at this brassy behavior. A man and woman with different last names, using the same suite and making no effort to conceal their association, were considered decadent, regardless of the number of bedrooms at their disposal. Alex didn't notice the raised eyebrows, but Joanna nudged him until he realized everyone was watching them surreptitiously. She was amused, and her unrepressed smile, interpreted as an expression of lascivious anticipation, only made matters worse. The registration clerk wouldn't look at her directly. But they were not turned away. That would have been unthinkably impolite. Besides, in any hotel catering to Westerners, the employees knew that almost any boldness could be expected of Americans.

Two shy young bellmen escorted her and Alex to the top floor, efficiently distributed their luggage between the bedrooms, adjusted the thermostat in the drawing room, opened the heavy drapes, and then refused tips until Alex assured them that he offered the gratuities only out of respect for their fine service and impeccable manners. Tipping had not yet taken hold in most of Japan, but Alex was so long accustomed to American expectations that he felt guilty if he didn't provide anything.

The accommodations looked pretty much like any good two-bedroom suite in Los Angeles or Dallas or Chicago or Boston. Only the view from the windows firmly established the Japanese setting.

When they were alone, she moved into his arms. They stood by the window, all of Tokyo below them, and just held each other for a while.

He kissed her once. Then again. They were lovely kisses, but the moment was not right for more than that. As he had said, their first time together must be special, because it was a commitment that would change both their lives forever.

"What about sushi for dinner?" she asked.

"Sounds good."

"At the Ozasa?"

"You know Tokyo better than I do. Wherever you say."

Beyond the window, in the rapidly deepening twilight, the great city began to put on dazzling ornamental kimonos of neon.

✪

The restaurant, Ozasa, was in the Ginza district, around the corner from the Central Geisha Exchange. It was upstairs, cramped, and noisy, but it was one of the finest sushi shops in all of Japan. A scrubbed wooden counter ran the length of the place, and behind it were chefs dressed all in white, their hands red from continual washing.

When Alex and Joanna entered, the chefs shouted the traditional greeting: "*Irasshai!*"

The room was awash in wonderful aromas: omelets sizzling in vegetable oil, soy sauce, various spicy mustards, vinegared rice, horseradish, mushrooms that had been cooked in aromatic broth, and more. Not the slightest whiff of fish tainted the air, however, though raw seafood of many varieties was the primary ingredient in every dish in the house. The only fish fresher than Ozasa's were those that still swam in the deeps.

Joanna knew one of the chefs, Toshio, from her days as a Tokyo performer. She made introductions, and there was much bowing all around.

She and Alex sat at the counter, and Toshio put large mugs of tea in front of them. They each received an *oshibori*, with which they wiped their hands while examining the selection of fish that filled a long refrigerated glass case behind the counter.

The unique and exquisitely tortuous tension between Alex and Joanna transformed even the simple act of eating dinner into a rare experience charged with erotic energy. He ordered *tataki*—little chunks of raw bonito that had been singed in wet straw; each would come wrapped in a bright yellow strip of omelet. Joanna began with an order of *toro sushi*, which was served first. Toshio had trained and practiced for years before he was permitted to serve his first customer; now his long apprenticeship was evident in the swift grace of his culinary art. He removed the *toro*—fatty, marbled tuna—from the glass case, and his hands moved as quickly and surely as those of a master magician. With a huge knife, he smoothly sliced off two pieces of tuna. From a large tub beside him, he grabbed a handful of vinegared rice and deftly kneaded it into two tiny loaves spiced with a dash of *wasabi*. Toshio pressed the bits of fish to the tops of the loaves, and with a proud flourish he placed the twin morsels before Joanna. The entire preparation required less than thirty seconds from the moment that he had slid open the door of the refrigerated case. The brief ceremony, which ended with Toshio washing his hands before creating the *tataki*, reminded Alex of the posthypnotic code words that Omi Inamura had used with Joanna: Toshio's hands were like dancing butterflies. Sushi could be a messy dish, especially for a novice, but Joanna was no novice, and while consuming the *toro*, she managed to be both prissily neat and sensuous. She picked up one piece, dipped the rice portion in a saucer of *shoyu*, turned it over to keep it from dripping, and placed the entire morsel on her tongue. She closed her eyes and chewed slowly. The sight of her enjoying the *toro* increased the pleasure that Alex took in his own food. She ate with that peculiar combination of dainty grace and avid hunger that one saw in cats. Her slow pink tongue licked left and right at the corners of her mouth; she smiled as she opened her eyes and picked up the second piece of *toro*.

Alex said, "Joanna, I . . ."

"Yes?"

He hesitated. "You're beautiful."

That wasn't everything he had intended to tell her, and it was surely not as much as she wanted to hear, but her smile seemed to say that she could not possibly have been happier.

They drank tea and ordered other kinds of sushi—dark-red lean tuna, snow-white squid, blood-red *akagai* clams, octopus tentacles, pale shrimp, caviar, and abalone—and between servings they cleared their palates with sliced ginger.

Each order of sushi contained two pieces, but they ate slowly, heartily, sampling every variety, then returned to their favorites. In Japan, Joanna explained, the complex system of etiquette, the rigid code of manners, and the tradition of excessive politeness ensured a special sensitivity to the sometimes multiple meanings of language, and the two-piece-and-only-two-piece servings of sushi was an example of that sensitivity. Nothing that was sliced could ever be served singly or in threes, for the Japanese words for "one slice" were *hito kire,* which also meant *kill,* and three slices was *mi kire,* which also meant *kill myself.* Therefore, if sliced food were presented in either of those quantities, it would be an insult to the customer as well as a tasteless reminder of an unpleasant subject.

So they ate sushi two pieces at a time, and Alex thought about how desperately he wanted Joanna. They drank tea, and Alex wanted her more with each sip that he watched her take. They talked, they joked with Toshio, and when they weren't eating they turned slightly toward each other so their knees rubbed together, and they chewed bits of ginger, and Alex wanted her. He was sweating slightly and not merely because of the fiercely hot *wasabi* in the sushi loaves.

His inner heat was almost acute enough to be painful. That pain was the risk of commitment. But nothing worth having could be had without risk.

More things than sushi came best in twos. A man and a woman. Love and hope.

✪

White faces. Bright lips. Eyes heavily outlined in black mascara. Eerie. Erotic.

Ornate kimonos. The men in dark colors. Other men dressed as women in brilliant hues, bewigged, mincing, coy.

And the knife.

The lights dimmed. Suddenly a spotlight bored through the gloom.

The knife appeared in the bright shaft, trembled in a pale fist, then plunged down.

Light exploded again, illuminating all.

The killer and victim were attached by the blade, an umbilical of death.

The killer twisted the knife once, twice, three times, with gleeful ferocity, playing the midwife of the grave.

The onlookers watched in silence and awe.

The victim shrieked, staggered backward. He spoke a line and then another: last words. Then the immense stage resounded with his mortal fall.

Joanna and Alex stood in darkness at the back of the auditorium.

Ordinarily, advance reservations were required by every kabuki theater in Tokyo, but Joanna knew the manager of this place.

The program had begun at eleven o'clock that morning and would not end until ten o'clock that night. Like the other patrons, Joanna and Alex had stopped in for just one act.

Kabuki was the essence of dramatic art: The acting was highly stylized, all emotions exaggerated; and the stage effects were elaborate, dazzling. In 1600, a woman named O-kuni, who was in the service of a shrine, organized a troupe of dancers and presented a show on the banks of the Kano River, in Kyoto, and thus began kabuki. In 1630, in an attempt to control so-called immoral practices, the government prohibited women from appearing on stage. Consequently, there arose the *Oyama*, specialized and highly accomplished male actors who took the roles of female characters in the kabuki plays. Eventually women were permitted to appear on stage again, but the newer tradition of all-male kabuki was by then firmly established and inviolate. In spite of the archaic language—which few members of the audience understood—and in spite of the artistic restrictions imposed by transvestism, the popularity of kabuki never waned, partly because of the gorgeous spectacle but largely because of the themes it explored—comedy and tragedy, love and hate, forgiveness and revenge—which were all made bigger and brighter than life by the ancient playwrights.

As he watched, Alex realized that the basic emotions varied not at all from city to city, country to country, year to year, and century to century. The stimuli to which the heart responded might change slightly as people grew older: The child, the adolescent, the adult, and the elder didn't respond to exactly the same causes of joy and sorrow. Nevertheless, the *feelings* were identical in all of them, for feelings were woven together to form the one true fabric of life, which was always and without exception a fabric with but one master pattern.

Through the medium of kabuki, Alex achieved two sudden insights that, in a moment, changed him forever. First, if emotions were universal, then in one sense he was not alone, never had been alone, and never could be alone. As a child cowering under the harsh hands of his drunken parents, he had existed in despair, because he'd thought of himself as isolated and lost. But every night that Alex's father had beaten him, other children in every corner of the world had suffered with him, victims of their own sick parents or of strangers, and *together* they had all endured. They were a family of sorts, united by suffering. No pain or happiness was unique. All humanity drank from the same river of emotion; and by drinking, every race, religion, and nationality became one indivisible species. Therefore, no matter what protective emotional distance he tried to put between himself and his friends, between himself and his lovers, perfect isolation would forever elude him. Whether he liked it or not, life meant emotional involvement, and involvement meant taking risks.

He also realized that if emotions were universal and timeless, they represented the greatest truths known to humankind. If billions of people in scores of cultures had arrived independently at the same concept of love, then the reality of love could not be denied.

The loud, dramatic music that had accompanied the murder now began to subside.

On the huge stage, one of the "women" stepped forward to address the audience.

The music fluttered and was extinguished by the *Oyama*'s first words.

Joanna glanced at Alex. "Like it?"

He was speechless. He merely nodded. His heart pounded, and with each hard beat, he came more awake to life.

❋

They went to a bar where the owner greeted them in English with three words: "Japanese only, please."

Joanna spoke rapidly in Japanese, assuring him that they were natives in mind and heart if not by birth. Won over, he smilingly admitted them.

They had sake, and Joanna said, "Don't drink it like that, dear."

Alex frowned. "What am I doing wrong?"

"You shouldn't hold the cup in your right hand."

"Why not?"

"Because that's considered to be the sign of a gross, impatient drunkard."

"Maybe I *am* a gross, impatient drunkard."

"Ah, but do you wish everyone to know it, Alex-san?"

"So I hold the cup in my left hand?"

"That's right."

"Like this?"

"That's right."

"I feel like I've been such a barbarian."

She blew on her sake to cool it slightly. "Later, when the time is right, you can use both hands on me."

✪

They went to the Nichiegeki Music Hall for a one-hour show that smacked of vaudeville and burlesque. Comedians told low jokes, many of them very amusing, but Alex was cheered more by the sight of Joanna laughing than he was by anything that the funnymen had to say. Between the variety acts, gorgeous young women in revealing costumes danced rather poorly but with unfaltering enthusiasm and energy. Most of the chorines were breathtaking beauties, but in Alex's eyes, at least, none of them was a match for Joanna.

✪

Back in the hotel suite, Joanna called room service and ordered a bottle of champagne. She also requested appropriate pastries, treats that were not too sweet, and these were delivered in a pretty red lacquered wood box.

At her suggestion, Alex opened the drapes, and they pulled the drawing-room sofa in front of the low windows. Sitting side by side, they studied the Tokyo skyline while they drank champagne and nibbled almond crusts and walnut crescents.

Shortly after midnight, some of the neon lights in the Ginza began to wink out.

"Japanese nightlife can be frantic," Joanna said, "but they start to roll up the sidewalks early by Western standards."

"Shall we roll up our own sidewalks?"

"I'm not sleepy," she said.

He wanted her but felt as awkward as an inexperienced boy. "We have to be up at six o'clock."

"No, we don't."

"We do if we want to catch the plane."

"We don't have to get up at six if we never go to sleep in the first place," she said. "We can sleep on the plane tomorrow."

She slid against him and put her lips to his throat. It wasn't exactly a kiss. She seemed to be feeling the passion in the artery that throbbed in his neck.

As he turned to her, she rose to him, and her soft mouth opened under his. She tasted like almonds and champagne.

He carried her into his room and put her on the bed. Slowly, lovingly, he undressed her.

The only light was that which came from the drawing room, through the open door. Pale as moonglow, it fell across the bed, and she lay naked in the ghostly glow, too beautiful to be real.

When he settled down beside her, the bedsprings sang in the cathedral silence, and then a prayerlike hush settled once again through the shadows.

He explored and worshiped her with kisses.

On their last night in Japan, they didn't sleep at all. They wrapped the hours of the night around them, as though time were a brightly shining thread and they were a wildly spinning spool.

44

In Zurich, in the magnificent house above the lake, Ignacio Carrera was working diligently on his calves, thighs, buttocks, hips, waist, lower back, and abdominal muscles. He'd been lifting weights for two hours, with little time off to rest. After all, when he rested there was no pain, and he wanted the pain because it tested him and because it was an indication of muscle-tissue growth.

Seeking pain at the limits of his endurance, he began his last exercise of the day: one more set of Jefferson lifts. He straddled the barbell, keeping his feet twenty-four inches apart. He squatted, grasped the bar with his right hand in front of him and his left hand behind, and inhaled deeply. Exhaling, he rose to a standing position, bringing the bar up to his crotch. His calves and thighs throbbed painfully.

"One," said Antonio Paz.

Carrera squatted, hesitated only a second, and rose with the bar again. His legs seemed to be on fire. He was gasping. His pumped-up muscles bulged like thick steel cables. While Paz counted, Carrera squatted, rose, squatted, and rose again, and the pain was at first a flame and then a roaring blaze.

Other men lifted weights to improve their health. Some did it just to have their pick of the women who pursued bodybuilders. Some did it to gain improved strength for martial arts, some merely to prove their perseverance, some as a game, some as a sport.

To Ignacio Carrera, those were all secondary reasons.

"Seven," said Paz.

Carrera groaned, striving to ignore the pain.

"Eight," said Paz.

Carrera endured the torture because he was obsessed with power. He enjoyed holding power of every kind over other people: financial, political, psychological, and physical power. His wealth would have meant nothing to him if he had been physically weak. He was able to break his enemies with his bare hands as well as with his money, and he enjoyed having that range of options.

"Ten," said Paz.

Carrera put down the barbells and wiped his hands on a towel.

"Excellent," Paz told him.

"No."

Carrera stepped in front of a full-length mirror and posed for himself, studying every visible muscle in his body, searching for improvement.

"Superb," Paz said.

"The older I get, the harder it becomes to build. In fact, I don't think I'm growing at all. Only thirty-eight, yet these days it's a battle just to stay even."

"Nonsense," said Paz. "You're in wonderful shape."

"Not good enough."

"Getting better and better."

"Never good enough."

"Madame Dumont is waiting in the front room," said Paz.

"She can continue to wait."

Carrera left Paz and went upstairs to the master suite on the third floor.

The ceiling was high, white, richly carved, with gold-leafed moldings. The fabric wallpaper was a two-tone gold stripe, and the wainscoting had been painted with a gray wash. The Louis XVI bed had a high headboard and a high footboard, and against the wall directly opposite the bed stood a matched pair of Louis XVI mahogany cabinets with painted tole plaques on the drawers and doors. One corner was occupied by an enormous eighteenth-century harp that was intricately carved, gold-leafed, and in perfect playing condition.

Carrera sometimes joked that he was going to take harp lessons in order to be ready for Heaven when he was called, but he was aware that in his elegant bedroom he looked like an ape that had lumbered into the middle of a lady's tea party. The contrast between himself and his refined surroundings emphasized his wild, animal power—and he liked that.

He stripped out of his sweat-damp shorts, went into the huge master bath, and spent ten minutes baking in the attached sauna. He thought about Madame Marie Dumont, who was surely tapping her foot impatiently downstairs, and he smiled. For another half an hour, he soaked in the big tub. Then he suffered through a brief icy shower to tone his skin, staying warm by picturing Marie down in the reception room.

He toweled himself vigorously, put on a robe, and walked into the bedroom just as the telephone sounded. Paz answered it downstairs but rang through a moment later. "London calling on line one."

"Marlowe?" Carrera asked.

"No. Peterson."

"The fat man's in London? Put him through. And make sure that Madame Dumont doesn't get a chance to pick up an extension."

"Yes, sir," said Paz.

A scrambler was attached to the incoming line, and it could be activated from any phone. Carrera switched it on.

Peterson said, "Ignacio? Safe to talk?"

"As safe as it ever gets. What're you doing in London?"

"Hunter and the girl will arrive here tonight."

Carrera was surprised. "Dr. Rotenhausen swore she'd never be able to leave Japan."

"He was wrong. Can you move fast? I want you to go to the good doctor in Saint Moritz."

"I'll leave this evening," said Carrera.

"We'll try to put Hunter on Rotenhausen's trail, as planned."

"Are you directing the show in London now?"

"Not all of it. Just this business with Hunter and the girl."

"Good enough. Marlowe isn't fit to handle that. It's made him hypertense."

"I've noticed."

"He broke some rules. For one thing, he tried to pry her name out of me."

"Out of me too," Peterson said.

"He made some silly threats. I've recommended his removal."

"So have I," Peterson said.

"If approval comes through, I'll take care of him myself."

"Don't worry. No one's going to deny you your fun."

"See you in Moritz?" Carrera asked.

"Certainly," said the fat man. "I think I'll take a few skiing lessons."

Carrera laughed. "That would be an unforgettable sight."

"Wouldn't it?" Peterson laughed at his own expense and hung up.

The telephone doubled as an intercom, and Carrera buzzed the front room downstairs.

Paz answered, "Yes, sir."

"Madame Dumont may come up now. And you should pack a suitcase for yourself. We'll be going to Saint Moritz in a few hours."

Carrera put down the receiver and went to a wall panel that concealed a fully equipped bar. It slid aside at the touch of a button, and he began to mix drinks: orange juice and a couple of raw eggs for himself, vodka and tonic for Marie Dumont.

She arrived before he finished preparing her vodka, and she slammed the bedroom door behind her. She strode directly to him, in one of her best confrontational moods.

"Hello, Marie."

"Who the *hell* do you think you are?" she demanded.

"I think I'm Ignacio Carrera."

"You bastard."

"I've made vodka and tonic for you."

"You can't keep *me* waiting like that," she said furiously.

"Oh? I thought I just did."

"I hope you get rectal cancer and die."

"Such a sweet-talking young lady."

"Stuff it."

She was uncommonly beautiful, and she knew it. She was only twenty-six, wise and sophisticated beyond her years—though not nearly as wise as she thought. Her dark eyes revealed strange hungers and an intensely burning pain deep in her soul. Her fine features and the elegant carriage that she'd learned in expensive boarding schools gave her a haughty air.

She was dressed beautifully too: Her well-tailored, two-piece suit was a five-thousand-dollar Paris original, brightened with a turquoise blouse and minimal jewelry. Her perfume was so subtle that it must have cost upward of a thousand dollars an ounce.

"I expect an apology," she announced.

"There's your drink on the bar."

"You can't treat me like this. No one treats me like this."

She had been spoiled all her life. Her father was a wealthy Belgian merchant, and her much older husband was an even wealthier French industrialist. She had been denied nothing—even though her demands were never less than excessive.

"Apologize," she insisted.

"You wouldn't like it if I did."

"Like it? I demand it, damn you."

"You're a snotty kid."

"Apologize, damn you."

"But a beautiful snotty kid."

"Listen, you greasy ape, if you don't apologize—"

He slapped her face just hard enough to sting.

"There's your drink," he repeated, indicating the bar.

"If you ever touch me again, I'll have you killed," she said.

He slapped her so hard that she staggered, almost fell, and had to grip the edge of the bar to keep her balance. Punishment was what she wanted. It was why she had come.

"Pick up your drink," he said ominously. "I made it for you."

"You make me sick."

"Then why do you come?"

"Slumming."

"Pick up your drink," he said sternly.

She spat in his face.

This time he *did* knock her down. She sat on the floor, stunned. Carrera quickly pulled her to her feet. With one big hand on her throat, he pinned her against the wall.

She was crying, but her eyes shone with perverse desire.

"You're sick," he told her. "You're a sick, twisted little rich girl. You have your white Rolls-Royce and your little Mercedes. You live in a mansion. You've got servants who do everything but crap for you. You spend money as if every day is the last day of your life, but you can't buy what you want. You want someone to say 'no' to you. You've been pampered all your life, and now you want someone to push you around and hurt you. You feel guilty about all that money, and you'd probably be happiest if someone took it away from you. But that won't happen. And you can't give it away, because so much of it is tied up in trusts. So you settle for being slapped and humiliated and debased. I understand, girl. I think you're crazy, but I understand. You're too shallow to realize what great good fortune you've had in life, too shallow to enjoy it, too shallow to find some way to use your money for a meaningful purpose. So you come to me. *You come to me.* Keep that in mind. You're in my house, and you will do what I say. Right now, you'll shut up and drink your vodka and tonic."

She had worked up saliva while he'd been talking, and again she spat in his face.

He pressed her against the wall with his left hand, and with his right hand he grabbed the drink that he had fixed for her. He held the glass to her lips, but she kept her mouth tightly shut.

"Take it," Carrera insisted.

She refused.

Finally he forced her head back and tried to pour the vodka into her nose. She tossed her head as best she could in his fierce grip, but at last she opened her mouth to avoid drowning. She snorted and gasped and choked, spraying vodka from her nostrils. He poured the rest of the drink between her lips and let her go as she spluttered and gagged.

Carrera turned away from her and picked up the mixture of orange juice and raw eggs that he had made for himself. He drank it in a few swallows.

When he had finished his drink, Marie was still not recovered from having been force-fed hers. She was doubled over, coughing, trying to clear her throat and get her breath.

Carrera seized her by the arm, dragged her to the bed, and pushed her facedown against the mattress. He pushed up her skirt, tore at her undergarments, shucked off his own robe, and fell upon her savagely.

"You're hurting me," she said weakly.

He knew that was true. But he also knew that she liked it this way more than any other. Besides, this was the *only* way he liked it.

The power to inflict pain was the ultimate power.

Sexual power over women was as important to him as financial, psychological, and sheer physical power. Before he finished with Marie Dumont, he would hurt her badly, degrade and humiliate her, demand things that would disgust her and leave her feeling totally worthless, because that would make *him* feel godlike.

As Marie wept and struggled beneath him, he thought of Lisa-Joanna. He wondered if he would have the chance to do to her all that he was now doing to Marie. The very thought of it made him drive even more ferociously into his current willing victim.

When he had first seen the Chelgrin girl twelve years ago, she had been the most beautiful and desirable creature he'd ever encountered, but because of who she was, he had not been able to touch her. Judging by the photos taken in Kyoto, time had only improved her.

Carrera ardently wished that Dr. Rotenhausen's treatment would fail this time, and that Lisa-Joanna would then be passed to him for disposal. There was a risk that a second mindwipe would leave her with the mental capacity of a four-year-old, and the thought of a four-year-old's mind in that lush body appealed to Carrera as nothing else ever had. If she ended up that way, he would tell them that he had killed her and buried her, but he would keep her alive for his own use. If he possessed her in such a retarded state, he would be able to dominate her and use her to an extent that he had never been able to dominate or use anyone, including Marie Dumont. She would be his little animal, and he would train her to perform some amazing tricks.

Under him, Madame Dumont was screaming. He was hurting her too much. She had her limits. He didn't care about her limits. He pushed her face against the mattress, muffling her cries.

In his possession, the Chelgrin girl would learn the limits of joy, and she would be thrust beyond the limits of pain in order to learn total, unquestioning obedience. She would know extreme terror, and from terror she would learn to be eager to please. He would use her until he had explored every permutation of lust, and then he would share her with Paz. Finally, when there was nothing left to demand of her, when she had endured every degradation, Carrera would beat her to death with his hands. He would take at least an entire day to murder her; in her prolonged agony, he would find a pleasure so intense that bearing up under it would be as challenging as bearing up under any weight he had ever put on his barbells.

Borne away by his fantasy of absolute domination, he almost killed Marie Dumont. He realized that he was jamming her face so hard into the pillows that she couldn't breathe. He let her up just enough to allow her to gasp for air.

He happily would have killed her, but at the moment, disposing of her body would have been a serious inconvenience. He would soon have to leave for Saint Moritz.

That was where his true destiny lay. In Saint Moritz. With the Chelgrin girl.

PART THREE

✤ ✤ ✤

A PUZZLE IN A PUZZLE

The winter tempest
Blows small stones
        Onto the temple bell.

—BUSON, 1775–1783

✦ ✦ ✦

45

After getting no sleep in Tokyo, Alex and Joanna also slept little and poorly on the flight to London. They were tense, excited about their new relationship, and worried about what might await them in England. To make matters worse, the plane encountered heavy turbulence, and they lolled in their seats as miserably as seasick cruisers on their first ocean voyage.

When they landed at Heathrow, Alex's long legs were cramped, swollen, and leaden; sharp pains shot through his calves and thighs with every step. His back ached all the way from the base of his spine to his neck. His eyes were bloodshot, grainy, and sore.

From the look of her, Joanna had the same list of complaints. She promised to get down on her knees and kiss the earth—just as soon as she was certain that she had enough strength to get up again.

Alex found it difficult to believe that less than twenty-four hours ago, he'd experienced the greatest ecstasy of his life.

At the hotel they unpacked none of his suitcases and only part of one of hers. The rest could wait until morning.

She had brought two handheld hair dryers. One was a lightweight plastic model, and the other was a big old-fashioned blower with a metal casing and a ten-inch metal snout. A small screwdriver was in the same suitcase, and Alex used it to dismantle the bulkier of the two hair dryers. Before leaving Kyoto, he had stripped the insides from the machine and carefully fitted a gun into the hollow shell: the silencer-equipped 9mm automatic that he had taken off the man in the alleyway more than a week ago. It had passed through X rays and customs inspection without being detected.

He took a large tin of body powder from the same suitcase. In the bathroom, he stooped beside the commode, put up the lid and the seat, and sifted the talc out of the can, through his fingers. Two magazines of extra ammunition had been concealed in the powder.

"You'd make a great criminal," Joanna observed from the doorway.

"Yeah. But I've done better being honest than I'd ever have done on the other side of the law."

"We could rob banks."

"Why don't we just buy control of one?"

"You're a regular stick-in-the-mud."

"Dull," he agreed. "That's me."

They ate a room-service dinner in the suite, and at ten o'clock London time, they crawled under the covers of the same bed. This time, however, before they slept, they were too exhausted to share more than a single chaste goodnight kiss.

Alex had a strange dream. He was lying in a soft bed in a white room, and three surgeons—all in white gowns, white face masks—stood over him. The first surgeon said, "Where does he think he is?" The second surgeon said, "South America. Rio." And the third said, "So what happens if this doesn't work?" The first surgeon said, "Then he'll probably get himself killed without solving our problem." Alex grew bored with their conversation, and he raised one hand to touch the nearest doctor, hoping to silence him, but his fingers suddenly changed into tiny replicas of buildings, five tiny buildings at the end of his hand, which then became five *tall* buildings seen at a distance, and then the buildings grew larger, became skyscrapers, and they drew nearer, and a city grew across the palm of his hand and up his arm, and the faces of the surgeons were replaced by clear blue sky, and the city wasn't on his hand and arm any more but below him, the city of Rio below him, the fantastic bay and the sea beyond, and then the plane landed, and he got out. He was *in* Rio. A Spanish guitar played mournful music. He was on vacation and having a good time, having a very good time, a memorable and good, good time.

At seven o'clock in the morning, he was awakened by a loud pounding. At first he thought the sound was inside his head, but it was real.

Joanna sat up in bed beside him, clutching the covers. "What's that?"

Alex strove to shake off the last shroud of sleep. He cocked his head, listened for a moment, and said, "Someone's at the door to the hall, out in the drawing room."

"Sounds like they're breaking it down."

He picked up the loaded pistol from the nightstand.

"Stay here," he said, getting out of bed.

"No way."

In the drawing room, dim gray daylight seeped in at the edges of the closed drapes. The writing desk, chairs, and sofa might have been sleeping animals in the gloom.

Alex felt for the light switch, found it. He squinted in the sudden glare and held the gun in front of him.

"There's no one here," Joanna said.

In the foyer, they found a blue envelope on the carpet. It had been slipped under the door.

As Alex picked it up, Joanna said, "What's that?"

"A note from the senator."

"How do you know that?"

He blinked at her. Even after nine hours of sleep, he was still fuzzy-minded.

"How?" she persisted.

The envelope was unmarked by typewriter or pen, and it was sealed.

"I don't know," he said. "Instinct, I guess."

46

♣ ♣ ♣

London was rainy and cold. The bleak December sky was so low and heavy that the city seemed to huddle beneath it in expectation of being crushed. The tops of the tallest buildings disappeared into gray mist.

The taxi driver who picked up Alex and Joanna in front of their hotel was a burly man with a neatly trimmed white beard. He wore a rumpled hat and a heavy green cardigan. He smelled of peppermint and rain-dampened wool. "Where can I take you this morning?"

"Eventually," Alex said, "we want to go to the British Museum. But first you'll have to lose the people who'll be following us. Can you do that?"

The driver stared at him as if unsure he had heard correctly.

"He's perfectly serious," Joanna said.

"He seems to be," said the driver.

"And he's sober," she said.

"He seems to be."

"And he isn't crazy."

"That remains to be seen," said the driver.

Alex counted out thirty pounds to the man. "I'll have thirty more for you at the other end, plus the fare. Will you help us?"

"Well, sir, they tell you to humor madmen if you meet one. And it seems especially wise to humor one with money. The only thing that bothers me— is it coppers watching you?"

"No," Alex said.

"Is it coppers, young lady?"

"No," Joanna said. "They're not good men at all."

"Sometimes neither are the coppers." He grinned, tucked the bills into his shirt pocket, stroked his white beard with one hand, and said, "Name's Nicholas. At your service. What should I be looking for? What sort of car might they be using?"

"I don't know," Alex said. "But they'll stay close behind us. If we keep an eye open, we'll spot them."

The morning traffic was heavy. Nicholas turned right at the first corner, left at the second, then right, left, left, right.

Alex watched out the back window. "Brown Jaguar. Lose it."

Nicholas wasn't a master of evasive driving. He weaved from lane to lane, slipping around cars and buses, trying to put traffic between them and their tail—but at such a sedate pace that his passengers might have been a couple of frail centenarians on their way to their hundred and first birthday party. His maneuvers were not sufficiently dangerous to discourage pursuit. He turned corners without signaling his intent, but never at even a high enough speed to splash pedestrians standing at the curb, and never from the wrong lane, which made it easy for the Jaguar to stay with him.

"Your daring doesn't take my breath away," Alex said.

"Be fair, sir. It's London traffic. Rather difficult to put the pedal to the metal, as you Americans say."

"Still, there's room for a bit more risk than this," Alex said impatiently.

Joanna put one hand on his arm. "Remember the story of the tortoise and the hare."

"Yeah. But I want to lose these people quickly. At the rate we're going, we'll only lose them after eight or ten hours—when they're too tired to bother with us any more."

A London taxi was not permitted to operate if it bore any mark of a collision—even a small dent or scrape. Obviously Nicholas was acutely aware of that regulation. The insurance company would pay for repairs, but the car might be in the garage for a week, which would be lost work time.

Nevertheless, even at his stately—not to say snail's—pace, he managed to put three cars between them and the Jaguar. "We're going to lose them," he said happily.

"Maybe. As long as they play fair and stop for lunch at the same time we do," Alex said.

"You have a funny man here, miss," Nicholas told Joanna. "Quite a sense of humor."

To Alex, it appeared that Nicholas was being *allowed* to lose the tail. The driver of the Jaguar wasn't handling his car as well as he had at the start.

A surveillance unit only willingly detached itself from a target when it was confident that the target's ultimate destination was known. It was almost as if the men in the Jaguar knew that Alex and Joanna were going to the British Museum to meet the senator and were tailing them only so they could gradually fall back and ultimately appear to have been shaken off.

They came to an intersection where the traffic signal had just gone from green to red, but Nicholas screwed up enough courage to round the corner illegally. The tires even squealed. A little.

The cars behind them stopped, and the Jaguar was boxed in. It wouldn't be able to move again until the light changed.

They were on a narrow street flanked by exclusive shops and theaters, amid fewer cars than there'd been on the main avenue. Nicholas drove to the middle of the block and swung into an alley before the Jaguar had a chance to round the corner after them. They went to another alley, then onto a main street once more.

As they continued to wind slowly from avenue to avenue through the slanting gray rain, Nicholas glanced repeatedly at the rearview mirror. Gradually he broke into a smile, and at last he said, "I did it. I actually lost them. Just like in those American police shows on the telly."

"You were marvelous," Joanna said.

"You really think so?"

"Simply terrific," she said.

"I guess I was. I quite *liked* that. Not good for the heart on a regular basis, mind you, but an invigorating experience."

Alex stared out the back window.

At the British Museum, Joanna got out of the cab and ran for the shelter of the main entrance.

As Alex paid the fare, Nicholas said, "Her husband, I suppose."

"Excuse me?"

"Well, if it wasn't coppers—"

"Oh, no, not her husband."

The driver stroked his beard. "You aren't going to let me hang like this?"

"Indeed I am." Alex got out of the cab and slammed the door.

For a moment Nicholas stared at him curiously through the rain-streaked window, but then he drove away.

Alex stood in the cold drizzle, shoulders hunched, hands in his coat pockets. He looked both ways along the street, studying the traffic, but he saw nothing suspicious.

When he joined Joanna in the doorway, out of the rain, she said, "You're soaked. What were you looking for?"

"I don't know," he said. He was still reluctant to go inside. He surveyed the street.

"Alex, what's wrong?"

"Getting rid of the Jaguar was too easy. Nothing's been this easy so far. Why this?"

"Isn't it time our luck changed?"

"I don't believe in luck."

Finally he turned away from the street and followed her into the museum.

47

They were standing in front of an impressive array of Assyrian antiquities, to which Chelgrin's note had directed them, when they were finally contacted. The senator's representative was a small, wiry man in a peacoat and dark-brown cap. He had a hard face with eyes squinted in perpetual suspicion, and his mouth appeared to have been surgically sewn into a permanent sneer. He stood beside Alex, pretending to appreciate a piece of Assyrian weaponry, and then said, "Yer 'unter, ain't yer?"

The stranger's Cockney accent was nearly impenetrable, but Alex understood him: *You're Hunter, aren't you?*

Occasionally Alex's interest in languages extended to especially colorful dialects. Richer in slang, more distorted in pronunciation than any other regional usage of the English tongue, Cockney was nothing if not colorful. The dialect had evolved in the East End of London, but it had spread to many parts of England. Originally it had been a means by which East End neighbors could talk to one another without making sense to the law or to outsiders.

The stranger squinted at Alex and then at Joanna. "Yer butchers like yer pitchers. Both of yer."

Alex translated: *You look like your pictures. Both of you.* The word "butchers" meant "look" by virtue of Cockney rhyming slang. A "butcher's hook" rhymed with "look"; therefore, by the logic of the code, "butchers" meant "look" when used in the proper context.

"And yer butchers bent ter me," Alex said. "Wot yer want?" *And you look like a less than honest man to me. What do you want?*

The stranger blinked, astonished to hear an American speaking the East End dialect with such confidence. "Yer s'pposed ter be a Yank."

"'At's wot I am."

"Yer rabbit right good." *You talk very well.*

"Tar," said Alex. *Thanks.*

Joanna said, "I'm not following this."

"I'll explain later," Alex promised.

"Yer rabbit so doddle . . . 'ell, nofink surprise me no more," said the stranger.

Sensing that the Cockney didn't much *like* the idea of a Yank talking to him as though they were mates, Alex dropped the dialect. "What do you want?"

"Got a message from a right pound-note geezer."

Alex translated: *from a man who speaks real fancy,* which usually meant a man with a la-de-da Oxford accent, though not always.

"That doesn't tell me much," Alex said.

"Geezer wif a double of white barnet." *A man with a lot of white hair.*

Barnet Fair was a famous carnival outside London. Since Barnet Fair rhymed with hair, the single word "barnet" meant "hair."

"What does this geezer call himself?" Alex asked.

"Tom. He gimme a poney ter bring yer a message. Seems 'ee's stayin' at the Churchill in Portman Square, and wants to see yer."

It was Senator Thomas Chelgrin who was waiting in a room at the Churchill Hotel. It could be no one else.

"What else?" Alex asked.

"'At's all der was, mate." The little man started to turn away, then stopped, looked back, licked his lips, and said, "One fink. Be careful of 'im, 'ee's dodgey, that one. Maybe worse an dodgey—'ee's shnide."

Dodgey. *No good.*

Shnide. *Slimy.*

"I'll be careful," Alex said. "Thanks."

The stranger pulled on his cap. "It was me, I wouldn't touch him less 'ee was wearin' a durex from 'ead ter foot of 'imself."

Alex translated and laughed. *I wouldn't touch him unless he was wearing a condom from head to foot.* He shared the Cockney's opinion of the senator from Illinois.

48

✪ ✪ ✪

From a public telephone at the museum, Alex called the Churchill Hotel in Portman Square.

Joanna fidgeted beside him. She was frightened. The prospect of meeting her duplicitous father couldn't be expected to fill her with joy.

Alex asked the hotel operator for Mr. Chelgrin's room, and the senator answered on the first ring. "Hello?"

"It's me," Alex said. "I recognize your voice, so I figure you recognize mine."

"Is . . . she with you?"

"Of course."

"I can't wait to see her. Come on up."

"We're not in the hotel. Still at the museum. I think we should have a nice long chat by phone before we get together."

"That's not possible. The situation is too urgent. I don't know how much time I have."

"We need to know a few things. Like what happened in Jamaica. And why Lisa became Joanna."

"It's too important to discuss on the phone," Chelgrin said. "Much more important than you can have guessed."

Alex hesitated, glanced at Joanna. "All right. Let's meet just inside the entrance to the National Gallery in half an hour."

"No. That's impossible," Chelgrin said. "It has to be here in my room at the Churchill."

"I don't like that. Too risky for us."

"I'm not here to harm you. I want to help."

"I'd prefer to meet on neutral ground."

"I don't dare go out," Chelgrin said, and the uncharacteristic tension in his voice wound tighter. "I've taken every precaution to conceal this trip. My office is telling everyone that I've gone home to Illinois. I didn't fly out of Washington because I could be traced too easily." He spoke faster, running the words together. "Drove to New York, flew from there to Toronto in a chartered jet, then in another charter to Montreal, and in a third from Montreal to London. I'm wiped out. Exhausted. I'm staying at the Churchill because it's not my usual hotel. I usually stay at Claridge's. But if they discover I've come to London, they'll know I've changed sides, and they'll kill me."

"Who is they?"

Chelgrin hesitated. Then: "The Russians."

"You need a better story, Senator. The Cold War's over."

"Nothing's ever over. Listen, Hunter, all I want is a chance to make up for what I've done, for the past. I want to help you and my daughter . . . that is . . . if she'll allow me to call her my daughter, after what I've done. Together we can expose this whole dirty thing. But you've got to come to me. I can't risk showing my face. And you've got to make *damned* sure you aren't being followed."

Alex thought about it.

"Hunter? Are you still there? My room number's four-sixteen. Hunter?"

"Yeah."

"You have to come."

"We don't *have* to do anything."

The senator was silent for a while. Then he sighed. "All right. Trust your instincts. I don't blame you."

"We'll come," Alex said.

49

They took a taxi to Harrod's. Even that early in the day, the huge, world-famous store was aswarm with shoppers.

Harrod's Telex address had long been "Everything, London." In two hundred departments, the legendary store carried everything from specialty foods to sporting goods, chewing gum to Chinese art, from rare books to rubber boots, faddish clothes to fine antiques, nail polish to expensive oriental rugs— a million and one delights.

Alex and Joanna ignored all the exotic merchandise as well as most of the mundane stuff. They purchased only two sturdy umbrellas and a set of plain but well-made steel cutlery.

In the privacy of a stall in the ladies' room, Joanna unwrapped the package of cutlery. She examined each piece and chose a wickedly sharp butcher's knife that she concealed in her coat pocket. She left the other knives behind when she departed.

Now both she and Alex were armed. Carrying concealed weapons was a more serious offense in London than it would have been almost anywhere else in the world, but they weren't concerned about spending time in jail. Walking *unarmed* into Tom Chelgrin's hotel room would have been by far the most dangerous course they could have taken.

Outside Harrod's they hailed another cab and followed a winding, random course through rain-slicked streets, until Alex was certain that they were not being followed. They got out of the cab three blocks from the Churchill.

Using the umbrellas to hide their faces as much as to shield them from the rain, they approached the hotel from its least public aspect. Rather than barge through the front entrance and across the Regency-style lobby, where they were most likely to be spotted by a lookout, they used an unlocked rear door meant for hotel deliveries, and they quickly found a service stair-well.

"Better leave your bumbershoot here," Alex said. "We'll want our hands free when we get there."

She stood her umbrella beside his, in the corner at the bottom of the stairs.

"Scared?" he asked.

"Yeah."

"Want to back out?"

"Can't," she said.

Though they were whispering, their voices echoed in the cold stairwell.

He unbuttoned his coat and withdrew the 9mm pistol that had been jammed under his belt. He put it in an overcoat pocket and kept his hand on the grip.

She put her hand on the butcher's knife in her pocket.

They climbed the stairs to the fourth floor.

The corridor was brightly lighted, deserted—and too quiet.

They hurried along the hallway, glancing at room numbers. In spite of the elegant decor, Alex couldn't shake the feeling that he was in a carnival funhouse and that a monster was going to spring at them suddenly from a door or out of the ceiling.

Just before they reached 416, Alex was stopped abruptly by a vivid premonition: an intense vision like the brief but commanding burst of a camera's electronic flash. In his mind's eye, he saw Tom Chelgrin spattered with blood. Never before had anything like that happened to him, and he was shaken both by the weirdness of it and by the wet, red *vividness* of the image.

Joanna stopped beside him, gripped his arm. "What's wrong?"

"He's dead."

"What? The senator? How do you know?"

"I just . . . I do. I'm sure of it."

He took the pistol from his coat pocket and continued along the corridor. The door to 416 was ajar.

"Stand behind me," he said.

She shuddered. "Let's call the police."

"We can't. Not yet."

"We have enough proof now."

"We don't have anything more than we had yesterday."

"If he's dead—that's proof of something."

"We don't *know* he's dead," Alex said, though he knew. "Besides, even if he is—that's not proof of anything."

"Let's get out of here."

"We don't have anywhere to go."

He used the pistol to push the door all the way open.

Stillness.

The lights were on in the suite.

"Senator?" he said softly.

When no one answered, Alex stepped across the threshold, and Joanna followed him.

Thomas Chelgrin was facedown on the drawing-room floor.

50

⊕ ⊕ ⊕

Tom Chelgrin was unquestionably dead. The quantity of blood alone was sufficient to eliminate any doubt.

The senator was wearing a blue bathrobe that had soaked up a great deal of blood. The back of the garment was marred by three bloody holes. He had been shot once at the base of the spine, once in the middle of the back, and once between the shoulders. His left arm was extended in front of him, fingers hooked into the carpet, and his right arm was folded under his chest. His head was turned to one side. Only half his face remained visible, and that was obscured by smears of blood and by a thick shock of white hair that had fallen across his eye.

Alex closed the door to the hall and cautiously inspected the rest of the small suite, but the killers were not to be found. He had known they would be gone.

When he returned to the drawing room, Joanna was kneeling beside the corpse. Alarmed, he said, "Don't touch him!"

She looked puzzled. "Why not?"

"It won't be easy to walk out of here and into our hotel if you're covered with bloodstains."

"I'll be careful."

"You've already got blood on the hem of your coat."

She glanced down. "Damn!"

He pulled her to her feet and away from the corpse. With his handkerchief, he rubbed at the stain on her coat. "It doesn't look good, but it'll have to pass."

"Shouldn't we check him over? Maybe he's alive."

"Alive? Look at those wounds. They used a weapon with a hell of a punch. All this blood. He's dead as a man can be."

"How did you know he'd be here like this? Out there in the hall, how did you know what we'd find?"

"Hard to explain," he said uneasily. "I'd call it a premonition if that didn't sound too crazy. But it does sound crazy, and I'm no clairvoyant."

"So it wasn't just a hunch, professional instinct, like you've said before?"

He recalled the alarmingly vivid mental image of the blood-spattered corpse, and although the position and condition of the real body did not perfectly match the details of the vision, the differences were not substantial.

"Weird," he said.

She stared at the cadaver and shook her head sadly. "I don't feel a thing. No grief."

"Why should you?"

"He *was* my father."

"No. He surrendered all those rights and privileges a long time ago. He didn't mourn for Lisa. He let them do . . . all they did to you. You don't owe him any tears."

"But *why?*" she wondered.

"We'll find out."

"I don't think so. I think maybe we're in some sort of gigantic Chinese puzzle. We'll keep climbing into smaller and smaller boxes forever, and there won't be answers in any of them."

Alex wondered if she might go to pieces on him after all. He wouldn't blame her if she did. She was right: This was her father, after all. She appeared to be calm, but she might be suppressing her feelings.

Realizing that he was worried about her, Joanna conjured a ghost of a smile. "I'll be okay. Like I told you—I don't feel a thing. I wish I did. I wish I could. But he's a stranger to me. They took away all memory of him." She turned away from the body. "Come on, let's get out of here."

"Not yet."

"But what if they come back—"

"They won't be back. If they'd known Chelgrin had made contact with us, and if they'd wanted to kill us, they would've waited right here. They think they got to him before he got to us. Come on. We have to search the place."

She grimaced. "Search for what?"

"For anything. For everything. For whatever little scrap might help us solve this puzzle."

"If the maid walks in—"

"The housekeeper's already been here this morning. The bed's freshly made."

Joanna took a deep breath. "All right, let's finish this as fast as we can."

"You follow me," Alex said. "Double-check me, make sure I don't overlook something. But don't touch anything."

In the bedroom, Chelgrin's two calfskin suitcases were on a pair of folding luggage racks. One case was open. Alex pawed through the clothes until he found a pair of the senator's black socks. He pulled them over his hands: makeshift gloves.

Chelgrin's billfold and credit-card wallet were on the dresser. Alex went through them, with Joanna watching closely, but neither the billfold nor the wallet contained anything unusual.

The closet held two suits and a topcoat. The pockets were empty.

Two pairs of freshly shined shoes were on the closet floor. Alex slipped the shoe trees out of them and searched inside. Nothing.

A shaving kit stood beside the sink in the bathroom: an electric razor, shaving powder, cologne, a comb, a can of hair spray.

Alex returned to the open suitcase. It also proved to contain nothing of interest.

The second suitcase wasn't locked. He opened it and tossed the clothes onto the floor, piece by piece, until he found a nine-by-twelve-inch manila envelope.

He took off the makeshift gloves and emptied the contents of the envelope onto the dresser: several age-yellowed clippings from *The New York Times* and *The Washington Post;* an unfinished letter, apparently in the senator's handwriting, addressed to Joanna. Alex didn't take time to read either the letter or the newspaper pieces, but from a quick scan of the clippings, he saw that they were all fourteen or fifteen years old and dealt with a German doctor named Franz Rotenhausen. One of the articles featured a photograph of the man: thin face, sharp features, balding, eyes so pale that they appeared to be all but colorless.

Joanna flinched as if she had been bee-stung. "Oh, God. It's him. The man in my nightmare. The Hand."

"His name's Rotenhausen."

"I've never heard it before." She was shaking badly. "I . . . I never thought I'd s-see him again."

"This is what we wanted—a name."

She looked toward the open door between the bedroom and the drawing room, as if Rotenhausen might walk through it at any moment. "Please, Alex, let's get out of here."

The face in the grainy photograph was hard, bony, vampiric. The pale eyes seemed to be staring into a dimension that other men couldn't see.

Alex felt the hairs bristling on the back of his neck. Perhaps it *was* time to leave.

"We'll read these later," he said, stuffing the clippings and the unfinished letter back into the envelope.

In the drawing room, the dead senator still lay where they had last seen him. Alex had half expected the corpse to be missing. Or standing up, swaying, grinning at them. After recent developments, anything seemed possible.

51
✪ ✪ ✪

Alex and Joanna ate lunch in a busy café near Piccadilly Circus.

Heavy rain sluiced down the windows, blurring modern London until only the ancient lines of the city were visible. The inclement weather was a time machine, washing away the years.

Over thick sandwiches and too many cups of tea, they read the old clippings from *The New York Times* and *The Washington Post.*

Franz Rotenhausen was a genius in more than one field. He had degrees in biology, chemistry, medicine, and psychology. He'd written many widely recognized and important papers in all those disciplines. When he was twenty-four, he lost his hand in an automobile accident. Unimpressed with the prostheses available at that time, he invented a new device, a mechanical hand nearly as functional as flesh and bone, controlled by nerve impulses from the stump and powered by a battery pack. Later, he'd spent eighteen years as a lecturer and research scientist at a major West German university. He was mainly interested in brain function and dysfunction, and especially in the electrical and chemical nature of thought and memory.

"Why would they let anyone work on this?" Joanna asked angrily. "It's George Orwell time. It's *1984,* for God's sake."

"It's also the route to ultimate power," Alex said. "And that's what all politicians are after. So of course they funded his work."

Fifteen years ago, at the peak of a brilliant career, Franz Rotenhausen had made a terrible mistake. He'd written a book about the human brain with an emphasis on recent developments in behavioral engineering, contending that even the most drastic of techniques—including brainwashing—should be used by "responsible" governments to create a dissension-free, crime-free, worry-free Utopian society. His greatest error was not the writing of the book but his subsequent failure to be contrite after it became controversial. The scientific and political communities can forgive any stupidity, indiscretion, or gross miscalculation as long as public apologies come loud and long; humble contrition doesn't even have to be sincere to earn a pardon from the establishment; it must only *appear* genuine, so the citizenry can be allowed to settle back into its usual stupor. As controversy grew in the wake of the publication, however, Rotenhausen had no second thoughts. He responded to critics with increasing irritation. He showed the world a sneer instead of the remorse it wanted to see. His public statements were given an unusually threatening edge by his harsh voice and his unfortunate habit of making violent gestures with his steel hand. European newspapers were quick to give him nicknames—Dr. Strangelove and Dr. Frankenstein—but those soon gave way to another that stuck: Dr. Zombie. He was accused of wanting to create a world of mindless, obedient automatons. The furor increased. He complained that reporters and photographers were hounding him, and he was intemperate enough to suggest that they would be his first choice for behavior modification if he were in charge. He steadfastly refused to back down from his position, and thus he was unable to take the pressure off himself.

"I can usually sympathize with victims of press harassment," Alex said. "But not this time."

"He'd like to do to everyone what he did to me."

"Or worse."

The waitress brought more tea and small cakes for dessert.

The lunch crowd was thinning out.

Beyond the windows, the rain was coming down with such force that London had been blurred back into the eighteenth century.

Alex and Joanna continued to read about Rotenhausen:

In Bonn, back in that time before reunification, the West German government was exceedingly sensitive to world opinion. Rotenhausen was widely viewed as Hitler's spiritual descendant. The brilliant doctor ceased to be a national treasure (not so much because of his work but because he'd been unable to keep his mouth shut about it), ceased to be even a national asset, and became a distinct liability to the German state. Pressure was brought to bear on the university that gave him a research home, and eventually he was dismissed on a morals charge involving a student. He denied all wrongdoing and accused the university and the girl of conspiring against him. Nevertheless, he was weary of wasting time on politics when so much research awaited. He departed gracelessly but without challenging the powers that had gone after him with such success, and eventually the morals charge was dropped.

"He might not have been guilty of molesting that girl, but he was probably guilty of molesting others. I know him well. Too well."

Unable to endure the haunted expression in her eyes, Alex stared for a moment at the half-eaten cake on the plate in front of him, and then he took another yellowed clipping from the stack.

Six months after Dr. Zombie was forced out of the university, he liquidated his holdings in West Germany and moved to Saint Moritz, Switzerland. The Swiss granted him permanent residency for two reasons. First, Switzerland was a country with a long and admirable tradition of providing asylum for prominent—though seldom ordinary—outcasts from other countries. Second, Rotenhausen was a millionaire many times over, having inherited a fortune and later having earned substantially more from his dozens of medical and chemical patents. He reached an agreement with the Swiss tax authorities, and each year he paid a tithe that was meager to him but that covered a substantial percentage of the government's expenses in the canton where he lived. It was believed that he continued to do research in his private laboratory in Saint Moritz, but because he never wrote another word for publication and never spoke to newsmen, that suspicion couldn't be verified.

"With time he's been forgotten," Joanna said.

"Too many new monsters to excite the media every day. No time to keep track of the old ones."

Finished with the clippings, they turned to the unfinished, unsigned, hand-written letter from Chelgrin to his daughter. It was two pages of half-baked apologia: an ineffective, self-justifying whine. It provided no new information, not even a single fresh clue.

"How does Rotenhausen connect with the senator and with whatever happened in Jamaica?" Joanna wondered.

"I don't know, but we'll find out."

"You said the senator mentioned Russians when you spoke to him on the phone."

"Yeah, but I don't know what he meant. It seems ridiculous. The Cold War was still on in those days, but it's over now."

"What would Rotenhausen have been doing in a deal with the Soviets, anyway? He sounds more like a Nazi than a communist."

"Nazis and communists have a lot in common," Alex said. "They want the same thing—absolute control, unqualified power. A man like Franz Rotenhausen can find sympathy in both camps."

"Now what?" she asked.

"Now we go to Switzerland."

52

♣ ♣ ♣

As a hard wind blew shatters of rain against the café windows and as London seemed to dissolve toward prehistoric rock formations, Joanna leaned across the table. "No, Alex. Please, let's not do that. Not Switzerland. Not into . . . into his lair. We can turn this whole thing over to the police now."

"We still don't have enough proof."

She shook her head adamantly. "I disagree. We've got all these clippings, this letter, a dead body at the Churchill Hotel, and the fact that my fingerprints match Lisa's."

Alex reached across the table and put his hand over hers. "I understand your fear. But what police should we go to? The Jamaican police? The Americans? Chicago police? The FBI, the CIA? Japanese police? The British? Scotland Yard? Or maybe the Swiss police?"

She frowned. "It's not so simple, is it?"

"If we go to *any* cops now, we'll be dead by morning. These people, whoever they are, have been hiding something big for a long time. Now the cover-up isn't working any more. The whole thing's falling apart. And they know it. That's why they killed the senator—they've finally decided to clean up the mess before anyone notices it. Right now they're probably looking for us. Whatever immunity you might have had is gone—gone with your father. If we go public with the case now, we'll just be targets. Until we've got the entire story, until we understand the why of it, until we can blow them out of the water, we'll stay alive only as long as we stay out of sight."

Joanna seized on that. "But we'll be extremely visible if we go hunting Rotenhausen in Switzerland."

"We won't blunder straight over there. We'll be discreet."

She wasn't impressed. "The senator tried to sneak into London. It didn't work for him."

"It'll work for us. It has to."

"But even if it does—what'll we do after we get to Saint Moritz?"

He sipped his tea and thought about her question. Finally he said, "I'll find Rotenhausen's place, look it over. If it isn't too heavily guarded, I'll get in, find his file room. If he's the careful, methodical man of science he seems to be, maybe he'll have a record of what he did to you, how he did it, and why."

"What about British-Continental Insurance?"

"What about it?"

"If we follow up on that lead, maybe we won't have to go to Saint Moritz."

"Now that we know where they put you through this 'treatment,' we don't have to pry into British-Continental. Besides, that would be just as dangerous as going to Switzerland, but we wouldn't be likely to find as much there as at Rotenhausen's place."

She slumped back in her chair, resigned to the trip. "When do we leave London?"

"As soon as possible. Within the hour, if we can manage it."

53

When Alex and Joanna returned to the hotel for their passports and luggage, they didn't go to their suite alone. They stopped at the front desk, ordered a rental car, told the clerk that they were checking out sooner than originally anticipated, and took two bellmen upstairs with them.

Although the bellmen served as unwitting guards, and though the senator's killers were not likely to strike in front of witnesses, Alex paced nervously in the drawing room and watched the door, alert for the silent turning of the knob, while Joanna got their bags ready to go. Fortunately, when they had arrived the previous night from Tokyo, they had been too tired to unpack more than essentials; and this morning, awakened by Tom Chelgrin's noisy messenger, they'd had no time to hang up their clothes and transfer their things from the suitcases to the dresser drawers, so repacking only required a couple of minutes.

On the way downstairs, the elevator stopped to take aboard more people at the tenth floor. As the doors slid open, Alex unhooked one button on his overcoat, reached inside, and put his hand on the butt of the pistol tucked under the waistband of his trousers. He was half convinced that the people waiting in the corridor were not merely other hotel guests, that they would have submachine guns and would spray the elevator with bullets. The doors rolled open. An elderly couple entered the cab, conducting an animated discussion in rapid-fire Spanish, hardly aware of their fellow passengers.

Joanna smiled grimly at Alex. She knew what he'd been thinking.

He took his hand off the 9mm automatic and buttoned his coat.

They had to wait in the lobby fifteen minutes for the rental car to arrive, but by a quarter past three, they drove away into rain so silver that it appeared to be sleet. Gray mist as thick as smoke settled lower with the waning of the day, engulfing the tops of the tallest buildings, and in the strange pewter light, London seemed medieval even where the buildings were all of glass and steel and modern angles.

For a while they weaved through a Byzantine complexity of rain-lashed streets that branched off from one another with no discernible logic. They were lost but didn't care, because until they identified their tail and lost it, they had no specific destination.

Turned in her seat, staring out the back window, Joanna said at last, "Another Jaguar. A yellow one this time."

"All these bastards seem to travel in style."

"Well, they knew the senator," Joanna said sarcastically, facing forward and engaging her seat belt, "and the senator always moved in the very best circles, didn't he?"

Alex swerved right, in front of a bus and into thinner traffic. The tires squealed, the car shot forward, and he whipped from lane to lane, as if trying to make a car do what an Olympic skier could accomplish in a giant slalom. Motorists braked in surprise as the rental car swerved around and flashed past them, a truck driver blew his horn angrily, and pedestrians stopped and pointed. But the clog of London traffic didn't permit a protracted car chase like those in the movies, and the lanes ahead quickly began to jam up. Alex hung a hard left at the first corner and darted in front of a taxi with only centimeters to spare. At midblock he swung the wrong way into a one-way backstreet and stomped the accelerator. Building walls flashed past in a stony blur, two feet away on either side. The small car bounced and shimmied on the rough cobblestones, severely testing Alex's grip on the steering wheel. If anyone entered the alleyway ahead of them, a head-on crash couldn't be averted; but luck was with them, and they exploded out of the cramped street onto a main thoroughfare, fishtailing across the wet pavement in front of oncoming traffic and into a cacophony of squealing brakes and blaring horns. Alex turned right and sped through a red traffic light as it changed from yellow.

The Jaguar was no longer in sight.

"Terrific!" Joanna said.

"Not so terrific." He kept glancing worriedly at the rearview mirror. "We shouldn't have lost them. Not that easily."

"Easily? You think that was easy? We nearly wrecked half a dozen times!"

"They kill like professionals, so they ought to be able to run a tail like professionals. Should've kept on top of us every minute. They had a better car than this one. And they must be a lot more familiar with these streets than we are. It's just like this morning with the other Jaguar. It's as if they *wanted* to let us get away—so we'd feel safe."

"But why would they be playing a game like that?"

He scowled. "I don't know. I feel like we're being manipulated, and I sure don't like the feeling. It scares me."

"Maybe they don't have to take exceptional risks to keep us in view," she said, "because they've got this car bugged. A concealed transmitter. Or am I being paranoid?"

"These days," Alex said, "only the paranoid survive."

❂

Somewhere in the suburban sprawl, as the storm diluted the last light of dusk and washed it into a deep ocean of night, they stopped in the loneliest end of a shopping-center parking lot. Joanna stayed in the car and kept watch while Alex removed the license plates from their rental car and put them on a nearby Toyota. He didn't put the Toyota plates on the rental but kept them for later use.

A few miles farther on, they stopped at a busy roadside supper club. Over rolling thunder and the incessant roar of the rain, big-band music and laughter drifted through the drenched night.

Alex checked parked cars for unlocked doors, then looked inside each accessible vehicle in hope of finding keys in the ignition. In a silver-gray Ford, he discovered what he was looking for under the driver's seat.

Alex drove away in the stolen vehicle. Joanna stayed close behind him in the rental car. As far as he could tell, no one followed them.

In an apartment-complex parking lot, they quickly transferred their bags to the Ford. They abandoned the rental, sans license plates, and went in search of a quiet residential neighborhood.

Ten minutes later, they parked on a street lined with relatively new, identical, single-family brick houses with shallow front lawns and bare-limbed trees, where Alex removed the Ford's license plates and replaced them with the set he had taken from the Toyota in the shopping center. He dropped the Ford's tags into a drainage grate at the curb, and they splashed into the dark water below.

The owner of the Toyota was unlikely to notice immediately that his plates had been replaced with those from the rental car. And when the Ford was reported stolen back at the supper club, police would be looking for a car with the plates that were now lost in the storm drain.

By the time they were on the move again, Alex and Joanna were soaked and shivering, but they felt safer. He turned up the heater to its maximum setting. It was going to take a while to chase away the chill, because he was cold all the way into his bones.

✪ ✪ ✪

54

Joanna fiddled with the car radio until she located a station playing Beethoven. The beautiful music relieved her tension.

Using complimentary road maps provided by the car-rental agency, they got lost only three times before they were headed south on the correct highway. They were going to Brighton, on the coast, where Alex intended to spend the night.

For years Joanna had thought that the highway they now traveled was the same on which Robert and Elizabeth Rand had lost their lives. But both London and this outlying landscape were new and strange to her. Hard as it was to accept, she now knew that she had never spent her childhood and adolescence in London, as she had believed for so long; this was her first visit to England. Robert and Elizabeth Rand had existed only in a handful of phony documents—and, of course, in her mind.

As the windshield wipers thumped like a heartbeat, she thought of her real father, Thomas Chelgrin, lying dead on that hotel-room floor, and she wished that the image of the bloodied senator could reduce her to tears. Feeling grief would be better than feeling nothing at all. But her heart was closed to him.

She put one hand on Alex's shoulder, just to reassure herself that he was real and that she was not alone.

He glanced at her, evidently sensed her mood, and winked.

The storm continued without surcease. On the black highway, the headlights shimmered like the lambent glow of the moon reflecting off the glassy surface of a swift-flowing river.

"Just west of Brighton," Alex said, "on the way to Worthing, there's a quaint little inn called The Bell and The Dragon. It's a couple hundred years old but beautifully kept, and the food's quite good."

"Won't we need a reservation?"

"Not this late in the year. The tourist season is long past. They ought to have a few nice rooms available."

When they arrived at The Bell and The Dragon a short while later, the only sign announcing it was a large wooden billboard hung from a crossbar between two posts near the highway—no neon, no well-lighted announcement panel advertising an early-bird dinner special or a piano bar. The inn was tucked in a stand of ancient oaks, and the parking lot was nearly as dark as it must have been in the days when the guests arrived in horse-drawn coaches. It was a rambling structure, pleasing to the eye, half brick and half plaster with a crosswork of rugged, exposed beams. The front doors were fashioned from oak timbers and featured hand-carved plaques indicating that beds, food, and drink were offered inside. In the lobby and public rooms, soft electric lights hidden in converted gas lamps imparted a marvelous luster to the polished, richly inlaid paneling.

Alex and Joanna were given spacious quarters on the second floor. White plaster walls. Darkly stained beams. A pegged oak floor protected by plush area carpets.

Joanna examined the griffin-head water spouts in the bathroom, was pleased to find that the stone fireplace in the bedroom would actually work if they chose to use it, and finally threw herself on the four-poster bed. "It's absolutely delightful."

"It belongs to another age—one more hospitable than ours."

"It's charming. I love it. How often have you stayed here?"

The question appeared to surprise him. He stared at her but didn't speak. She sat up on the bed. "What's wrong?"

He turned slowly in a full circle, studying the room. At last he said, "I've never stayed here before."

"Who told you about it?"

"I haven't the slightest idea. I've never been to Brighton before, can't remember ever talking to anyone about it—except to you, of course. This is the third time today."

"The third time what?" Joanna asked.

He went to the nearest window and gazed into the rainy darkness beyond. "It's the third time I've known about something I shouldn't know about. Have no way of knowing about. Creepy. Before I opened that note this morning, I knew it was from the senator."

"That was just a good guess," Joanna said.

"And before we ever got to his hotel room, before I saw that his door was ajar, I knew Tom Chelgrin was dead."

"Intuition."

Alex turned away from the window, shaking his head. "No. This place is more than a hunch. I knew the name—The Bell and The Dragon. I knew exactly how it would look, as if I'd seen it before."

"Maybe someone told you about it, but you just don't recall. Or you read about it in a travel article—one with photographs."

"No. I'd remember," he insisted.

"Not if it was a few years ago. Not if it was casual reading. Maybe a magazine in a doctor's office. Something you skimmed and pretty much forgot, except this place stuck in your subconscious."

"Maybe," he said, though he was obviously unconvinced.

He turned to the window again, put his face close to the glass, and stared into the night, as if certain that people were out there staring back at him.

55

✪ ✪ ✪

With the descent of night in London, the temperature had dropped ten degrees. It now hovered at the freezing point. The wind had grown stronger, and the rain had become sleet.

On his way home from the Fielding Athison offices in Soho, Marlowe—previously in charge of all Soviet operations that had used the importing company as a front, now working for post-Soviet forces that still dreamed of a Russian Marxist Utopia—drove slowly and cursed the weather. He kept his head tucked down and his shoulders drawn up in anticipation of a collision. Everywhere he looked, cars slid on the icy pavement, and as far as he could tell, he was the only motorist in all of Greater London who wasn't driving like a suicidal maniac.

In a line of work that demanded caution, Marlowe was one of the most cautious men he knew. He had committed himself to a life of treason, which was, thank you very much, more than enough risk for any man. Having made that one dangerous decision, he tried thereafter to ensure that espionage would be as thoroughly safe and serene an occupation as floral arrangement or managing a tobacco shop. He abhorred taking any action without first thinking through all the ramifications, and he was always markedly slower to act than any of his associates. He kept four stashes of false passports and getaway cash at various places in England, as well as secret bank accounts in Switzerland *and* Grand Cayman.

His aversion to risk extended beyond his working world into his private life. He participated in no leisure sports that were likely to result in broken bones or torn ligaments. He didn't hunt, because occasionally one saw stories in the press about hunting accidents, chaps shooting themselves or one another, either out of carelessness or because they'd mistaken one another for game. He had acquaintances who enjoyed hot-air ballooning, which he considered no safer than bungee jumping off high bridges, so he refused to join them on their mad weekend flights. He faithfully followed a low-fat, low-salt diet. He never drank alcoholic beverages or any beverage containing caffeine. He ate only trace amounts of refined sugar, always bundled up well and wore a hat in cold weather, underwent a complete physical examination twice a year, never had sex without a condom, and drove as sedately as an octogenarian vicar.

On the roadway ahead, another driver stood on the brakes, and the car fishtailed wildly on the ice-sheathed pavement.

Marlowe tamped his brakes judiciously and congratulated himself on having left enough room to stop short of a collision.

Behind him, the brakes of another vehicle squealed horribly.

Marlowe winced, gritted his teeth, and counted the seconds until impact. Miraculously, no crash ensued.

"Morons," Marlowe said.

He cherished life. He intended to die no sooner than his one hundredth birthday—and then in bed with a young woman. A very young woman. *Two* very young women.

At the moment his anxiety was exacerbated by his inability to concentrate on his driving to the degree he would have liked. In spite of the constant fear that some lunatic would plow into him, he couldn't prevent his mind from wandering. The past few days had been filled with signs and portents, bad omens—and he couldn't stop mulling them over, trying to decide what they meant.

First, he had come out of the confrontation with Ignacio Carrera less well than expected. When he'd tried to learn Joanna Rand's real name, he had been operating on his long-held conviction that he and Carrera were equals in the eyes of the masters whom they served. Instead, he'd been slapped down. Hard. Then word had come from Moscow that Marlowe was to back off the Rand situation, obey Carrera, and leave the mysterious woman unharmed even if she blundered into the offices of Fielding Athison and threatened to disrupt the entire operation.

Marlowe was still smarting from that loss of face when the grotesque Anson Peterson swept in from America and began issuing commands with royal arrogance. Marlowe wasn't permitted to see the Rand woman, not even a photograph of her. He was told not to speak to her if she should call British-Continental again. He was not even supposed to *think* about her any more. Peterson was in charge of the operation, and Marlowe was instructed to go about his other work as if he knew nothing whatsoever about the crisis.

But Marlowe was reluctant to surrender even a single minor prerogative of his position. He jealously guarded his authority and privileges; it was dangerous to relinquish even a small amount of hard-won power. One backward step on the ladder could turn into a long, bone-crunching fall to the bottom, because everywhere there were schemers who envied their betters and were willing to give them a killing push over the brink at the first sign of weakness.

Marlowe was jolted out of his reverie by the mighty blast of an air horn. A big lorry loaded with frozen poultry skidded and nearly sideswiped him. He glanced at the rearview mirror, saw that no one was close behind, and jammed his foot down on the brake pedal harder than he should have. The car began to slide, but he let the wheel spin as it wished, and a moment later he was in control again. The lorry slid past him, swayed as if it would topple, then regained its equilibrium, and sped on.

Taking heart from the way he handled the car, he told himself that he would manage the current crisis at work with equal skill, once he'd had time to think out all courses of action open to him.

Marlowe lived on the entire top floor of a large three-story, eighteen-room townhouse that had been converted into apartments. When he parked at the curb in front of the building and switched off the car engine, he sighed with relief.

As he carefully negotiated the icy sidewalk to the front door, he was pelted furiously by sleet, but it couldn't get under his coat collar because he'd wound a scarf around his neck and then buttoned the collar securely over it.

At the third floor, Marlowe unlocked his apartment door and felt for the light switch as he stepped across the threshold. He smelled the natural gas even as his fingers touched the switch. But in the fraction of a second that his mind raced frantically through all the ramifications of the situation in search of the safest action, his right index finger recklessly completed its small arc and flicked the switch. Marlowe was blown to Hell with a flash of remorse at all the potato chips never eaten, the beers never drunk, and the women never experienced without the desensitizing barrier of a latex sheath.

✪

Across the street from the apartment house, Peterson sat alone in a parked car, watching as the third-floor windows blew out, the wall exploded, and Marlowe arced out into the rainy night as though he were a clown shot from a cannon. Briefly the dead man appeared to be able to fly as well as any bird— but then he plummeted to the pavement and did less damage to it than it did to him.

A man and a woman ran from the front entrance of the building. No one was at home on the second floor, so Peterson figured these two were ground-floor residents. They rushed to Marlowe's crumpled body—but they hastily drew back, sickened, when they got a close look at him.

The fat man popped a butter-rum Life Saver into his mouth. He released the parking brake, put the car in gear, and drove away from that sorry place.

Peterson hadn't received permission to eliminate Marlowe. In fact, he had never expected to receive it, so he hadn't even bothered to ask for it. Marlowe's transgressions had been far too minor to generate a kill order from the directorate in Moscow.

Nevertheless, Marlowe had to die. He was the first of six primary targets on the hit list. Peterson had made promises to an extremely powerful group, and if he failed to keep those promises, his own life would end as quickly and brutally as Marlowe's.

He had worked for an hour to set up the gas explosion so it would appear to have been an accident. The bosses in Moscow, who demanded absolute obedience from Anson Peterson, might be suspicious about an "accident" that killed one of their major London operatives, but they would blame the other side rather than one of their own best agents.

And the other men, those to whom Anson Peterson had made so many commitments, would be satisfied. The first of his promises had been kept. One man was dead. The first of many.

56

Alex and Joanna ate dinner in the cozy, oak-paneled dining room at The Bell and The Dragon. The food was excellent, but Alex was unable to get a full measure of enjoyment from it. While he ate, he surreptitiously watched the other customers, trying to determine if any of them might be watching him.

Later, in bed in the dark, he and Joanna made love. This time it was slow and tender, and they finished like a pair of spoons in a drawer. He fell asleep pressed against her warm back.

The peculiar dream came to him again. The soft bed. The white room. The three surgeons in white gowns and masks, staring down at him. The first surgeon asked the same question he'd asked before—"Where does he think he is?"—and the same conversation ensued among the three men. Alex lifted one hand to touch the nearest doctor, but as before his fingers were transformed magically into tiny replicas of buildings. He stared at them, amazed, and then his fingers ceased to be merely replicas and became five tall buildings seen at a great distance, and the buildings grew larger, larger, and he drew nearer to them, dropping down from the sky, and a city grew across the palm of his hand and up his arm. The looming faces of the surgeons were replaced by blue sky. Below him was Rio, the fantastic bay and the ocean beyond. Then his plane landed, and he got out, and he was *in* Rio. The mournful but beautiful music of a Spanish guitar filled the Brazilian air.

He mumbled and turned over in his sleep.

And he turned into a new dream. He was in a cool dark crypt. Candles flickered dimly. He walked to a black coffin that rested on a stone bier, grasped the massive bronze handles, and lifted the lid. Thomas Chelgrin lay inside: blood-smeared, gray-skinned, as dead as the stone on which his casket rested. Heart pounding, overcome with dread, Alex gazed at the senator, and then as he started to lower the lid, the eyes of the corpse opened. Chelgrin grinned malevolently, exposing blood-caked teeth. He grabbed Alex's wrists in his strong, gray, cold hands and tried to drag him down into the coffin.

Alex sat straight up in bed, an unvoiced scream trapped in his throat.

Joanna was asleep.

He remained very still for a while, suspicious of the deep shadows in the corners. He had left the bathroom door ajar, with the light burning beyond it. Nevertheless, most of the room was shrouded in gloom. Gradually his eyes adjusted, and he could see that there were no intruders, either real or supernatural.

He got out of bed and went to the nearest window.

Their room offered a view of the sea. Alex could see nothing, however, except a vast black emptiness marked by the vague lights of a ship behind curtains of rain. He shifted his gaze to something closer at hand: the slate-shingled roof that slanted low over the window, creating a deep eave. Still closer: The windows had diamond-shaped panes of leaded glass, and each pane was beveled at the edges. Closer: In the surface of the glass, he saw himself—his drawn face, his troubled eyes, his mouth set in a tight grim line.

The case had begun with Joanna's repeating nightmare. Now he had a recurring dream of his own. He didn't believe in coincidence. He was certain that his dream of Rio harbored a message that he must interpret if they were to survive. His subconscious was trying to tell him something desperately important.

But for God's sake, what?

He had been to Rio for a month the previous spring, but he hadn't been hospitalized while there. He hadn't met any doctors. The trip had been perfectly ordinary—just one in a series of brief escapes from a job that had begun to bore him.

He shifted his attention from his own reflection and stared into the distance again.

We're puppets, he thought. *Joanna and me. Puppets. And the puppetmaster is out there. Somewhere. Who? Where? And what does he want?*

Lightning slashed the soft flesh of the night.

57

Rain was no longer falling. The morning air was piercingly clear. Judging by the window glass to which Joanna touched her fingertips, the day was also fearfully cold.

She felt refreshed and more at ease than she'd been in a long time. She could see, however, that Alex had not benefited from the night at the inn. His eyes were bloodshot and ringed by dark circles of slack skin.

He returned the 9mm pistol to its hiding place in the hollowed-out hair dryer and packed the dryer in Joanna's largest suitcase.

They checked out of The Bell and The Dragon at nine o'clock. The clerk wished them a swift, safe trip.

They went to an apothecary and purchased a tin of body powder to replace the one that Alex had emptied into the toilet in London. In the car again, he slipped the extra magazines of ammunition into the talc. Joanna put the resealed can in her suitcase.

They drove from the outskirts of Brighton to Southampton. No one followed them.

At the Southampton airport, they abandoned the stolen Ford in the parking lot.

Aurigny Airlines hadn't yet sold out the Saturday morning flight to Cherbourg. Alex and Joanna sat behind the starboard wing, and she had the window seat. The flight was uneventful, with such an utter lack of turbulence that it almost seemed as though they hadn't left the ground.

The French customs officials thoroughly inspected the luggage, but they neither opened the can of body powder nor took a close look at the hair dryer.

On the express turbotrain from Cherbourg to Paris, Alex's mood brightened somewhat, apparently because Paris was his favorite city. He usually stayed at the Hotel George V; indeed, he was so well known by the staff that he might have gotten a room without a reservation. They stayed elsewhere, however, in less grand quarters, precisely because they didn't want to go where Alex was well known.

From their hotel, he telephoned another hotel in Saint Moritz. Speaking fluent French and using the name Maurice Demuth, he inquired about reserving a room for one full week, beginning Sunday, two days hence. Fortunately, a recent cancellation had made a room available, and currently there was no waiting list for week-long accommodations.

When Alex put down the phone, Joanna said, "Why Maurice Demuth?"

"So if anyone connected with Rotenhausen should go around Saint Moritz checking advance bookings at the hotels, he won't find us."

"I mean, why Maurice Demuth instead of some other name?"

"Well . . . I don't know. It's just a good French name."

"I thought maybe you knew someone with that name."

"No. I just plucked it out of the air."

"You lied so smoothly. I better start taking everything you say with a grain of salt." She moved into his arms. "Like when you tell me I'm pretty—how can I be sure you mean it?"

"You're more than pretty. You're beautiful," he said.

"You sound so sincere."

"No one has ever done to me what you do."

"So sincere . . . and yet . . ."

"Easy to prove I'm not lying."

"How?"

He took her to bed.

Later, they ate dinner at a small restaurant overlooking the Seine, which was speckled with the lights of small boats and the reflected amber wedges of the windows in the buildings that stood along its banks.

As she nibbled flawless *oie rotie aux pruneaux* and listened to Alex's stories about Paris, she knew that she could never allow anyone or anything to separate her from him. She would rather die.

58

✣ ✣ ✣

In Saint Moritz, Peterson had a gray Mercedes at his disposal. He drove himself, continuously peeling a roll of Life Savers and popping a series of butter-rum morsels into his mouth.

Low over the towering mountains, the sky appeared to be nine months gone, bulging with gray-black storm clouds that were about to deliver torrents of fine dry snow.

During the afternoon Peterson played tourist. He drove from one viewing point to another, enchanted by the scenery.

The resort of Saint Moritz is in three parts: Saint Moritz-Dorf, which is on a mountain terrace more than two hundred feet above the lake; Saint Moritz-Bad, which is a charming place at the end of the lake; and Champfer-Suvretta. Until the end of the nineteenth century, Saint Moritz-Bad was *the* spa, but thereafter it lost ground to Saint Moritz-Dorf, which is perhaps the most dazzling water playground in the world. Recently, Moritz-Bad had been making a concerted effort to recapture its lost position, but its ambitious recovery program had led to a most unlovely building boom.

An hour after nightfall, Peterson kept an appointment in Saint Moritz-Bad. He left the Mercedes with a valet at one of the newer and uglier hotels. Inside, he crossed the lobby to the lakefront cocktail lounge. The room was crowded and noisy.

The hotel's day-registration clerk, Rudolph Uberman, had gone off duty fifteen minutes ago and was waiting at a corner table: a thin man with long, slim hands that were seldom still.

Peterson shrugged out of his overcoat, hung it across the back of a chair, and sat facing Uberman. The clerk was nearly finished with a brandy and wanted another, and Peterson ordered the same.

After they were served, Peterson said, "Any word?"

Uberman was nervous. "Monsieur Maurice Demuth telephoned four hours ago."

"Excellent."

"He will arrive Sunday with his wife."

Peterson withdrew an envelope from an inside coat pocket and passed it to Uberman. "That's your second payment. If all goes well on Sunday, you'll receive a third envelope."

The clerk glanced left and right before quickly tucking the payoff out of sight—as if anyone who witnessed the exchange would immediately know that it was dirty business. In fact, none of the other customers was the least bit interested in them.

"I would like some assurance," Uberman said.

Peterson scowled. "Assurance?"

"I would like a guarantee that no one . . ."

"Yes? Go on."

"That no one will be killed."

"Oh, of course, dear man, you have my word on that."

Uberman studied him. "If anyone were killed in the hotel, I'd have no choice but to tell the authorities what I know."

Peterson kept his voice low, but he spoke sharply. "That would be foolish. You're an accomplice, sir. The authorities wouldn't deal lightly with you. And neither would I."

Uberman tossed back his brandy as though it were water. "Perhaps I should return the money."

"I wouldn't accept it. A deal is a deal."

"I guess I'm in over my head."

"Relax, sir. You've a tendency to melodramatize. It will all go very smoothly, and no one will ever know it happened."

"What do you want with them anyway?"

"You wouldn't care to know that. Just think of all those Swiss francs in the envelope and the rest to come, and forget the source of it all. Forgetting is always best. Forgetting is safe. Now, tell me, is the restaurant here any good?"

"The food is terrible," Uberman said.

"I suspected as much."

"Try Chesa Veglia."

"I'll do that."

"Or perhaps Corviglia at the top of the funicular."

Peterson put enough money on the table to cover the bill. As he stood and struggled into his overcoat, he said, "I'm a heeder of my own advice. I've already forgotten your name."

"I never knew yours," Uberman noted.

"Did someone speak?" Peterson asked, looking around as though he couldn't even see Uberman.

Smiling at his own joke, he left the hotel for dinner at Chesa Veglia.

59

✪ ✪ ✪

On Saturday they flew from Paris to Zurich. Their hotel, Baur Au Lac, stood in its own lakeside park at the end of Bahnhofstrasse.

In their room, Alex dismantled the hair dryer yet again and put the pistol under his belt. He took the spare clips of ammunition from the talcum powder.

"I wish you didn't have to carry that," Joanna said.

"So do I. But we're getting too close to Rotenhausen to risk going without it."

They made love again. Twice. He could not get enough of her—but he wasn't seeking sex as much as closeness.

That night he had the dream again.

He woke shortly before three o'clock, gasping in panic, but he regained control of himself before he woke Joanna. He couldn't go back to sleep. He sat in a chair beside the bed, the pistol in his lap, until the wake-up call came at six o'clock.

He was grateful for his peculiar metabolism, which allowed him to function well on little sleep.

Monday morning they boarded a train at Zurich's Haupbahnhof, and they headed east.

As the train pulled out of the station, Joanna said, "We're sure going roundabout. No one'll be able to track us down easily."

"Maybe they don't need to track us down," Alex said. "Maybe they knew our route before we did."

"What do you mean?"

"I'm not sure. But sometimes I feel . . . manipulated . . . programmed. Like a robot."

"I don't understand."

"Neither do I," he said wearily. "Forget it. I'm just edgy. Let's enjoy the scenery."

At Chur they changed trains to follow the fertile Rhine Valley downstream. In summer the land would be green with vineyards, wheat fields, and orchards, but now it lay dormant under a blanket of snow. The train chugged into the towering Rhaetian Alps, passed through the dramatic Landquart Gorge, and followed a new river upstream. After a long, winding, but for the most part gentle ascent, past a handful of resort villages, they came to Klosters, which was nearly as famous as Saint Moritz.

They debarked at Klosters and left their luggage at the station while they outfitted themselves in ski clothes. During the trip from Zurich, they had realized that nothing they'd packed was adequate for high-altitude December weather. Besides, dressed in the usual winter clothes of city dwellers, they were conspicuous, which was precisely what they did not want to be. They changed in the dressing rooms at the ski shop and threw away the clothes they had been wearing, which amazed the clerk.

After lunch they boarded a train to Davos. It was crowded with a large party of French skiers bound for Saint Moritz. The French were happy, noisy, drinking wine from bottles that were concealed in plain paper sacks.

A fine snow began to fall. The wind was but a breeze.

The Rhaetian Railway crossed the Landquart River high on a terrifyingly lofty bridge, climbed through magnificent pine forests, and chugged past a ski center called Wolfgang. Eventually the tracks dropped down again to Davosersee and the town of Davos, which was composed of Davos-Dorf and Davos-Platz.

Snow fell fast and hard now. The wind had gained power.

From the train window, Alex could see that the storm concealed the upper regions of Weissfluh, the mountain that most dominated the town. Up there in the mists, behind a heavy drape of falling snow, skiers began the descent along the Parsenn run, from Weissfluhjoch—at the 9,000-foot level—down to the town at 5,500 feet.

In spite of the charming village beyond the train window, a sense of absolute isolation was unavoidable. That was one of the qualities that had attracted people to this place for more than a century. Sir Arthur Conan Doyle often had come to escape London and perhaps to think about Sherlock Holmes. In 1881, Robert Louis Stevenson had sought the solitude and the healthful air of Davos in which to finish his masterpiece, *Treasure Island.*

"The top of the world," Alex said.

"I get the strange feeling that the rest of the earth was destroyed," Joanna said, "all of it gone in a nuclear war or some other great cataclysm. This might be all that's left. It's so separate . . . so remote."

And if we disappeared in this vastness, Alex thought uneasily, *no one would ever find us.*

From Davos the train went to Susch and Scuol. The French were singing reasonably well, and no one complained. In early darkness, the train moved up the Engadine Valley, past the lake, and into Saint Moritz.

They were in the middle of a blizzard. The wind was coming off the mountains at thirty—gusting to fifty—kilometers an hour. The preternaturally dense snowfall reduced visibility to a single block.

At the hotel when Alex and Joanna checked in, they were required to present their passports and, therefore, used their real names; but he asked that the Maurice Demuth nom de guerre be the only name kept in the registration file. In a town that was accustomed to playing host to privacy-conscious movie stars, dukes, duchesses, counts, countesses, and wealthy industrialists from all corners of the world, such a request was not unusual, and it was honored.

They had a small but comfortable suite on the fifth floor. When the bellmen left, Alex tested the two locks and double-bolted the door. He went into the bedroom to help Joanna with the unpacking.

"I'm exhausted," she said.

"Me too." He took the pistol out of the waistband of his slacks and put it on the nightstand.

"I'm too tired to stand up," she said, "but still . . . I'm afraid to sleep."

"We'll be safe tonight."

"Do you still have that feeling? That somehow we're being manipulated?"

"Maybe I was just wired too tight," he said.

"What will we do tomorrow?"

"Scout around. Find out where Rotenhausen lives, if we can."

"And then?"

Alex heard a noise behind them. He turned and saw a tall, husky man standing in the open doorway between the bedroom and the living room.

So soon! Alex thought.

Joanna saw the intruder and cried out.

The intruder was holding an odd-looking gun and wearing a gas mask.

Alex lunged for the pistol that he had left on the nightstand.

The man in the mask fired the gas-pellet gun. Soft, waxy bullets struck Alex and disintegrated on impact, expelling clouds of sweet fumes.

He picked up the 9mm pistol, but before he could use it, the world dissolved in whirling white clouds, as though the blizzard beyond the windows had swept inside.

60

In the front room of the suite, Ignacio Carrera and Antonio Paz loaded the luggage into the bottoms of two large hotel laundry carts. Then they placed Alex Hunter and Joanna Rand into the carts, on top of the suitcases.

To Carrera, the woman was even more beautiful than she appeared in photographs. If the gas could have been counted upon to keep her unconscious more than just another half hour, he would have undressed her and raped her here, now. Helplessly asleep, she would be warm and exquisitely pliant. But he didn't have time for fun just yet.

Carrera had brought two pieces of Hermes leather luggage with him. They belonged to the fat man. He put them in the bedroom.

Tomorrow, the day clerk would secretly alter the registration card. It would appear that Anson Peterson had checked in on Sunday. There would be no record of Hunter and the woman: They would simply have ceased to exist.

Paz covered the unconscious couple with towels and rumpled bed linens.

They wheeled the carts to the service elevator and rode down to ground level without encountering anyone.

61

✣ ✣ ✣

When Alex regained consciousness, he wished he hadn't. He tasted bile. His vision was blurry and tinted red, as if his eyes were full of blood. A demon donkey was inside his head, kicking to get out.

At least he was alive. Which was inexplicable. They had no use for him— only for Joanna—and should have wasted him by now.

He was lying on his left side on a white-and-black tile floor. A kitchen. A light glowed above the stove.

His back was against a row of cabinets, and his hands were tied behind him. Good, heavy cord. His feet were also bound together.

Joanna wasn't with him. He called her name softly but received no reply.

He despised himself for letting them take her so easily. In his own defense, he could only argue that no one could have expected such a bold assault in a busy hotel and only minutes after their arrival.

He listened for movement or voices in another room. Nothing. Silence.

Knowing that the restraints wouldn't break or come loose easily, nevertheless hoping for a bit of luck, he tried to jerk his wrists apart. Incredibly, impossibly, the rope snapped on the third try.

Stunned, he lay motionless, listening and wondering.

Deep silence.

Fear sharpened his senses, and he was able to smell items that were shut away in the cupboards: cloves of garlic, soap, a pungent cheese.

Finally he brought his hands out from behind his back. The broken rope was loosely draped around his wrists. He pulled it off.

He scooted around on the shiny tile floor until he was sitting with his back to the cabinets. He untied the rope at his ankles, threw it aside, and got to his feet.

His skull seemed to be cracking under the punishing hooves of that indefatigable donkey. His vision dimmed-brightened-dimmed in a dependable rhythm, but gradually the red tint was fading.

He picked up the length of rope that had been around his hands and took it to the stove. Examining it under the small fluorescent light, he saw why he'd been able to snap it with so little effort: While he'd been unconscious, someone had cut most of the way through the line, leaving only a fraction of the diameter intact.

Manipulated. Programmed.

He had the uncanny conviction that everything that was going to happen during the next few hours had been planned a long time ago.

But by whom? And why?

He wondered if he and Joanna would be the winners or the losers of the game.

62

Joanna woke with a vile taste, swimming vision, and a fierce headache. When she began to be able to see, she discovered that she was in a hospital bed in a white room with a high window: the familiar setting of her nightmare. An electroencephalograph, an electrocardiograph, and other machines stood nearby, but she wasn't connected to them. The air reeked of a mélange of disinfectants.

Initially she thought that she was dreaming, but the full horror of her situation quickly became apparent. Her hammering heart pounded a cold sweat out of her.

Broad leather straps with Velcro fasteners restrained her wrists and ankles. She wrenched at them, but she was well secured.

"Ah," a woman said behind Joanna, "the patient's awake at last."

She had thought that the head of the bed was against the wall and that she was alone, but she was in the center of the room. She twisted her neck, trying to see the person who had spoken, but the straps and the inclined mattress foiled her.

After a taunting moment, a woman in a white smock walked around to the side of the bed where she could be seen. Brown hair. Brown eyes. Sharp features. Unsmiling. Rotenhausen's assistant. Joanna remembered the pinched face and hard eyes from one of the regression-therapy sessions in Omi Inamura's office.

"Where's Alex?" Joanna asked.

Without answering, the woman picked up a sphygmomanometer from a tray of medical instruments and wrapped the pressure pad around Joanna's arm.

She tried to struggle, but the straps rendered her helpless. "Where's Alex?" she repeated.

The physician took her blood pressure. "Excellent." She unwound the pad and put it aside.

"Unbuckle these straps," Joanna demanded, trying to quell her terror by focusing on her rage.

"It's over," the woman said, tying a rubber tube around Joanna's arm, forcing a vein to bulge. She swabbed the skin with alcohol.

"I'll fight you," Joanna promised.

"If it makes you happy."

The woman had an accent, as Joanna had recalled in regression therapy. It wasn't German or Scandinavian. A Slavic accent of some kind. Russian? The senator had said something about Russians when he'd telephoned Alex in London.

The woman tore open a plastic packet that contained a hypodermic syringe.

Joanna's heart was already slamming. The sight of the syringe made it throb painfully harder than before.

The physician thrust the needle through the sterile seal on the end of a small bottle that contained a colorless drug. She drew some of the fluid into the syringe.

When the woman took hold of her arm, Joanna twisted and jerked in the restraining straps just enough to make the vein a difficult target. "No. No way. Get away from me."

The doctor backhanded her across the face, and in the instant that Joanna needed to recover from the shock and pain, the needle slipped into her.

With tears running down her face, she said, "Bitch."

"You'll feel better in a minute."

"You rotten, stinking bitch," Joanna said bitterly.

"I'll give you a name to hate," the physician said with a small smile. "Ursula Zaitsev."

"That's you? I'll remember. I'll remember your name, and I'll destroy you."

Ursula Zaitsev's economical smile grew broader by a millimeter or two. "No, you're quite wrong. You won't remember it—or anything else."

63

Alex slowly pushed open the swinging door from the kitchen. The dimly lighted hallway was deserted, and he eased into it.

Five other doors opened off the corridor before it reached the head of the stairs. Three were closed. Past the two open doors were dark rooms.

He stepped to the closed door across the hall, hesitated, opened it, and peered into a bedroom with exquisite contemporary furnishings in lacewood and bird's-eye maple, which somehow didn't seem at odds with the considerable age of the house. The lamp on the nightstand cast warm light on a deeply sculpted, predominantly green carpet. He checked the adjacent master bath but found no one.

Beside the bed were half a dozen books. Five dealt with new discoveries in the behavioral sciences. The sixth was a heavily illustrated, privately printed collection of pornography: The subject was sadism; the beautiful, vulnerable-looking women in the pictures appeared to be suffering in earnest. The blood appeared to be real. It turned Alex's stomach.

In one of the bureau drawers were two pairs of fine leather gloves. No. Not pairs. When he looked closer, he saw that the four gloves were all for the same hand.

Unquestionably, this was Franz Rotenhausen's house.

In the corridor again, Alex went to one of the open doors. He found the light switch, flipped it on, and immediately snapped it off again when he saw that it was a deserted dining room.

The second open door led to a living room with more low modern furniture and what might have been two Picasso originals. The big casement windows framed a dramatic view of Saint Moritz at night, aswirl with snow, revealing that the house was slightly above the town and at the edge of the forest.

The fourth door led to a large guest bedroom with its own bath. It had not been used in a long time and had an unpleasant musty odor.

The house remained unnaturally quiet. The walls were so thick and the bronze windows so well made that even the howling of the storm wind was a distant threnody.

Alex was impressed with the size of the building. Evidently, Rotenhausen lived in this sprawling top-floor apartment, which left an enormous amount of space below for unknown purposes.

The final door opened on a library furnished in a traditional style more in keeping with the house itself: mahogany paneling and bookshelves, a magnificent antique desk with an intricate marquetry top, a few wing-backed chairs upholstered in well-aged red leather. A Tiffany desk lamp with twelve trumpet-flower shades cast a light so golden that it seemed palpable.

Alex stopped just over the threshold, overwhelmed by déjà vu, frightened almost to the point of immobility. Although he had never been in the house on any prior occasion, he had seen this library before. Even the smaller objects were eerily familiar: a carousel-style pipe rack on the desk, a huge globe softly lighted from within, a sterling-silver magnifying glass with a long ornate handle, a two-bottle brandy chest . . .

He had broken his paralysis and walked around behind the desk before he even realized that he was moving—as if half in a trance.

He opened a desk drawer and then another. In the second drawer he found the 9mm pistol that he had taken off the man in the alleyway in Kyoto several days ago.

The instant he saw the pistol, he realized that he had known it would be there.

After she administered the injection, Ursula Zaitsev left Joanna alone in the white-walled room.

The winter storm huffed at the high window that Joanna had recalled in one of her regression-therapy sessions with Dr. Inamura, but it also whined and whispered at another window behind her, which she could not see.

She strained against the straps once more, but she was so well secured that any attempt to pull free was useless. She finally fell back against the mattress, gasping for breath.

A minute passed. Two. Three. Five.

Joanna expected the drug to take hold of her, because Ursula Zaitsev had implied that it was a sedative or a depressant. She ought to be getting drowsy—but, instead, she was thinking faster and more clearly by the minute.

She figured she was on an adrenaline rush. It would fade in a minute or two, and the drug would begin to affect her.

But she was still clearheaded when Rotenhausen entered the room. He closed the door after himself. Locked it.

Sitting at the library desk, Alex thoroughly examined the gun. He was suspicious. They could have disabled the weapon.

The pistol appeared to be in perfect working order. Unless the ammunition had been replaced with blanks.

He assumed that he was being set up somehow. Suckered into a trap. But the nature of that trap seemed more incomprehensible the longer that he tried to puzzle out what it might be.

Though he was reluctant to be manipulated any further, he could not simply sit there all night. He had to find Joanna and get her out of the house.

He rose from the desk chair, pointed the silencer-equipped pistol at a row of books on the far side of the room, and squeezed the trigger.

Whump!

One of the books jumped on the shelf, and the spine cracked with a sound louder than the noise made by the gun itself.

The pistol wasn't loaded with blanks.

He left the library and went to the head of the stairs.

66
✪ ✪ ✪

The Hand.

He looked much the same as he had in her nightmares: tall and thin, clothes hanging loosely on him, balder than he had been twelve years ago but still without gray in his hair. His eyes were pale brown, almost yellow, and in them shone a controlled madness as cold as Arctic sun flickering on strange configurations of ice. The shiny, chitinous, gear-jointed fingers of his steel hand reminded her of the grasping legs of certain carnivorous insects.

Mariko had assured her that she'd find this man less frightening in reality than he was in her nightmares, but the opposite was true: She was weak with terror.

As he approached the bed, he said, "Sleepy, little lady?"

Though it was clear that he expected her to be in a stupor or on the edge of one, her mind wasn't in the least clouded. She wondered if Zaitsev had made a mistake and given her the wrong drug.

"Hmmm?" he said. "Sleepy?"

Fate—or someone in its employ—had given her a last, desperate chance, though it was as thin as an atheist's hope.

"Let me go," she said, slurring her voice as though sinking under the influence of the medication. Through her half-closed eyes, she thought that he was suddenly suspicious, and she said, "Wake up. Gotta . . . wake up."

"You think you're already asleep?" he asked, amusement replacing any suspicion that he might have had. "You think getting rid of me will be as easy as waking up? Not this time."

She closed her eyes and didn't answer him at once, pretending to slip away for a moment. Then she opened her eyes but squinted as if having difficulty focusing on him. "I . . . hate you . . . hate . . . you," she said with no edge of true anger, but in a dreamy voice, as though the drug had disconnected her mind from her emotions.

"Good," he said. "I like it when there's hatred."

The steel fingers clicked as he reached for her.

67
✪ ✪ ✪

The house was solidly built. Not one step creaked.

Alex paused at the second-floor landing. The deserted hallway was hung with shadows, illumined only by a weak amber mist of light that drifted into it from the stairwell. The air was redolent of disinfectants and medicinal odors, indicating that Joanna might have been imprisoned twelve years ago in one of these second-floor rooms.

He was about to investigate the first of the closed doors when he heard voices. He crouched, prepared to run or open fire, but then he realized that he was hearing a conversation in progress downstairs and that no one was approaching. Deciding to explore the second floor later, he descended toward the ground floor.

In the dimly lighted lower hallway, he edged close to a door from behind which the voices arose. It was ajar an inch, and as he reached it, he heard someone say Joanna's name and then his.

He risked looking through the crack between the door and the jamb. Beyond was a conference room. Three men sat at a large oval table that could have accommodated a dozen, and a fourth man stood at the tall windows with his back to the others.

The nearest man was extremely obese. He was opening the end of a roll of Life Savers.

Anson Peterson.

Alex heard the name as if someone had whispered it to him, but he was still alone in the hall. He had never seen the fat man before, yet he knew his name. He was intrigued and still frightened by the sense of being caught up in events as preordained as the course of a bobsled in a luge chute, but he was not surprised. He didn't think anything could surprise him after he'd found his gun in the library desk where he'd somehow known that it would be.

The next man at the table was unusually large but not obese. Even sitting down he appeared to be tall. Bull neck. Massive shoulders. His face was broad and flat beneath a low brow.

Again, an inner voice spoke the name: *Antonio Paz.*

The third man at the table had coarse black hair, a prominent nose, and deeply set dark eyes. He was shorter than Paz but even more powerfully built.

Ignacio Carrera.

The fourth man turned away from the windows and the cascading snow beyond them.

Alex was capable of surprise after all. The fourth man was Senator Thomas Chelgrin.

68

✥ ✥ ✥

With his mechanical hand, Rotenhausen grasped the sheet, pulled it off Joanna, and tossed it to the floor.

She was wearing only a thin hospital gown tied in back, but she was so cold inside that the cool air didn't chill her.

Faking the effects of the drug as she imagined they would have been, she let her eyes swim out of focus and murmured wordlessly to herself.

"Pretty," he said, looming.

She required all the courage that she could summon to continue to feign a drugged indifference.

The steel fingers gripped the neckline of her gown and tore the garment from her.

She almost gasped, but kept a grip on herself because she knew that he was watching her closely.

The steel hand touched her breasts.

69

✿ ✿ ✿

Peterson popped a butter-rum Life Saver into his mouth, savored it, and then said to Carrera, "So it's decided. You'll kill Hunter tonight, strip him, and dump his body into the lake, under the ice."

"I'll cut off the tips of his fingers so the police won't be able to print the body, smash out his teeth to prevent dental-record identification."

"Isn't that excessive? By the time the lake thaws and they find him next summer, perhaps even the summer *after* next—if they ever *do* find him—the fish will have left nothing but bare bones."

"Can't be too careful," Carrera disagreed. "I'll also disfigure his face so he can't be identified from a photograph."

And you'll enjoy every minute of it, Peterson thought.

Chelgrin hadn't said much during the past half hour, but now he walked to the table and faced Peterson. "You told me I'd be allowed to see my daughter as soon as they brought her here."

"Yes, Tom. But Rotenhausen must examine her first."

"Why?"

"I don't know. But he felt it was necessary, and he's the boss in this place."

"Not when you're around," Chelgrin said sourly. "Wherever you are, you're the boss. It's in your genes. You'll be in charge of Hell an hour after you get there."

"How very kind of you to say so," Peterson replied.

"Damn it, I want to see Lisa. I want—"

Carrera interrupted: "And there you have another problem. The girl. What do we do about the girl if she comes through the second treatment with a lot of mental damage?"

"That won't happen," Chelgrin said firmly, as though he could determine her fate by fiat.

"Fifty-fifty chance," Carrera said.

Refusing to confront that dreadful possibility, Chelgrin turned from Carrera, started toward the hallway door, but then halted and backed up a step. "Someone's there, listening."

70

The instant that he knew he had been seen, Alex pushed the door all the way open and stepped into the room, thrusting the pistol in front of him.

"Ah, hello," said the fat man with curious aplomb. "How're you feeling?"

Ignoring him, Alex stared at Chelgrin. "You're dead."

The senator didn't respond.

Sickened and infuriated by a profound and growing sense of violation, by having been so totally manipulated, Alex said, *"Why aren't you dead?"*

"Faked," Chelgrin said, nervously focusing on the muzzle of the gun. "We just wanted you to find the clipping about Rotenhausen."

"And the unfinished letter to Lisa—?"

"Nice touch, wasn't it?" Peterson asked.

Confused, Alex said, "Now that I think about it . . . at the time, I should've checked you for a pulse. Why didn't I check you?"

"The bullet wounds, the rabbit blood," Chelgrin said, "the hair over my eyes so you wouldn't notice any involuntary eye-muscle spasms—it was all very convincing. And I wore only the robe and left my wallet on the dresser so you wouldn't have any reason to search me."

Alex glanced at each of the men, then at Chelgrin again. "No. Doesn't wash. I made Joanna stay away from you too. As if I'd been programmed to keep us at a distance from you. Programmed not to shatter the illusion. Isn't that right?"

Chelgrin blinked. "Programmed?"

"Don't lie to me," Alex said, raising the gun a few inches until the muzzle was lined up with the senator's heart.

Chelgrin seemed genuinely baffled. "What're you talking about?"

Turning to the fat man, Alex said, "It's true, isn't it? I've been running around like a damn robot, programmed like a machine."

Peterson smiled. He knew the truth, even if Chelgrin didn't.

Alex thrust the pistol at him. "Last spring, when I went to Rio for a vacation—what in the name of God happened to me there?"

Before Peterson could answer, Antonio Paz reached under his jacket for a gun. Alex caught the movement from the corner of his eye, swung away from Peterson, and fired twice. Both shots ripped into Paz's face. Like perfume from an atomizer, a mist of blood puffed into the air. Paz and his chair crashed over backward.

Even as Paz went down, Carrera sprang to his feet.

That mysterious inner voice whispered to Alex again, *Kill him.* Before he could think about what he was doing, he obeyed, squeezing the trigger twice more.

One of the rounds hit Carrera, and he fell.

Shocked, wide-eyed, terrified, the senator backed away. He held his hands out in front of him, palms toward Alex, fingers spread, as if he thought he might be able to ward off the bullets meant for him.

Kill him.

Alex heard the interior voice again, icy and insistent, but he hesitated. Bewildered. Shaking.

He tried to think through to another, less violent solution: Paz and Carrera had been dangerous men, but they were dead, no longer any threat, and the senator wasn't a threat either, just a broken man, a pitiful specimen, begging for his life, so there was no need to waste him, no justification for it.

Kill him, kill him, kill him, killhim, killhim.

Alex couldn't resist that inner voice, and again he squeezed the trigger twice.

Hit once in the chest, Chelgrin fell backward into the window. His head struck the glass, and one of the thick panes cracked. He dropped to the floor and was as still as stone.

"Oh, God," Alex said, and stared at the hand in which he held the gun, as if he couldn't quite believe that it was his own hand. He was out of control, acting before thinking. "What am I doing? *What am I doing?*"

The fat man was still in his chair on the far side of the table. "The terrible angel of vengeance," he said with a smile. He appeared to be delighted.

Bloody but not mortally wounded after all, Carrera launched up from the floor, seized a chair, and threw it.

Alex fired, missed.

The chair struck him as he tried to dodge it. Pain speared through his right arm. The pistol flew out of his hand and across the room, clattered off the wall. He staggered backward, collided with the door, and Carrera charged him.

71

Gleaming, cold, humming, clicking, the steel hand caressed her. Squeezed her. Patted, stroked, pinched her. *Click, click, click.*

She was impressed by her own courage. She didn't flinch. She endured Rotenhausen's obscene explorations and pretended to be doped. She mumbled, murmured, sometimes feigned a dreamy pleasure at his touch, occasionally warned him off as if she had briefly surfaced from her delirium, but then drifted away again.

She'd just about decided that he was never going to stop petting her with that monstrous hand, when he finally reached across her and disengaged the strap on her right wrist. He freed her left hand as well, and then he moved to the foot of the bed to release her ankles. She was unbound.

He returned to the head of the bed.

She still did not make a break for freedom.

Taking off his white smock and draping it across the cart that held the syringes and other instruments, he said, "I remember you so well. I remember . . . how you felt." He took off his shirt.

Through half-closed eyes, Joanna studied the mechanical hand. A flexible steel-ring cable trailed up from the metal wrist and terminated in a pair of male jacks that were plugged into a battery pack. The pack was strapped to his biceps.

"This will be better even than before," he said. "With your father just downstairs."

Joanna seized the cable and tore the jacks out of the battery pack. The steel fingers froze. She rolled away from Rotenhausen. Naked, she dropped off the other side of the bed and ran for the door.

He caught her with his real hand as she touched the dead-bolt lock. Clenching a handful of her hair, he spun her around to face him, and his pale eyes were full of inhuman menace.

Screaming in pain and fear, she flailed at him, and her fists landed with satisfyingly hard, flat sounds.

Rotenhausen cursed her, dragged her from the door, and shoved her away.

She collided with the bed. Unbalanced, she grabbed the footrail to avoid falling.

Standing between her and the door, he plugged the jacks into the battery again. The hand purred. The steel fingers moved. *Click, click, click.*

72

Carrera came low and fast, like a human locomotive.

Without the pistol, Alex had no chance to get the best of the powerful bodybuilder. He had some knowledge of martial arts, but no doubt Carrera was even better trained.

He stumbled backward through the door, pulled it shut after him, and ran along the ground-floor hallway. The last room on the right was dark. He plunged across the threshold, slammed the door, fumbled frantically for a latch. He found a privacy-lock button in the center of the knob.

An instant later Carrera reached the other side, tried to get in, discovered that he had been locked out, and immediately threw himself against the door, determined to break it down.

Alex located the light switch. The overhead bulb revealed an empty storeroom that offered nothing he could use as a weapon.

He was loath to leave the house with Joanna held somewhere in it, but he would be no good to her if he got himself killed.

As Carrera battered the door, Alex crossed to the storeroom window and put up the blind. A fierce gust of wind fired a barrage of fine white granules against the glass.

Carrera hit the door again, again, and wood splintered.

With trembling hands, Alex unlatched the casement window and pushed the halves outward. Arctic wind exploded into the room.

Carrera rammed into the door. In the lock, tortured metal shrieked against metal.

Even wounded, the man was a bull.

Alex clambered over the window ledge and stepped into a foot of fresh snow. Wind howled along the valley wall, clocking at least seventy or eighty kilometers an hour; it bit his face, wrung tears from his eyes, and flash-numbed his hands. He was thankful for the insulated ski clothes that they had bought in Klosters.

In the room that he'd just left, the door went down with a thunderous boom.

Alex hurried away into the bitter darkness, kicking up clouds of snow as he went.

73

✪ ✪ ✪

By the time Peterson reached the storeroom, Carrera was climbing through the window in pursuit of Hunter. Peterson started after him, but then he changed his mind and crossed the hall to Ursula Zaitsev's private quarters.

She refused to answer when he knocked.

"Ursula, it's me. Anson. Hurry."

The door cracked open on a security chain, and she peered at him fearfully. "What's all the noise? What's gone wrong?"

"Everything. We have to get out of here now, right away, before the police arrive."

"Go?" She was a strange, self-involved woman even in the best of times, but in her bewilderment she had the wild-eyed look of an asylum inmate. "Go where?"

"Damn it, Ursula, *hurry!* Do you want to go home—or spend the rest of your life in a Swiss jail?"

She had left Russia twenty years ago and had been Rotenhausen's assistant—and watchdog—for fifteen, from the day that his funding had been provided exclusively by Moscow. Since she'd been away from home, the old order had fallen, and judging by her expression, the home to which she would be going was one that she either found unappealing or could not quite comprehend.

"*Ursula,*" Peterson hissed with red-faced urgency. "The police—do you hear me?—the *police!*"

In a panic, she undid the security chain and opened her door.

Peterson drew the silencer-equipped pistol from the shoulder holster under his jacket, and he shot her three times.

For such a severe-looking, even mannish woman, Ursula died gracefully, almost prettily. The bullets spun her around as if she were twirling to show a new skirt to a boyfriend. There wasn't much mess, perhaps because she was too thin and dry to contain any substantial quantity of blood. She sagged against the wall, gazed at Peterson without seeing him, allowed a delicate thread of blood to escape one corner of her mouth, let go of her icy expression for the first time since he had known her, and slid down into death.

Four of the six people on Anson Peterson's hit list had been eliminated. Marlowe. Paz. Chelgrin. Ursula Zaitsev. Only two others awaited disposal.

He sprinted across the hall and into the storeroom with that peculiar grace that certain very fat men could summon on occasion. He climbed through the open casement window and groaned when the bitter night air slapped his face. The only thing he disliked more than exertion and an unsatisfied appetite was physical discomfort.

He was having a very bad evening.

The wind was busily scouring the footprints from the newly fallen snow, but he was still able to follow Hunter and Carrera.

74
❖ ❖ ❖

Shouting and a series of muffled noises arose in a distant part of the house. At first, Joanna hoped it was Alex coming for her—or someone from outside coming for both of them. But Rotenhausen ignored the uproar, either because he was so focused on her that he didn't hear it or because there were other people to deal with whatever was happening; and when quiet quickly returned, she knew that she was finished.

He backed her into a corner, pinned her there with his body, spread his steel fingers, and gripped her throat. He placed his real hand over the battery pack to prevent her from pulling out the jacks.

She couldn't look away from his extraordinary eyes: They now seemed as yellow as those of a cat.

He cocked his head and watched her quizzically while he squeezed her throat, as though he were observing a laboratory animal through the walls of its cage. His expression was not bland; on the contrary, in his face was a cold passion that defied description and, most likely, understanding.

When she began to choke, and when she saw that her choking only elicited a smile from him, she struggled fiercely to break free—twisted, thrashed, kicked ineffectually with her bare feet. She was too tightly pinned to be able to go for his eyes, but she clawed at his arms and flanks, drawing blood.

Until now, she'd held fast to the hope of being saved from both Rotenhausen and his treatments, but his unexpected reaction to her counterattack stole all hope from her. He flinched and hissed each time that she drew his blood—but each pain that she inflicted seemed only to arouse him further. Crushing her against the wall, he said excitedly, "That's it, yes, fight for your life, girl, fight me, yes, fight me with everything you've got," and she knew then that each wound she inflicted would have no effect other than to give him even greater pleasure later, when he subjected her to various tortures on the bed.

The steel hand tightened inexorably around her throat, and black spots glided like dozens of ink-dark moths across her vision.

✪ ✪ ✪

75

Great surging rivers of snow poured out of the Swiss mountains, and Alex seemed to be carried through the deep night by the powerful currents of the storm almost as he would have been swept away by a real river. With the buoying wind at his back, he crossed a hundred yards of open land before he reached the shelter of the forest. The mammoth pines grew close together, providing relief from the wind, but a considerable amount of snow still found its way through the evergreen canopy.

He was on a narrow but well-established trail that might have been made by deer. The heavy white crusts that bent the pine boughs and the white winter mantle on the forest floor provided what meager light there was: He navigated the woods by the eerie phosphorescence of the snow, able to distinguish shapes but no details, afraid of catching a tree branch in the face and blinding himself.

He stumbled over rocks hidden by the snow, hit the ground hard, but scrambled up at once. He was certain that Carrera was close behind.

As he came to his feet, he realized that he had one of the loose rocks in his hand. A weapon. It was the size of an orange, not as good as a gun but better than nothing. It felt like a ball of ice, and he was concerned that he wouldn't be able to keep a grip on it as his fingers rapidly continued to stiffen.

He hurried deeper into the woods, and thirty feet from the spot where he had fallen, the trail bent sharply to the right and curved around an especially dense stand of shoulder-high brush. He skidded to a halt and quickly considered the potential for an ambush.

Squinting at the trail, he could barely discern the disturbance that his own feet had made in the smooth skin of softly radiant white powder. He weighed the rock in his hand, backed against the wall of brush until it poked him painfully, and hunched down, becoming a shadow among shadows.

Overhead, wind raged through the pine and fir boughs, howling as incessantly as the devil's own pack of hell hounds, but even above that shrieking, Alex immediately heard Carrera approaching. Fearless of his quarry, the bodybuilder made no effort to be quiet, crashing along the trail as though he were a drunk in transit between two taverns.

Alex tensed, keeping his eyes on the bend in the trail just four feet away. The subzero air had so numbed his hand that he couldn't feel the rock any more. He squeezed hard, hoping that the weapon was still in his grip, but for all he knew, he might have dropped it and might be curling his half-frozen fingers around empty air.

Carrera appeared, moving fast, bent forward, intent on the vague footprints that he was following.

Alex swung his arm high and brought the rock down with all his strength, and it caught Carrera in the face. The big man dropped to his knees as if he'd been hit by a sledgehammer, toppled forward, and knocked Alex off his feet. They rolled along the sloping trail, through the snow, and came to a stop side by side, facedown.

Gasping air so bitterly cold that it made his lungs ache, Alex pushed onto his knees and then to his feet again.

Carrera remained on the ground: a dark, huddled, vaguely human shape in the bed of snow.

In spite of his still desperate circumstances and even though Joanna remained captive in the house, Alex felt a thrill of triumph, the dark animal exhilaration of having gone up against a predator and beaten him.

He looked up the trail, back through the woods, but he'd come too far to be able to see the house any more. Considering Carrera's size and ferocity, the other men wouldn't give Alex much chance of getting out of the woods alive, so his quick return would take them by surprise and might give him just the advantage he needed.

He started to go back for Joanna, but Carrera grabbed his ankle.

76

Joanna rammed her knee into Rotenhausen's crotch. He sensed it coming and deflected most of the impact with his thigh. The blow made him cry out in pain, however, and he bent forward reflexively, protectively.

His mechanical hand slid down her throat as his cold, clicking fingers loosened their grip on her.

She slipped out of his grasp, from between him and the wall, but he was after her at once. His pain forced him to hobble like a troll, but he wasn't disabled nearly enough to let her get away.

Unable to reach the door in time to throw the lock and get out, she put the wheeled cart between them instead. In addition to an array of syringes, a bottle of glucose for the IV tree, a packet of tongue depressors, a penlight, a device for examining eyes, and many small bottles of various drugs, the instrument tray on the cart held a pair of surgical scissors. Joanna snatched them up and brandished them at Rotenhausen.

He glared at her, red-faced and furious.

"I won't let you do it to me again," she said. "I won't let you tamper with my mind. You'll either have to let me go or kill me."

With his mechanical hand, he reached across the cart, seized the scissors, wrenched them away from her, and squeezed them in his steel fingers until the blades snapped.

"I could do the same to you," he said.

He threw the broken scissors aside.

Joanna's heartbeat exploded, and the governor on the engine of time seemed to burn out. Suddenly everything happened very fast:

She plucked the glucose from the tray, thankful it wasn't in one of the plastic bags so widely used these days, but the robotic hand arced down, smashing the bottle before she could throw it. Glass and glucose showered across the floor, leaving her with only the neck of the bottle in her grip.

He shoved the cart out of the way, toppling it, scattering the instruments and the small bottles of drugs, and he rushed her, pale eyes bright with murderous intent. Desperately she turned. Scanning the floor. The litter. A weapon. Something. Anything. He grabbed her by the hair. She already *had* the weapon. In her hand. The bottle. The broken neck of the bottle. He yanked her around to face him. She thrust. Jagged glass. Deep into his throat. Blood spurting. Oh, God. Pale eyes wide. Yellow and wide. The robotic fingers released her hair, plucked at the glass in his throat—*click, click, click*—but only succeeded in bringing forth more blood. He gagged, slipped on the glucose-wet floor, fell to his knees, reached for her with his steel hand, working the fingers uselessly in the air, fell onto his side, twitched, kicked, made a terrible raspy effort to breathe, spasmed as if an electrical current had crackled through him, spasmed again, and was still.

77

✤ ✤ ✤

Alex fell, jerked free of Carrera, rolled back down the trail, and sprang to his feet, acutely aware that he was not likely to get up again if he gave the big man a chance to get atop him.

The bodybuilder was badly enough hurt that he wasn't able to reach his feet as quickly as Alex. He was still on all fours in the middle of the path, shaking his head as if to clear his mind.

Seizing the advantage, Alex rushed forward and kicked Carrera squarely under the chin.

The thug's head snapped back, and he fell onto his side.

Alex was sure the kick had broken his adversary's neck, crushed his windpipe, but Carrera struggled onto his hands and knees again.

The bastard doesn't quit.

Alex took another kick at Carrera's head.

The bodybuilder saw it coming, grabbed Alex's boot, toppled him, and clambered atop him, growling like a bear. He swung one huge fist.

Alex wasn't able to duck it. The punch landed in his face, split his lips, loosened some teeth, and filled his mouth with blood.

He was no match for Carrera in hand-to-hand combat. He had to regain his feet and be able to maneuver.

As Carrera threw another punch, Alex thrashed and bucked. The fist missed him, drove into the trail beside his head, and Carrera howled in pain.

Heaving harder than before, Alex threw Carrera off, crawled up the slope, clutched a tree for support, and pulled himself erect.

Carrera was also struggling to his feet.

Alex kicked him squarely in the stomach, which gave no more than a board fence.

Carrera skidded in the snow, windmilled his arms, and went down on his hands and knees again.

Cursing, Alex kicked him in the face.

Carrera sprawled on his back in the snow, arms extended like wings. He didn't move. Didn't move. Still didn't move. Didn't move.

Cautiously, as though he were Dr. Von Helsing approaching a coffin in which Dracula slept, Alex crept up on Carrera. He knelt at the bodybuilder's side. Even in that dim and eerily phosphorescent light, he could see that the man's eyes were open wide but blind to any sight in this world. He didn't need to fetch a wooden stake or a crucifix or a necklace of garlic, because this time the monster was definitely dead.

He got up, turned away from Carrera, and ascended the trail, heading back toward the house.

Anson Peterson was waiting for him in the open field just beyond the forest. The fat man was holding a gun.

78

Rotenhausen was dead.

Joanna felt no remorse for having killed him, but she didn't experience much in the way of triumph either. She was too worried about Alex to feel anything more than fear.

Stepping carefully to avoid the broken glass scattered across the floor, she found her ski clothes in a closet.

As she was hurriedly dressing, she heard the steel fingers—*click-click-click-click*—and she looked up in terror, frozen by the hateful sound. It must have been a reflex action, a postmortem nerve spasm sending a last meaningless instruction to the mechanical hand, because Rotenhausen was stone-cold dead.

Nevertheless, for a minute she stared at the hand. Her heart was knocking so loudly that she could hear nothing else, not even her own breathing or the wind beyond the windows. Gradually, as the hand made no new move, the fierce drumming in her chest subsided somewhat.

When she finished dressing, as she knelt on her left knee to lace up the boot on her right foot, she spotted the small bottle from which Ursula Zaitsev had filled the syringe. It was among the litter on the floor, but it had not broken.

She laced both boots, then picked up the bottle and pulled the seal from it. She shook a couple of drops of the drug onto the palm of her hand, sniffed, hesitated, then tasted it. She was pretty sure that it was nothing but water and that someone had switched bottles on Zaitsev.

But who? And why?

Puppets. They were all puppets—as Alex had said.

Cautiously she unlocked the door and peered into the hall. No one in sight. But for the background noise of the storm, muffled by the thick walls, the house was silent.

Room by room, she inspected the rest of that level but found no one. For almost a minute she stood on the second-floor landing, looking alternately up and down the steps, listening intently, and at last descended to the ground floor.

A corpse lay in the hallway. Even in the poor light and from a distance, Joanna could see that it was Ursula Zaitsev.

Several doors led off the hall. She didn't want to open any of them, but she would have to search the place if she had any hope of finding Alex.

The nearest door was ajar. She eased it open, hesitated, crossed the threshold—and her father stepped in front of her.

Tom Chelgrin was ashen. His hair was streaked with blood, and his face was spotted with it. His left hand was pressed over what must have been a bullet wound in his chest, for his shirt was soaked with blood as dark as burgundy. He swayed, almost fell, took one step toward her, and put his bloody hand on her shoulder.

79

✪ ✪ ✪

On the snow-swept slope, less than a hundred yards from the house, above the storm-dimmed lights of Saint Moritz, Alex and Peterson stared at each other for a long, uncertain moment.

Alex couldn't speak clearly or without pain, because his mouth was swollen and sore from the punch he'd taken, but he had questions and he wanted answers. "Why didn't I kill you when I killed Paz and Chelgrin?"

"You weren't supposed to," said the fat man. "Where's Carrera?"

"Dead."

"But you didn't have a gun," Peterson said incredulously.

"No gun," Alex agreed. He was weary. His eyes watered from the stinging cold. The fat man shimmered like a mirage in the night.

"It's hard to believe you could kill that mean bastard without a gun."

Alex spat blood onto the snow. "I didn't say it was easy."

Peterson let out a short bray of laughter.

"All right," Alex said, "all right, get it over with. I killed him, now you kill me."

"Oh, heavens, no! No, no," Peterson said. "You've got it all wrong, all backward, dear boy. You and I—we're on the same team."

80

✪ ✪ ✪

Chelgrin had been dead in London. Dead on a hotel-room floor. Now he was here in Switzerland, dying again.

The sight of the blood-smeared specter immobilized Joanna. She stood in shock, every muscle locked, while the senator clung to her shoulder.

"I'm weak," he said shakily. "Can't stand up any more. Don't let me . . . fall. Please. Help me . . . down easy. Let's go down easy."

Joanna put one hand on the doorjamb to brace herself. She dropped slowly to her knees, and the senator used her for support. At last he was sitting with his back against the wall, pressing his left hand against the chest wound, and she was kneeling at his side.

"Daughter," he said, gazing at her wonderingly. "My baby."

She couldn't accept him as her father. She thought of the long years of programmed loneliness, the attacks of claustrophobia when she'd dared to consider building a life with someone, the nightmares, the fear that might have been defeated if it could have been defined. She thought of how Rotenhausen had repeatedly raped her during her first stay in this place—and how he had tried to use her again this very night. Worse: If Alex was dead, Tom Chelgrin had directly or indirectly pulled the trigger. She had no room in her heart for this man. Maybe it was unfair of her to freeze him out before she knew his reasons for doing what he'd done; perhaps her inability to forgive her own father was itself unforgivable. Nevertheless, she felt no guilt whatsoever and knew that she never would. She despised him.

"My little girl," he said, but his voice seemed colored more by self-pitying sentimentality than by genuine love or remorse.

"No," she said, denying him.

"You are. You're my daughter."

"No."

"Lisa."

"Joanna. My name's Joanna Rand."

He wheezed and cleared his throat. His speech was slurred. "You hate me . . . don't you?"

"Yes."

"But you don't understand."

"I understand enough."

"No. No, you don't. You've got to listen to me."

"Nothing you have to say could make me want to be your daughter. Lisa Chelgrin is dead. Forever."

The senator closed his eyes. A fierce wave of pain swept through him. He grimaced and bent forward.

She made no move to comfort him.

When the attack passed, he sat up straight again and opened his eyes. "I've got to tell you about it. You've got to give me a chance to explain. You have to listen to me."

"I'm listening," she assured him, "but not because I have to."

His breath rattled in his throat. "Everyone thinks I was a war hero. They think I escaped from that Viet Cong prison camp and made my way back to friendly lines. I built my entire political career on that story, but it's all a lie. I didn't spend weeks in the jungle, inching my way out of enemy territory. I never escaped from a prison camp because . . . I was never in one to begin with. Tom Chelgrin was a prisoner of war, all right, but not me."

"Not you? But *you're* Tom Chelgrin," she said, wondering if his pain and the loss of blood had clouded his mind.

"No. My real name is Ilya Lyshenko. I'm a Russian."

Haltingly, pausing often to wheeze or to spit dark blood, he told her how Ilya Lyshenko had become the Honorable United States Senator from the great state of Illinois, the well-known and widely respected potential candidate for the presidency, Thomas Chelgrin. He was convincing—although Joanna supposed that every dying man's confession was convincing.

She listened, amazed and fascinated.

81
✜ ✜ ✜

At the height of the Vietnam War in the late 1960s, in every Viet Cong labor camp, commandants were looking for certain special American prisoners of war: soldiers who shared a list of physical characteristics with a dozen young Russian intelligence officers who had volunteered for a project code-named "Mirror." None of the Vietnamese assisting in the search knew the name of the project or what the Russians hoped to achieve with it, but they did not allow themselves to be in the least curious because they understood that curiosity killed more than cats.

When Tom Chelgrin was brought in chains to a camp outside Hanoi, the commandant saw at once that he somewhat resembled a member of the Russian Mirror group. Chelgrin and the Russian were the same height and build, had the same color hair and eyes. Their basic facial-bone structures were similar. Upon his arrival at the camp, Chelgrin was segregated from the other prisoners, and for the rest of his life he spent mornings and afternoons with interrogators, evenings and nights in solitary confinement. A Vietnamese photographer took more than two hundred shots of Chelgrin's entire body, but mostly of his face from every possible angle, in every light: close-ups, medium shots, long shots to show how he stood and how he held his shoulders. The undeveloped negatives were sent to Moscow by special courier, where KGB directors in charge of the Mirror group anxiously awaited them.

Military physicians in Moscow studied the photographs of Thomas Chelgrin for three days before reporting that he appeared to be a reasonably good match for Ilya Lyshenko, a Mirror volunteer. One week later, Ilya underwent the first of many surgeries to transform him into Chelgrin's double. His hairline was too low, so cosmetic surgeons destroyed some hair follicles and moved the line back three quarters of an inch. His eyelids drooped slightly, thanks to the genetic heritage of a Mongolian great-great-grandfather; they lifted the lids to make them look more Western. His nose was pared down, and a bump was removed from the bridge. His earlobes were too large, so they were reduced as well. His mouth was shaped quite like Tom Chelgrin's mouth, but his teeth required major dental work to match Chelgrin's. Lyshenko's chin was round, which was no good for this masquerade, so it was made square. Finally, the surgeons circumcised Lyshenko and pronounced him a fit doppelgänger.

While Lyshenko was enduring seven months of plastic surgery, Thomas Chelgrin was sweating out a seemingly endless series of brutal inquisitions at the camp outside Hanoi. He was in the hands of the Viet Cong's best interrogators—who were being assisted by two Soviet advisers. They employed drugs, threats, promises, hypnosis, beatings, and torture to learn everything they needed to know about him. They compiled an immense dossier: the foods he liked least; the foods he liked most; his favorite brands of beer, cigarettes; his public and private religious beliefs; the names of his friends, descriptions of them, and lists of their likes, dislikes, quirks, foibles, habits, virtues, weaknesses; his political convictions; his favorite sports, movies; his racial prejudices; his fears; his hopes; his sexual preferences and techniques; and thousands upon thousands of other things. They squeezed him as though he were an orange, and they didn't intend to leave one drop of juice in him.

Once a week, lengthy transcripts of the sessions with Chelgrin were flown to Moscow, where they were edited down to lists of data. Ilya Lyshenko studied them while convalescing between surgeries. He was required to commit to memory literally tens of thousands of bits of information, and it was the most difficult job that he had ever undertaken.

He was treated by two psychologists who specialized in memory research under the auspices of the KGB. They used both drugs and hypnosis to assist him in the retention of the information he needed to *become* Thomas Chelgrin, and while he slept, recordings of the lists played softly in his room, conveying the information directly to his subconscious.

After fourteen years of English studies, which had begun when he was eight years old, Lyshenko had learned to speak the language without a Russian accent. In fact, he had the clear but colorless diction of local television newsmen in the Middle Atlantic States. Now he listened to recordings of Chelgrin's voice and attempted to imprint a Midwest accent over the bland English that he already spoke. By the time the final surgeries had been performed, he sounded as though he had been born and raised on an Illinois farm.

When Lyshenko was halfway through his metamorphosis, the men in charge of Mirror began to worry about Tom Chelgrin's mother. They were confident that Lyshenko would be able to deceive Chelgrin's friends and acquaintances, even most of his relatives, but they were worried that anyone especially close to him—such as his mother, father, or wife—would notice changes in him or lapses of memory. Fortunately Chelgrin had never been married or even terribly serious about any one girl. He was handsome and popular, and he played the field. Equally fortunate: His father had died when Tom was a child. As far as the KGB was concerned, that left Tom's mother as the only serious threat to the success of the masquerade. That problem was easily remedied, for in those flush days when the Soviet economy had been largely militarized, the KGB had a long arm and deep pockets for operations on foreign soil. Orders were sent to an agent in New York, and ten days later, Tom's mother died in an automobile accident on her way home from a bridge party. The night was dark and the narrow road was icy; it was a tragedy that could have befallen anyone.

In late 1968, eight months after Tom Chelgrin had been captured, Ilya Lyshenko arrived by night at the labor camp outside Hanoi. He was in the company of Emil Gotrov, the KGB director who had conceived of the scheme, found funding for it, and overseen its implementation. He waited with Gotrov in the camp commandant's private quarters while Chelgrin was brought from his isolation cell.

When the American walked into the room and saw Lyshenko, he knew immediately that he was not destined to live. The fear in his haggard face and the despair in his eyes were, of course, a testimony to the work of the Soviet surgeons—but the doomed man's anguished expression had haunted Ilya Lyshenko across three decades.

"Mirror," Gotrov had said, astounded. "A mirror image."

That night the real Thomas Chelgrin was taken out of the prison camp, shot in the back of the head, tumbled into a deep grave, soaked with gasoline, burned, and then buried.

Within a week, the new Thomas Chelgrin "escaped" from the camp outside Hanoi and, against impossible odds and over the period of a few weeks, made his way back to friendly territory and eventually connected with his own division. He was sent home to Illinois, where he wrote a best-selling book about his amazing experiences—actually, it was ghost-written by a world-famous American writer who had long been sympathetic to the Soviet cause—and he became a war hero.

Tom Chelgrin's mother hadn't been a wealthy woman, but she had managed to pay premiums on a life insurance policy that named her son—and only child—as the sole beneficiary. That money came into his hands when he returned from the war. He used it and the earnings from his book to purchase a Honda dealership just before Americans fell in love with Japanese cars. The business flourished beyond his wildest expectations, and he put the profits into other investments that also did well.

His orders from the men behind Mirror had been simple. He was expected to become a business entrepreneur. He was expected to prosper, and if he could not turn a large buck on his own, KGB money would be funneled into his enterprises by various subtle means and an array of third parties. In his thirties, when his community knew him to be a respectable citizen and a successful businessman, he would run for a major public office, and the KGB would indirectly contribute substantial funds to his campaign.

He followed the plan—but with one important change. By the time he was prepared to seek elective office, he had become hugely wealthy on his own, without KGB help. And by the time he sought a seat in the United States House of Representatives, he was able to obtain all the legitimate financial backing he needed to complement his own money, and the KGB didn't have to open its purse.

In Moscow the highest hope was that he would become a member of the lower house of Congress and win reelection for three or four terms. During those eight or ten years, he would be able to pass along incredible quantities of vital military information.

He lost his first election by a narrow margin, primarily because he had never remarried after the loss of his first wife, who had died in childbirth. At that time, the American public had a prejudice against bachelors in politics. Two years later, when he tried again, he used his adorable young daughter, Lisa Jean, to win the hearts of voters. Thereafter, he swiftly rose from the lower house of Congress to the upper—until he developed into a prime presidential candidate.

His success had been a thousandfold greater than Moscow had ever hoped, and even after the collapse of the Soviet Union, the surviving Marxist element in the new government of Russia held a tight rein on Tom Chelgrin. He was more valuable than diamond mines. Where once he had labored to obtain and pass along highly sensitive military information, he now worked somewhat more openly to transfer billions of U.S. dollars in loans and foreign aid into the grasping hands of his masters, who had lost the Cold War but still prospered.

Eventually his success became the central problem of his life. Even while the Cold War had still been under way, Thomas Chelgrin—who had once been Ilya Lyshenko—had lost all faith in the principles of communism. As a United States Congressman and then as a Senator, with his soul secretly in hock to the KGB, he was called upon to betray the country that he had learned to love. By then he didn't want to pass along the information they sought, but he could find no way to refuse. The KGB owned him. He was trapped.

82

"But why was my past taken from me?" Joanna demanded. "Stolen from me. Why did you send me to Rotenhausen?"

"Had to." The senator bent forward, racked by a vicious twist of pain. His breath bubbled wetly, hideously in his throat. When he found the strength to sit up straight again, he said, "Jamaica. You and I were . . . going to spend a whole week down there . . . at the vacation house in Jamaica."

"You and Lisa," she corrected.

"I was going to fly down from Washington on a Thursday night. You were at school in New York. Columbia. A senior. Summer term. There was a project you had to finish. You couldn't . . . get away until Friday."

He closed his eyes and didn't speak for so long that she thought he had lost consciousness, even though his breathing was still ragged and labored. Finally he continued:

"You changed plans without telling me. You flew to Jamaica . . . on Thursday morning . . . got there hours ahead of me. When I arrived that evening, I thought the house was deserted . . . but you were in your bed upstairs . . . napping."

His voice grew fainter. He was striving mightily to stay alive long enough to explain himself in hope of gaining her absolution.

"I had arranged to meet some men . . . Soviet agents . . . in the last years of the Soviet Union, though none of us realized it then. I was handing over a suitcase of reports . . . important stuff related to the strategic defense initiative. You woke up . . . heard us downstairs . . . came down . . . overheard just enough to know I was a . . . a traitor. You barged into the middle of it . . . shocked and indignant . . . angry as hell. You tried to leave. You were so naive, thinking you could just leave. Of course they couldn't let you go. The KGB gave me a simple choice. Either you . . . had to be killed . . . or sent off to Rotenhausen . . . for the treatments."

His account of the events in Jamaica did not stir even the shadow of a memory in her, although she knew he must be telling the truth. "But why did Lisa's entire life have to be eradicated? Why couldn't Rotenhausen just remove all memories about what she . . . about what I overheard . . . and leave the rest untouched?"

Chelgrin spat blood again, more and darker than previously. "It's comparatively easy . . . for Rotenhausen to scour away . . . large blocks of memory. Far more difficult . . . to reach into a mind . . . and pinch off just a few . . . selected pieces. He refused to guarantee the results . . . unless he was permitted to erase all of Lisa . . . and create an entirely new person. You were put in Japan . . . because you knew the language . . . and because they felt it was unlikely . . . that anyone there would spot you and realize you were Lisa."

"Dear God," Joanna said shakily.

"I had no choice."

"You could have refused. You could have broken with them."

"They would've killed you."

"Would you have worked for them after they killed me?"

"No!"

"Then they would never have touched me," she said. "They wouldn't have had anything to gain."

"But I couldn't . . . couldn't go up against them," Chelgrin said weakly, miserably. "The only way I could've gotten free . . . was go to the FBI . . . expose myself. I'd have been jailed . . . treated like a spy. I would've lost everything . . . my businesses, investments, all the houses . . . the cars . . . everything . . . everything."

"Not everything," Joanna said.

He blinked at her, uncomprehending.

"You wouldn't have lost your daughter," she said.

"You're not . . . not even . . . trying to understand." He sighed as if in frustration, and the sigh ended in a wet rattle.

"I understand too well," she said. "You went from one extreme to the other. There wasn't room for humanity in either position."

He didn't reply.

He was dead. For real this time.

She stared at him, thinking about what might have been. Perhaps there never could have been anything between them. Perhaps the only Tom Chelgrin who could have been a decent father was the one who had never left Vietnam, the one whose charred bones were still buried in a deep, unmarked grave.

At last she got up from beside the dead senator and returned to the ground-floor hallway.

Alex was there, coming toward her. He called her name, and she ran to him.

83

As if the bodies littering the house were of little concern, Peterson insisted on a cognac. He led Alex and Joanna to the third floor, into the library where Alex had found the pistol. They sat in the red leather chairs while the fat man poured double measures of Rémy Martin from a crystal decanter. He sat in a chair opposite them, nearly overflowing it, and clasped the brandy snifter in both thick hands, warming the Rémy with his body heat.

"A little toast," Peterson said. He lifted his glass. "Here's to living."

Alex and Joanna didn't bother to raise their glasses. They just drank the cognac—fast. Alex hissed in pain as the Rémy stung his cut lips, but he still took a second swallow.

Peterson savored the Rémy and smiled contentedly.

"Who are you?" Joanna asked.

"I'm from Maryland, dear. I'm in real estate there."

"If you're trying to be funny—"

"It's true," said Peterson. "But of course I'm more than just a Realtor."

"Of course."

"I'm also a Russian."

"Isn't everyone?"

"My name was once Anton Broskov. Oh, you should have seen me in those days of my youth. Very dashing. I was so thin and fit, my dear. Positively svelte. I started getting fat the day that I was sent to the States from Vietnam, the day I began impersonating Anson Peterson in front of his friends and relatives. Eating became my way of coping with the terrible pressures."

Joanna finished her cognac. "The senator told me about the Mirror group before he died. You're one of them?"

"There were twelve of us," Peterson said. "They made us into mirror images of American prisoners of war, Alex. Sent us home in their place. They transformed us—not unlike the way in which this dear lady was transformed."

"Bullshit," Alex said angrily. "You didn't endure pain like she endured. You weren't raped. You always knew who you really were and where you came from, but Joanna lived in the dark."

She reached out and touched Alex's arm. "The worst is past. You're here. It's okay now."

Peterson sighed. "The idea was that all twelve of us would go to the States, get rich with the help of the KGB. Some of us needed that help, some didn't. We all made it to the top—except the two who died young, one in an accident, the other of cancer. Moscow figured that the perfect cover for an agent was wealth. Who'd ever suspect a self-made multimillionaire of plotting to overthrow the very system that made him a success?"

"But you said you're on our team," Alex reminded him.

"I am. I've gone over to the other side. Did it a long time ago. I'm not the only one. It was a possibility that the fanatics behind Mirror didn't consider carefully enough. If you let a man make his mark in a capitalistic society, if you let him achieve all that he wants in that society, then after a while he feels grateful toward that system, toward his neighbors. Four of the others have switched. Dear Tom would have come over too, if he could have gotten past his fear of having his millions stripped from him."

"The other side," Joanna said thoughtfully. "So you're working for the United States?"

"The CIA, yes," Peterson said. "Years and years ago, I told them all about Tom and the others. They hoped Tom would turn double like I did, of his own free will. But he didn't. And rather than try to turn him, they decided to use him without his knowledge. All these years, they fed subtly twisted information to dear old Tom, and he dutifully passed it on to Moscow. We've been quietly misleading first the communists, then the hash of ideologues who replaced them. In fact, we had a lot to do with the fall of the Soviet. Too bad it couldn't continue with Tom."

"Why couldn't it?"

"Dear Tom was going too far in politics. Much, much too far. He had a better than even chance of becoming the next President of the United States. Think of that! With him in the Oval Office, we couldn't hope to continue to deceive *any* faction in the Russian government."

"Wouldn't it be even easier to deceive them?"

"You see, when intelligence analysts in the Kremlin occasionally discovered a mistake in the information passed on to them by *Senator* Chelgrin, they figured it was because he wasn't in a sufficiently high position to acquire the entire unvarnished story. But they never lost faith in him. They continued to trust him. However, if he rose to the presidency, and if they discovered errors in the information passed to them by *President* Chelgrin, they would know something was rotten. They'd go back and painstakingly reexamine everything that he'd ever given them, and in time they'd realize that it was all doctored data, that they'd been played for fools."

Joanna shook her head, perplexed. "But why does it matter any more whether they find out or not? The Soviet Union is gone. The new people in charge are all our friends."

"Some of them are friends. Some of the old thugs are still around, however, still riddling the bureaucracy, still in some key positions in the military—just waiting for an opportunity to come storming back."

"No one really believes they'll get into power again."

Peterson swirled the remaining cognac in his crystal snifter. "You're perceptive, dear lady. Let's just say . . . we didn't merely feed them false information. For years, we engaged in a masterful charade that deceived them into a reckless expenditure of their national wealth on unnecessary military projects, leading to poverty and unrest in the civilian population. Furthermore, we played upon their systemic paranoia, giving them reason to believe they needed to make greater use of the Gulag, and the more people they dragged away to prison in the dead of night, the more their fragile system cracked under the strain of the people's fear, resentment, and anger."

"You *encouraged* them to put more people in concentration camps?" she asked, disbelieving.

"We didn't encourage it so much as provide them with information that led them to believe it was necessary for their survival."

"Are you saying you fingered people as enemies of the state who actually weren't spies or provocateurs? You provided phony evidence against them, condemned innocent Russians to suffering just to cause more internal turmoil?"

Peterson smiled. "Don't get moralistic, dear lady. It *was* a war, even if cold, and the Soviets were a formidable enemy. In a war, some sacrifices must be made."

"Sacrifices of innocent people."

He shrugged his big round shoulders. "Sometimes."

"Dear God."

"But you can see why we wouldn't want to have light thrown on the whole operation. Some pretty nasty stuff happened here. Let's just say . . . it would taint the victory we so well deserved and won. So when Tom began to seem not merely like a credible candidate for the presidency but like an inevitable successor to the current bumbler, he had to be removed."

"Why not just kill him in a staged accident?" Joanna asked.

"For one thing, the other side would have been alarmed and highly suspicious. In this line of work, we tend not to believe that there are *ever* any genuine accidents."

"But why did *I* have to do the removing?" Alex asked.

Peterson finished his cognac and, incredibly, took a roll of butter-rum Life Savers from his pocket. He offered them to Alex and Joanna, then popped one into his mouth. "The CIA determined that maximum propaganda value should be gotten from the senator's death. They decided that his status as a former Soviet—and now Russian—intelligence operative should be revealed to the world—but in such a way that the Russians would think the Mirror network of deep-cover agents had not been uncovered, just Tom. The Cold War is over, yes, and we're all chums with the Russians now, skipping hand in hand toward the carefree and glorious dawn of the millennium, but we still spy on them and they still spy on us, and thus will it always be among powerful nations with big nuclear arsenals. We don't want to damage my position or that of the other turncoat Mirror agents in the States. If the CIA itself tore the mask off Tom Chelgrin, the Russians would be convinced that he had been made to tell everything about Mirror. But if a civilian—such as you, Alex—stumbled across Chelgrin's double identity through a chance encounter with his long-lost daughter, and if Chelgrin were killed before the CIA could have a chance to interrogate him, the Russians might think that Mirror was still safe."

"But the senator told me all about it," Joanna said, "and now it isn't a secret any more."

"You'll merely pretend that he didn't tell you a thing," the fat man advised. "In a few minutes, I'll leave. What we would like you to do is wait half an hour, giving me time to make myself scarce, and then call the Swiss police."

"We'll be arrested for murder," Alex objected, "in case you've forgotten the carnage downstairs."

"No, you won't be arrested when the whole story comes out. You see . . . you'll tell them how you tracked backward through Joanna's life to London and then to here, how you discovered that Lisa was made into Joanna because of what she heard in Jamaica all those years ago, and how you shot these people in self-defense." He smiled at Joanna. "You'll tell the press that your father was a Soviet agent, that he told you his pathetic story as he lay dying. But you'll make no mention of Mirror or of the other doppelgängers like him. You must pretend to believe that he *was* Tom Chelgrin, the *real* Tom Chelgrin, who just fell into a secret love of Marxism after Vietnam."

"And what if I *do* mention Mirror and the other doubles?" she asked.

Peterson looked distressed. "Most unwise. You'd destroy the most spectacular counterintelligence operation in history. There are people who wouldn't take that lightly."

"The CIA," Alex said.

"Among others," Peterson said.

"You're saying they'd kill me if I told it all?" Joanna asked.

"Dear lady, they would certainly regret having to do it."

Alex said, "Don't threaten her."

"I didn't make a threat," Peterson said placatingly. "I merely stated an incontrovertible truth."

Putting down his empty brandy snifter, tenderly blotting his hand against his bloody lips, Alex said, "What happened to me in Rio?"

"We stole a week of your vacation. Like the KGB, the Agency has long sponsored a few behavioral psychologists and biochemists who have been expanding upon Rotenhausen's research. We used some of Franz's techniques to implant a program in you."

"That's why I went to Japan on vacation."

"Yes. You were programmed to go."

"That's why I stopped in Kyoto."

"Yes."

"And went to the Moonglow Lounge."

"We implanted that and a lot of other things, and I must say you performed perfectly."

Joanna slid forward on her chair, filled with a new fear. "How detailed was the program?"

"How detailed?" the fat man asked.

"I mean . . . was Alex . . . ?" She bit her lip and then took a deep breath. "Was he programmed to fall in love with me?"

Peterson smiled. "No, I assure you that he wasn't. But by God, I wish I'd thought of it! That would've been a surefire guarantee that he'd follow the rest of the program."

Alex got up from his chair, went to the bar, and poured more of the Rémy Martin into his glass. "Moscow will wonder why you weren't killed too."

"You'll tell the press and police there was a fat man who got away. That's the only description you'll be able to give. You'll say I shot at you, and you returned my fire. When I ran out of ammunition, you chased me, but I had quite a lead, and I got away in the darkness."

"How do I explain Ursula Zaitsev?" Alex asked bitterly. "She wasn't armed, was she? Don't the Swiss frown on killing unarmed women?"

"We'll put the 9mm pistol in her hand. Believe me, Alex, you won't wind up in jail. The CIA has friends here. It'll use them on your behalf if necessary. But that won't even be called for. All of this killing was strictly in self-defense."

They spent the next fifteen minutes constructing and memorizing a story that would explain everything that had transpired without mentioning Mirror or the fat man's true role in Chelgrin's downfall.

Finally Peterson stood up and stretched. "I'd better get out of here. Just remember . . . give me half an hour before you call the police."

84

✪ ✪ ✪

They stood at the open door of Rotenhausen's house and watched the fat man drive out of sight in his gray Mercedes, down toward the lights of Saint Moritz.

When Alex closed the door, he looked at Joanna and said, "Well?"

"I guess we have to do what he wants. If we talk about Mirror, if we spoil their fun and games, they'll kill us. I don't doubt that. You know they will."

"They'll kill us anyway," Alex said. "They'll kill us even if we do exactly what they want. We'll call the Swiss police, tell them our story. They won't believe us at first, but in a day or two or three, they'll match your fingerprints to Lisa's. And other things will fall into place, so then they'll accept what we've told them. They'll let us go. We'll tell the same story to the press, just the way Peterson wants it told, with no mention of Mirror or Lyshenko. Newspapers all over the world will front-page it. War hero, Senator Tom Chelgrin, was a Russian agent through the two decades of the Cold War. Big news. The former members of the KGB will gloat and preen about how clever they were, and the current government of Russia will pretend to be embarrassed and distressed that such a thing could have been done by their predecessors. In time everything will quiet down. We'll start to lead normal lives again. Then someone in the CIA will begin to worry about us, about a couple of civilians walking around with this big secret. They'll send someone after us, sure as hell."

"But what can we do?"

He had been considering their options while Peterson had been helping them create a slightly altered version of the truth for the police. "It's a cliché, but it'll work. It's the only thing we *can* do. We won't call the cops. We're going to walk out of here, go to Zurich tonight or in the morning, hole up in a hotel, and write a complete account of this, all of it, including Mirror and everything Peterson just told us. We'll make a hundred copies of it and spread them among a hundred attorneys and bank trust departments in ten or twenty countries. With each sealed copy, we'll leave instructions that it be sent to a major newspaper, each copy to a *different* major newspaper in the event that we're killed—or in the event that we simply disappear. Then we'll send a copy to Peterson at his real-estate office in Maryland and another to the Director of the CIA, along with notes explaining what we've done."

"Will it work?"

"It better."

For twenty minutes they moved rapidly through the house, wiping everything that they might have touched.

In the garage they found the van in which they'd been brought unconscious from the hotel. Their luggage was still in the back.

Exactly half an hour after Peterson left, they drove away from Rotenhausen's clinic. The windshield wipers thumped metronomically, as if counting cadence for the dead; snow caked on the blades and turned to ice.

"We can't drive through these mountains tonight," Joanna said. "The roads won't be passable. Where will we go?"

"To the depot," he said. "Maybe there's another train out."

"To where?"

"Anywhere."

"Whose life will we live?"

"Our own," he said without hesitation. "No disguises. No running. In our own ways, we've been running for a long, long time. Neither of us can do that any more."

"I know. I just meant—your life in Chicago or mine in Kyoto?"

"Kyoto," he said. "You can't be asked to start over yet again. And there's nothing for me in Chicago if you're not there. Besides, I really do like big-band music. It's not a taste they programmed into me. And on a winter night, I like the way that snow falls like powdered starlight on the Gion. I like the pure notes of temple bells and oiled-paper lanterns that make shadows dance in a breeze."

Within the hour, they were sitting in a nearly empty passenger car, holding hands, as the last train out clattered toward midnight and then, finally, beyond.

Afterword
✪ ✪ ✪

The Key to Midnight was the first novel that I wrote under the pen name Leigh Nichols, which I now no longer use. The other Nichols novels included *Shadowfires, The Servants of Twilight,* and *The House of Thunder,* which have previously been put under my real name, and one other that will be reissued in paperback in 1996.

Like all my pen names, Leigh met a tragic end. (Please see the Afterword to *The Funhouse* for the story of the death of "Owen West," who also wrote *The Mask.*) I used to tell people that while taking a tour for research purposes, Leigh had been killed in an explosion at a jalapeño-processing plant. Later, I insisted that Leigh died in a catastrophic rickshaw pile-up in Hong Kong. The truth, of course, is uglier. After drinking too much champagne one evening on a Caribbean cruise ship, Leigh Nichols was decapitated in a freak limbo accident.

This first Nichols book was meant to be my stab at an action-suspense-romance novel with a background of international intrigue, because I like to read stories of that kind when they are well done. Before giving Berkley Books the go-ahead to reprint *Key,* I reread it. Although many readers who discovered this novel through the years wrote to say that they enjoyed it, I decided that I hadn't succeeded with the original version as well as I'd thought at the time. Furthermore, it needed to be updated to reflect world events since its initial publication.

I am my own worst critic and a full-blown obsessive-compulsive, which is a bad combination in a line of work that requires me to meet deadlines. I swore that I would only lightly revise *Key,* but as is often the case, I was lying to myself. After all these years, one might think that I would no longer trust myself, but I continue to be a sucker for my own lies. I have this wide-eyed, puppy-dog look that I give myself in the mirror, when I'm lying, and I'm always fooled by it. I could sell myself the Brooklyn Bridge. In fact, I have.

And I've no idea what I did with the money that I swindled from myself. I hope I had fun with it. Anyway, by the time I'd finished revising *The Key to Midnight,* I'd cut 30,000 words from it, added about 5,000 new words, and reworked it nearly line by line.

Nevertheless, I resisted the demonic urge to write an entirely new version of the story—even though the satanically induced desire to do so was so strong that at one point my head was spinning around 360 degrees on my shoulders. In spite of all these changes, *Key* is still largely the novel that it was on first publication. The plot and the characters have not been changed materially, and I have not altered the style in which it was written, but I believe and hope that the story is much more smoothly told and more fun to read than it was in its previous incarnation.

None of my other books is in the genre or the style of *The Key to Midnight,* but lurking in these pages is the Dean Koontz you know. I can't repress a love of twist-and-turn storytelling, and a certain characteristic eeriness creeps in, as with the scenes involving Omi Inamura, in spite of the intentionally spare (essentially Japanese) tone. I hope you enjoyed this change of pace. And remember, when you drink, don't limbo.